ADVANCE PRAISE FOR *ROAR*

"Wow. Wow. Wow. I want to roar, READ T[illegible] superlatives. *ROAR* is simply stunning: a courageous book the world needs right now and forever. Masterfully crafted. Sentences that steal your breath. Characters so richly imagined, they follow you around and occupy your heart. Microscopic detail that lures us into every scene, breaks us open, provokes, informs, heals, transforms. Raw and tender, heartbreaking and joyful. Infused with love, compassion, and unblinking truth. Above all else, *ROAR* is unforgettable. A debut novel it may be, yet it introduces the voice of an enlightened, gifted storyteller."

–SHEREE FITCH, award-winning, bestselling author of *Kiss the Joy As it Flies*

"Fire and ash, breath, spirit and mist, forest, river and sea, earth wafting sweet scents of peony, honeysuckle. Shelley Thompson's *ROAR* is a beautiful, deeply immersive story of a family's resilience through loss and their work of healing, and rebuilding, as we follow Don's journey to becoming Dawn and, as her name suggests, a new beginning. A story of thresholds, transformations, and the power of love, *ROAR* is also a story about community; Thompson resists romanticizing it, doesn't shy away from exposing its underbelly—but she also reveals its capacity for acceptance and change. We've always needed this story but now we need it more than ever."

–JEANETTE LYNES, author of *The Apothecary's Garden*

"Fierce, tender, brave, and incendiary, *ROAR* is a story for these fractious times that couldn't be more true. Here, absence = presence = love, the kind that outweighs gender biases and ugly assumptions about how things "should" (or shouldn't) be that divide a family and a community. Set against the bucolic and the brutal—all that's good and depressingly bad about rural Nova Scotia—here's a righteous shredding of the ignorance that underlies transphobic, and by extension all, hatred. As Thompson so compellingly shows us, keeping silent only nurtures it."

–CAROL BRUNEAU, award-winning author of *Brighten the Corner Where You Are*

"*ROAR* is a model for finding a road back to your family. It reminds us that the process of repairing relationships sometimes asks us to take a trust fall."

–RONNIE ALI, registered psychotherapist

Vagrant Press is an imprint of
Nimbus Publishing Limited
3660 Strawberry Hill St, Halifax, NS, B3K 5A9
(902) 455-4286 nimbus.ca

Nimbus Publishing is based in Kjipuktuk, Mi'km'aki, the traditional territory of the Mi'kmaq People.

Printed and bound in Canada

NB1675
Editor: Whitney Moran
Cover design: Jenn Embree
Typesetting: Rudi Tusek

Library and Archives Canada Cataloguing in Publication

Title: Roar / a novel by Shelley Thompson.
Names: Thompson, Shelley (Actress), author.
Identifiers: Canadiana (print) 20230217958 | Canadiana (ebook) 20230217982 | ISBN 9781774712368 (softcover) | ISBN 9781774712375 (EPUB)

Classification: LCC PS8639.H64665 R63 2023 | DDC C813/.6—dc23

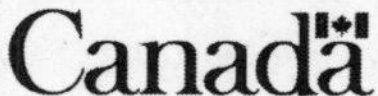

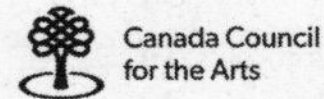

Nimbus Publishing acknowledges the financial support for its publishing activities from the Government of Canada, the Canada Council for the Arts, and from the Province of Nova Scotia. We are pleased to work in partnership with the Province of Nova Scotia to develop and promote our creative industries for the benefit of all Nova Scotians.

a novel by

SHELLEY
THOMPSON

Vagrant
PRESS

This book is dedicated to trans individuals around the world who, for lack of the loving support of family and community, have lost their potential, their livelihoods, their lives.

Reading reflections of one's own life can re-bruise.
Please, go gently into these places.

Prologue

From where she leaned against a wall, reverberations of the slamming back door still hanging in the humid early summer air, Miranda could see hill after soft green hill layered into the distance: a misty, silk-screened image.

The dining room window gave her a surreal perspective: on the wall beside her, generations of the MacInnes family were captured in their timeless squares and appeared to float in a white-blue sky broken only by one tiny cloud. Parading through decades but concluding with the high school graduation pictures of Miranda's children: Tammy, two years ago, and Donald, not even finished school yet, really, but still hanging with the rest, defiant. Miranda knew Donald would never cross the stage of the regional high school. Wouldn't climb the stairs and shake a hand and raise a scroll in the air triumphant like Tammy had done, like Miranda had done years before, and even John Andrew—though barely.

Breathe. This was just the beginning of what she must give up.

Something crashed against the door she was closest to—Donald's bedroom. She took another deep breath and tapped. Waited.

"Come in."

On the floor beneath the door, bits of...something crunched, and she struggled to move it past whatever the casualty was. Honestly, Donnie.

Outside, an engine turned over, started, spluttered, then revved. Crossing to the window, Miranda watched the ancient pickup throw gravel as it left the driveway to join the lane from the farmhouse to the main road. John Andrew was gone to the workshop till dinnertime now.

Breathe, she thought. He's got no tools for this. He never imagined it.

She sat on the end of the bed, close to her child. Donald, as he often did, had made himself smallsmallsmall, back against the bed hugging his knees, surrounded on the floor by makeup and brushes. Eyeshadow. Blush. Mascara. None of it Miranda's. She toyed gently with the blond curls escaping his striped headband, pushed them back so she could see the delicate face of her youngest child, the carefully made-up eyes now tear-smudged. Softly—

"This can't go on, lovely boy."

"I'm not—"

So much sadness in him.

"—a boy."

Such relief in finally saying it out loud, looking up at Miranda.

She stroked and stroked the face.

"I know."

Everything seemed to be about breathing. Miranda would hold her breath when John Andrew started in on Donald; she let it go when he left the house. She held it again as she totalled the columns of figures—feed, vet bills, farmhands—that told her over and over again, not enough, never enough. She let it go when she finished and knew there was nothing, nothing she could do better. And now—

"Mom?"

Miranda looked up from where she'd settled at her desk in front of another view of hills and—gasped was wrong, that signalled shock, she thought, or fear or anger, no—she hiccupped. Drew breath in and sent it out again, astonished at the marvel before her. Soft clear skin, generous perfect lips, eyes like—like hers, she thought. So that's what I could look like.

I'm looking at a better version of myself.

Oh, Donald. What should she call him, her—what should she—

"Mom? Do you hate me too, now?"

On her feet, her arms around—Donald. Don. Donnie.

Dawn.

"Oh, my darling, no, never. No. I'm just a little—"

Not a little, thought Miranda, a lot. I'm just a lot moved. Touched. Surprised. Shocked. Amazed. Bewildered. Dawn watched her as she rejected words, so hard to find the right one. Miranda touched Dawn's face.

"You're lovely."

Dawn waited.

"So absolutely you, and—"

Miranda saw the bag. Her own ancient carpet bag that she never took anywhere now.

"Oh."

"I'm sorry, Mom. You know I have to go."

She knew it, she did, but Miranda couldn't stop looking at that bag, thinking of what might have gone into it, if she and John Andrew had gone to the city, say, for a night or two, to pretend they were kids again and not folks who had made children they didn't understand, who only wanted to leave, and now...would her husband ever put his arms around her again, ever forgive her for DonaldDonDonnieDawn, ever lift that bag into the cab of their ancient truck, ever take her anywhere again?

Her breath, she thought was just. Not. There.

Usually, she could count on the drawing in and the letting go to get her past these moments of fear, of longing, and recently, of pain, but now, today, it wasn't working.

"Mom?"

"I'm sorry, darling. I know. I know you do. But what about—" Miranda nodded towards the grad picture on the wall.

"Graduation?" Dawn shook her head "I don't care. I've got the bit of paper, the marks, and the stupid hat. None of it matters. That school's been hell."

Miranda was nodding, listening, nodding.

DonaldDonDonnieDawn.

"Okay."

"Okay, I can go?"

"Okay, you're going to go."

"Yes. But..."

Of course. DonaldDonDonnieDawn needed—

"Would you lend me some..." Dawn chewed her lip. "I'll need some money."

"Of course." Miranda reached into her empty pockets. "Where will you go?"

"The city. I'll get the bus."

Miranda looked at her watch. "You've only got an hour."

"Less," said Dawn.

"Your dad has the truck. I can't drive you to town."

"I'll walk."

"Oh god." Miranda leaned on the wall, defeated.

"Don't, Mom. I have to." Dawn reached for her mother's hand. "I have to leave before Dad sees me like this. He'd kill me."

"Don't—that's—of course he wouldn't." She held Dawn's face. "Your father loves you."

"My father loves an idea of me. He loved the little-boy me. The version-of-him me. He doesn't know me."

Miranda couldn't argue. She started down the hall, paused by the bag. "Do you have everything you need?"

"I think I can go to a shelter, or a friend..."

Miranda disappeared into her bedroom, but Dawn kept talking. To the heavy air, Miranda thought, and to the grandfather clock that was just now chiming the hour when DonaldDonDonnieDawn would leave.

"I promise I'll keep in touch," came Dawn's voice from the other room. "I'll let you know where I am, and what I do. I have a friend in the city."

"Who? Where did you meet them?" Miranda reappeared with a coat, a multicoloured silk scarf, and a small blue velvet box in her hands.

Dawn was studying a picture of sixteen-year-old Miranda standing behind her father on his Ford Jubilee tractor. Grandad Vic, who Dawn couldn't remember meeting but knew all about. She turned back to her mother. "The tournament. Last month. A goalie. We've been messaging."

Miranda handed Dawn the bright scarf she'd played with as a child, and Dawn tucked it in the pocket of her mom's old coat, pulled from the closet just now, transforming DonaldDonDonnie into Dawn.

Miranda's hands were trembling as she opened the velvet box and turned Dawn around.

"She'll help me. Mom? Are you okay? What are you doing?"

Miranda was clasping a set of pearls—her only treasured thing—around Dawn's neck.

"Mom. These were for..." Dawn touched the pearls as if afraid they'd shatter. "Tammy thought she'd have them someday."

"She'll be fine. Here." Miranda tucked a roll of bills into Dawn's pocket. "I'll make sure you're okay. Come on."

Miranda picked up the carpet bag that held bits of her past and all of her child's future and walked onto the deck, scanning the road. In case John Andrew had forgotten something or was coming home to apologize for losing his temper again with the son who bewildered him.

"Go now," she said, holding the bag out to Dawn. "I love you. Go. Call me? Email me?"

Dawn held on and held on and held on until Miranda was sure that the bus would go without DonaldDonDonnie.

"Dawn. Go. Go."

Dawn went, without a look back.

Miranda sat on the porch step, trying and trying to breathe again like she used to: in for four, hold for four, out for four, wait for four. Then starting the cycle again, but crying for four, crying for eight, crying for twelve, like she would cry forever.

Tammy

"I wish you'd let go."

Byron spoke gently, the first sound in the car for the last half hour, apart from the thrum of traffic, as he negotiated the teeming 401. Tammy looked up at her right hand, drained of colour. She couldn't remember when she'd reached for what Byron called the 'oh shit!' handle above the door, but she realized now that it felt like if she let go, she'd fly apart.

She looked at Byron. "I can't."

He turned his focus, just for a moment, from the behemoth eighteen-wheelers that surrounded them, dwarfing them, to give her a look so suffused with sympathy and love that it nearly set her off. Again.

"The blood that should be in your hand goes rushing straight to your armpit, you know that, right?" he said. "And it creates a kind of reservoir behind your sweat glands, and as it gets hotter—which it's going to because it's supposed to get up to at least thirty today, and this air conditioning is crap—you may start to sweat blood."

"Byron."

"It could be true. Take your hand down, Tam. I worry."

Tammy's eyes filled. She looked at him. He got it.

"Hold on to me," he said.

She took her right hand down and put both her hands into the pink palm that lay on her lap. Open, available. Soft. Softer than hers.

"Your expensive hand cream seems to be working."

He grinned. "I know, right? You're not laughing now, are ya?"

He winced. Oops. She looked away.

"Tammy. I'm sorry. I'm just trying to..."

"I know."

She turned from Byron and focused on the President's Choice truck beside them, fighting a wave of loss as thick as the yellow custard pictured on the side of the huge—Woah! The truck gave a teasing swing to within inches of her. So close. Mr. Big PC was like an undisciplined dance partner to their tiny red car, the white dashes on the road between them a magical shield of protection. She hoped.

Byron squeezed her hands tighter. "Do you want to stop?"

"We're not even to Quebec."

"I know," he said, "but maybe just a breather."

"Let's just get there?"

Another glance at her. "Okay."

She knew she wasn't easy. Not even at the best of times, and this was definitely not that. She never relaxed—or rather, she never *used* to relax. Work, home; work, home; strain up the ladder. Save for a car, buy a car. Save for a condo, save, wait, watch. Save, work, wait. Whatever and whatever and whatever's next. Until Byron.

Then something somewhere deep and distant said, Take a breath, Tammy. Take a deep, sweet breath. And she did. She relaxed enough to be funny sometimes, and then warm, sometimes, and, as Byron would say now, to take her prickle off. She took her prickle off and let him in, so he was here with her now, after nearly two years of reserving her prickle for some of her workmates who knew that really, Tammy was a chestnut. Smooth as silk and sweet sweet sweet on the inside, if you had the patience and dexterity, like Byron, to get through the tiny spikes. And sometimes—and Byron took a lot of pleasure in reminding Tammy of this—it took a *lot* of patience.

Byron was twisting the diamond he'd given Tammy just before they'd headed to Nova Scotia for his first visit with her family, six months before. Christmastime. Very traditional, Tammy had teased him, just a plain old diamond solitaire. Like her mother's, she'd said, which was made from her grandmother's engagement ring.

"Don't you want to wait and ask my dad for his permission?" she'd asked him.

He'd thought she was joking. She wasn't. Tammy realized now that he'd been careful with his reply.

"What if he said no?"

"Why would he?"

She remembered that conversation again now, looking at her small, pale hands in his large, dark one. Why would he? She thought about her quiet father, how she had hoped he would like Byron, and been relieved. She hadn't realized until she'd said those words, *why would he*, that there was a possibility John Andrew's "still, dark waters," as her mother called them, might contain some vestige of racial...what? Discomfort? Fear? Resistance to his small (Tammy was only five-foot-four) girl-child, his only daughter, being partner to this large Black man? Did the father she loved and admired harbour those notions she knew still lingered? Thought bubbles she saw floating above strangers' heads on the street as Tammy and Byron walked hand in hand. Difference was meant to be celebrated now. It was supposed to be so easy, acceptance.

But it wasn't, really. Not in her big city and certainly not in her tiny hometown, population three thousand. Where there had not been a single person of colour in her grade, right through to graduation. Where you didn't belong unless you had three generations in the graveyard and a Mc or a Mac at the front of your last name. Where the first question when you were introduced to someone new was, Who's yer father? followed by a swift yup-yup-ing intake of approving breath when you replied.

So, on reflection, *what if he said no?* was a fair question, and she'd struggled as she imagined what shape her life might have taken if her gentle father *had* said no. But he hadn't said anything. What John Andrew did instead when they told him was quite un–John Andrew-like. His eyes moistened and he pulled Byron into a long hug. Tammy had never seen her father hug anyone outside of their family. He'd rarely hugged her. Her mother, sometimes. Almost never Donald, her younger brother.

Donald.

Don't, she told herself. Don't go there. Soon enough, soon enough. She returned to the comfortable landscape of her life with Byron.

Byron had told her things at Christmas he hadn't shared before, about his two other significant relationships. She knew about them of course: she'd creeped the women on Facebook, then confessed.

Both were beautiful, accomplished, and white. And then, of course, Tammy and Byron had done what new lovers do, deep into night after night: recounted, dissected, and analyzed their former relationships. But still, she hadn't known exactly what had happened with Byron's exes, or who had finished with whom. Byron always circled the details: he was circumspect and fair to a fault. There's no blame, he used to say, although it seemed clear to Tammy that there *was* blame, Byron just wasn't going to lay it.

At Christmas, though, with Byron getting a little moist-eyed himself, what was revealed was that the parents of both of his former partners, who at first had been welcoming and kind, and who didn't see colour, suddenly did.

He couldn't pin the ending of either relationship on a single event, but both were terminated in remarkably similar ways. He'd grieved each, and then, as Byron did with anything he couldn't be responsible for, he let them go.

This was probably the trait that Tammy loved most in him. Next to his smell. Laundry in from a sunny, breezy line. A kind of magic she couldn't explain. Even when he was dirty and sweaty and gross—his words—he always smelt to her like clean, windblown sheets. She knew it was the stuff of clichéd romance. Like something from one of her mother's old Harlequin novels that lived wedged into the bookcase under Miranda's night table alongside an assembly of strange bedfellows: the graduation present from Miranda's parents, an ancient and massive Oxford English Dictionary. T. S. Elliot and Robert Frost. Donald Westlake and Raymond Chandler, and Margaret Atwood and Carol Shields and Ann Patchett and Iain Rankin and Harold Robbins's *A Stone for Danny Fisher*. All of which Tammy had devoured as an impressionable teenager, searching for sex in every publication—including the dictionary. She found heat and promise in the Harlequin romances and actual educative sex in the Harold Robbins books, then dismissed both in her late teens as misogynist. When she met Byron, though, the imagery and certainty and the glorious hot sensuality that she remembered from those books came rushing back, and she wondered if they had in fact got it *all* wrong.

So, she had felt sure the thought bubbles wouldn't be hovering in her home, because her parents understood deep and abiding love and sex. Tammy saw their still-present heat. She watched them watch each other with an itch she knew would be scratched, despite the fact that since Donald had left, there was tension between them: anger from her father, resignation from her mother, and sadness from both of them. And yet, the itch remained. Their love remained. She knew they would see Byron watching her, with clear admiration and delight. She felt sure they would never look at Byron's colour as anything worthy of thought or comment; never make him an outsider, never reduce him. Her parents were expert non-judgers, borne, she thought, of decades of 4-H, first as participants, then leaders: where children came from such a variety of complex situations, bringing their outrageous plans and talents and passions for animals and farm implements. Those children, who had for years included her and her brother, would never be judged; must only ever feel the warmth of acceptance and their own special brilliance, as amplified by John Andrew and Miranda.

4-H. Donald. Acceptance. Christmas. Tammy's thoughts danced through the monkey-mind her meditation teacher was teaching her to love, bouncing back and forth now between Donald, who hadn't been home at Christmas last year, or the year before, or the year before that, or... Settle, monkey brain. Warm thoughts. Good thoughts.

Last Christmas, Tammy remembered, was brilliant and magical for so many reasons. Because her mother was well again. Because her parents were so warm and ready for Byron. Because Sarah and Mattie, her two closest high school friends, had come home with their partners, too, and were exactly what they'd always been: witty and acerbic, generous and spontaneous, showing Byron how fun a small town in the snow could be. And Tammy knew that for Byron, the magic was in the knowledge that they had claimed one another, asking no one's permission or opinion.

But last Christmas was also so deeply sad and poignant because it wasn't just last Christmas. It was the last Christmas.

John Andrew

Heat waves were rising from the hood of his muddy pickup. John Andrew thought he might have been here for hours, that the temperature of the day had been rising as he stood there. Morning seemed to have turned to noon and found him where he'd started the day, looking through the kitchen window to the driveway and back garden.

What had he come in here for? Cup of tea. Why? Something to do, something to fill the next minute.

He could hear the next minute. And the next. And the next.

In the humid silence, the clock—a wedding present from Aunt Leny; he remembered unwrapping it twenty-nine years before with absolute clarity—seemed to be shouting the reluctant departure of every second. Nothing moved in the kitchen; nothing moved outside, not the lightest leaf on the topmost branch of the tallest tree. Betsy, the border collie, crouched tense on her bed, panting in the heat.

He pushed aside a casserole and plugged in the kettle. He looked at the macaroni salads and beef stews and read the note on one: *MOUSSAKA*. What was moussaka when it was at home? The food should go in the fridge, but he knew it was already full. Just looking at it all made him nauseous. How could he eat when she wouldn't?

He stood behind her chair, his rough hand catching threads on the pale pink throw still draped where she'd left it days ago. Weeks ago? He didn't know.

John Andrew shifted his weight. Betsy lifted her twelve-year-old self to her haunches, all attention and readiness. She seemed to be willing him away from the window, so that their day could be what their day usually was. Now though, with an incredible economy, John Andrew lifted his hand and reached for a mug, and then was motionless again for a moment before raising his head to a swell of cicadas, breaching the stillness with their electric hum. Betsy settled again, prepared to be patient. Finally, John Andrew turned and switched off the kettle. A view from a different window might ease the clenching in his gut.

He opened the front door and stepped onto the porch. It was shaded this late in the afternoon. He could hear his cattle moving from the far pasture: Jerry and his son Andy were driving them in for the late afternoon milking. There was a breeze now that carried the herd's chorus and teased the ancient two-seated swing into a gentle creaking to and fro. The humid air held the smell of the tidal river not far off, and warm rugosa roses. Sweet. Cinnamon.

He sat on the swing. The rugosa hedge was the same age as Tammy. He saw Miranda twenty-seven—or twenty-eight?—years ago: belly full, knees in the dirt, gently easing one tiny bush after another into the trench he'd dug, and his young self following behind, heeling in. One pink, one white, pink-white, pink-white. He'd protested: the hedge would look like the fancy striped toothpaste she liked.

That's right, she said.

And then she'd nursed Tammy on the swing, where she could smell the eight or ten blooms that came late that first summer.

Tammy Rose. In spite of everything, John Andrew felt something lift at the thought of his daughter. But with Tammy came Donald—following his big sister as he had from the day he was born, on her heels and in her hair. And the tiny moment of relief was gone.

John Andrew stood and went back inside. One last glance through the oval glass of the front door to the long driveway and he turned to climb the stairs. Where to go, what to do, why. Looking down, he realized he still had his boots on. He could hear her: Don't bring the farm in, J'n Andrew! That would never do. He sat on a step to take them off, but something caught his eye. He reached for the bright, glinting strand and carefully picked it up to study it. A single long silver-blond hair.

He breathed. She was still here. Now he knew where he was going, and why. Boots still on, he stood and carried the hair into the bedroom, to where the ancient silver-backed brush Miranda had used every night lay on the crowded dresser. Her mother's. Her grandmother's. Decades of grooming MacLean women, now done. He laid the gossamer thread gently across the brush. A gift bestowed by her, but still, another ending. This seesaw of grief was exhausting.

He hadn't realized before that death was not absence, but presence. Every other passing he remembered had him looking for something he'd lost. His mother, first. Where had she gone when he was six? Gone and not come back. His first very own dog, Bronco—he'd wanted a horse—at ten. Disappeared and gone for a week, Bronco was returned by a neighbour who'd found him at the roadside miles away. The pain of that lost-forever companion was buried under a rock-marked mound in the back field, the loss growing less pronounced each day until it wasn't an ache anymore, just a story.

Then his father, growing yellow and unsteady, finally succumbing to a fall.

Now he enumerated the deaths. The tiny baby boy Marcus that Jenny, Miranda's best friend, had buried a week after his birth; the unwed mother grieving her so-wanted child, her family not-so-secretly relieved. Those nights of ugly weeping, the two women holding each other in a way he could never imagine holding another man. Miranda's cousin Leonard, Leny's eldest son, caught in a grain auger. Horrible. Miranda's father: that was a complicated departure. Even now, John Andrew's dislike for his wife's father brought guilt and shame. The freedom, though. The welcome absence.

But this. This was a light hand on his shoulder, a shadow that shifted when he turned. A hair he'd never have noticed. A hairbrush unremarkable until now. Smudged glasses on her bedside table. The book she'd been reading—what was that book? *Variations*. Pink-and-blue-and-white-striped cover. He'd never seen it before. She used to tell him about the books she was reading all the time, but lately, almost never. The dresses he was pushing aside now in the closet, looking for something for her to wear. Jesus. He'd never seen these dresses on her. Where had they all come from?

He selected one, pale pink like the throw in the kitchen, held it up. Did he remember it? Had she liked it? Had he? Did it matter?

He sank onto the bed. What happened now? Who would order the feed? Do the books? Settle arguments? Find the answers and always, always! be right? His chest tightened, wondering as he had so many times, how Miranda, so much smarter and quicker and brighter than he, had been content to lie nose to nose with him, stroking his face to coax him to sleep, for years?

Would he spend every minute now of every day following one question with another? Why did she get ill? Why didn't she get better? Where was his son when he needed someone to lean on?

Something disturbed Betsy, now barking at the bottom of the stairs, then running to and from the back door. He stood and pulled the curtain aside to see Tammy's tiny red car pull up, and his gut unclenched a little.

Byron

That last stretch was too long, Byron thought, pushing the door open and swinging his feet out first. He often felt like a cartoon clown, easing his large frame out of Tammy's tiny car. Perfect for her, ridiculous for him.

The contrast between the somewhat air-conditioned vehicle and the humming, moist heat of Nova Scotia summer hit him with the same force that emerging from a plane onto a tarmac in Greece had once delivered, but with a completely different expectation. This was not going to be a holiday.

He looked past the kitchen garden, the outbuildings, and across the field to the dairy. Trees. Birds. Heat waves hovering above fields dotted with wildflowers. Eighteen hours from the collection of small rooms in the mostly glass structure that was their Toronto condo, and this might as well have been Greece. A different world.

He turned back to Tammy, still sitting, unmoving, in the passenger seat. Processing, she'd say.

Almost half an hour ago now, they'd pulled into the end of the long, treed driveway. "Stop," she said. He did, and they sat a distance from the house, silent, until she turned to him and said, "How do I do this?"

He reached for her hand, shaking his head. He felt helpless, exhausted after hours of driving, pulling over to snooze for an hour and then starting off again. He hadn't wanted Tammy to drive. She'd cried quietly, and sometimes not so quietly, most of the way through Ontario and Quebec, then slept through New Brunswick.

Now he considered. "Not sure," he said. "Whatever you do..." He felt inadequate. He'd never had someone close to him die. "Whatever you do will be the right thing."

She turned back again. Yeah right, her look said. Then, "Don't let me be a bitch to Donald."

He held her gaze, took a deep breath. She could be complicated. She could make fantastic, dramatic, uncomfortable scenes. She wore her heart on her sleeve but covered it with broken glass that had to be so carefully picked off.

"You won't be. Give him a chance, though. He'll be struggling too."

She looked forward, her eyes filling again. "Oh God, this house."

"Tammy, c'mon, your dad will be looking for us."

She nodded. Took a breath. Byron restarted the car and eased it to the end of the drive, finally pulling up around the corner of the house.

Now, feet on the ground, waiting, he turned to watch her reach for the handle as the back door of the house opened. A black-and-white fur bomb exploded towards Tammy, nearly knocking her over. Following Betsy was John Andrew.

Byron stood and reached out. "Mr. MacInnes. I'm so sorry for your loss."

John Andrew held on to Byron's hand, both of them still for a moment, before letting go to watch Tammy talking quietly to Betsy. Tammy stood up and looked at her dad and then, a bit like Betsy had, threw herself at him.

John Andrew was not a hugger or a holder, but now, Byron thought, he looked like he wanted to pick his daughter up and cradle her. As it was, they rocked gently, Tammy's head on her father's chest. Finally, she asked, "Dad, why didn't she say come? Didn't she want me—"

"Tammy—don't."

John Andrew was holding the reins of his grief very tight. He continued, "She couldn't. It was so fast, Tam. So fast."

Byron stood, barely breathing, waiting for his cue. Move? Don't move?

"They didn't think, till the last minute, that she was going." Then, delicately, "She kept rallying, and I—I wasn't there, Tammy."

Tammy eased from her father's arms to stand away and look at him.

"I wasn't there." John Andrew pulled her back into him and buried his face in the top of his daughter's head. "Jenny was."

So much crying. Tammy would make herself sick, Byron thought, taking a step towards her.

John Andrew drew a sleeve across his eyes and straightened up.

"Okay. Okay, now. We have to— Come on, Tam let's get inside. Get you settled."

Betsy, who'd been watching from a respectful distance, knew she had to lead. She crept in and nudged Tammy's hand, herding her gently towards the door.

Byron was glad Betsy had taken responsibility. For the moment, anyway. He opened the hatchback, grabbing Tammy's bags, John Andrew reaching for Byron's case.

"Have you heard from Donald?" Tammy asked her father.

John Andrew was nearly through the back door, pausing for a split second before answering. "Not yet. Sent an email. Found an address in your mother's desk. Didn't get an answer. Maybe the wrong one."

And he was gone inside.

Tammy turned back to the car to grab her handbag from the trunk, then, almost accusing, fired at Byron, "You see?" and followed her dad inside.

Byron stood where he'd been shot, wondering what, exactly, he was supposed to see except that Donald, poor Donald, was already failing at whatever was expected of him, because he wasn't here first.

The air above Byron buzzed, galvanic with a thousand male cicadas serenading their potential mates. And Tammy called—

"Byron? You coming in?"

So he went inside: past hooks with hats, overalls, and jackets. A mat crowded with workboots, sneakers, women's rubber boots and sandals, and in a basket, a variety of garden tools, a pair of women's gardening gloves, and seed packs all ripped at the top as if they'd been opened just yesterday. He glanced through a window at the small kitchen garden, where a few inches of green shoots declared the seed packs had been opened weeks before.

Byron came into the kitchen, much cooler than outside. A relief. Betsy had settled on her bed. Tammy and John Andrew leaned on opposite counters—counters groaning with a variety of casserole dishes and trays and plates, tinfoil throwing little reflective barbs of light around the walls and ceiling.

Byron stopped in the doorway, amazed. "Woah."

John Andrew followed Byron's sweeping gaze: from the *MOUSSAKA*, to all the other mystery dishes. "Yeah. Don't know where to put this—" He waved his hand at it all.

"In here," Tammy said as she opened the fridge. Then closed it. It was already packed. "Maybe not," she said. "We'll figure it out. Have you been eating?"

Her dad shrugged.

Silence in the kitchen. A clock ticked. Byron watched the tiny second hand. He was surprised to find the same ease now that he'd felt at Christmastime. This house was...open. Warm. Full of interesting—he searched for a word—*relics*, he thought. Of everyone's life and talents. Pictures of Tammy's successes at horse shows. Donald holding up a 4-H trophy, standing with a sweet-looking golden calf that gazed at him with huge, adoring dark eyes. A much younger, delighted John Andrew on a brand-new, bright green, shiny tractor. Byron had never seen John Andrew smile like that. And everywhere, Miranda's work.

Just off the kitchen was Miranda's tiny, bright sewing room, with views to the fields on two sides and, on the walls with no windows, floor-to-ceiling shelves of coloured fabric and a rainbow of thread in every hue. Her old Elna still sat open, threaded, ready. His mom had an Elna too, so they'd talked about sewing machines at Christmas. He loved that room. The cat (what was the cat's name? Did it have a name?) slept on the window seat in the sun. He'd never wished to be a cat once in his life but he did in that moment: to be able to lie near Miranda, in that room, in that pool of winter sun.

He'd fallen, he knew, a tiny bit in love with his partner's mother. She'd connected him back to things he'd wanted, things he admired. Miranda was—she'd *been*, he corrected himself—a sewer and a weaver and a *maker* of things. Her words, when he asked what she did. Her creations, woven and collaged and patchworked, hung throughout the house. And, Tammy had told him with pride, all over the town.

Stunning glimpses of a woven field in winter. A patchwork piece of the cliffs and beach beyond the grazing fields, assembled from scraps of fabric in only pale greens and golds. Hers was a talent he didn't see often, though he worked with visual artists, of a type, all the time at the agency. Not just a way of seeing the world around her but working to find the best medium to capture it. She was, as an artist, the whole package. Visualizer, conceptualizer, creator. He told her that, and she just smiled and said that Tammy had to get her painting and drawing ability from somewhere, and it wasn't her dad. John Andrew couldn't draw breath, she'd laughed.

Byron had leaned by the door talking with Miranda while she was mending. Tammy mended, too. Byron had loved that discovery. Tammy mended and darned using a light bulb. They kept one of the old incandescent bulbs like some kind of sacred object; she lived in fear of it breaking. She couldn't bear to throw a sock away; couldn't bear, Byron discovered, to waste anything. They ate leftovers for days.

He was hungry. He eyed the casseroles.

"So, Dad," said Tammy, "nothing then from Donald."

Her dad shook his head.

"Have you been in touch at all?"

Again, John Andrew shook his head. Byron felt the ease of the kitchen beginning to slip away. "Your mom was. Seems like. She had an email for him in her desk."

"Well then..."

Byron knew Tammy was going to push this moment towards some kind of answer, even if there wasn't one. And John Andrew, Byron thought, hadn't the energy for that.

"Hey, Tam, let's take our stuff up and get a wash, okay? I'm pretty grubby. Then we can have a cuppa?"

"Right. Okay. Back in a sec, Dad."

Tammy always knew when she was being diverted. She never liked it, but she must have seen the relief it brought her dad. She reached for her bags, Byron reached for his, and she led him upstairs, pushing open a door right at the top of stairs. Not where they'd slept before.

A tiny box-room with a single bed and an even tinier closet. He'd not even noticed this room at Christmas.

"Here you go," she said.

"Here *I* go? Where do you go?"

And instead of waving at the guest room across the hall where they'd stayed last time, she gestured to her childhood bedroom. He weighed his next words. Word.

"Okay."

Her eyes filled. "I can't. I just—with Dad next door and—I can't. When he's alone."

This, thought Byron as his heart lurched. He didn't know what to call it, but it was the contrast between the pugnacious, sharp-fanged woman she left at the office and the insecure, intuitive empath that bemused and captivated him. He loved her for *this*.

He took her bags, put them down, and reached for her. She was shaking, working to contain herself so her dad wouldn't hear her sobs. She folded into him and they stood like that beside the single bed until the storm passed, Tammy drawing deep breaths, then hiccupping. He held her away, brushed the hair from her face, and said, "Hiccup punctuation?"

She nodded. "I'm done. Thank you."

"I'm gonna wash," he said, "then meet back downstairs? I'm sorry but I'm—"

"Starving," said Tammy

"Like a—"

This was a game. He was always hungry.

"Bear?" she said. "Hummingbird?"

"Hummingbird?" This was new, he thought.

Tammy picked her bags up and turned to the door. Over her shoulder: "They eat twice their own weight every day."

She'll be all right, he thought, heading for the bathroom.

A few minutes later, Byron was bounding back down the stairs when there was a knock at the front door. He could hear Tammy and John Andrew in the kitchen, ease restored. He called down to them: "Shall I get the door?"

Jill

"She wouldn't want black."

Dawn rejected the dress Jill was holding out and turned back to the tiny suitcase lying open and partly packed on the bed beside her.

Jill returned it to the crammed closet and continued pushing clothes aside, searching. Silently she offered Dawn something pink (no), then a pale, flowered skirt, which was considered and accepted. Dawn rolled it and tucked it into the suitcase, added a shirt, then reached for a photo sitting on the bookcase. She examined it as if she'd never seen it before: the young woman standing behind an older man at the wheel of a red and white tractor. It seemed, Jill thought, that the intensity of Dawn's focus was intended to transport herself into the photo, with that laughing woman wearing the rough plaid shirt and string of pearls.

Jill hadn't thought she'd ever care about the origin story of a tractor—or, actually, anything to do with one. Until last fall, when she'd seen this photo of the beautiful young woman on the tractor for the first time, and learned that this was Dawn's mother, Miranda.

They'd come back to Dawn's place after a match to change before joining the rest of the team to celebrate. Dawn's studio flat was the closest to the grounds where they'd just won their semi-final, so, adrenaline still running high, Dawn and Jill and a couple others took turns in the shower. Dawn, the most recent addition to the team, microwaved popcorn for the women and Jill had picked up the picture.

"Is that you? Nice tractor."

Dawn looked over Jill's shoulder at the picture.

"Isn't it? No, that's my mom. She's sixteen there. She learned to drive on that. It's a Ford Jubilee."

"Why Jubilee? Do you know?"

Dawn was looking at the tractor like a proud parent.

"Why yes, ma'am, I do."

She knew about *all* the Ford tractors—her knowledge was encyclopedic—but her favourite was this one, the one they had at home, built in the fiftieth year of the Ford Motor Company. It was different for lots of reasons, Dawn explained, but in particular, tire size and the impact on their handling. Furtive yawns from her audience as she continued with the scintillating details: the Ford Jubilee had 28-inch rear tires and 16-inch front tires compared to its close cousin, the Ford 8N, with its 28-inch rear tires and *19-inch* front tires. So, Dawn said, the 8N was probably faster but the Jubilee was more elegant, had more personality.

Jill studied this young woman, who was saying the most words Jill had heard from her yet. Incongruous words: Dawn, so delicately featured and fair, so athletic and dancer-like, was clearly a dweeb when it came to farm machinery.

"Really. *Personality*. A tractor."

"Yes, ma'am."

"Why do you know this?"

"I'm a 4-H kid." Dawn took a little bow to the group, who'd stopped their chatter to listen.

Jill squinted at the picture. "She's gorgeous. Your mom, not the tractor. And exactly like you—well, you like her."

Dawn nodded. "I know," she said, her words tinged with sadness.

Dawn kept herself very much to herself, and Jill never pried.

Jill was expert at being open, still, and available. Jill knew animals (and children: former teacher Jill felt children under twelve were a separate and distinct species; children over twelve, well—how long do you have, she'd say) the way that Dawn clearly knew machines. Maybe preferred them to people. Jill's particular talent came from her understanding that no creature was caught by reaching for them. They would only come of their own volition, from flight to a place of stillness; when they felt safe, they would settle and open, too. So Jill stayed still, and waited for Dawn to settle.

Jill knew some of Dawn's story, as she suspected Dawn knew some of hers. Like so many in Halifax's small trans community, they'd both run away from home to find safety and fellowship. *Fellowship* was the word Jill chose to describe what she'd searched for: odd, considering the masculine etymology of the word. *Fellow*ship. Not *person*ship, which when she really considered, she thought she might have preferred. But.

Coming from a large Ugandan family made up entirely of boys, Jill had begun with the notion of finding fraternity, and only after she'd recognized who she truly was did she realize she was searching for a like-minded sorority—sisters who would love and respect her. But eventually the fine distinctions became only words she'd been trying to fill with meaning, and fellowship became her ideal. It was broad and generous and welcoming. And in Halifax, she discovered, there was a portal—Pier 21—that represented all of that. The entry point for so many newcomers to the continent in years gone by. Even though it wasn't how she or any of her friends had arrived here, it personified the city. An open door that seemed to promise a new world of possibility and safety. So many queer individuals drawn, like Jill, by the romance of the compact city by the sea, looking for something they couldn't name till they'd found it in Halifax. Like Dawn, moving from rural Nova Scotia to Toronto, but eventually to Halifax after years in Montreal. And like herself: from Uganda to Kenya to the UK to Kenya to Toronto to Montreal and eventually to Halifax. Looking for that fellowship, and finally discovering community.

Jill had landed at The Haven, Halifax's hostel for queer kids, at the right time, offering herself as a tutor and games specialist before honing her skills as facilitator, counsellor, and then in outreach. With a degree in English from Cambridge, a love and talent for nearly every sport, reservoirs of empathy for refugees like herself—Jill believed every trans person was a refugee—she was embraced. Now, eight years after arriving in town with a backpack and only one name in her notebook, Jill was looked up to—at six-foot two, way up to—as the heart of the city's trans community.

That one name she'd carried with her belonged to the woman who'd met Jill off the plane and tucked her under her capacious wing. Tula became Jill's solace and strength, and eventually, her partner. Now Jill worked both inside and outside of The Haven. She built programs and connections for the BIPOC and queer communities and had become a spokesperson for both. She had a nose for opportunity and the tact and intelligence to seize it for herself and her peers, without grasping. The Haven became her life; safety and respect for her community, her mission. And that was where, nearly a year ago, she'd met Dawn.

Dawn had come to volunteer, when she was still just barely making enough each month to pay rent. Despite having the love and support of her mother, Dawn struggled with the estrangement from her dad and ached for the kids arriving at The Haven searching for connection to replace the families that had rejected them. She was a sought-after listener.

Perspective, thought Jill with admiration, and like Tula had done for Jill, she tucked Dawn firmly under her wing.

Jill discovered that Dawn played soccer, and in the spring urged her to try out for the all-female team she played on. Mostly cis women, she told Dawn, but also, said Jill, "...a few of *us*."

A long pause from Dawn, then, "Really?"

"Really. They judge our skills, not—" and Jill waved towards her crotch with a wry grin.

With a bit more coaxing, Dawn had come, and played, and excelled. She was by far the most talented member of the team, and modest. After her first game, which Dawn had won for them with a last-minute, dramatic goal, Jill had dubbed Dawn Aurora, lifting her high in the air before the victory lap. This win heralded a new and surprising chapter of success for the team.

Later Dawn asked Jill, "Where's it from? Aurora?"

"Latin. Roman goddess of the dawn."

And Dawn, so quiet and self-contained, roared with delight, determination, and possession when she connected with a ball aimed at the goal, so Dawn's nickname was shortened to *Roar*.

When Jill learned, shortly after that semi-final game, that the lovely woman in the tractor photo was ill, she offered to come with Dawn to the hospital. Just to wait for her, so that when Dawn finished a visit she'd have someone to report to. Weeks passed as Miranda came and went from the Halifax hospital for treatment, and finally Dawn asked if Jill would come up to meet her. Jill realized Dawn needed someone in her community to know her mother, to understand where Dawn had come from.

Those visits taught Jill a lot about Dawn and gave Dawn such pleasure in sharing her mom. Miranda treated Jill like another daughter immediately, delighted by all they had in common. Music. Politics. But books, mostly. They had both read voraciously and discussed endlessly, with Jill bringing books or articles about books every time she came, for Miranda to read in "business class."

That's what Miranda had dubbed her chemo chair. She'd never flown business class—or any class, really; she could count the flights she'd taken on her thumb, she said—but she'd lean back with a tube in the top of one hand and a book in the other, telling Dawn she was on her way to some exotic destination where she'd step out of business class into health and a new world. Jill knew Miranda was working hard to hide her exhaustion from Dawn, who insisted Miranda was growing stronger every day.

Miranda worried about Dawn but never ever said so to her daughter. Only to Jill.

She worried about every possibility, every piece of ugly news: 'Don't Say Gay'; trans athletes whose rights to compete were being attacked; governments that were prepared to put a whole state on hiatus to ban a single child from a public bathroom; *Roe v. Wade*, which might have made a world of trouble for cis women but, Miranda knew, could spell unspeakable danger and disaster for trans men, who were her children now, too. More lost lives plotted on a graph measuring the hopelessness and fear of trans people across the continent. Every sadness for her child's community presented a world of fear to Miranda. Who would speak for Dawn, if Miranda couldn't?

Dawn was resilient, Jill told Miranda. She had community; she would manage. Even the grief that might come—and Jill could see that it was coming—wouldn't diminish Dawn's quiet resolve or destroy the dreams and goals she had been building. Dawn, Jill reminded Miranda, had already met her biggest challenge. She'd had the courage to step into herself, and to speak for herself.

Those early days of getting to know Dawn, and then Miranda, turned into weeks, then months.

Miranda recovered, somewhat—they stopped short of calling it remission—and went home to the farm. Dawn was glad her mother was better of course, but now that she'd left the city and only came in once a month for a wellness check, Dawn missed her. Jill felt her absence too. She realized that the curiosity and intellectual rigour that Miranda applied to everything had fed her in a way Jill hadn't been fed since college, as they discussed all they had in common and much they didn't. Rare and delicious, their conversations, she told Miranda in her precise, earnest way.

And when Miranda went home, the chance that Dawn might reconnect with her father receded, too. A mixed blessing: Jill knew that Dawn armed herself on every visit for the unlikely chance of an accidental meeting with her dad, which could be devastating. The thing about the possible meeting, Jill discovered one day, was that Dawn's protective armour had not been grown just against the possibility of disaster. She balanced likely catastrophe with an imagined, rosy-hued reconnection, one that would give her back her father. She had to fight against that, too—the implausibility of it. Jill discovered this after one particularly hardscrabble game, coming out of a triumphant huddle to find Dawn crouched behind the now empty bleachers, distraught. Sobbing.

"What?! Hey—" What on earth had happened. Had she been assaulted? "Roar, baby! Are you hurt?"

Dawn shook herself. "It's ridiculous. Couldn't have been...so I don't know why—"

A paroxysm of sobbing. Jill held her.

Finally, Dawn calmed. Jill had never seen this from her before. "I thought I saw my dad," Dawn said. "And it wasn't him. I just..." She was silent a long time and then, "I want to see my dad."

It had been over five years since Dawn had seen John Andrew, and every day that passed made the idea of reconnection more unlikely. Impossible, Dawn told Jill. The turning of one season to the next brought with it specific longing: birthday and holiday rituals that had meant so much growing up went uncelebrated now, away from the farm and her family. And as the year grew dark, the comfort of physical contact with Miranda was gone: she didn't come in to the city in the winter. Doctors seemed to prefer the new online-care model, and it meant no more snowstorms on the highway. Wins for everyone, except Dawn.

Christmas passed with a brief visit in the city, shopping. Quiet January. Long, cold, and snowy February: Miranda sent a crazy Valentine. March. In April a courier delivered an Easter basket to Dawn's little studio, and then, in May...

Miranda was sick again. Her best friend Jenny brought her in for consults first, and then more radical treatments. John Andrew was about to start planting and there would be more calving soon, but he came with her for the start of a weekly drug trial, on which everyone was pinning their hopes. Then Jenny would bring her, mostly, though whenever he could get Jerry and his son Andy from across the road to help with the herd, John Andrew would drive in, then turn around and drive back: five hours on the road, then two or three in the hospital, at the busiest time of year. Mostly he'd been managing the farm alone—well, with Jerry, who'd been a farmhand for years and helped as much as he could. But Jerry had built up his market garden with his son's help, and now Andy was juggling spring prep and planting with another job too, so like John Andrew, Jerry was looking for help.

Nothing simple about rural life. Neighbours helping neighbours hold families together. Jill had gathered—mostly from Miranda's overly cheerful responses to Dawn's questions—life on the farm these days was unusually tough. Especially when the team contracted dramatically, as it had with Miranda gone again. She and John Andrew were partners: Miranda was the money manager, the strategizer, appointment maker and keeper, the negotiator with bankers and the milk-marketing folks, while John Andrew, Miranda said with pride tinged with concern, did everything else. It was a small farm, but these days a small farm meant a lot of big issues.

The drugs drip-dripped into Miranda as she laid back in business class, with Jenny and Dawn on either side of her. The three women were planning. Like the most committed generals, they were laying the groundwork for a complicated and delicate campaign: reconnecting Dawn and her dad. When one of them would comment on the military metaphors they were using, they'd remind each other that John Andrew was not the enemy; he just didn't know. *When* he knew, when Miranda was well enough to have that careful conversation, to bring Dawn and John Andrew back together, they would start again: all adults now, making their way through a new landscape.

And Miranda began to improve. The drug, so hideously toxic at first, seemed magically effective. Every day a little more possibility, a little more strength. When Miranda had an extended stay as the doctors changed things up, John Andrew called two or three times a day when he couldn't be there. They were all hopeful: Miranda kept getting better.

Then, after nearly three weeks with a positive, bright trajectory, the ground rolled under all of them, a crevasse forming in their landscape of hope.

Something small, manageable it seemed. An infection, unrelated to 'the main event,' except that Miranda seemed to have no resources to fight it, developed when she was in for a three-day stint. They kept her there, managed it. Four, five, six days. It was a tenacious bug. Tests were up and down. Then one evening, Miranda did what she had never done: she told Dawn and Jill to go, she was too tired to talk, or listen. The next morning Miranda woke up, but barely. Sick and getting sicker fast. Whatever was galloping through her was taking down every fence it attempted. She was failing on a day John Andrew wasn't going to be there; he was doing some of the most back-breaking work of his season: delivering two calves himself, hoping to avoid getting a vet in. Money. Always money. So, in the morning Miranda told Jenny no, no, don't call him. She just needed a drop of water; a breath of air; to see Dawn; her shawl, it was cold. It was June, and it was hot, beyond hot, and Jenny called John Andrew and couldn't reach him. By noon, Miranda was silent, concentrating, as if she was in labour, Jenny thought. Jenny tried calling John Andrew over and over, voice mails until John Andrew's mailbox was full. She called Jerry. Then Jerry's wife, Sandra. And Jerry's son, Andy. And...Jenny felt like the whole community had been swallowed.

Dawn didn't leave her mother's bedside. Late in the afternoon, doctors spoke quietly outside the door and then came in to make sure Miranda was comfortable. Nurses checked back, asking Jenny quietly if a chaplain was wanted.

That Miranda was going soon was absolutely clear now to Jenny and Jill. Dawn kept telling them all that her mom was looking better and better. Never had Jill known such a long day: minutes that felt like hours, hours that ballooned to nearly bursting, feeling like days, or weeks even. Miranda slipped in and out now. Every time she came back to herself, she'd ask, Where is John Andrew? Jenny called again.

It was getting dark when Jill began to sing quietly.

Jill had told Miranda the best part of college was singing evensong in the college choir, so now she sang softly through every piece she could remember—the alto parts. Walton, Vaughan Williams, Thomas Tallis. Then, pulling words up on her phone, she started on Miranda's particular hero.

Miranda moved her head from one cheek to the other. For a moment absolutely there, she lifted the corners of dry lips and whispered, "Forever Young"? Then, exhausted by that effort, she closed her eyes to Bob Dylan.

Roar, Jill thought now, watching the quiet young woman as she wrapped the cherished photograph in a T-shirt, sliding it between layers of clothes then zipping the suitcase shut.

"Doesn't seem like much," said Jill.

Dawn shrugged. "Won't need much."

She lifted the case, picked a bus ticket off her desk, and turned to the door.

Miranda

The room was dim. She'd straddled this peculiar space all day, feeling Dawn so close, Jenny with her hand on her foot as though she was trying to hold her in the bed, which Miranda felt herself above, observing dispassionately. Jill's voice so gentle in her ear—but also, she thought, surrounding her, like...

The water in the Strait, near the farm in late summer. Just before hurricane season, when it was impossible to tell where you ended and the ocean began: the heat, the blood temperature of it. The beat, beat, beat of the waves.

Beat. Beat. Beat. In utero.

She was swimming, rolling, reaching up and away from the narrow white bed, not her bed, not her home—where was John Andrew?

Tammy. Oh, Tammy would ache for this.

She hovered above the women, knowing she couldn't linger, but curiosity kept her there.

What next?

Dawn and Jill were holding her hands, and each others', across her chest—which was so curiously absent, she thought. She'd never got used to having that plateau of bone instead of the gentle roll of her breasts. It's only topography, she thought, and then considered that a strange description of her body, now that she'd vacated.

Could she let them know? How easy it was? Like a swim on an August day? What was she now, she wondered—and then knew.

She was breath, she discovered, feeling Jill's song against her ear, Dawn's sighs on her face. All those times when she'd struggled to control it, to hold it, to gather it, and now, she *was* it.

Dawn touched her hair, looking up.

Aaaaah, breathed Miranda. Thought, becoming air. Zephyrs all: memory, longing, pain, discovery. Jenny's silk scarf moved as Miranda recalled how they'd met: grade three, new girl Jenny, friends forever.

What is forever, Jenny was wondering. Where is forever, as she turned to see where the draft came from.

Aaaaah, Miranda considered again, and knew that now, and perhaps forever—was this forever?—she could be breath. Or wind. Or thought.

Oh DonaldDonDonnieDawn.

Oh Tammy.

John Andrew—oh.

Dawn

Dawn looked back to Jill, still waving, and raised her hand before turning forward, pulling her sweater tighter. The air conditioning sent a frigid waft through the nearly empty bus as it edged into the traffic, lining up to cross the bridge over the harbour. She loved that bridge. That bridge, and the sun throwing shafts through it as it set, had taught her which way was west. Directions in Halifax were perplexing: South should be the harbour, North towards the Citadel. Neither was true, but now she knew which direction was where; watching the sunsets from her tiny studio window had set her personal compass. A kind of miracle, the way those green girders and orange cables, reminding her of her dad's ancient Meccano set, held the huge weight of the roadway, all the cars and trucks and cyclists and pedestrians and buses—

What is wrong with me, thought Dawn. It's a fucking bridge. My mother is dead.

She touched the string of pearls around her neck. She thought she used them like a rosary, then considered she didn't really get how Catholics used their rosaries. What did they count? Blessings? Dawn certainly wasn't.

Instead, as she touched each pearl, she went over and over the things she wished she'd been able to say to her mom, if things hadn't happened so fast. If they hadn't all believed, to the very last moment, that Miranda would rally; when she didn't. But after her last breath, Miranda had stayed with them, they all knew it. Jill and Jenny left Dawn alone with her mother because they knew it. They knew Dawn only had until...whatever happened next in a hospital happened, and Dawn needed to ask her mother about everything. Leaving everything behind.

Dawn had sat silent in that thrumming room. Having that conversation meant Miranda was going. Gone. And even when Dawn was led from the room, she wouldn't acknowledge it. So. Still so much left unsaid; so many questions unanswered. And no way to know when Miranda got there.

Dawn could hear her mother, now—

Get where?

Miranda, a non-believer who attended church every Sunday, praying, she told Dawn, to any available goddess who'd provide maternal intercession for friends or neighbours in need, would be gentle, but practical.

Get where, darling? Don't wait up. Don't leave the lights on.

Dawn shook her head now, thinking there were few parts of her mother's life that contained the tangle of contradictions Miranda's spiritual life had. Me, maybe, Dawn thought. And whatever made me. She wondered if her transition had impacted her mother's beliefs; if her mom had turned over responsibility for Dawn to one of those available goddesses. Now she'd never know. Dawn's stomach lurched with the finality. All the questions she hadn't asked.

Get where?

Wherever it is you go. You *know* Mom, Dawn would have replied, not crying.

She would cry for her mother eventually. She cried about other things. Odd things. A broken plate she hadn't even liked. Strangers with tiny animals on the internet: this morning, a blind ferret being bottle fed, and the beautiful relationship between an Australian shepherd and a cow. A Jersey. She wept for the ferret that would never see the person who loved them enough to keep them alive, and for the deep and abiding cross-species love between a dog and a cow, but she didn't cry at her mother's bedside, or when she left Miranda in that room alone forever.

Now Dawn touched the pearls, one at a time, turning them gently, doing as Miranda had suggested when she gave them to Dawn years before, leaving home. Touch these, she'd said, and remember all the good things: a sunny day we had, a beautiful place we found, an unexplainable thing we saw, a joke, a song, a goal.

If she'd been able, at the end, she would have told Dawn to be specific. Miranda had tried to live her Mantra of "Be Here, Now," even when the "Here, Now," was uncomfortable or inconvenient. She would take Dawn's phone away sometimes—Dawn heard her now—Sit in the moment. Name it. That is being alive.

Now, Dawn thought, as she turned each pearl, it's being *not* alive. But I have to believe in each of these tasks she gave me and believe that each memory *is there*. She's there, here.

The air conditioning gave a gentle moan, and the cold breeze became just cool. Comfortable.

The pearls made Dawn think of Tammy, and she'd been trying not to. As long as she could remember, Tammy had believed those pearls would be hers. Dawn found it hard to imagine that meeting her sister after five years with these pearls around her neck could become a memory that would sit easily on this string of creamy recollections. There was no avoiding it though: this was the day she'd see Tammy again, and Tammy would see her, after five years of what she was sure Tammy would consider a deplorable drip-drip-dripping from the family reservoir of trust and good faith. Dawn suspected the reservoir was a tangible, measurable thing to Tammy, and her sister would feel that Dawn's disappearance and silence was somehow a reflection on her, because how could someone vanish without letting THE BEST BIG SISTER IN THE WORLD know where, or why, they had gone. Tammy by that time had already skedaddled—her words—to the big city for university. Not too long before Tammy left, Dawn had given her a small silver trophy celebrating that special Big Sister status, with the words *so much love from*, and her deadname, engraved on the wooden plinth.

Now a million emotional years away from her fifteen-year-old self—though only actually seven—Dawn knew so much more about her sister. She remembered that while Tammy had always been quick to claim credit whenever credit was lying around waiting to be assigned, she was weirdly, equally inclined to assume blame, and any drama occasionally associated with blame. She wondered if her sister was still doing that thing: looking to be told she must *not* shoulder responsibility that wasn't in any way hers, but then, martyr-like, being absolutely prepared to wear any and all culpability. An exhausting dance. Dawn hadn't known the descriptor *high-maintenance* in those days, and would never have applied it to THE BEST BIG SISTER IN THE WORLD if she had, but she was curious whether the steps to Tammy's tango remained the same. Idly Dawn wondered whether the gifted trophy was where Tammy had left it, in pride of place next to her 4-H riding ribbons on her dresser, or if she'd eventually taken it to her new home in Toronto.

Despite her quirks, Tammy really had been the best big sister Dawn could imagine. Never really, *really* mean (though Dawn remembered a couple *really* mean occasions), but quick to take offence. But with Dawn, patient and funny. Great at diversionary tactics of every kind. She'd be a good mom. Dawn had followed her like a shadow, learning about who *Dawn* really was, as she watched Tammy come into herself. Dawn didn't talk much about Dawn in those days—didn't have the words to explain, didn't know what she felt, or what she was, or what she wanted to be. But, one day—Dawn replayed this memory like a movie when she needed proof that she could go home, could meet her sister in this new incarnation—they were listening to music in Tammy's bedroom while Tammy got dressed to go out, and Dawn watched as she made herself up, oh so carefully. If it was too much, their dad would send Tammy back to wash her face and she'd have to start over again, so she'd quickly learned the subtle art of elegant enhancement and had become expert at it.

That day, Tammy turned to Dawn, and for the first time said directly, "You like this, right? Like, watching me do my makeup?"

Dawn nodded.

Now Tammy tiptoed on, so gently. "Do you like girls?"

Dawn didn't know what to say. She knew what the right answer was, but she also knew it might commit her to something that perhaps she wasn't. Dawn wanted so badly to be truthful with someone. So she said, "I do, but..."

And then she stopped.

She knew what she wanted to say: that she did like girls, one girl. Anya. Who made Dawn's heart race and her face heat up, but so did one of the boys, Curtis, on the soccer team. Dawn didn't know why or how her feelings for one were different from the other. Who she liked, Dawn thought, wasn't really the problem. It was who she *was*.

Tammy sat silently, waiting for what would be the most revealing thing her sibling had ever shared. Dawn felt the pressure of that moment like a band around her chest and balked. Tammy was watching her.

"But?" Tammy said.

Dawn took a deep breath and...lied. "But I don't like anyone *now*."

Tammy had paused in her toilette and Dawn felt her laser focus examining every moment of heat Dawn had felt for any individual in her class, her school, her town. Secrets Dawn kept secured in her heart's strongbox. In that moment, the lock had been broken and Tammy knew—something.

But Tammy would never tell, and she didn't press any further, because she was THE BEST BIG SISTER IN THE WORLD.

Oh god. Tammy.

Breathe, feel the pearl, breathe, feel another, breathe.

Look out the window. Almost no one on the bus, but there was a guy sitting opposite, studying her. Fuck off. Fuckofffuckofffuckofffuckoff.

Does he know? Does he know me? Breathe. Look out the window. Fuck. Off.

She whirled—as much as she could whirl in that confined space—and glared blades at the guy: her age, handsome in a self-conscious, carefully scruffy way. He held her gaze for moment, felt the edges of it, and turned away. She'd won. That.

She turned back to the window. Impassively, she watched her reflection, elegantly enhanced—Jesus, Tammy again—superimposed on summer-green hills slipping past the bus; subdivisions that turned to single homes, dotted more and more sparsely on the landscape; on sky, and water, and on a herd of Jerseys in a lush field. That cheered her up. She had missed cows.

She'd tried to explain to Jill one evening about the comfort of cows. Their gentle, simple curiosity. The sweet breath and the visceral sound of a lowing herd: call and response in every key, every emotion somehow present. Longing first. Hunger. Loneliness. Irritation and chastisement. Love songs. She told Jill about being a 4-H foster to a beautiful Jersey calf, so out of place in her father's Holstein herd. Dawn understood that little cow. How separate sweet Martine must have felt sometimes, her warm gold against all that black and white.

Martine. What a beauty she was. Light brown-gold, with smoky eye shadow encircling huge dark eyes, and what Miranda had called comedy eyelashes. Martine batted those inch-long beauties and butted Dawn's head, catlike, when Dawn arrived with an orange or pear. Martine loved a pear. Dawn loved Martine. She wondered what had become of Martine when she'd left home. Her mother had never once mentioned her, which, Dawn supposed, didn't bode well. Like so much else, though, silence had just become the default.

The guy across the aisle was humming tunelessly to something banging in his headphones. Dawn inserted her own earbuds. The drone of the bus was replaced by her most recent musical crush. "Go first," sang the burgundy-voiced woman, "go first. Either way it's going to hurt, but I want you to go first."

Shit. Dawn pulled the earbuds out. If she was going to cry for her mother it would not be here, on the bus, manipulated by a beautiful voice who didn't know her or Miranda, or care that Miranda *had* gone first.

They crossed a tidal marsh. The windmills on the hills grew from tiny whirling toys to massive, sci-fi uniped creatures with a flailing tri-pronged limb as the bus passed close. They waited in the predictable summer road-repair queues, the sign-holding traffic controllers turning tired, bored faces towards them, sunburned and dripping in the heat. The hoodoos whizzed by, a community of tall sandstone elders with faces drawn down in anger and consternation. No one is happy, Dawn thought. Water runs earthward and takes the stone faces with it.

That's the last thing she thought before she fell asleep.

Dawn woke with a jolt as the bus jerked to a stop and her head bumped the window, the front door of a farm market coming into focus. The ice cream stand a mile from her home. The guy across the aisle was already up and at the door. Good. She gathered her things, waited for him to get down the steps and away from the bus. The driver was watching her now.

"Need a hand there, miss?"

Ah. See, Dawn, she thought, don't judge. Open the door, open the door, look for the good, she heard her mother say into her ear.

"Thanks," she said. "I'm fine."

She climbed down into the thick heat of the late afternoon. Holy... she began the thought, and then her dad, who always said Holy something, was in the ear her mother had been whispering in the moment before, his deep quiet voice pronouncing, Holy Moley. Holy Mackerel. Holy Toledo. A new sanctified something every time he expressed anger, or pleasure, or incredulity, and with her hand on the metal door of the farm market, she thought, Holy Hotcakes as guy-across-the-aisle came out, Coke in hand. Coke in a bottle, not a can. Mm. She was thirsty for summertime Coke-in-a-bottle. He held the door for her, giving her a careful, appraising look. Maybe, she thought, she'd been too hasty. He reminded her of...someone. The door swung behind her, she paid for the drink, and headed back out into the sun, ready to walk home. Half an hour, she thought. Half an hour, then it all starts.

In the parking lot in front of the market, an open-topped Jeep scattered gravel as it slid to a halt, radio cranked all the way up to "Watch Me," so she did.

Aisle-Guy jumped up into the Jeep, bumped and punched and physically macho'ed the other guys greeting him with absolute joy—it made Dawn smile. And then: a face she knew at the wheel. God. She turned away quickly. She hadn't thought about Marty Stewart for...ages.

The misery he'd caused her. Marty had a special talent for disruptive shit-spreading. Godgodgod. Fuck. The sickening stomach roil that only Marty Stewart produced. How far away, Dawn wondered, did she have to go, and for how long, before she'd exorcize that particular humiliation and pain?

Aisle-Guy fell back into his seat as the Jeep lurched forward, speeding to the exit, then braking suddenly to avoid oncoming traffic. Aisle-Guy, and all of them, turned to throw a last look at Dawn, now pulling her small suitcase. She heard the back and forth of ribald chatter tossed above the music, deep and dirty laughter, and then, as a gap in traffic let them race off, Aisle-Guy hollered, "Why don't you pull *me*, sexy!"

Receding laughter and music and a testosterone-generated twister of heat and gravel dust whirled around Dawn and she thought, What's the collective noun for a group of assholes? A group of porcupines, she remembered—why remember this now?—was a prickle. A group of skunks was a surfeit. Or a stench. Some wit had come up with those, and Dawn thought either would work here, as any number of skunks was too many. Frankly though, she thought *shits* a better collective than stench for a group that included Marty Stewart.

Brushing dirt from her eyes, she thought, Sorry, Mom.

But also, some tiny place inside her warmed with something like satisfaction. She was home, she was Herself, and they had seen that and added her to a whole world of women, theirs to abuse. Wow. Had she set that low bar when she moved to the opposite side of the binary, or had they?

They had. Fuck the patriarchy.

She was on the bridge and now she paused in the middle of this "nearly home" landmark, setting her suitcase at her feet to lean on the rails, out over the river. Sandstone cliffs with toes in the water. Willows with their lowest branches floating, gently coaxed towards the sea: the tension of being rooted yet pulled by the tide. The sweet briny scent, languid on the warm breeze. Ah, Mom, Dawn thought, inhaling the beauty she'd missed, but still chewing on Fuck the patriarchy.

Her mother wouldn't have approved of that thought. She'd be turning the other cheek and smiling as she did. Dawn shook herself and thought, Next time. New leaf turned, other cheek, turning...now. Miranda, she realized, now rode on her shoulder. That's where *there* is, she thought. My shoulder. Guiding or watching or—less comfortable thought—judging?

The river was sluggish: a chocolate milkshake melted under the bridge. She knew the water was salt now with the tide so high, and the reddish-brown clay lining the riverbed would be sticky and slippery. Suddenly, Dawn saw her young self sliding through the ooze with Tammy into the fresh tide farther down the river, and the memory of the skinny little boy with the mud-coated legs and the white concave chest made her feel nauseous.

Would it always be like this? Would every corner reveal another version of that person, so alien to her now?

The breeze off the river lifted her hair, teased it lightly across her face, almost a caress. The air was urging her onward. It would be all right. She picked up her suitcase and strode on.

The long driveway to the farm was the same.

The avenue of enormous sugar maples was nearly unchanged. One gap, where a stump remained. Her dad told her once that the trees were probably two hundred years old, and that conversation had prompted a grade-six science fair project. Dawn learned those maples could live for up to four hundred years, so theirs were, by maple standards, only middle-aged. Someone in her mother's family had planted those trees one by one down the long drive, imagining what they would become. That, Dawn had always thought, was some kind of miracle. The foresight. The imagination. The faith. The literal roots of her family ran beneath her. From tree to tree, and—probably—reaching sinewy tendrils into the foundations of the house, tying the maples and the home on land tended for two hundred years, together.

That school project, Dawn thought as she paused in the gap by the stump—running her hand across the rings and then wondering, front door or back?—was probably the most time she and her dad had ever spent working on something together, just the two of them.

For years, John Andrew had tried to get Tammy involved in tapping and boiling the syrup—they'd made and bottled buckets of it to give to neighbours and family as gifts—but she wasn't interested. She'd paint or draw the trees, collect their red leaves, and make collages every year, but that was as far as Tammy's arboreal interest went. Dawn and her dad tapped the driveway trees, and then John Andrew took Dawn deep into their woods to a stand of wild sugar maples, where they tapped again. They went daily for nearly a month, sitting in silence together with patches of snow still on the ground, watching the comings and goings of deer, mink, coyotes, hare, a bobcat (they named him Robert; he didn't come often), and, once, a black bear.

Dawn had been dozing, her father sitting in silence smoking—back when he rolled his own, before Miranda put her foot down and the "evil weed" disappeared—and Dawn felt a dig in her ribs. Nothing said. Her eyes flew open to see a bear, very large, very still, and very close.

Too close. Watching them.

"Do we play dead?" Dawn had whispered.

Her dad shook his head no and reached, without hurry or apparent concern, for a fallen branch near him. Then he slowly rose, unfolding to his full height, his back against the tree they'd tapped. Dawn crouched at his feet, trembling.

The bear stood still.

John Andrew, stretched to his full six-foot-two, stood still.

Dawn imagined herself invisible and held her breath.

Her dad took a step forward, not looking directly at the bear but raising the huge branch above his head. The bear looked undecided, then shuffled a step backwards. John Andrew took another step towards the bear, never looking directly at the creature. This dance was agony to Dawn, who was still trying not to breathe.

And then her father roared.

Not high and sharp; not a yell, but a long, guttural ululation, from the deepest part of himself. The bear seemed a little...flummoxed, they decided later, and the flummoxed bear made a decision and turned, in an unhurried, considered sort of way, taking herself back into the forest.

That was her father, whom she'd loved and idolized at twelve years old: fearless bear vanquisher, a mild-mannered farmer who roared to protect his child and himself.

If Dawn had heard the conversation later that night after everyone was in bed—the tale having first been presented to Miranda as an encounter with a Winnie the Pooh–like critter—she would have heard her father, the bear-battler, say how frightened he'd been; how his arms had been shaking as he raised the branch; how he knew the situation could end very badly; that he'd never dealt with a bear in his life; how his next plan was to scream at his child to run, run, run while he fought for their lives. Miranda held John Andrew as he told her that their child might have seen their father killed. Dawn would have heard her father say that he'd roared because he was afraid, not because he was brave.

Now, not being privy to that conversation between her parents, Dawn stood at the bottom of the front porch wondering if she could still turn back, turn away from the promise she'd made to Miranda, because what would they possibly have to say to each other, when she thought, *that*. We have—thinking of Jill, who she wished was there now, who'd given her a new name—*that* in common.

We roar.

She walked up the porch steps and reached to open the front door. Then stopped and knocked instead. After a minute the door was opened by a handsome, tall—as tall as her father—young Black man.

"Hi. Can I help you?"

Dawn was startled. Was this her home? Had something happened that Miranda had somehow forgotten to tell her? Had they lost the farm, left, someone else moved in?—rapid-fire thoughts she knew were impossible, but but but...and then she knew that of course this handsome man watching her with a puzzled expression had to be the young man attached to—

Tammy. Who appeared through the dining room doorway, closely followed by John Andrew.

Tammy gasped, in recognition and shock. "Jesus!"

John Andrew stopped like invisible reins had pulled him up short, fixed on the young woman, still neither in nor out, but on the threshold in front of him. He seemed unable to speak, but finally he did: he whispered, "Miranda?"

The tall young man watched this exchange, looking to Dawn, then to Tammy, then to John Andrew, then back to Dawn. A peculiar emotional tennis match. Dawn felt herself removed, flying above this moment she'd imagined, feared, for so long. She was numb and yet too present. Every sense heightened. The silence was a molasses pool, and she clawed her way to its surface to say, "No, Dad. It's me. Dawn."

Cicadas. Crows. A cow in the distance. A car passing.

Then John Andrew turned away. Going, Dawn assumed, to the kitchen. Dawn watched Tammy take in every detail of her: clothing, shoes, suitcase, pearls. The pearls. How much information, Dawn wondered, were the pearls giving her? The amount of time Dawn had spent with her mother that Tammy hadn't known about? The role that Dawn had assumed as second *daughter*, rather than second *child*? How, wondered Dawn, did it change a family when the youngest child, the baby, was a girl instead of a boy? Dawn's thoughts tumbled as Tammy turned and followed her father. The young man was left where the strange scene had begun for him: cast as the gatekeeper, responsible for allowing access to the family.

"Hold on. Like...Don, Tammy's brother?"

Dawn wanted for a moment to employ her blade-vision to cut this man down to size, to hold her space that was so hard won, but instead she heard herself think, Open the door, and smiled slightly as she registered that the two of them stood with an open door between them. She was surprised when he smiled too, so she was able to say, with no blades, "No. Like Dawn, her sister."

He looked at her then with such kindness and such a lack of judgment that she just liked him. He picked up her suitcase, clearly expecting her to follow him into the kitchen. He turned back to say, "I'm Tammy's fiancé. I'm Byron."

"Right. Congratulations," she said, and thought, Good luck.

Now she remembered what Miranda had said about Byron: a lovely young man who worked with Tammy at the agency. But Miranda had never mentioned he was Black. Dawn thought for a moment about what that revealed about her mother, and then her sister, and most of all, her father.

Byron carried on into the kitchen, providing a buffer for her. He didn't deserve to be sucked into this, but he'd picked up her bag, and gone in first.

Watching him go, Dawn gathered all her reasons for coming here into one golden-threaded carpet bag of longing and responsibility. Clutching it tight tight tight, she turned to the picture of her parents on their wedding day in the hallway gallery; studied the school pictures of her sister and young Donald from primary to graduation; touched the beautiful hanging her mother had created from her family's old T-shirts; and with a breath in and a breath out, Dawn reminded herself that this was the place where she had been made.

Move forward. Be here, now.

In the kitchen, her father was standing by the farthest window, holding back the net curtain as if it was a responsibility he'd undertaken, looking out. Tammy sat at the kitchen table, crowded with casserole dishes. Why weren't they in the fridge? Dawn wondered.

Byron lifted the kettle. "Tea, anyone?"

Without waiting for a response—there wasn't one—he set the kettle on the stove and turned it on, then took up his place again, leaning against the counter. Not sitting with Tammy, not standing like John Andrew, not assuming any kind of status. Leaning. Minimizing his six-foot-two frame. Being careful not to occupy any of the family space owned by Tammy and John Andrew and now Dawn, who crossed the kitchen slowly towards her father, stopping short to hang her purse over a chair back, and kind of float for a moment. Where to go: sit, stand, lean, leave?

She looked to Tammy, who studied their father. Dawn felt the curtain stir with a breath of air through the window into the warm, still room. She locked eyes with Betsy, who studied her but did not budge from her bed, then looked from one family member to the other, trying to decide exactly what this dynamic was.

"Betsy," called Dawn gently. "Bets?"

Betsy considered Dawn with a long, slow look, but didn't budge.

Dawn spoke to the air: "She must have forgotten me."

No one replied. Every sound that Dawn remembered of the house was amplified. Ticking. Fridge hum, and cicadas—so loud. She hadn't remembered how raucous they were in the heat. Tammy's chair squeaking as she shifted. The water in the kettle beginning to bubble.

Dawn reached for the roar that came when she ran for a goal: for strength, focus, presence. For proof she should be exactly where she was. She gathered it and said softly, "Dad."

John Andrew moved his head slightly, an animal straining to hear something in the distance.

"I missed you, Dad." Not for Tammy to hear, or Byron, but for John Andrew. And her mother.

The kettle began to shriek. John Andrew lunged for it, took it off the heat. He reached into a cupboard for a tea caddy and pot. He pulled a mug tree closer to the tea things and then, with two large steps, he was at the coat stand. He lifted his hat and disappeared into the little back hallway, leaving Dawn and Tammy and Byron in the silence punctuated by heavy-footed steps, and the bang of the back door.

John Andrew

He took the steepest path from the beach to the clifftop. Every stone that rolled under his foot, sending him slipping, was a chastisement deserved for rushing out, for leaving Donald's—Jesus—statement hanging in the air.

Missed him, he said. She said. Well, John Andrew had missed his son, though he realized he'd never known him. He could have tried harder, done better. Of course. But the boy had been sandpaper against his skin for so long, and John Andrew had never been able to look at why. Miranda had. John Andrew knew she'd watched her husband turning into his own silent, judgmental father. She tried so many times to gently broach it. And when Donald left, she'd known why and where and how and had never told him. Now he thought, and I never asked.

"Dawn, her sister," he'd heard from the front hall. At the clifftop now, he reached for the small poplar on the edge to haul himself up and then made for the bench, placed years ago by Miranda's parents for the view across the Strait to Cape Breton. He and Miranda had courted here.

Courted. What did that even mean now? Did people court anymore?

They'd sat here for hours, talking, necking, imagining, planning. As a farmhand starting out, when he'd had the first of what would become many set-tos with Miranda's father, walking away thinking he wouldn't be back, she'd come here to find him. When she'd found she was pregnant with Tammy, she'd lain, head on his lap, crying: happy, frightened, determined to be the best of mothers. And she had been, from the moment she knew they were coming, to when each of them left. And beyond, he thought.

He'd struggled sometimes with the distance that grew between Miranda and himself with the arrival of each child: a strange, elastic space that expanded and then shrunk again as the children grew and made their way through every new crisis. But with Donald...well. The elastic stretched and then stretched some more. And with all the adjusting and readjusting Miranda had done to keep the peace between John Andrew and his son, a son in whom he recognized so little of himself, their own connection, their partnership, had been fractured. Despite the shared belief that every disagreement could be ended in bed, when Donald left home the elastic had come so close to breaking that there were long, silent nights of each working *not* to touch, *not* to let their night clothes even brush, as they lay listening for sleep to come to the other. Even falling asleep first became a kind of failing, he felt, and months went by in an exhausting blur.

She'd been distant, but not evasive. She wasn't punishing him; she told him that. She needed him to know she didn't blame him for his discomfort, but she wouldn't take sides. Not against her husband, and not against her child, so it was hard for her to be exactly who she'd been before Donald left. John Andrew must recognize that.

John Andrew couldn't talk about things that way; he didn't analyze his feelings, he just felt them till he didn't. To him, Miranda was there, and then she wasn't fully. And Donald was there, and then he wasn't, and with Donald went a lot of things John Andrew couldn't name, didn't know he'd cared about so deeply, but now understood. What might have been, what could have happened. What it meant to have a son.

All Miranda had ever said to him was "gay." She thought Donald was gay but wouldn't talk about it. It wasn't for her to have opinions on, she said. And John Andrew thought maybe Donald would get over it.

But not by leaving home, with help from his mother.

So he went silent and she did too, apart from the necessaries. The quiet house, without Donald there—no flashes of anger, no fighting, just smouldering regret—it was a relief, really. As time went on, John Andrew figured Miranda knew where Donald was, but she wouldn't talk about it unless John Andrew asked, and he wasn't going to. He wondered if he'd always be angry at Donald for creating these holes in his life, never admitting they were holes in his heart. He'd never tell Miranda that he missed his son, and everything he once hoped Donald would be. Growing up without much of a father himself, John Andrew had planned to be *such* a father, so much better than his own. Miranda would have helped him, he knew now, too late. And then, he missed Miranda so much because they never again were quite what they had been.

But he worked at it, John Andrew did.

After she'd been ill and come home again, he took to bringing home a bottle of wine Fridays. He didn't care for wine, but Miranda preferred it to beer, though she rarely had more than a sip or two. He'd lay in a fire, fall and winter, and they'd eat in front of it. They'd talk about every other thing in the world, and she let him know, without telling him a single fact, that his son was okay. Fridays were enough, for now. Someday, John Andrew thought, there would be more.

Slowly, with tiny kindnesses, they grew back towards each other, and when they started to make love again after a long desert of space and illness and silence, to feel her hand on him again was almost too much. But even with that return, he'd sometimes feel a look from Miranda that seemed a gentle dig, and he understood it, because he felt it in himself. Disappointment.

Dawn. Her. Her, she, hers. *Gay* seems like it would be easy to grasp now, he thought. But this. What even was *this*? What did it mean? How did *he* become *she* now? Could people just choose, now, what they wanted to be? John Andrew would never know, though, because he could never ask this person who looked exactly like his—shit!—*her* mother. Miranda.

Miranda. Help me do right here.

He stood up. He sat down. He stood again, and went to the cliff's edge to study the beach below. Other people, he thought, deal with this stuff. I will. He could hear his wife saying, Just be nice, you.

Nice wasn't enough, he thought. He started back home, then changed direction, heading to the barn.

Jerry was seeing the last of the herd into the dairy for the evening milking. John Andrew hollered inside making Jerry turn and answer, "What are you doing here?" as he urged the last cow into the milking parlour. His son Andy was hooking and unhooking the cows from the milkers, and the dairy was alive with sound: whooshing, clicking, and soughing, all with the radio chatting and laughing beneath. Jerry thought the cows liked the radio and milked easier and happier when it was on. "Happy cows, good milk!" he said. John Andrew thought Jerry was a bit fanciful, but he left him to it.

"Ah, you know, just... They behaving?"

Jerry studied his friend for a moment, then said gently, "Little lambs. We're fine here. Go on, go home now. We got this." Jerry started towards the door, knowing his friend would follow.

They walked, heads down, the rhythmic milking machines punctuated by the occasional bovine complaint, as they were released from the machine and urged out of the parlour.

"Whose car?" Jerry asked. "Tammy home?"

John Andrew nodded. "And her boyfriend."

"Must be serious."

"Yeah. Fiancé," John Andrew corrected himself.

They walked on, nearly back at the entrance to the barn now. John Andrew had to say something, to someone. So he said, tasting the name, "Dawn's home."

"Don! Well, that's good." With a sideways glance, Jerry added, "Isn't it?"

John Andrew nodded then said again, with all the difference he could muster: "Dawn."

"That's what you said," responded Jerry. "Don's home."

Perhaps John Andrew was losing the plot a bit, thought Jerry. Repeating himself. Came on with the grief sometimes.

"Dawn," said John Andrew again, then added, "like sunrise."

Now Jerry stopped walking, turning, bemused, to John Andrew, who lifted his hands and gave up, heading towards the big barn door and saying over his shoulder as he went, "You'll see."

Tammy

The only one in the kitchen who moved when the door slammed was Betsy. She went to the back door, then returned to the kitchen and sat with a disappointed, tired look, examining the three who remained. It was the look, Tammy thought, that her mother would wear at the end of a long day negotiating with her and Donald—shit, Dawn. Although, Tammy thought, I don't know that she did that much peacekeeping with us. We were pretty good. We got on.

Byron had a way of saying "next?" when he thought it was time to change the subject, smooth things over. She dearly wanted to say "next," but she couldn't walk back her response at the door. Still, speaking might be a start. She took a breath and looked at Dawn, so beautiful, so like her mother. Dawn was watching her, patient. Like Byron.

"What?" she said to both of them.

Shit. Did that sound aggressive?

Dawn pulled a chair opposite her. Byron turned to finish tea-making and delivered a cup to each.

Receiving hers, Tammy said, "Milk?" with a note of acid expectation.

He looked at her and narrowed his eyes.

"Please," she added. Then, "Sorry."

It was a multipurpose sorry, and she sprayed it towards Byron, then turned it towards Dawn. Dawn raised one elegant eyebrow as she settled opposite Tammy, waiting. Tammy lifted her mug towards the milk Byron poured, as did Dawn. Then all three sipped silently until Tammy said, "You look exactly like her. It's a...shock."

"I know." Did Dawn think Tammy wanted her to apologize? God, it was quiet. Tammy broke the silence again.

"Where did you go?"

"Toronto, first. Then, Montreal eventually."

"Do you speak French?" Byron asked.

"I do now." Dawn looked at Tammy, who was chewing her lip. She offered gently, "Go ahead."

Tammy shook her head. She wasn't insensitive; she knew there were things she had no right to know, but still. "I don't know...did you go alone?"

Dawn lifted one side of her mouth, almost a laugh, and said, "Well, I didn't have a buddy."

Tammy felt that as a criticism. How could she know the right thing to say? What were the allowed questions? Why didn't Dawn help her, make it easy? And even as she scrambled through these thoughts, she also heard them answered for herself: Don—shit, Dawn—doesn't owe you any explanations. You have no right to expect anything, until she's prepared to share. Why should things be easy for you when they can't have been for him—shit, her. This can't feel like a very safe space. All correct thoughts, Tammy congratulated herself.

Tammy had always considered herself very *woke*—though she hated that word—and recently she'd done a week of sensitivity training at work. The handsome queer man who came to lead them through the new territory had been elegant and crystal clear. He never came from a place of guilt or humiliation, only kindness and availability. When he talked about gender identity, equity, and the importance of creating a workplace that wasn't sexually charged or judgmental, she'd realized this was *not* a comfortable environment for some of her colleagues. The casual sexism, the vacuous assumptions about a world they viewed and sold as a heteronormative paradise—they were advertisers, after all—were, she realized now, harmful.

All these thoughts were pinging like a marble in a pinball machine as she tried to decide what she could, should, and absolutely mustn't, ask her sibling.

Sister.

Who looked like her mother.

Who was dead.

She started to cry again, and Dawn reached a hand towards her.

Tammy pushed her chair away and stood and said exactly what she didn't want to say: "Well, you're here. Five years of figuring out how and when to come back, but you picked a great time and I guess now we all have to be grateful."

"Tam!" Byron stood and took a step towards her.

Dawn turned to him. "It's okay."

"It's not!" Tammy barked, thoroughly ashamed of herself now, watching all her good intentions fly hither and yon—something her mom would say, Tammy thought—as she found it impossible to get this moment right. So why not just keep on talking. And she did, sending off a final sour little salvo: "This is supposed to be all about her, but now, of course, it's just about you."

And Tammy fled the kitchen as she had countless times as a teenager, when she really didn't know how to fix the mess she had just made.

Tammy sat on the bed waiting. In the past when she'd thrown such an undignified tantrum, it wasn't long before Byron would come show her what an ass she'd been. She didn't exactly look forward to that moment, and she certainly wasn't proud of the behaviour that prompted it, but she was always relieved when the knock came at the door—and she was now.

Only it wasn't Byron, it was Don—shit—Dawn.

Dawn came into her sister's bedroom and gently pushed the door so it was nearly closed, then just stood. There was a long moment, and Tammy realized that unlike Byron, Dawn wasn't there to make things easy for her; she was just there. Nor was she going to start this conversation. So Tammy did.

"I'm not an asshole," she said.

Dawn raised that eyebrow again.

Tammy responded with a kind of *what?* shrug.

Dawn replied with a gentleness that, Tammy had to admit, she hadn't expected. "It's an adjustment," she said.

Tammy looked down and studied her manicured hands, waiting for what would come next. Waited. And...waited. It was clear to Tammy now that Donald—shit, Dawn. Jesus, how long was this going to take? Dawn, Dawn, Dawn—was gathering his—shit—her thoughts.

Wow. Had that training really not taken? And what a lot of thoughts she—there I did it, Tammy thought—she had to gather.

Tammy, looking up again, found Dawn focused on her, considering, before she said, "I'm...comfortable."

Pause. Gather.

"More, now," Dawn added.

Tammy understood, but didn't know what she could ask, or answer in response, so she reverted to accusation. Blame seemed a reliable refuge.

"You never called. Birthdays. Christmas."

"I did," said Dawn. "I hung up. I thought I'd lose you forever if you knew."

"You didn't *have* me. You never gave me a chance—" She threw this at Dawn, trying not to see the sibling she had so missed. She studied the sculpted brows, full-lipped mouth, elfin chin, the long pale neck...and—

What?

Pearls. There was a set of pearls that Tammy recognized around Dawn's beautiful neck.

"Are those Mom's?" she asked.

Dawn nodded.

"I thought she'd lost them."

Dawn shook her head.

Ah, thought Tammy. That hurt. A lot.

"She said they'd be her *daughter's* one day."

Tammy saw that hurt Dawn, and felt the satisfaction of a well-timed jab, quickly replaced by shame as she watched a deep flush spread over Dawn's fair neck and face as she replied without rancour, "They are."

"Wow," said Tammy.

Perhaps the cruellest single word ever spoken.

In that one syllable, Tammy discovered the incredible value of regret. She learned about the complexity of knowing the price of something compared to its value. She learned about how hurt lodges;

that the place hurt burrows becomes a dark and dangerous hole filled with bubbling and boiling history, and if you fall into that place—or worse, if you *push* someone into that place—unless they're pulled out again so fast, and with such care, an important part of their heart will not survive. Tammy understood all of this, wishing that she could take back the ugliest thing she had ever said to her baby brother, now her baby sister, who had even copied the way Tammy plucked her eyebrows.

"I knew..." Tammy started, trying to explain, or engage, or redeem herself. "...something. I spent the whole drive wondering how I was going to tell Dad you were gay, but this..." She stopped. Again, the right words, the kind words, the *woke* words were eluding her.

Dawn leapt on her: "This?!"

Tammy took a breath. She heard her mother saying, breathe first, then speak. "I don't know how to do...this. I've never—I don't understand...this." She waved her hands in a general *you-me* wash. She followed, as her eyes started to fill again with, "I wish..."

Dawn was listening.

"I'm sorry. I am. I wish Mom was here. I wish—" She hiccupped.

"I know," said Dawn. "I know you don't know. And I thought, we thought—" Dawn paused, weighing something. Then— "She seemed so much better at Christmas."

"Wait—you saw her at Christmas? We were here at Christmas. I thought—you said Montreal."

"I came back to Halifax when she got sick."

"You've been in Halifax for, like, two years? Where? At school? Or—what?"

"I came back when she had the first mastectomy. Sort of school. I worked, but I've been studying. I need courses and money so I can go to school for sports physio, so when she was in the hospital, if Jenny brought her in for treatment—"

"Hold on," said Tammy, almost standing. "*Jenny* knew? *We* didn't know but *Jenny* did? Jesus."

This felt like betrayal. And if she felt this, what would her father feel?

The loss of her position as only daughter, the pearls, her brother —shit—sister: these were all a lot, but the secret that her mother had kept, guarding it from her and her father...the knowledge was a hand squeezing her heart. The pain of it was stopping Tammy's breath.

"Tammy," Dawn said quietly, "Mom didn't want Dad being the only one who didn't know about my transition, so we couldn't tell you. I was afraid of him seeing me. He hates me. You saw. He can't bear to be in a room with me. I didn't want Mom caught between us. Not then. I knew you'd be mad, and I—I thought that everyone hating me would make her sicker. Mom wanted to put all of us back together but I felt like the whole thing was killing her. I knew it would just be too hard then for her, and for me so...Jenny did what Mom wanted, and Mom did what I wanted. Tam—"

That "Tam" sounded like little Donald. Little, loving, baby brother Donald. Oh, she'd loved him so much.

"Tam. I was trying to keep her from exactly this. It wasn't about my love for you, though I do. I do love you. I never stopped loving you. But in that exact moment it was only about my love for her. You need to understand that."

Dawn moved from where she had been bolted in the middle of the room to sit on the bed beside Tammy. Tammy moved sharply away. The bed creaked. More than creaked.

"Woah!" Dawn said. They both felt it give unnaturally. Dawn studied Tammy before she said, "I don't think Byron will be very comfortable in this bed."

"Don't be disgusting. Byron's sleeping in the box room."

"What? Why? Don't you two live together? And why not the spare room?"

"I didn't know if you'd...and Dad is in the next room and he's alone, and I don't want—" She broke off. As Dawn waited, Tammy's eyes started to fill. "...don't want anyone to ever touch me again," she said.

Dawn reached towards her, just one finger, and lightly touched Tammy on the arm. Tammy stopped her ramp up to tears and shouted, "Stop it."

Dawn touched her arm again, twice this time, harder.

"Donald!—Shit!—sorry, sorry, sorry—Dawn! Don't. Touch. Me!"

Dawn reached for her with both hands now. Tammy lurched away on the bed, Dawn lurched towards her, arms open, to enfold her, as Tammy threw herself farther away and—

The bed gave way, the bottom separating with a loud crack, spilling the girls onto the floor, Tammy, falling into Dawn's arms, was shouting, "Stop it. Stop! I hate you! I want Mom, I want her, I want her, I want her!"

Dawn's arms tightened around her and slowly, Tammy stopped flailing as she felt the comfort in her sibling's strength, letting Dawn become the grown-up sister-in-charge. Dawn's blond head rested on Tammy's darker one for a long time.

They heard steps in the hallway; cautious feet climbing, then descending, the stairs; quiet bass voices downstairs; the chatter of the birds outside as dusk fell, and night sounds beginning to drift in.

Oh, thought Tammy. I'm not woke, I'm ridiculous and awful and I'll never get it right. And as if she'd said it out loud, her sister said, "We just have to want to get there, Tam. Wanting's more than half way."

John Andrew

Someone had let Betsy out, and when John Andrew arrived back in the yard she ran to greet him as though he'd been gone weeks. He bent to stroke her. No judgment here, he thought. What a relief a dog was.

In the kitchen, Byron was at the table scrolling on his phone. John Andrew had to resist his knee-jerk reaction: a nose breath. Miranda always said to him, Don't do that. Don't do your sniffing thing or everyone will know you think they're idiots.

"It's breathing," he'd say back. "I'm just breathing. You're always telling people to breathe."

"You're breathing *reproof. Judgment.* Please don't?"

So now he found himself holding his breath, because he really liked every single thing about Byron, except Byron's love for his devices.

Byron looked up, and then jumped up. "Hey. I hope it's okay, but I put one of these"—he waved at the multitudinous casseroles—"in the oven."

"It's fine. You must be starved, that long drive. I'll go up and have a quick wash. Where's Tammy and uh—"

"Dawn followed her upstairs. I think they're, you know, having a chat."

"Oh. Right. Well, I'll go up. Maybe give a shout when you think it's ready?"

Byron nodded as John Andrew headed up the stairs, sat back down and continued to scroll.

At the top of the stairs John Andrew could hear the—he stopped himself from thinking *kids* and substituted *girls*. Then revised again: *women*. He could hear the women—oh, that was difficult—in Tammy's room. Dawn was speaking. John Andrew started towards the bathroom then stopped, realizing how clearly he could hear them. Tammy was annoyed about something. He listened.

"You saw her at Christmas? We were here at Christmas. I thought—you said Montreal," said Tammy.

What? Thought John Andrew. So close? And then caught enough of the next exchange to realize, shocked, like Tammy, that his wife's best friend—his best friend too, really—she'd known, too.

He felt sick.

Jenny who he'd thought of as his sister. Who'd been a rock to him through all of this. She'd known about his son, and hadn't told him? Where Donald was? What he'd done? *Who* he was? Shit. Shit.

And then this: "I was afraid of him seeing me. He hates me, you saw..."

He missed a lot of what they said next but he heard this, spoken so quietly he had to creep closer to Tammy's bedroom to hear the end of it.

"Jenny did what Mom wanted, and Mom did what I wanted. Tam—"

John Andrew struggled to breathe—nose-breathe, anything. His chest felt, even as he stood, as if a great weight pressed on it, emptying him. In that "Tam," John Andrew heard his little son, six or seven or eight, pleading with his sister. His head felt light. He silently went back to the stairs and sank onto the top one, hand on his chest. Was this what having a heart attack felt like? Dawn was still speaking just barely above a whisper and yet he heard this ring out, bell-like: "...it was only about my love for her. You need to understand that."

Someone moved in the room and John Andrew thought they might be coming out, so he stood, ready to pretend he'd just arrived on that top step. But they were muffled now; he only heard Tammy saying, "Stop it."

Then louder, "Donald! Shit!—sorry, sorry, sorry. Dawn! Don't. Touch. Me."

And next, an enormous bang, something heavy crashing, and after a minute, muffled crying. Was someone hurt? Tammy? But before long the sobbing stopped, then...silence. A long, long silence. During which John Andrew turned and crept towards the bathroom, gently closing the door.

He splashed his face, and from the mirror a red-eyed man, lost in a labyrinth of grief and—he saw it in his own eyes—fear, stared back. Where on earth did he go next?

Was it possible he could hate his own child?

Possible or not, if his child believed it, it was true, and the only truth that mattered.

Five years of avoidance, of eggshell conversations with family and friends, of losing his wife, or part of her, before he *lost* her. How could he possibly fix this? Oh, death was terrible and absolute. He didn't know, he never knew! He put his head back, wanting to howl at the injustice of loving so deeply and for so long and finding no comfort for this loss now, nothing but anger and confusion.

The window was open, and the sun as it departed was leaving behind a bruised sky. Peach, fuchsia, mauve, and purple, with navy blue at the edges. The last breaths of the day rattled the metal loops of the shower curtain against the rod. John Andrew stood at the window and let the breeze, just starting to cool after the day's heat, dry his face.

Tammy

Dinner was fine. Byron had chosen a vegetable casserole, thank goodness, as they'd all just discovered Dawn was vegetarian, considering veganism. Tammy had nearly laughed out loud watching her father's face contorting as he grappled with that revelation, harder maybe, she thought, than Dawn's gender, while Dawn and Byron chatted. Byron was a self-described "vegetarian sympathizer." That meant, Tammy was always quick to point out, that when it suited him to be self-righteous about what he ate, he embraced it; otherwise, he was not giving up Sunday brunches with a side of bacon at Frankie's Diner. Fortunately, Byron and Dawn were sensitive enough not to sit at a dairy farmer's table and debate the environmental impact of keeping cattle or the relative health qualities of dairy products. Those kinds of conversations generally became fraught in this house, Tammy knew. Passing behind her fella as she collected the dishes, she gave him a peck on the head. She felt proud of Byron, and her...sister, who at this moment, having broken that bed together, she loved so much.

Byron followed Tammy to the kitchen, prepared to help with clean-up, but she released him and he headed to the yard. He disappeared briefly, then reappeared with a soccer ball and began to juggle and dribble to entertain Tammy. Dawn arrived at Tammy's shoulder to watch him out the window.

"Oh my god," said Dawn. "Really?"

Tammy felt protective. "What?"

"He's...enthusiastic."

Tammy knew what that meant, and flicked the dishtowel she was holding at her sister. She thought, my sister. I will never get it wrong again.

"Go on," said Tammy, giving Dawn a nudge. "Show him a thing or two. You know you want to."

Dawn sped outside to join Byron, surprising him with a quick-footed reach that won her the ball, then juggling it masterfully as Byron tried to steal it back.

Now John Andrew arrived to take Dawn's place at Tammy's shoulder, watching with her.

"Like puppies," said John Andrew.

Tammy grinned at her dad.

"He's awful and...she's great. She is great, isn't she, Dad?"

John Andrew said nothing. Just kept watching, while Tammy watched him.

Dawn expertly stole the ball again, then nutmegged Byron and collected the ball on the other side of him while he collapsed onto the ground before rolling onto his back, pretending to be hurt.

John Andrew snorted. "Big baby."

"Yeah. He is." Tammy smiled fondly, watching Dawn as she bent over, laughing at Byron, who grabbed at Dawn's foot while she still had control of the ball. Byron rolled on, faking. Really, he was pathetic. Tammy laughed.

Her dad looked at her and she sobered, instantly.

"Sorry."

"No," he said, "We have to..." And he waved a hand, failing to find words for the notion of going on, going forward, living.

Tammy considered what should come next. Everything from now on, she knew, was a careful building of one bridge after another, leading to a new landscape, so different from the terrain their family had inhabited before.

"She's on a women's team in the city. Top scorer—I squeezed that out of her. She loves it. She wants to be a sports physio, didja know that?"

"How would I?" John Andrew didn't leave the window despite the edge in his voice.

"Well," said Tammy carefully, wondering how to place the next girder for this particular bridge, "she's here now, and I'm glad."

Except for the muffled laughter outside, and Betsy's barking joy at the roughhousing, everything was still. Tammy and her dad stood side by side, saying nothing until Tammy decided she wouldn't let this go. She turned to her dad and challenged him. "I missed her. I'm glad she's here. Are you, Dad?"

John Andrew didn't turn away, didn't sniff or say anything offhand or cruel, he just...thought and watched, while his daughter waited. After what seemed an age, he left the room silently.

Tammy decided in that moment she could forgive her father almost anything. She felt so much sympathy for him; these two huge losses, his wife, his son, were changing everything he'd known about himself and his life. She was the adult now in their relationship. She was the fixed point, the North Star, and she understood that John Andrew might not yet know if he was happy, or pleased, or relieved that Dawn had come home, but he was definitely not indifferent.

Bridge one, day one.

Miranda

The house was still now, in the kinetic way old buildings are. The floorboards contracted from their hot-day stretch, yawning and creaking as the night cooled them. The windows bowed and returned. The slight breeze whistled warm where it found a loose window frame. The pets moved, soft-pawed, from room to room, checking on the occupants and choosing: Betsy finally settling with Tammy, and the cat, generally known only as "the cat," tucked in close to Byron's sleeping S.

John Andrew turned to Miranda's pillow when the curtain stirred, and a breath of air seemed to lift the edge of the sheet—too hot tonight for anything more. He buried his face in the pillow. Her scent was still there. These sheets had been on now for weeks, he thought. He could add that question to his endless list: how often had Miranda washed the sheets? How many things had he still to discover that just got done, that he'd never questioned or asked for? Tammy would feel that changing the sheets would be part of his way forward.

Miranda agreed. Change the sheets, darling. He heard her, bell-clear.

Change the sheets, and hang them on the line for me to dry.

He smiled at a memory, remembered that now it would always only be a memory, and laid his beautiful, ruddy arm with its red curling hairs over his eyes. Miranda loved her husband's arms: the landscape of flesh and fur, the sweep of his long forearm, and the brawn of his biceps and shoulders.

His eyes filled as he thought of the last time they'd made gentle, careful love. Every part of her was tender. Mindful of her fragility, he'd found himself exploring her body with such delicacy, and she'd tried not to mind the strange, deflated nature of her chest that once, so curvaceous and cushioned, had brought such pleasure. How he'd loved her breasts. How *she* had loved them, their beauty and practicality: she'd found nursing her babies so easy, so joyful, triumphant almost.

And how kind John Andrew had been, how matter of fact, when they were gone. She remembered with a wrench the moment she had taken off her shirt in front of him for the first time after the mastectomy, watching his face for...disgust is what she had feared most. She saw only sympathy, and relief—they both thought she was safe, then. He'd taken her hand and brought her to bed.

Ah bed, she thought. She had loved to love him, and regretted how that world would be lost to him—for how long, she wondered?

John Andrew pulled the pillow in and hugged it tight. He closed his eyes, dreading another day breaking without Miranda. Another dawn, he thought wryly. Sunrise, thinking of Jerry's bemused face. And fell asleep.

Miranda hadn't yet discovered if there was a way to be in more than one place at a time. She'd like to watch her husband sleep—he'd had so little of late—but remembering how she would creep from room to room when her children were small, to cover them and enjoy their baby beauty in repose, she found herself with Tammy, curled around Betsy. She admired Tammy's decision to sleep alone, imagining the discomfort for her father—for now, not always—in sleeping alone while his daughter curled against her lover next door. Thank you, she breathed over her daughter, and Tammy, still awake, stirred, tightening her grip on Betsy who protested a little. Love hurts. Tammy believed in pretending you were sleeping to bring on sleep, and she was pretending hard, eyes shut tight, then opening again as she imagined waking in this house for the first time without Miranda there. How could it be home? she asked Betsy.

It's home, Miranda breathed. It's home. You're building it again, Tammy, and it's work. Sleep.

Miranda urged Tammy's heavy lids to close, and they did.

Dawn lay so awake. Listening for Miranda in every sough and creak of the house, in every rustle of the old maple outside her bedroom window. She and Tammy had made an imperfect start, she thought, but she could see a way back—she corrected herself—a way forward. And Byron, well...Byron was excellent, and Dawn wondered whether Tammy had any idea how fortunate she was to be so loved by him.

And John Andrew.

John Andrew. Dawn had not corrected her father once at dinner when he'd misgendered her, and the one time he'd addressed her he'd called her by her deadname. *Dead name*. She hated that nomenclature. Melodramatic. Inaccurate. She understood the politics of it and why things had to be overstated to make any kind of impact. But in this particular moment, anything else would be better. Former. Old. Birth name. In any case, when John Andrew misspoke, he'd been corrected by Tammy, then stayed silent for the rest of the meal.

Dawn had seen him watching Byron and her through the window as they'd fooled with the ancient soccer ball. Had it pleased him, she wondered, to see that she still loved a game they were both passionate about, and that she was still skilled? Her father's fervour for her games through high school bordered, her mom used to say, on the religious: he'd lead the crowd roaring for her goals, and celebrated each win with an enthusiastic whack on the shoulder—the closest he got to demonstrations of affection. She asked her mother now: did it please him? To see I still play? And Miranda breathed, It will.

Dawn laid her arm, the exact replica of her father's forearm, bicep, shoulder, over her eyes, blue blue blue like Miranda's, and for the first time since her mother had gone, she cried, and wondered if she'd ever be able to stop; if she'd ever sleep again; if this longing to be held and truly known, and really seen, as her mother had held, known, and seen her, would ever abate. She watched the little clock on her bedside table turn from one to two to three to—did she see four o'clock? Or did she sleep then? Miranda watched. Her daughter slept.

John Andrew's pillow was damp, but he slept deeply now, the grip on his heart easing with every breath.

Betsy, knowing that Tammy was actually asleep, eased herself carefully from under Tammy's arms, nosed the door open, and lay at the top of the stairs where she listened to all the family and Miranda, breathing.

Finally, Betsy slept too.

Dawn

Whispering voices passing her door woke her, though Dawn was also aware that her phone was vibrating repeatedly on the bedside table. A series of texts. She sat up, focused on the door and the voices as she reached for the phone, and threw back the sheet. Stepping onto the landing, she could just see her father's departing head as he rounded the stairs towards the kitchen, closely followed by Tammy.

"Good morning," Dawn called, feeling she'd already missed whatever was underway. Tammy came back to the bottom of the stairs.

"Hey. Sleep okay?"

Dawn shrugged. "Ish. You?"

"Ish. Sleeping's fine. Waking up is—"

From the kitchen, their dad's voice cut in: "We need to go, Tammy."

John Andrew came back, just into sight. Tammy looked at him, then back up to Dawn.

"We're going into town. Dad has to do some stuff—"

"Should I come?"

Dawn had barely got the question out as her father answered, "We're good. Your sister's just helping me sort some things. Gotta go."

At that moment, Byron yanked the box-room door open and bounded down the stairs like a bright-eyed retriever.

"Coming, Dawn?" He paused mid-staircase for her answer.

As Tammy quickly answered, "No, we're fine," John Andrew's voice cut in with, "No, he's"—pause, pause—"-*she*'s stayin'." John Andrew turned away and headed back to the kitchen, and then, with a bang of the back door, the yard. Tammy stood awkwardly for a moment before turning and following him.

Byron studied Dawn. He glanced over the railing to where Tammy had gone, debating, Dawn realized, whether he should follow her.

Dawn released him. "I'm good. See ya later." With a kind of salute that Dawn knew put them securely on the same 'outsider' team, Byron rounded the foot of the stairs, letting the back door bang one last time with his exit.

Dawn went back into her room, gently closing the door behind her, holding the knob then letting it slowly grab—no click—then wondered why was she being so quiet, now, when there was no one to hear. But she knew. That old habit of taking as little space, using as little oxygen as possible, creating no disturbance or discomfort for anyone, she thought, but herself. She went back to the door, opened it, and slammed it. With relish. Then she stood in the middle of the room, pressing her right heel hard on her left foot's toes until it became unbearable, as she had for years in school in response to bullying. Well—to Marty Stewart. She'd discovered that inflicting hurt on herself pulled her attention away from whatever cruel barbs he sent her way. It had kept the tears at bay, mostly. Deprived him of the satisfaction. Now, though—

Her eyes, which for days had seemed immune from the infection of grief, were filling again. Dawn dropped to the bed and lay looking up at the model airplane she'd built and hung when she was twelve. A World War II Avro Lancaster. All the information she'd compiled came back to her, and she could see—she felt she could almost project it onto the wall—the social studies report in her careful, cramped handwriting. Her eyes were still tear-filled, blurry, but focusing on the gently swaying aircraft, they cleared enough for her to count the contents of her bookcase—breathe in for four, hold for four, out for four, repeat—till she had counted every single book. Now she was okay, she thought. Cristiano Ronaldo agreed. She swore he was nodding at her from the poster above her bed—maybe not reassurance, but their signal for a pass that would see her tearing down the field, roaring to a goal he would celebrate by lifting her high in the air—like Jill did all those months ago. Poor Cristiano. Proof you can't go back. He'd become the best soccer player in the world the first time he was at Manchester United, when Dawn was tiny, but now, his return seemed to signal the team's downward spiral. Dawn wondered if her father still watched all the Man U games like they used to.

Her phone buzzed again. Text after text lined up from Jill, and now the phone rang.

"Sorry," said Dawn, answering. "Oh no, wait. Sorry, sorry, sorry, sorry, sorry—is that 7 yet?—sorry. Now it is."

Jill laughed. "I know. Too many texts, but my stomach said don't leave her alone. Did you get there all right? And did your family—you know..."

Her stomach. Jill had second sight, a gift from her mother—it was one of the ways she had known incontrovertibly that she was trans, because in her family, second sight passed from mother to daughter. And it very definitely had passed to Jill. But in this case, thought Dawn, Jill's stomach might be...overreacting.

"...Murder me and stow me in the freezer?"

"Dawn!"

"Sorry."

"Not funny. At all."

"I know. Sorry. I'm fine. They're...fine."

"So, not awful."

Offal. Dawn considered the homonym: organs; guts and hearts. Surely this homecoming was all about guts and hearts but...

"They're trying," said Dawn. "It is awful, but it could be worse. My sister is—she's turned...almost into a grown-up. Her fiancé is amazing. Adorable, really. My dad, though..." Dawn heard Jill's empathy in her silence. She swallowed and continued, "I don't know, Jill."

"You'll find out. Be still. Let him come to you. You can do that."

"I don't think he's going to."

"Give him a chance," urged Jill. "This is outside his world. Be kind, Dawn."

Dawn glanced at the T-shirt on top of the pile she'd pulled from her suitcase sitting on a chair, waiting to be put in a drawer. Her favourite: black with a rainbow arching above just those words: *Be Kind.* Words she wore across her chest at every practice, and—she ran her fingers over the same words, tattooed in white—on her wrist. "Right," she said.

A long pause, then Jill said, "Tula says make sure you know we love you and we're here. She says keep your pecker up."

Dawn laughed. "Oh my god. Tell Tula she has got to bench that expression. Tell her I love her too, and I will do my best. Okay?"

"Okay. Your best is—we'll take it. We'll see you...not too soon, okay?"

Not too soon. How long would she last here? Dawn stood, reached for the towels on the dresser, and started to the door, realizing she was anticipating with pleasure a shower with actual pressure, and probably really hot water—neither of which her flat had. So, check mark there. Turning back, she took a second to lay the pearls across the corner of the photo of her mom on the back of the tractor. Everything in its place.

Later, scoured by glorious, abrasive pressure in a shower with apparently endless hot water, Dawn went downstairs in search of breakfast. She paused at the doorway of her mother's sewing room. Sunlit and dappled with the shadows from the maples, it looked as though Miranda had just popped out for a minute, to a neighbour's or to the garden. A pile of mending waited on one end of the sewing machine and something was under the machine's presser foot, as though she'd expected to be back in a minute to finish.

Don't. Don't.

Before Dawn could think it a third time, a squeak from the window seat. A small grey cat was lying in a cluster of tiny rainbows, cast by a cut-glass jar full of coins. The cat had its serious, leaf-green eyes on Dawn and drew her over to sit and stroke...her? Him? Them? Dawn settled on gender-neutral as the silky beastie butted her gently. What was going on? She'd never met this cat. She hadn't grown up with cats in the house—her dad thought they were barn animals. Dawn wondered how on earth this little one had wormed its way into someone's affections, and then into the house. Into the coziest room in the house, with sunbeams from two directions, and with all the fabric, pillows, and clothing, soft landing spots everywhere.

"Hello, Cat," said Dawn. "What's up?" The cat looked Dawn right in the eye and answered with a tentative squeak. "Ah, you talk. Did she give you a name?" Another squeak, this time a definite statement. "Okay, that's it then: Squeak," said Dawn. "I'll make sure everyone knows."

Betsy had come to the door to see who Dawn was speaking to in the empty house. Discovering Dawn's conversation was with a cat, the dog retired, disgusted, to her bed in the kitchen. Dawn laughed, surprising herself, and went to sit cross-legged on the floor beside Betsy. Equal time.

The house, though empty, didn't feel it. The music of dust floating on the sunbeams, the wedges of light through the windows...they were vibrating. And there was something else, Dawn thought. Something beyond the hum of the fridge and the tick of the clock. She stood still to listen. No leaves moving outside the window. Some subdued birds. Cows far in the distance but also—

"Mom?" she said and felt foolish. But said it again, louder with more urgency, as if calling was enough to bring Miranda down the stairs or through the door. "Mom?!"

Nothing. Of course, nothing.

Dawn went into the pantry. A jar of blueberry jam—*Miranda's Finest*, the jar proclaimed—and a loaf of bread from the freezer with a label in Miranda's handwriting. Dawn knew then how meticulously her mother would have prepared. The fridge might be full of casseroles from neighbours at the moment, but Dawn knew the old chest freezer would be full of bread and buns and scones and all the baked goods her father was partial to and her mother loved to provide. Dawn cut a slice of bread, put it in the toaster, then opened a cupboard to reach for a mug. She stopped, hand in the air, catching sight of the red and blue mugs labelled *Tammy* and *Donald* in childish script. Oh.

She leaned on the counter, then remembered how comforting it was to sit on the floor in this pantry, back against one set of cupboards and feet against the ones opposite, so she slid to the ground, to think. To wonder how much, how many *things* were still to be discovered, recovered, remembered: cat, fabric, jam, bread, mugs.

Was her mother and Dawn's own history everywhere, in everything? How could it be excised? How could anything be easy again in this house, where things were so hard for so long and the past jostled for a place alongside the present. Where *nothing* got left behind: the opposite of Dawn's mission for the last five years.

She would not, she promised her mother, stay in this puddle on the floor of the pantry. She wouldn't—

A knocking on the front door. Barking from Betsy.

Dawn stood, gathered, and moved towards the door to see who that firm, determined summons was coming from.

Tammy

Leading the way into Murray's Funeral Home, Tammy paused when she realized her dad wasn't right behind her. He'd got to the top step and just...stopped. Tammy went back to the screen door. "You coming?" John Andrew seemed to be focused on the sign next to the door. A sign that Tammy knew simply said, *Murrays' Funeral Home. Arthur Murray, Funeral Director.* He was reading and re-reading it.

"Tammy." She turned towards the voice: Arthur. Long-time family friend and, when all was said and done, an undertaker. She couldn't remember ever having the Murrays to dinner. Maybe you just didn't invite an undertaker to dinner, thought Tammy, though she knew Arthur's wife, Joy (even her name seemed to call uncomfortable attention to itself), was one of her mother's friends. Had been. It must be so hard, she mused as Arthur watched her being silent and her father glued to the porch, knowing that people are afraid, or worse, a bit disgusted by your vocation. But someone has to...

"Tammy? Are you okay?" Arthur reached a hand towards her, and she—she was ashamed—recoiled.

"Sorry. Sorry," she said. Sorry for being silent, sorry for that slight step backwards. Now she had to do better. "I'm still a bit—"

"Of course you are. Hang on." Arthur walked to the door, opened it as Tammy had done, and stood on the threshold. "John Andrew," he spoke with such compassion and warmth, "would you rather talk out here? It's fine if—"

"No. Sorry," said John Andrew. "I'm a bit..." and he stopped too.

The three of them stood tongue-tied, poorly rehearsed actors. Then John Andrew stepped in, held out his hand to Arthur, and said, "It's all a bit of a shock. We were so sure that she was improving." Arthur was nodding and nodding as he touched John Andrew's elbow, then led the way into the main room. Large chairs, a sofa. Attractive, simple. A comfortable living room, thought Tammy. And then: oh god.

Arthur was motioning John Andrew to one of the big chairs near a desk and Tammy wondered how long this was going to take. As if he'd heard her, Arthur cleared his throat and started gently. "Look," he said, "this won't take long, because you don't need it, and because, frankly, Miranda was very clear about what she wanted. And Tammy, I got the obit you sent from the road—"

"Okay. Good. Was it..."

"It's beautiful," said Arthur. "Exactly her. I don't know how you wrote it so quickly."

"She writes for advertising," said John Andrew, and then must have thought that sounded odd. "I mean—she has to write fast."

"I do," said Tammy, reaching for her dad's hand, and then realized. "Arthur, have you got a printed copy here? Could I...?"

"Of course." Arthur stood. "I'll grab it. I just printed it off. It hasn't gone anywhere yet."

"Great." Tammy was looking at John Andrew. "That's great."

Arthur left the room. Tammy was still holding her father's hand. John Andrew was looking into the distance. Through the archway into the next room, Tammy could see what her father was focused on. A row of coffins: different sizes, colours, wood types. One after another, placed so a person could walk in between them, compare the padded interiors, the grains of exotic wood. Like furniture in an expensive shop. And along the wall, a shelf unit full of urns of various shapes, each in their own little square. It reminded Tammy of the IKEA shelves she and Byron had recently installed in their condo. A series of boxes, really, with a vase in each square. Vases with lids. And boxes with handles. And locks? she wondered. Do coffins have locks? Then shook herself mentally. How strange death is, she thought. All about containers.

Arthur came back with a sheet of paper. Tammy scanned it, pulled a pen from her purse, stroked something out, wrote something in, and handed it back. Arthur laid it on the desk without looking at it, keeping his focus on them.

"So. The church is booked. I've spoken to Alice Markham—the minister," he added for Tammy's benefit, and John Andrew nodded.

"She's taking care of all the bits and pieces, music and so on. Miranda left pretty clear instructions with Alice and with me. I'm sure you knew, John Andrew." Tammy looked at her dad. She was pretty sure he *didn't* know. She was pretty sure her parents had never talked about it, despite her mom's illness and despite John Andrew's work being threaded through with death on a daily basis. "Alice'll call you, Tammy, if that's okay?" She nodded. "I've given her your number. Very simple service. Jenny will do the eulogy."

Tammy felt her dad's hand stiffen. What was that?

"And then readings for you, Tammy, and for..." Arthur was delicate. "Is Donald back? And able to participate?"

Tammy had rarely been lost for words, and she didn't expect help from her father in this moment, but he said, "Yes. Dawn's back. We'll check." Tammy squeezed his hand. That, she thought, was enough. And she stood. "I'll give you a call later, Arthur, if I think of anything," she added. "Alice and I might speak first, but the simpler the better, so..." Arthur was nodding, relieved.

Small towns might have lots going for them, Tammy thought, but in this instance the cold, impersonal big city won out. It must be so much harder to bury people you knew and liked: family friends whose children had gone to school with yours; who'd smoked with them and gone to dances; necked with them. (Once: Danny Murray. It didn't go anywhere—because, well, he lived in a mortuary. His bedroom was literally above dead people in a fridge.) Tammy thought all of this, but said, "Anything else we should know?"

"Well, the wake will be here, day after tomorrow. Again, all sorted, between Miranda and Jenny and—" Arthur waved his hands as if the whole world had been involved in the plans. The whole world, but not John Andrew, thought Tammy. He'd continued holding her hand even after they'd stood. Tighter than she'd ever felt him hold it. Now, though, John Andrew was reaching into his breast pocket. He pulled out a chequebook and Arthur waved again—this time waving it away, back into the pocket it had come from.

"John Andrew," he spoke so gently. "Miranda took care of it. Six weeks ago."

All the air was sucked out of the light-filled room then, and Tammy felt as though her father had fallen into a dark hole while she stood, toes over the edge, watching him get smaller and smaller as she yelled, What? What?? after him.

And Arthur saw that John Andrew needed to find his way out of that crevasse, so he turned away from the two of them and said, “I’ll go next door for a few minutes. I’ve left a few urns on the table there for you to have a look at. If you don’t like them or need—anything—just, ah...I’ll see you in a minute or two at the door.” And he left them there.

As if choreographed, John Andrew and Tammy turned together to study the line of urns they’d not registered before on the table behind the desk. Tammy reconsidered, realizing that some of the squares on the shelf next door had been empty. She wondered what Arthur’s criteria was for her mother’s urn. She saw four completely different styles, including one that looked like it might have been made for a cowboy. Kind of saddle shaped. Maybe Arthur really didn’t know her mother after all. He should have let Joy pick them out.

Her father said, so quietly she could almost not make out the words, “I can’t put...” and Tammy led him out of the room.

Arthur was waiting by the door, holding the obituary. Tammy wondered if he’d read it yet. “I can’t tell you,” he said, “how sorry I am.” Tammy drew breath in slowly and he added, “How much we’ll all miss her.”

John Andrew nodded and kept walking through the open front door. He paused on the porch where he’d gotten stuck on his way in and Tammy passed him, heading for the truck. He turned back. “Arthur,” he said, with a pleading note in his voice that made Tammy turn from the open door of the truck. “Do we have to have a wake?”

“Well, you can do what you like, John Andrew, of course you can,” said Arthur apologetically, “but the town loves a wake, and,” he paused, searching John Andrew’s face as if he was about to give up some long withheld secret, “the town loved Miranda.”

John Andrew knew he was beat. He turned away. Tammy got into the truck, closed the door, and as her dad came round, raised her hand to Arthur through her open window. But Arthur was looking down at the obituary, squinting as he read and, Tammy knew, re-read where she had scratched out *daughter, Tammy, and son, Donald* and written in *daughters, Tammy and Dawn*, before he looked back up at her.

John Andrew started the truck and Arthur, focused on Tammy now, raised his hand too. “See you Thursday,” he said.

Dawn

Oh no, thought Dawn as she saw, through the glass oval, a face she remembered.

Sandra Betz, their nearest neighbour and Jerry's wife, was complicated, Miranda had always said. Grating, her father said. She came from a family that had fought for everything that was theirs and a lot that, according to local gossip, wasn't. They lived a raggle-taggle existence on the back of the mountain in a house too small for a family of eleven, and someone in the family was always at odds with someone else in the community or the law. Disputes and ancient vehicles were the crops they tended; both thrived and multiplied. Somehow they turned their fractious energy to a living that had very little to do with farming, though they kept animals. Few and poorly cared for, but they sold chickens and eggs, and raised some pork and beef—for their consumption only—and those animals often seemed to be the source of their troubles. Someone had cheated them on the price, or they hadn't paid what was agreed, or the animal was sick. Sandra's father, Ronald, was interested in law, and so took every case that he could to court, defending or prosecuting the cases himself. As a result he'd also cultivated a massive debt—that no one ever seemed to call in. Dawn had grown up hearing gossip about the family; they were a reliable source of contempt in the town. That hard bunch up the hill.

But Sandra had taken a daring step outside the expected family connections and claimed Jerry and—the more unkind faction in the town would say—the large mixed farm that he would inherit. After nearly forty years together, Jerry remained utterly devoted to her. They had two sons: Andy, who'd been Jerry's adoring shadow from the moment he could follow him, emulating his dad's kindness and solid reputation, and Michael, Sandra's sweet-faced darling and constant companion: a sunny, inquisitive man with Down syndrome.

Miranda said Michael had taught Sandra everything she'd needed to learn about mothering, as she hadn't learned much from her own mother. Unlike her chronically uninterested parents, Sandra had been determined that Michael should try everything he felt drawn to. So she stood close while he fell in love with horses and learned to ride, embracing the whole cowboy world: learning lassoing and calf roping, and every country song referencing horses that he heard. He adored his mother and she him, both of them joking they were lassoed together. But even rising to meet the challenge of caring for Michael, Sandra still wasn't welcomed by a certain strata of the community. John Andrew reckoned she had a leather cheek which she turned with every snub. She slowly put distance between her extended family and Jerry's. She worked, John Andrew said, like a man digging a firebreak: helping Jerry with the farm; caring for his ailing, aging parents and Michael; then taking a job in the local pizzeria "to get out a bit." Eventually she had earned, and was offered, more than a grudging respect.

Sandra understood conflict and trouble, and was always among the first who knocked on the door to make sure that folks who were struggling had what they needed. But she always had opinions, and wasn't shy about voicing them.

"Hello!" Sandra was chirpy, but as the door opened and she saw Dawn, also startled. "Well, my goodness, you can certainly tell that you are related. You're the spit of Miranda."

Okay, just see where this goes. Dawn could see Michael sitting on the stump of the old maple partway down the drive, waiting for his mother. Don't presume, don't anticipate, make room, thought Dawn, and said out loud, "Yeah. People say."

Sandra replied by cocking her head—Dawn thought of Betsy when she was puzzled—and saying, "Huh. I didn't know Miranda had any nieces."

Okay.

"She doesn't. Didn't." Deep breath. "I'm Dawn."

"Dawn?" Sandra was computing. "Dawn. Oh." And then the penny dropped. "Don. Oh God. Jesus."

"No," Dawn let herself be pissed enough to say, "nope. Just her daughter." And then with something like pleasure, she watched as Sandra, so out of her element that even her leather cheek couldn't save her, turned, flustered, casserole still in hand, back to the steps and down them, looked at her hands, realized she still had the dish, came back to drop the casserole on the top step, and scuttled down the driveway, only pausing to pull Michael with her, without even a toodle-oo or wave.

Well. That should be out round town in about fifteen minutes, Dawn thought.

She heard a car giving a gentle beep as it turned into the drive, some brief chatter, and then a bright green Volkswagen rolled into sight. Dawn felt her shoulders—way too high and her chest too tight and her breathing too fast—descend, release, slow.

She knew that car.

Jenny

Jenny knew exactly what had happened when she turned into the drive and saw Sandra. Now it begins, she thought. She slowed and set her face into an only-slightly-strained greeting and rolled down the window. She'd just opened her mouth when Sandra blurted, "Is that what I think it is?" Sandra was out of breath and personally affronted.

"What? Is what, what you think?"

"That. That—Don."

Jenny thought of how Miranda had gently educated her about language and pronouns and just—Jenny mentally shook her head—basic respect for difference. But she didn't have the energy or patience or sympathy that Miranda had at the best of times, and certainly none now to waste on beginning that process with Sandra. So instead she bit out, "She is not an *it.* That person is Dawn, the daughter of Miranda, your close friend and neighbour, living as her true self after years of hiding and struggling. That's a concept you can probably get your head around? So, excuse me now, Sandra, but I have to go: the child of my best friend is grieving her mother."

Jenny rolled the electric window back up and eased the car gently up the drive—with Sandra turning to look after her, jaw actually dropped—when what she wanted to do was spin gravel into Sandra's face.

She felt ashamed. She hadn't helped anything. Sandra wasn't stupid, Jenny knew. Anyone who'd managed to escape that family's machinations and deal with the complexities of her own life couldn't be. And perhaps, Jenny thought, Sandra would have done better, wouldn't have hurt Dawn as Jenny expected Dawn had just been hurt, if that not-stupid person had had a little warning.

But wait, warning? Jenny was debating with herself now, as she would have sparred with Miranda. Really? Why do strangers deserve to be forewarned of something that has nothing to do with them, except as it piques their curiosity? Growing more pugnacious without Miranda, the yin to her yang, she continued on this defensive/aggressive path. "More to the point," she said to Miranda-in-her-head, "and I don't need to tell *you* this"—"But you will," Miranda answered—"their discomfort with the unexpected or unfamiliar, especially in this town, is due to their own ignorance. That they aren't *interested* in adjusting." Jenny's vehemence often resulted in italics. "And that is *wilful* ignorance. *So much worse. Criminal, nearly.*" And Miranda would say gently to Jenny, as she had a hundred times before: "Honey, isn't that a little intolerant? Exactly what you're bridling against?"

"So, I get it," Jenny would reply. "So, I speak from *experience*. So, I'm right." And Miranda would say, "Oh my god, I give up."

And now who would say that, Jenny thought, and not give up. Shit. She bit down on the possibility of tears: I am only going to get worse and worse without her to stop me.

Tolerance had never been Jenny's strong suit. She could make a list of folks who'd agree. Including her ex-husband. And her present one. Ah well. Tolerance was for her next life.

Jenny and Miranda had gone back and forth on the idea of tolerance as opposed to respect, in relation to Dawn and her community; complex and revealing conversations that Jenny wished they had been having years before. When she had first realized that something was happening with Miranda's youngest child that wasn't going to be easy. Something that would have to be respected, not tolerated. This, around the same time she was discovering the difference between tolerance and respect for herself—enough to leave husband number one.

But then the world had changed so fast and so dramatically: Me Too and Black Lives Matter upended everything. Nothing was off limits now, as far as truth-telling. Jenny and Miranda joked that change was a steel-toed stiletto that kicked their little town from the end of the 1950s into 2020. And it seemed like it happened almost overnight, culminating in rainbow crosswalks in front of town hall. Some people still stopped traffic in the middle of the block to avoid using them.

But of course it wasn't overnight, or over a few months, or even a couple of years, and it wasn't easy at all. It fractured the town, and came with a lot of discomfort and disillusionment, in particular with the church, which sat geographically and symbolically in the heart of the town. Revelation after revelation; tectonic events, upending so much. For the good, thought this Catholic girl who'd got herself in trouble, left her family forever, kept her baby and then lost him in days and was, on that very day, reclaimed by the church. She was silent that day but saved her pain and anger, and when she was old enough to know better, told the parish priest he could go fuck himself—in front of his housekeeper. A memory that still brought Jenny satisfaction. She liked to think the housekeeper found the idea of the priest fucking *himself* a relief, as most of the town knew he'd been fucking *her* for the better part of thirty years, all while wringing his white hands over fornication. Ah well, he was gone now. As was his housekeeper. No one knew where, or if they did, they weren't saying. All the duties of a wife for thirty years but none of the status. Poor woman.

The last few years had released more than a few people from ill-fitting, long-unexamined convictions. They'd certainly taken the lid off Jenny's particularly uncomfortable box. So she believed she understood Dawn a little, the freedom and exhilaration she must feel in finally being able to be herself. Jenny knew that coming from this town, in that time, Dawn had only had one option.

So when Dawn left, Jenny wasn't surprised. Except at her bravery and Miranda's stoicism in letting her youngest go. And Miranda had known she could count on Jenny: to help her get information to share with Dawn, to be a shoulder, and the hardest thing—to respect Dawn's wishes, knowing it was going to tear things apart. Keeping the secrets of who Dawn was and where she'd gone from John Andrew, whom Jenny had long loved like a brother, was uncomfortably complicated. Constantly weighing what she owed John Andrew against what this young person deserved. But the scales tipped every time in favour of Dawn's chance to be happy. Next to her own daughter, Tessa, Dawn was the youngster Jenny most loved, and had been her pet since the first time she'd held the little scrap with the huge eyes that looked straight into Jenny's soul—or what passed for one, she'd joke.

Now, Dawn straightened up with a casserole in her hands—left by Sandra on the porch, Jenny realized, when she took off down the driveway. Jesus. Dawn was looking at her—waiting for her to speak.

"Oh, fer fuck's sake," said Jenny as she climbed the steps. Dawn actually grinned.

"Jenny. You look so pretty and you talk so dirty. I'll get a swear jar started for you. Come inside?"

"You shouldn't need to. There's one in your mom's sewing room—but I think it's labelled *Margarita Night*. No. I'm good here." And she sat on the porch swing.

Dawn opened the door and said over her shoulder, "Right back. Tea or anything?"

"Something cold?"

"I'll see what's there." And the door swung closed behind her.

Jenny knew Dawn wouldn't offer up chapter and verse on how things had gone so far. Dawn took her time; you had to wait for her to share anything personal. Unlike her Tessa, who was a chronic over-sharer. Jenny often wished she knew less about her daughter's life. And Dawn, despite the breach between her and her father, was loyal. She loved him and wanted a way back, so acquiescing to Miranda's request to repair things with John Andrew had not been a hardship. The heart was willing, but the timing, they all felt, had to be just right.

This timing could not possibly be just right.

When Jenny and Miranda had broached coming up with a plan, Dawn had agreed. But the earnestness with which the three of them approached "the plan" became impossible. The conversation that needed to happen had such enormous stakes attached that the prospect of it became too fraught to manage except with a kind of hysteria, which was when Dawn started referring to it as her "Gender Reveal." She and Jill would riff on the planning of this reality TV–type event: the cake, the balloons, the pink, blue, and white fireworks letting all the neighbouring farms know what was happening so they could join the celebration—and they got exactly nowhere. And the result was whatever fallout Dawn was dealing with today. Her father. And her sister. And Sandra. And and and.

Jenny wished now that the Gender Reveal *was* going to happen. A little mad foolishness. A little joy and celebration instead of—

Dawn pushed the door with a tray containing two glasses, a selection of drinks, and a couple of Miranda's scones, heated.

"The freezer is stuffed, right?" Jenny said as she picked one up.

Dawn nodded. "Every single thing any of us ever liked. There's probably hundreds of scones. When did she do all this?"

Jenny shrugged. "She went crazy baking back in February—I thought it was a Valentine's throwback, but it must be when she started feeling rough again. We were away nearly all the next month and when I got back she just looked, well. You know. She didn't say anything till she'd been back to her doctor and knew about the drug trial."

"She never told anyone anything."

"That's not quite true, Dawn." They sat silent for a bit before Jenny said, "Who did you want told what?"

"Me. How sick she was. That she was planning to die and leave us."

Jenny reached for Dawn and rocked her as she cried, the old swing squeaking until it slowed and, finally, stopped.

Jenny pushed the hair off Dawn's face. "You know if she told you it would have made it real, don't you? She had to keep believing it wasn't true and she was getting better. She couldn't say anything, so instead she organized and planned and stuffed the freezer, because if it didn't happen it didn't matter, and if it was going to, well, she could try to ease her exit by—"

"Making scones."

"You'll be finding lots of things she sorted, I imagine." Jenny hugged Dawn hard. When she released her, Dawn set the swing going again by sliding to the end of it and reaching down to pet Betsy. "How's your dad?" Jenny asked.

"Who knows?" Dawn didn't look up from stroking the dog. "He's not okay, but he doesn't talk about anything. He and Tammy have gone to town for—stuff."

"How's Tammy seem?"

"She is actually sort of okay. To me, I mean. But sad and—well, she has Byron, who is fantastic."

"He is."

"Jenny—" Dawn paused, then, "I can't do this. This town. The wake, the funeral."

"You can."

"They didn't want me in town with them. How can I—"

"That was today. First day. It's an adjustment."

"I told Tammy that."

"You were right. Dawn, the wake, the funeral...they aren't about you."

"Tammy said they've become about me."

"She said that yesterday? Like, just after she'd seen you for the first time in five years? After driving day and night from Toronto to her mother's funeral, wondering if her brother would turn up? What did you think she was going to say? Dawn, you know Tammy—she talks first and thinks after."

"I *knew* Tammy. But I was a—"

"A kid. Her brother. Not her sister who's her equal now. Maybe—don't tell her I said this." Jenny stoked the side of Dawn's face. "Maybe *more* than equal. Maybe someone who's had to grow and flourish despite circumstances compared to someone who's been able to grow and flourish *because* circumstances provided." Dawn was studying the porch floor. Jenny said gently, "So. Be the bigger sister. Cut her some slack."

Dawn looked at Jenny, her eyes filling. "You sound like Mom."

"That's the best thing you could say to me." She hugged Dawn again then held her out by the shoulders. "You can do the wake and the funeral. It won't be the most comfortable thing you've ever done, but it won't be the worst. Think about the worst. And all those people who want a good look will get it, and say *isn't he*—I know!" she added as Dawn raised her head to protest— "They'll say, isn't *he* like *her* mother, the idiots, and you'll hear it, and it'll be awful and also great because you *are* like her: *so* like her. This awful time will turn into the story you'll tell one day about your mother helping you come home and make things right with your dad. Because that was the most important thing she could give you at the end. Not a freezer full of scones."

Dawn

"See you tomorrow night," Jenny said before turning the little green car to head off down the drive. Dawn watched her go, giving a final wave when she reached the last bend before the main road.

The bang of a door to the machine shed closest to the house startled Dawn and pulled her around. There wasn't a breath of wind; had an animal had knocked it? She set out, Betsy herding her as she went: lying down in front of her, then up around behind her till Dawn got to the door.

"I got here, okay? Relax, Bets."

Betsy came to heel, looking with Dawn around the door that was still closed. Nothing. Nobody there. She looked for movement in the tops of the trees: none.

It was going to be another hot day with no breeze bringing relief.

"Weird." Dawn took a step in to the gloomy shed. It felt as though no one had been in there for a very long time. Light was fighting its way in, squeezing through cracks in the siding, illuminating the contents with shards of sun. Metal chairs. Ancient tools on a bench and in boxes. An old bicycle. A tetherball stand. At least a dozen saws of all sizes and eras, hanging handle up, blade down, according to size and looking, Dawn thought, like a xylophone.

And in the corner, partly covered with a burlap sack and a blanket of spider's webs, was the old Ford Jubilee tractor from the picture that she'd carried everywhere with her for years: to Toronto, then Montreal, then Halifax, and now back here, where it sat on her bedroom dresser. The tractor Miranda had loved because it was her father's. She'd learned to drive on it, and now, Dawn remembered, had fought with John Andrew about it—more than once. Why, Dawn couldn't remember, and wasn't sure she wanted to.

Now she laid her hand on it as if gentling a restive horse, and her touch conjured a memory. A summer day like this, Miranda stuffing her hair under a ball cap before climbing into the seat and reaching down to help small Dawn clamber onto her lap. She remembered her hand touching the hot side of the tractor as she climbed up. She remembered the scent of her mother. Linden, humidity, and beeswax. What had they been doing? The heat waves had shimmered above the field and little Dawn was mesmerized: the air was bending itself. Did she ask her mother why? Did Miranda answer? She couldn't remember, but that scent enveloped her now. Where was it coming from?

Nowhere. Her longing.

She patted the pony-tractor.

"Oh, buddy," Dawn breathed. "You look so sad and lonesome."

She tugged the burlap sack off the tractor. Underneath, the fender over the flat back tire looked like a lichen-covered log. You could still see the raised *FORD* scrolled across the top, but the paint was flaking and the rust was definitely winning. Dawn slipped her fingers down along the fender's edge: the metal was rusty but not jagged or breaking off. Savable, she thought, humming a little as she began to make her way around the tractor. At the back, she stepped up behind the seat like her mother in the picture. She touched the pearls around her neck. Then got down again, moving around it slowly, taking in every detail. At the front, she anatomized, viewing the tractor like a patient. Grille, not too bad: sound but flaking, not disastrous. The rims on the small front wheels: disastrous. The big bug-eye lights on each side: one broken, one gone. Aw, man. Made her look so pathetic, Dawn thought. But the Jubilee medallion between the eyes—was there! Intact and readable. She went round to the other side and swung herself up into the seat. So sweet. Everything the right size, the right level.

"Little beauty. Why would he just...let her go?" she wondered to herself, but Betsy made a distinct whine in defense of John Andrew giving up on something well past its prime. "She's fixable," retorted Dawn and jumped down in search of the key.

The ledge under the closest window, thick with dust, was the likeliest spot—but no key. A selection of old tins, bottles, and incongruously, a silver baby cup. No name engraved. Dawn picked it up to inspect it more closely—such an odd find—and tipping it, it gave the gentlest clink. She reached in and—presto!—a key. More magic: it fit into the rusty ignition. Dawn tried to turn it, but feeling a rusty crunch, stopped, not wanting to break it off. She scanned the ramshackle shed, then crossed to the cluttered workbench beneath the saw-xylophone and spotted an ancient tin of WD-40, the farmer's friend. She pushed a nail through the plugged top hole, tipped the can, and waited. A drop of honey-thick oil fell on the key. This time she managed to jiggle it in, and carefully she turned it. Not even a cough.

"No surprise. Probably no gas," Dawn said to Betsy. "But the key's here. It turns. Waddya think, girl? Could she go again?"

If Betsy had an opinion she didn't share it, because at that moment the shed door gave another almighty bang, sending poor Betsy scrambling to crouch against Dawn's leg. But Dawn understood now, and called to her mom: "You think so?"

Miranda's reply was to smack the door against the shed one last time, then ease it wide open, flooding the dark space with dusty light.

Byron

If Byron was to measure things by percentages, today had probably been twenty-five percent better than yesterday, which was perhaps five percent better than the day before. So, how many days before back to—and what was?—one hundred percent? Where, he thought, toying with his fork, should the percentage improvement be measured *from*? John Andrew's phone call four, no, five days ago? The moment they decided to drive to Nova Scotia? The moment they got in the car?

Tammy gently took the fork from Byron's hand, stacked his plate with the others already expertly balanced on one hand—you could see she'd waited on tables all through university—and gave his hair a gentle tug.

"Delicious." He smiled up at her.

"Okay for artichokes," she said, reaching for John Andrew's plate.

"What's wrong with artichokes?" Byron was genuinely puzzled. They always had them on their pizza at home.

She shrugged, throwing a glance at her dad. "You just don't expect country folk to eat fancy casseroles with artichokes."

John Andrew looked up and took the bait. "Country folk?"

"Yup," she responded, and moved around to gently tug *his* hair. "Unsophisticated, red-necked, meat-eating folk like you." She dropped a kiss on his head and took the plates into the kitchen with John Andrew's response—"We did meatless Mondays every week"—following her out.

Dawn had been quiet for much of the meal, but now looked up. "Pretty tasty, considering the source."

Byron and John Andrew turned to her.

"Sandra," she responded to the unspoken question. "She gave it to me this morning. Well," she considered, "dropped it on the porch and ran."

Tammy came back into the doorway between the kitchen and dining room. "Jerry's Sandra?"

Dawn took a moment, then shrugged and said, "Yeah. She meant well."

Byron might have been the only one to hear John Andrew say under his breath, "Poison, that woman," because a knock on the back door pulled Tammy out to the kitchen and Dawn started piling up the rest of the dishes. But they all heard Tammy say, "Jerry! Hi. We're just finishing up, come on through." Tammy led Jerry into the dining room, where he stood, twisting his hat, still in his barn overalls. Tammy leaned on the door frame, widening her eyes at her sister. Dawn looked down, John Andrew looked at Dawn, Byron looked from Tammy to John Andrew to Dawn. All around the table, Byron realized, there was a feeling of complicity—as if together they were responsible for conjuring Jerry, at that moment, to defend his wife.

John Andrew turned in his chair to speak to him. "Everything okay, Jerry? Milk truck come?"

"Yup. Test was fine."

"Good. Didn't need another load dumped." John Andrew drained his glass of beer. Jerry lingered. That wasn't what he'd come to say.

"Yeah. Yeah, hey, listen. I'm not nuts or anything?" That came out like a question and then Jerry paused; he clearly had doubts about that. "Listen," he said again, "I hope you don't mind, but...God's truth, this. Five o'clock, funerals come on the radio. Miranda's name for the wake tomorrow." He took a breath. "Every cow in the barn stopped chewing."

John Andrew was fixed on him.

"Milkers going, chugging away—not another sound. They stopped breathin' to listen. Never seen it." He looked from one face to another with something like defiance, but also reverence. They all were silent. Then, Tammy finished drying the casserole dish she'd rinsed and passed it to Jerry, the giving and receiving far more delicate than warranted. Jerry took it from her with relief and said, "Ah. Thanks. Sandra said at lunch she'd brought something. That the artichokes?"

"Yes," said Tammy. "Delicious."

"Bit fancy for me." Jerry tucked the dish under his arm. "Anyway, glad you ate it! Night, John Andrew. Tammy. And ah..." He turned and Tammy joined Byron, hands on his shoulders.

"Byron. My fiancé."

Byron smiled up at her. It never got old.

"Byron," said Jerry. "Good to meet you." Jerry's gaze moved on now, landing on Dawn. "And uh..."

Dawn jumped in, a little strong, a little tight. Byron felt for her as she said firmly, "Dawn."

"Dawn," Jerry repeated. "Of course." He studied her. What, Byron wondered, had Sandra actually said? Jerry continued, his focus still unwavering on Dawn.

"Of course. You were just a kid last time I seen ya. All growed up now."

"Yes," she answered, and waited. Was there more?

"Different person now." Jerry looked down for a minute, then raised his head to continue. "Good yer home for yer mom. Bless ya." With one last nod, he put his hat back on as he left the family sitting in silence.

Later, dishes done, the house quiet with everyone busy or pretending to be, Byron was finally taking clothes out of his suitcase and hanging them in his tiny cupboard. He was, Tammy told everyone, a bit of a dandy. He couldn't help it. His mother had pressed his boxers, he told her, and when you have that kind of start, it's hard to let your standards slip. Not true: in fact, his mother, with her full-time job and six children, had been vehemently anti-ironing despite—or maybe because of—her seamstress skills. He'd ironed his own boxers. So, two days without ironing anything—Tammy mended, he ironed—he was feeling a bit twitchy and hoped that hanging things might be enough to get the wrinkles out for the wake, at least. He didn't feel it was quite right to ask for the ironing board at the moment, and he didn't know the dress expectations. He'd never been to a wake.

Tammy came in and sat on the bed. Uh-oh, he thought. Today's percentage improvement might be about to take a dive.

"Hey. No knock?" he joked, continuing to hang things up.

"In case you're, what? Taking a meeting?" She took one of the pillows and hugged it the way she always did when she was upset. He waited. Finally, she said, "I can't believe she didn't tell him."

"About Dawn?"

"About everything. How sick she was." She buried her face in the pillow for a moment, then, "Byron."

"Yes." He shook out a shirt.

"Please look at me."

Byron turned to her.

"Byron," she said, "we have to share everything."

"We do," he said, then quipped rashly, "except for a bed round here."

Tammy started to protest and he stopped her with, "It's okay. It's fine. Your bed's toast anyway. Plus, I wouldn't dare, you know"—he swung a little hip action back and forth—"next to your parents' room."

"Byron!"

Shit. Stop hips. "Your dad's..." Shit shit. "Sorry. Sorry, Tam." He put down the shirt and sat beside her on the bed, tentatively putting an arm around her.

"Sorry. I was just trying—I'm stupid, Tam."

She leaned into him and they sat, Tammy with her face in the pillow, Byron with his chin on her head. The cat pushed the door open and slipped quietly in, sitting directly in front of them, studying them and then a paw, which she began to wash. Tammy raised her head to watch.

"I don't know where this cat came from. Mom never said. All these secrets."

"I don't expect the cat was a secret, Tam. Maybe an oversight. More important things, ya know?"

The cat paused to listen.

Tammy drew a shaking breath and said, "I'm afraid of life without her."

Byron nodded silently. “Yeah. She was...” She was so much, Byron didn’t know how to begin. “Imagine,” he said, “how Dawn feels.”

Tammy turned to him with her what? look. “Well...” Now he wished he hadn’t started, but “...your mom was her only family for years. And now—”

Tammy’s response came swiftly: “She chose.”

“Tammy.” Byron withdrew his arm so he could turn to her, resisting his impulse to say Holy shit, Tammy. Sometimes she was unlikeable, and his job was to get through those moments. But as he turned to her, she said with irritation, “Why is it so easy for you?”

“No history. She’s a new person.” Then added, trying to lighten things, “A gorgeous, blond person.”

“Jesus, Byron.”

“Tam, come on.” He put the arm back, tried to pull her in to kiss her. “I’m joking.”

“Nothing about this”—she flung his arm off as she stood—“is funny.”

And she left the room. The cat stopped grooming to watch Tammy go, then, starting her quiet purr, she turned to wind in and out of Byron’s legs.

Dawn

Dawn looked up from her computer, where she'd been following a Ford Jubilee thread into a deep cyber-pit, when she heard Tammy huffing out of Byron's room. In Dawn's head the room was now "Byron's hole," as in "hidey-hole," and Dawn worried about accidentally calling it that out loud: she was pretty sure her sister would misunderstand. But Byron kept reminding her of animals: that retriever she came back to, but also creatures who'd retire to a cave or burrow to lick wounds, regroup, and re-emerge, ready to face...whatever. Tammy. Tammy's family. Tonight at dinner, clearly starving but with his careful manners, he'd reminded her of a koala she'd seen online, eating an apple. Little bite, wait, look up, was anyone going to take it away? Little bite, wait, repeat.

Dinner was extraordinary for lots of reasons; Byron was the least of them, really, but he was such a comforting presence for Dawn. He'd turn to *see* her before he talked to her. To truly connect. She didn't know many people who managed their communication like that. Even Jill would kind of spray her speech like a firehose sometimes, and whether it soaked you or brushed you was dependent on whether you felt inclined to put yourself directly in its path. Not Byron. Nothing random about it, and if you were there with him and he engaged, you wanted to respond in kind. You could see his process: thought, consider, connect, check, speak, listen, absorb. Repeat. So unusual in a guy his age. So unusual in a *guy*. But he's Black, thought Dawn. He's like Jill: not sitting in a place where he expects things to come to him. Neither of them, she thought, could assume any kind of privilege, but they would not accept subservience. A beautiful balance. Dawn checked herself. Byron isn't a saint and this was not, she spoke sternly to herself, a crush on her sister's man. But his interaction with Jerry tonight was pretty demonstrative of who he was. The way he listened without judgment as the older man talked about the cows: no eyebrow raised, no suggestion of a smirk, just an open-faced "Yes." From all of them, Dawn realized. The look on her father's face—what was that, she mused. Pride? Reverence? Wonder?

Wonder. More things in heaven and earth than are dreamt of in our philosophies.

Something remarkable no one would taint by examining.

Byron accepting, Tammy receiving, John Andrew grateful, and, Dawn thought, me knowing. Of course the cows knew and understood grief. Of course their lives were lesser now. Miranda had gone to the dairy every day; she'd loved the herd, known them by name, helped many of them into the world, so of course. Of course. Thank you, Jerry.

And one more gift, so different from what his wife had brought to the door. His "bless you" was the benediction she'd never dreamt she'd receive here, and so much sweeter for that.

Now Tammy's door slammed. Dawn looked up: Tammy must have stood on the landing for ages, deciding whether to go make up with him or not. That slam was a pretty solid *I want to be alone until you seek me out, which better happen immediately* statement. Dawn wondered if she should go see her sister. But then it might look like she was taking sides, and she wasn't going to do that.

Dawn gathered up the physio textbooks she'd been pretending to study while actually searching for blogs on tractor restoration, gave Betsy a scratch, and switched off the kitchen light. At the bottom of the stairs, just outside the den that had always doubled as the farm office, she paused, hearing the low brown sound of John Andrew speaking. On the phone?

But then she heard, "Miranda." He was talking to her mother.

"...when you knew? Did you have to manage it all? Finding the boy—Jesus. Girl. D'ya know...how this feels? Jesus. Jenny. Arthur. All these secrets. What else, Miranda?"

Dawn wanted to pass the door and head upstairs. Her father seemed close to tears, and that wasn't something she thought she could bear, or that he'd want her to witness. Caught.

"Ya think I couldn't do better? I could. I would." Then silence, broken by, "Fucking cows stopping chewing." Dawn heard a long, ragged breath and then papers moving on his desk, a drawer closing. She waited then went to the doorway.

"Dad?" He looked up. "I'm going up. Are you milking in the morning or is Jerry?"

"I am."

"Want some help?"

John Andrew busied himself with some papers. "I'm good."

"I'd like to. I don't mind getting up —"

"Go on," said John Andrew. "Get yer beauty sleep."

Slap. Dawn felt her centre collapse, all her air gone. She didn't take the time to decide if it might *not* be an intentional slight. She couldn't have replied if she'd wanted to.

She found her breath and climbed the stairs, leaving Betsy behind in the doorway watching John Andrew with reproachful eyes as he put his head in his hands. Betsy was the only one to hear his "Shit, shit, shit."

The buzz of her phone alarm pulled Dawn from sleep. Surprisingly, she'd fallen asleep as soon as she hit the pillow. She hadn't chewed over her dad's parting comment. She'd made a decision, put it away, and now she was going to get on with it.

She pulled aside the curtain: light was just beginning outside. She dug through her clothes for jeans, a T-shirt, and something warm. Not much to choose from. She wondered if her mom had stuff downstairs.

In the back hallway, a pink hoodie of Miranda's hung with other barn gear. Dawn pulled it on and went back to the kitchen, measured out coffee, and scooped it into the French press. As the kettle began its wail, she reached to silence it, and heard her father's heavy steps. He stopped short, pulling on his workshirt, and she realized he'd seen her mother in the pink hoodie. He was white-faced, but he gathered himself. "Have you got any boots?" he asked.

"I think my old ones are there." Victory.

He watched as she poured water onto the coffee, went to the fridge for milk, and opened a cupboard for mugs. They both turned to footsteps on the stairs, and Tammy entered—sweet as a child in her flowered pyjamas, pillow lines pressed onto her face.

"What's going on?" she asked, pulling a chair out. "Why's everybody up?"

Dawn and her dad stopped what they were doing and turned. "It's a farm, Tammy," said Dawn. "We're doing farm things." And John Andrew added, "Go back to bed, girl. Get your beauty sleep." The room was illuminated for a moment: an infusion of understanding. Dawn saw: her father hadn't belittled her last night; he'd elevated her to Tammy's status. Daughter, girl, woman. Dawn opened another cupboard, looking for honey: simple task and result—the honey was where it had always been. Ease. Home. Her father saw her. They were on their way.

Now Byron came in, dressed and alert as if he'd been up for hours. "What's going on?"

Tammy waved with one hand, covered her yawn with the other. "They're doing farm things. Go back to bed."

"I'm up now. Can I do farm things?"

John Andrew considered. "I don't know. Can you?"

"I'm a quick study." He grinned. John Andrew grinned back. Dawn grinned at both of them.

Tammy looked from one to another, amazed. "Wow. Before coffee."

Dawn lifted the French press in one hand and a mug in the other and offered it to Tammy. "Want some?" Tammy nodded; Dawn poured. A cardinal sang outside the kitchen window.

"He wants some." Byron nodded to the bird on the branch, taking the cup John Andrew was offering. In the dim, warm kitchen, the family listened to the call and response from the cardinal and his mate. Then John Andrew reached for his hat, pushed it on his head, looked from Byron to Dawn, and said, "Right then."

The day officially began as they followed him out the back door.

Everything about the dairy was as Dawn remembered. She felt relieved. Jerry was there this morning too and greeted them like family: big slap on the back for Byron, a gentle pat for Dawn. John Andrew seemed surprised but glad to see him. Jerry was a master cowman: he kept the bovine river flowing into the dairy, and with three of them to settle the cattle, clean the teats, attach the milker, and send them off again, it was going smoothly. Byron was enraptured, capturing the process and the cows—faces; udders; back ends (which seemed to be his favourite)—on his phone, annoying her dad.

John Andrew wasn't a fan of technology. If he had his way, Dawn thought, they'd be in here doing it by hand. And she understood that. The connection between person and cow, pressing your head against a warm, trusting flank, was like nothing else. The perfect version of milk collection came with human and cow in sync as the cud was chewed and udders gently pulled, a pulsing relief as the milk emerged.

Byron, though, loved technology of any kind and was fascinated by the cows' cooperation with the mechanized milkers. And, Dawn realized, he enjoyed doing what he was told. She grinned to herself: that explained him and Tammy. John Andrew was showing him how to dip the teats in iodine and wipe them with newspaper, and Byron was grinning like a kid who'd just performed his first magic trick.

The cows left the dairy one by one to return to the barn, and eventually they were watching the last black-and-white rump depart. Byron and Dawn sluiced the troughs on the raised milking platforms, the floor of the dairy, and the archway back into the barn with the high-pressure hose—and Byron was suddenly five years old, sliding around the barn floor in an old pair of John Andrew's boots, arms in the air like an ice dancer. When Jerry laughed at Byron's "shitty pirouette" in the cow dung, John Andrew gave a single, barking guffaw, then stopped, almost surprised at the noise he'd made, and turned back to work. The other three carried on with cleanup, easy with each other now, the music of the cows moving from barn back to yard, a gentle underscore to their chores.

The rising sun flooded the dairy with beams through the high windows, catching the drops of water in webs spun across the ancient frames. Dawn looked up and nudged Byron: the angle of the rays lit the hanging crystals, bouncing the light from one shiny metal surface to another. The dairy was alive with dancing rainbows. They beamed at each other: alive, too.

The morning chatter of the birds had settled by the time they headed back to the house, but coming out of the barn, Byron looked up to spot an eagle.

"Hey, look!"

John Andrew glanced up. "Bald eagle. Chicken farm down the road."

Byron looked puzzled. Dawn explained: "They throw the chicken carcasses into the field sometimes. The eagles hang around for them."

"Why the field?"

John Andrew shrugged. "They plough them in. Fertilizer."

"Wow. Gross." Byron made a city-boy face.

"But the eagles pull them out."

"Not just the eagles." Dawn looked at her dad, grinning. He grinned too, knowing what she was remembering.

Byron looked from one to the other. "What?"

"When Betsy was little—like, eight months, Dad?—she ran off to the chicken farm and found a full carcass. She came tearing home to show us, so proud. Got to the door and Dad came out, wearing new Birkenstocks that Mom had just got him—you didn't want them, right?—"

"Hippy shoes. Never wore 'em."

"He couldn't keep them on. But he ran after Betsy, Birks falling off, trying to grab her and get the chicken out of her mouth." John Andrew was shrugging as she continued. "Betsy knew Dad wanted the chicken—chicken bones splinter; they can be deadly to dogs—"

"Probably full of maggots," John Andrew added.

"—but no way was she going to let him get it. She took off around the property, just fast enough to keep out of Dad's reach, somehow eating as she went, starting at the head, with Dad trying to keep the Birks on and get the chicken out of her mouth... It *was* funny."

"Yeah," John Andrew replied. "Hilarious. "I caught the dog just as she got to the end of the chicken, two feet sticking out of her mouth. I reached for them and she swallowed and sat down in front of me, looking some sick."

"But proud," Dawn laughed.

“That was a night.” John Andrew shook his head. “Up till morning. Stupid dog.”

“Not *so* stupid,” said Dawn. “She won’t eat anything with chicken in it now,” she told Byron. He laughed.

“Martine was glad to see ya,” John Andrew said to Dawn.

Dawn nodded. “She’s a beauty. I wondered if she’d still be here. Mom never said.”

“Who’s Martine?” asked Byron.

“The Jersey that nearly knocked him”—John Andrew stopped and looked right at Dawn and said, clearly—“*her* over, butting...her. Sorry. Martine was a 4-H project when Dawn was fifteen.”

“I loved that calf.” She loved her dad.

Byron looked surprised. “4-H is a real thing? I thought it was just, like, a movie thing.”

John Andrew and Dawn both turned to him.

“Where did Tammy find you?” Dawn asked, and for the second time that day, her dad laughed. “Yeah. It’s a real thing. Dad and Mom were both leaders. We did all sorts. Animals, public speaking, small-machine stuff...”

They were nearly back at the house now, passing the machine shed. Dawn turned to John Andrew. “Speaking of machines, Dad, what’s the deal with that tractor? You and Mom talked about fixing it up?” She turned to Byron, gesturing to the shed where the tractor was just a shape in the dim, far corner. “See it? Mom loved that tractor. Her dad taught her to drive on it.” She turned back to her father. “I’m good with engines. I thought I might be able to get it going—”

“It’s garbage,” John Andrew cut her off. “I’m not wasting time or money on garbage.” And he strode away, leaving a cold front where Dawn and Byron stood.

“What was that?” Byron sounded shocked at the vehemence of John Andrew’s response.

Dawn watched her dad disappear round the corner, then turned towards the shed. “I guess girls don’t fix tractors.” She pulled the door hard behind her and left Byron blinking, wondering what had just happened.

Tammy

The last four meals, Tammy realized, had been prepared, served, and tidied away by her. What the hell. She knew her mother's role had to be filled somehow, but this needed to be sorted. Though maybe—she scanned the very closed-off faces at the table after a silent, tense breakfast—this wasn't the time.

Dawn stood and picked up her plate with its half-eaten breakfast, then Byron's, moving around the table towards her father. As she reached for John Andrew's plate, he moved it away, stood, and took it to the kitchen himself. A deep flush spread up Dawn's neck. Tammy watched Byron trying to decide whether to speak and thought at him: Don't please, don't make this worse. He turned, opened his mouth, and Dawn put the plates down quietly, and exited before anyone could speak. Byron looked after her, unmoving.

This fucking family, Tammy thought. And it's me...again. Tidying up, making nice. She knew she was glowering when she rose to pick up the plates Dawn had left and said, "Right. Guess I'll do the dishes then." She could feel Byron suppressing his frustration with her and her dysfunctional tribe when he said, "I'll do them. Don't pout."

"I'm not pouting." But of course she was. "Fuck this." And she slammed the plates down and left too.

Tammy didn't follow her sister upstairs, or her father into the office. She wasn't going to sort them out. She went into her mom's sewing room, joining the cat on the window seat. She didn't know where this latest storm had blown in from—they went out happy and light and came back miserable. What happened? She assumed her dad was the root of it, but she couldn't ask him. And now she was annoyed with Byron, so she wouldn't ask him either—

The back door slammed. Tammy looked out and saw Dawn crossing the backyard, towards the shed. She disappeared inside, then emerged with a bicycle and pump and began fiddling with them.

Tammy remembered this. When Dawn was small, his—shit, her—go-to comfort was mechanical: something to take apart, or put together. She told the cat, "I never used to ask what was going on, because—why?" The cat stared steadily at her, offering the answer: because teenage girls aren't interested in feelings that aren't theirs. But now—Tammy stood up, and the cat stood too—now I am, and I'm going to pull this fucking family back together.

The cat jumped onto the shelf that held her mother's swear jar. Fucking perfect.

Byron was at the sink, washing and carefully stacking dishes on a tea towel. Tammy walked past, feeling him turn to watch her scan the mat at the back entryway for outdoor shoe options: her mother's rubber boots, Birkenstocks, garden clogs. Her mother never let an argument fester, Tammy thought, studying the shoes. If she really was going to move this whole family forward, she had to grow up.

Tammy went back into the kitchen, stood behind Byron, and slipped her arms through his, reaching up to kiss the back of his neck. He carefully set down the dish he was drying and turned to her.

"Hey." He held her away from him.

"Hey. Sorry."

"No need."

She hugged him and they stood quietly, connected, before she eased away and said, "Back in a bit."

Another thing she loved about Byron, she thought, stepping outside the back door: he let things lie. He didn't dig and pick and dissect. In this way, he was the antithesis of her, and that patience kept him popular at work with colleagues and clients: letting others have their time to weigh things, yet remaining available. Open. How did she manage to find—and keep—someone so different from her? Tears again. Oh my god, she thought, stop. Maybe, she considered, taking a step towards the shed and stopping, this wasn't the time to try to talk to Dawn. The warm breeze shifted. Hair blew into her face now, and the wind was the slightest pressure against her back. No, she should go, she would, and she went.

Dawn had left the bicycle outside, upside down, and was in front of the workbench, digging through boxes full of ancient tools with an old bike pump in one hand. Tammy spoke to her back: "That bike's ancient. Probably won't blow up." Nothing from Dawn. Tammy took a breath and tried again, gently. "I didn't do anything. Why aren't you talking to me?"

"I'm not *not* talking, I'm just not saying anything." And the bike pump flew through the air, just missing the window and crashing against the wall. Tammy stepped back, shocked. Her sibling had always retreated, withdrawn from their own anger. This was—healthy. Tammy stood her ground and Dawn stormed to the tractor, swung her leg up, and sat, watching the shed door swing to and fro. Tammy turned too, then turned back to Dawn to say, "Woah."

"He wants me gone. He wants this over."

"Those are two different things; you know that, right? We all want this over, but not for the reasons you think."

Tammy could nearly hear her sister's inner monologue: How does she know what I think? for starters. So she addressed that first. "...and I don't know exactly what you think, but it's more about him than you. I mean, this isn't making it—"

"*This* again."

"You, then. Who you've become, what he's lost, these..." She was careful not to say *things*. "...these facts make it hard. Come on. Give him a chance. It's day three."

Dawn sat silent. Tammy turned to the box Dawn had been digging through, removing item after rusted item. Fencepost thingy, jumper cables, a ball-peen hammer. She looked at the ball-peen, remembered a long-ago 4-H session, something to do with metal and engines and...

She studied Dawn, head down, hair moving in a slight breeze. The tractor was sitting in a shaft of light provided by the open shed door. Tammy went to her sister and tapped gently on her leg with the ball-peen. "Hey. What's this for?" she asked.

Dawn raised her head, took the hammer, and examined it, still silent.

Tammy waited, then: “Dawn. Are you gonna fix it?” Now Dawn turned to her sister. “The tractor? Mom wanted it fixed, remember? You could—”

“Dad doesn’t want it fixed.”

“Today, maybe. But he will. Remember the carriage clock?”

“Yeah. He nearly killed me.”

“He was pissed when he saw the pieces all over the den, but then it worked, right? You made it work and he was like, ‘My boy the mechanical genius.’”

Dawn shot her sister a furious look. Dawn’s hackles, just beginning to settle, were rising again.

“Okay,” said Tammy, knowing she sounded impatient and petulant, but geez. “So, do we just forget you were someone else? Have you got some kind of rulebook you can provide so I can start to get it right?”

Dawn jumped off the tractor and stepped towards her sister, so angry, so intense, so...Tammy didn’t even have a word. She stepped back. She’d never seen this.

“I wasn’t someone else,” Dawn spat. “Google it. And no, I don’t run my life by a rulebook. I’m just hoping for basic...respect. Intelligence. Not stupid fucking questions. What century are you in? I forgot what a jerk you can be.” And she left.

That went well, thought Tammy. She sat on an old milk crate. Fuck.

She was trying. She wanted her sibling back, she wanted to get things right, she wanted to be a good person. But this—shit. *THIS*. She had to excise that word, or at least in this context, because despite her best efforts, it seemed impossible to uncouple it from the ignorance and judgment intertwined with her feelings for Dawn.

Oh my god, she thought, how do I fix this? Shit. *This*. How do I realign our relationship so that she trusts I’m trying to do better. Trying to help.

Tammy felt proud of constructing those two sentences without *THIS*.

A little eddy had formed at the door, and the cat—she hadn’t realized she’d been followed out of the house—was swiping at...a leaf? a petal? caught in the tiny whirlwind of dust. Tammy watched the absorbed little beast, then reached over for the box again. More garbage: wires, paper bags of nails and screws, and a plastic hardware-store bag. Containing a brand new bike pump, still in its packaging. She took it out of the bag and opened it. Tested it. Puff-puff-whizz. Everything has its own breath, Tammy's yoga teacher would say. She glanced to where the passé pump had landed, felt pleased with giving it that title and sorry for it no longer having its puff-puff-whizz, then laid the new pump on the tool bench where Dawn was sure to see it.

Dawn

Dawn leaned against the sink in the bathroom, replying to Jill's texts. Yes, she was fine. Trying to be herself in this environment was exhausting and sad. Jill's reply, that it surely must be better than trying to be who she used to be, was, of course, correct but not really helpful at this particular moment, just before Dawn's first public outing—literally—in her hometown.

Early evening sun was slanting through the bathroom window. The afternoon had been hot, quiet, everyone doing their own thing and dripping: John Andrew bent over the piles of papers on his desk, Tammy and Byron facing each other across the dining room table, trying to "keep a finger in the dyke"—the dyke being the advertising agency where they were both, apparently, indispensable. Dawn had winced at the word she'd heard climbing the stairs after her long walk to cool down after the shed. She *had* cooled down, but not enough to go into the dining room after hearing that and make nice with Tammy.

Words. The world was full of snares—seen and unseen. Real and imagined.

So much of this area had farmed land for centuries that was reclaimed from the sea, surrounded by dykes, so Dawn knew her sensitivity was ridiculous. Really, the whole issue with her sister had to do with words. Dawn knew that Tammy's heart was fully engaged in working everything out between them. That Tammy loved her. Wanted to understand her. But trying to squeeze emotion, longing, history into available words, and trying to separate those words from years of other misunderstood or misused words, consistently fucked things up. Dawn didn't consider herself militant or an activist—not the way Jill and Tula were. In their eyes, just existing in a world that wanted you invisible was activism. And in her community, she was surrounded by people who relished a fight. Who defined themselves by those confrontations. They fought because they had grown accustomed to being abused, or told no, or ignored, and now they expected those things; assumed a fight was necessary even before a question was asked. Dawn understood that, had experienced it, but she found it stressful and, ultimately, unproductive. Her mother used to say how much simpler it was to assume the best, and deal with the worst from people if you had to, instead of pressing them into the worst versions of themselves through distrust or judgment. Yeah. Yeah. But. Easy for beautiful Miranda to say, who'd always been who she'd always been. You got it, Mom, thought Dawn, but also you didn't.

Buzz went the phone again. *Dawn?????* Dawn wasn't good being in two places, whatever her mother had thought when she used to take her phone away. She sent a last text to Jill—*All good, getting ready for the wake, talk tomorrow, K?*—and turned back to the mirror. She liked the way she looked now. She turned sideways. Were her breasts bigger than Tammy's? Oh my Jesus, she thought. Where did that come from? Pathetic. But—she turned to look at the other side—were they? What did Byron see when he looked at her? Dawn, she said to the girl in the mirror, stop that. You don't even like guys.

She studied herself again—the whole picture. What were her long-lost family at the wake and funeral going to see? She still found looking in the mirror and thinking she could see her mother unsettling, but Miranda was definitely there. More so, thought Dawn, since she wasn't. But so was John Andrew. Miranda's eye colour, her father's nose and eye shape. A person was such a strange assemblage of others, she thought. Features lost in time, relatives she'd never known but recognized from ancient photographs. She grinned, thinking "ancient," and saw her Aunt Leny. Aunt Leny rarely grinned, but when she did, it was in an unnerving, Cheshire cat fashion. Tammy used to say Freddy Krueger before Dawn knew who that was. But Dawn grinned now and saw the Cheshire cat. Yikes.

She opened her tiny makeup bag and dug for her staples: mascara, little bit of blush, lip gloss. She hated base but had worn lots of it until the hormones and electrolysis—which hurt—had helped change the way her skin looked. Jenny gave her electrolysis vouchers for every occasion: birthday, Christmas, Easter, Halloween. Who gave Halloween gifts? Fortunately, her dad never had a blue beard so it wasn't as bad, and didn't hurt as much, as some folks had said it would. Her dad still had a kind of baby face. A sweet face. Oh. She put the mascara down, dabbed at her eyes. She did love him. She wanted them to be...okay. Grown-ups. Humans.

More dabbing. This was hard, she knew, because every thought, every memory was like DNA, linked to another strand of history, another echo of who she'd been—or hadn't been. This mirror: he'd come in here and caught her, practicing with makeup. The look on his face. Disgust. Anger. Failure. He thought who she was, was down to him—his poor example of maleness. What a fucked-up world. She felt so much sympathy for him, remembering. At seventeen she hadn't understood, and certainly couldn't explain, complicated genetics. And maybe she wouldn't try even now, because somewhere in that explanation there would still lie fault: he'd made her. She wondered if he'd ever see the fact of her, rather than the fault. Sympathy wouldn't have mattered then. She wondered if it mattered now.

A knock. "Dad? You in there? We need to go." Tammy gave another tap when Dawn didn't answer. "Dad?"

"He already left for the funeral home." Dawn put the mascara away, took out a lipstick.

"Oh. He didn't say." A pause and then, "Dawn?"

Throwback to school days, with Tammy banging on the door and Dawn trying to reconcile what she felt with what she saw in the mirror. Now it was Dawn's teenaged self who snapped, "I'm going as fast as I can!"

"No. It's fine, I just..." Dawn stopped doing her lips. Tammy said quietly, "I googled it." Dawn turned to the door. From behind it, Tammy continued. "But I know who you are. I always have. I'm just not good at...communicating how much I care about you."

No kidding, but okay. Dawn opened the door.

"Woah," Tammy gasped.

Oh no, Dawn thought. She was going to have to start over—like Tammy years ago when her father had sent her to wipe off her face. "Too much?"

Her sister shook her head and still didn't speak for a moment. Then—

"Perfect."

Dawn had longed for an impossible moment like this. She leaned against the door, lightheaded with joy. Tammy reached out to steady her, then took her hand and led her down the stairs.

Tammy

"Byron! What are you doing?"

Byron stopped short, one step onto the porch of the funeral home. "What?" he said, framing up a photo of the sign.

Tammy looked around, mortified. No one coming in behind them. Now he was taking pictures of his feet. "Stop. Byron, honestly," Tammy was hissing. "Put your phone away."

He turned to her, a little chagrined. "You guys. Come on. Look at that." And he pointed.

Tammy and Dawn had seen the sign dozens of times: *Murray's Funeral Home, Arthur Murray, Funeral Director*. They looked at the sign, at each other, back at Byron.

"Really?" he said. "Really? It's Arthur Murray. Arthur Murray is a famous dance school. My parents went every Saturday night. They put their feet on paper footprints and," he did a little turn, putting his feet on invisible guides, "they danced. I can't believe—"

"I can't believe you're doing this, here. Now. Stop it." Tammy passed him on the porch, imperious.

Chastened, but now a bit pissed, Byron straightened his tie, tucked his phone in his pocket, and moved to the door, holding it open for the sisters. Tammy stepped into the hallway, then whirled to catch Dawn, giving the tiniest curtsy to Byron as she passed him in the doorway, and he whispered, "Hey. Dying to dance?"

"You two, for f—"

"Tammy! Don't," said Dawn, moving aside to make room for strangers now squeezing past her. Tammy shot black looks at the two of them and hissed over her shoulder to her sister, "Well, don't encourage him," then turned back to deliver the double whammy: "And don't draw more attention to yourself."

Dawn passed her like a blast of winter wind.

Byron put a hand on Tammy's shoulder and pulled her around. "That was great. Get a fucking grip, Tammy." And he swiftly followed Dawn, leaving Tammy to make space for folks coming through the door.

Honestly. One step forward and two—then caught herself. Arthur Fucking Murray. Tammy was dancing on eggshells now. She edged into the main room, determined to keep her distance from Dawn and Byron. They seemed to have coalesced into a team, and she was sitting on the sidelines waiting to be picked. This was not what she'd expected. And that begged the question: what she had expected? And she realized she'd assumed she'd be supporting Dawn as the victim here. What kind of a shitty person had she become? Suddenly. Not suddenly? Fuck. As if all of this wasn't bad enough without a deep soul-dive. She pulled her shoulders back.

The wake was a wake. Subdued voices sharing recollections of Miranda—almost all humorous, certainly light and positive, but presented in doleful tones resulting in a weird incongruity. Nothing matched. The photo of Miranda was bright and smiling, wind whipping her hair back, the energy palpable, but everyone in the room was subdued and downcast. So far from what her mother would have wanted, Tammy thought, heading for the punch table. She looked to see where Byron was as she ladled a glass of what looked and smelled like liquefied raspberry Jell-O. There was Byron, with Dawn, in a corner with someone Tammy didn't know: a young woman, really cute, funky hair with a streak of bright green and a face that lit up the place. She was anything but subdued. Tammy wondered who she could be and watched how engaged Dawn was. Byron too. Her stomach tightened. How engaged *was* Byron? She twisted her ring.

A sudden flurry of chat near the door pulled Tammy around. People were moving aside to let someone in. Someone important, Tammy thought, as an aisle appeared, splitting the room, which went silent for a moment. Because the important person was Aunty Leny, the ancient, outspoken—rude, actually—self-appointed matriarch of the family. Older sister to Miranda's father: soothsayer, truth-teller, keeper of family secrets, arbiter of family feuds—not that there were many. Leny felt her age gave her absolute license. At ninety-six, she still lived in her own home, drove her own car (at a glacial pace), and took care of herself, so she felt entitled to her own opinions and the right to share them. With vigour and without—in legal terms—any "let or hindrance." And here they came.

"Well, this is pretty dull," Leny pronounced. "Miranda would have hated it. Where's the music? Is there liquor in that punch? Give me a glass."

John Andrew moved swiftly—one always moved swiftly after a 'request' from Leny—to ladle a glass to the brim. "Arthur, this isn't a funeral, it's a wake. Where's the fiddles?" Arthur scuttled—Tammy had never actually seen someone scuttle before—out of the room. John Andrew handed Leny the punch and was rewarded with her scrutiny. "J'n Andrew." She paused. Was Leny considering condolences? "I didn't know you had a suit." Another pause. The whole room wondering if she had something kind to say. "Is someone feeding you? You look peaky. Where are those gadabout children of yours?" She looked around. "Tammy! Tammy!" Tammy moved swiftly to her side, thinking oh god, she hasn't met Byron yet, what is she going to say, and oh god. Dawn. If Byron thinks *my* responses are inappropriate—

"When did you get here? Are you feeding your father? Your mother said you were engaged—I hope he's better than the last one." That was really unfortunate as the "last one," Alex MacDonald, and his family, were in the room, staring daggers at her now, after she and Alex had only just managed to start speaking again. Thanks, Leny.

"Ah," Leny sighed as Byron stepped up beside Tammy. "Are you it?" She didn't pause for Byron's response. "Well, you're a good-looking fella. Strapping. You'll have pretty children, the two of you, that's for sure. Will you earn enough to keep them? She's a princess," nodding at Tammy, "you know that?" Byron turned to give Tammy a slightly cool, appraising look. Then Byron nodded back to Leny with a smile and shook the hand she held out, but she was far from done.

"And where's—" Now Leny was scanning the room and Tammy knew she was looking for Dawn. Shit. Fiddle music started, loud. There is a God, Tammy thought, and He just turned the fiddles on so the room wouldn't hear whatever Leny had to say about Dawn. But fiddles were no competition for Leny. "Now then," her voice easily overpowering the music, "come and let me see you." There was no doubt to whom that command was issued. Dawn crossed the room like she was headed to the gallows, stopping in front of her ancient aunt.

"Well." Leny's gaze swept Dawn from toes to beautiful eyebrows and lingered there. "The world's gone to hell in a handbasket, hasn't it?"

Silence in the room. Leny, master of the dramatic pause, practiced her art.

Then: "You know." Pause, shifting all around the room, not a single breath or cough or word. "You were the prettiest little boy I ever saw." A sharp intake of breath from the young woman with the green-streaked hair in the corner. "And now you're the most beautiful woman. The soul of your mother." The room deflated slightly. An overblown balloon releasing air.

"Your dad called this morning—"

Tammy looked over to her father, his face inscrutable.

"He said you were in the barn first thing, never missed a beat, best cowhand he ever had. You'll be a credit to him. To her. Make sure you are." Leny seemed to grow a couple of inches as she opened her arms. "Hug me."

Tammy realized she'd been holding her breath, and the green-haired young woman in the corner let out a strange, strangled whoop—half cheer, half laugh. Dawn reached tentatively towards Leny, who grabbed her and held her, the grip saying everything anyone needed to hear: This family is family. This family keeps our own safe.

Tammy didn't need to put her family back together. Leny had just done all the heavy lifting.

Dawn

It was a lot, Dawn thought later, aiming for a door to the outside and navigating a crowd of people who, after Leny's introduction, all thought they knew her. She was grateful for the intercession that had landed her back in the bosom of her family, but it was just...a lot.

Closing the door to the funeral home behind her, she was faced with a massive barbeque taking up much of the tiny patio. Really? Everything today lay just on the edge of absurd.

During the few seconds Aunt Leny had hugged her, despite the resounding endorsement that pre-empted it, Dawn couldn't help imagining Leny pouring vitriol into her ear, Shakespearean poison oozing from the warm gesture. It was a moment of real panic—palpitations, flushing—but Leny said nothing more, just held her tight. Finally, as the hushed room watched, she'd released Dawn and held her at arm's length and Dawn realized that her aunt recognized her discomfort. Leny did whisper then, leaning in—and she never whispered—"You're home now. Stay a bit. For your dad, eh?" Grateful, Dawn nodded as the crowd started its slow buzz again and became a kind of kaleidoscope, a shifting, brightly clothed assortment of kin she didn't recognize, perhaps had never known, with her and Leny at its centre. Someone seemed to have sent a memo about not wearing black: it was a rainbow room. That brief thought made Dawn smile. Rainbows, she could embrace.

She walked the four steps to the edge of the patio. Ahh. Unperfumed air. Well, not quite. The trees around the building were moving slightly and wafting the scent of—she recognized it—lindens. Her mother, of course. Dawn sat and swung her legs over a low bench, facing the river that ran past the funeral home towards the harbour. She heard the gentle click of the door but didn't turn.

"Dawn?" she heard behind her. "D'you mind me joining?"

She turned. No. She didn't mind at all.

Banu, the young woman with the green stripe in her hair, surveyed the river too before joining Dawn on the bench. “I thought you might need some company, but if you don’t, let me know and I can go.”

“Thanks. It’s fine. It’s all a bit—”

“Intense? Yeah. That old gal smiles like Freddy Krueger.”

Dawn laughed. “I didn’t think anyone else would ever think that.”

“Well, I did. And I think your sister did, too. She looked pretty freaked out.”

“I don’t think she’s ever seen Aunt Leny hug anyone. It’s rare.”

“So. Quite a statement.”

Dawn considered. “Definitely.”

The two sat quietly. The ease, Dawn thought, of not feeling she had to speak to entertain, or explain, or fill space, was a relief. Banu had a presence like Jill’s. Except—she’d been hyper-aware of this fact since they first met inside—Dawn found the androgynous, non-binary Banu really, seriously sexy. Dawn had felt like the whole room could feel her think so, so she’d immediately rejected the thought. Super inappropriate observation to have at her mother’s wake. But. Here it was again. This time she let it linger.

Was this silence charged? Or just...silent?

“How long were you treating my mom?” Banu had told her and Byron they were Miranda’s massage therapist.

“Nearly three years.”

“Oh.” Dawn was surprised. She’d only very recently heard Miranda mention Banu.

“Yeah. I came through here when I was travelling, liked it, and came back. I met her doctor in the café—where I work now—and I guess Miranda asked her for a recommendation. I was new, there aren’t many massage therapists in town, so...folks took a flyer on me.”

“She told me about you. You helped, she said. She liked you.”

“I liked her. Loved her. And...” Banu took a little case out of their pocket, removed a joint, and dug in another pocket for a lighter. “She told me about you.” They grinned. “She liked *you*.” Dawn smiled carefully back. Banu waved the joint. “Is this okay?”

Dawn nodded. Banu lit up, offered it. Dawn shook her head. "I get emotional when I'm *not* emotional. Today it might be..."

"Too much? I get it." Banu looked out to the river, then: "I'm going to miss her a lot." A long, slow drag. "Everyone in there, everyone in general, talks about her like she was a kind of saint. I know she wasn't. She struggled, like all of us, but—she was...available."

"Yeah." Dawn didn't know if she could talk about Miranda this way with a person she had only just met. Who didn't think Miranda was a saint. Who knew about her struggles when Dawn wasn't sure that *she* did. What did Miranda and Banu talk about, she wondered. Her? What details had Miranda confided?

Dawn stood up; something tugged at her. Miranda having a relationship with a person Dawn's age, a relationship based on touch and an intimate knowledge of her mother's body—it was discomfiting. Especially given how sexy Dawn found Banu. Miranda had told Dawn that Banu found a lump under her arm when they were treating her, and that's what had sent Miranda back to her doctor. Not soon enough, Dawn thought. She felt Banu watching her as they smoked. Every pull on the joint seemed to define more clearly who Banu was. Confident. Decisive. Relaxed. Undemanding.

The door opened behind them and Banu tapped the joint out (considerate), putting it away as Byron appeared, looking relieved to see them.

"Oh good, you found her," Byron said to Banu, who nodded as the door opened again and Tammy joined them.

"Here you guys are," Tammy said tentatively as she turned to her sister. Dawn remembered Tammy reaching for her outside the bathroom, and now she did the same to Tammy, saying warmly, "Here we are. Barbeque?" Everyone turned to the supersized grill. A line of faces registering the incongruity of the thing, and no one even trying to find something clever to say. United in mild disbelief. The door clicked once more, and John Andrew joined. He stopped in the doorway. Probably wondering if there was room for him on the patio. He stared at the barbeque too. Five faces in the line now.

John Andrew broke the strange spell it was casting. "I'm going to take Leny home now. She's—"

"Drunk?" said Tammy.

"Emotional," said John Andrew.

Tammy shrugged. "She had a gallon of punch in, like, half an hour."

"Banu said there's music at the pub tonight." Byron looked down the line. "What do you think?"

Dawn flicked a look to Banu and then John Andrew before saying, "I don't think—" but her dad interrupted.

"That's a good idea," said John Andrew. "Just"—looking at Byron—"not too late? I'll get you up for milking again tomorrow."

Byron beamed like a kid. Dawn realized he was proud to be asked, *told,* she corrected herself, that he was milking in the morning.

"Great. King of the teats, that's me!"

"Oh my god." Tammy started back towards the door. "This is a sick reality show, created to demonstrate why I shouldn't marry you."

Byron reached for Tammy and pulled her into a tight hug. She struggled, sort of, to get away until he planted a loud, wet kiss on her cheek and said, "Come on, Tam. Let's go get emotional."

Banu

It was dark by the time they finally extracted themselves from the wake, which now felt much more like a party. The spiked Jell-O–flavoured punch had definitely had its effect, and the vibe as Dawn, Tammy, Byron, and Banu made their exit was a whole lot looser than a couple hours earlier.

They walked the kilometre into town along the river, Byron and Tammy in front, holding hands, Dawn and Banu behind, deep in conversation.

"...I'd been travelling—my parents paid for me to go to massage school in their hometown—Goa, in India? They've been in Ontario since before I was born, but you know, home is home...anyway. I saw lots of places but I fell in love with...here." Banu threw an arm out, embracing the town and the river. "Weird. This totally non-gay town felt more like home than anywhere else I've been." Banu stopped for a moment, looking to the river. "And I've loved my work. Building up my clientele."

"Is it your own practice?" asked Dawn.

"*Practice* is a bit grand. I rent a room from another therapist when they're not using it—at the Wellspring—and I have about six regulars now. Three of them are pals of your mom."

"Jenny, Debby, Joy?"

Banu nodded, then—"Your mom said—are you still going into sports physio?"

"Oh, she told you? Hope so."

"Do you have to go back to school? Or—study remotely? Are you staying long?" Banu took a breath. "Sorry, twenty questions."

Dawn bit her lip. "It's okay, but I don't know. Any of it. Except I'm not in school. I just—"

"Sorry," said Banu. "Probably too soon to know exactly what comes next."

Dawn nodded. Tammy had paused ahead and turned to watch them and, Banu thought, definitely listen. Banu's dad had an expression, "ears out on stalks," and Tammy's definitely were. She pointed to the pub sign at the bottom of the street. "Dawn?" she called, "you feel okay about this?"

Dawn waved her sister on, and Tammy turned and kept walking. It landed on Banu, looking at Dawn, what an ordeal this day, night, week must be for her. She seemed so self-assured, self-contained. She projected this quiet, confident exterior that must be hell to maintain while being made to jump through one hoop after another. And now a pub full of strangers. Or worse, Banu thought, people who'd known Dawn before, and heard about her homecoming. Banu knew half the town had: gossip this spicy spread here like a cold in a kindergarten. Dawn must know that Miranda's passing and her own arrival after such a long absence would be an eleven out of ten on the town's gossip scale. And, Banu considered, taking a sideways glance at her, Dawn's looks were just complicating things. Dawn was undeniably gorgeous and so like her mother—with whom everyone had been a little in love, including Banu—that it was, frankly, a bit weird. Poor Dawn. What a strange and uncomfortable burden. Banu paused and reached for Dawn's hand, stopping them both, then dropped it again as Dawn turned. No liberties, they thought.

"Hey," Banu said, "we really don't have to do this, we could just keep walking, or, whatever, but—"

Dawn shrugged. "It'll have to happen sometime." She carried on towards the neon pub sign swinging off the wall in front of Tammy and Byron, who waited for them.

"New sign," Tammy said, indicating the neon-blue-and-white *The Watering Hole* that buzzed above them. Dawn studied it. Banu wondered if she was having second thoughts when she said, "I have never been in here."

"Oh right," said Tammy. "You left before you were legal."

"Being legal was never the issue," said Dawn as she reached for the door.

A tangy fusion of warm bodies, fried food, and beer was released into the summer night. The Celtic-themed pub had a fire burning—like midwinter, not mid-July—under a pair of crossed swords hung on draped tartan. And to ensure you couldn't mistake the flavour of the space, a couple of elderly men straight from central casting were wearing kilts—Banu never got tired of this town—and playing cribbage under pictures of caber tossing and pipe and drum bands on the town's streets. It was as if they'd stepped through a door to a different time and country.

It was busy, not crammed, still a table or two. Heads turned when the group came in but then turned back to conversations. It didn't go silent or feel uneasy. Maybe it'll be okay, Banu thought. But then they saw who was behind the bar—and worse, sitting with a group of pals at the end of it.

"Tammy-bo-bammy!" shrieked the person behind the bar.

"Oh my god. Oh. My. God!" Tammy squealed. Byron, under his breath: "Oh my god, oh my gaawwwdd!" to Dawn and Banu, who grinned at him.

"Oh, Tammy, I'm so sorry. Your beautiful mom. Everyone loved her so much."

"Ah, thanks, Ali." Tammy reached to hold hands with Ali Stewart across the bar. "Everyone's been so nice. It's been great to see people and—holy cow!"

Ali looked down. "I know, right? Hang on, I'll come round," and she did.

What looked like a massive beach ball arrived before Ali did. The size of her belly wasn't a surprise to Banu—Ali came into the café regularly—but for someone who had known Ali as the stick insect she'd been before getting pregnant, this version of her would be quite a shock.

"Ali! You're about to pop!" Did Banu detect disgust or longing in Tammy? To be explored, they noted for themselves. Always fascinating, conflicted peeps, these breeders.

"Not quite: seven and a half months, but *cow* is right, I know."

Byron looked anxious. "Are you having twins?"

Tammy turned to him, mortified. "Oh my god, Byron!" She turned back to her friend. "Ali, sorry, sorry. This is Byron—he's my fiancé and a man and an idiot—"

"And right," said Ali. "I'm having twins, a boy and a girl."

"Wow," said Tammy.

"Wow, *wow*," said Dawn.

Ali turned her attention to Dawn then. Her gaze was laser-focused and, from Banu's perspective, didn't feel truly warm, kind, or welcoming, though Ali was working hard to create the illusion of all those things. Banu knew this look, having been on the receiving end of it every time Ali came into the café, interacting with them or Ethan. Ali clearly had a problem with queer folks. She managed to balance on the edge of polite, but never climbed right into the middle of it. She had a permanent head tilt: curious. As though she were examining a bug on a slide. It was not a comfortable place to be, under her microscope.

"Hiiii," said Ali, drawing out the word, a long downhill slide, and then, "Don, right?" Banu could hear the name being spelled D-O-N and was sure everyone else could too. "I heard you were back in town."

"Yup, I am. And this is Banu."

Ali gave Banu a cursory glance and said, "Yeah, I know her. Sorry. Them. Them."

Banu smiled. "*Her* is fine. I prefer they/them, but either works."

"Man, that's so hard, right?" Ali said to Tammy, who, Banu noticed, was starting to go a bit pink.

"Is it?" said Banu.

"Well, yeah, 'cause technically the *they* thing is grammatically incorrect, right? And, I mean, you're so clearly a *she* that, like, isn't it a bit sort of, I don't know, do you really need, like, both of them? She and they? It's confusing, right?"

"Gosh," said Banu, who had this conversation with Ali every time she came into the café—so, daily—"is it? Really? Still?"

Ali turned her faux friendliness back to Dawn. "You must remember Marty, right? My little brother? You guys were in school together, and on the soccer team?"

"Yeah," said Dawn, and it was plain to Banu that Dawn remembered Marty very clearly and that the Marty-Dawn connection hadn't been a dreamy one. She turned to Banu and Byron and said, "I'll grab a table."

"Well, he's here," said Ali, pointing. "End of the bar. Go over. Say hi. I know he'd be super interested to see you."

"It's okay. We're good. He looks busy. Let's, um—" Dawn turned and headed towards an empty table, but Ali wasn't giving up. She shouted above the music, just coming to the end of a number. "Hey, Marty, look who's here. Don MacInnis!"

What Banu had been dreading on Dawn's behalf, happened. The bar went quiet. The musicians on their platform all turned to look, and anyone who'd been watching the band turned to look too. The patrons' heads were on strings, pulled from Ali to Marty to Dawn, where Marty was looking, and back round the circle until Marty stood, gestured to the pal with him, and started across the room. And with what Banu realized was a family specialty, Marty was raising his voice to greet Dawn with same faux friendly ease that his sister had.

"Wow," said Marty. "Donald MacInnes! After all these years. Crazy, eh? Some crazy shit going down, eh?"

Banu wanted to hit him. Or say, *Like what crazy shit, bro? Like the assault on Washington? Like North and South Korea at odds again? Like the ice caps melting? What's worrying you most, buddy?* But they knew what he was actually saying and wouldn't, as Miranda used to say, give him the satisfaction. And if Banu had started the night being, a) curious about Dawn and, b) a bit attracted, with every exchange Banu observed they became, a) *more* curious and, b) REALLY attracted. Dawn managed to be aloof, but also direct, and she never dropped her eyes from Marty's. Now she said, "Definitely. Good to see you, but if you don't mind—"

Marty didn't mind and didn't move. His pal moved behind Dawn and Banu, who stood next to her.

Marty said, "Think you were on the bus with Jimbo?"

"Yeah. Wow." Jimbo leaned in and sniffed Dawn. Sniffed. She

turned slowly to him and said, "Oh, Aisle-Guy. Right." Marty seemed annoyed that Dawn had a name for his pal.

"So," said Marty. "Huh."

Dawn sat down. Marty pulled out a chair and sat opposite. Banu sat beside Dawn. Aisle-Guy loomed between them. Tammy arrived at the table and pulled out the chair beside Marty, looked back at Byron at the bar and Ali serving him, and seemed undecided about whether to sit or not. Marty looked at Tammy. She sat.

Banu did a little survey of the bar: who was watching, who was not. Mostly, folks who realized they'd been caught gawping looked away. The table of young women next to them—including a dental hygienist Banu knew—didn't, but also didn't say anything. Mental note: she won't clean my teeth again. Banu looked back to Marty who was—was that as a leer? Yes—leering, at them. He spoke to Dawn but looked at Banu.

"Amazing. The way you folks find each other. Just got here and buddies already with little Banu. Kind of a club, eh? Sort of like Tammy's"—he nodded towards Byron—"fiancé? Is that right, Tammy? Like the way his folk usually find each other." He scanned the pub. "Not here, really. But we're a little bit boring here—right, Jimbo? A little bit...samey. But, hey! Welcome!" He spread his meaty paws: the welcome came from him and all his fellow townsfolk! "This is something, Donny, after all this time."

"Dawn," she said, cool as a long, elegant, English cucumber.

Marty widened his eyes, innocent. "That's what I said. Hey—still playing soccer, Donny?"

"Dawn," said Banu.

Dawn glanced from Banu to Tammy, who was silent, watching Byron at the bar. She turned back to the table, with a small *I hear you* smile at Banu.

Dawn answered Marty's question: "A bit."

"Huh," Marty grunted again. He gets some mileage out of that sound, thought Banu. Then he continued, "Isn't that tricky? Like, the team thing?"

"Why?" Cucumber gal, quietly puzzled, didn't drop her eyes from Marty.

"Well," he drawled, "which side d'you play for now?"

Nothing from Dawn. She simply lifted her eyes from Marty's face to Byron's, to where he stood now, behind and above Marty, with a pitcher of beer and a pile of plastic glasses. People around them were torn: watch the trans girl and her androgynous, brownish pal, or the only actually Black guy in a bar full of white people. Banu felt the connection between the three of them, her otherish face beside Dawn's fine-featured composure and Byron's imposing, handsome presence: no shit taken here.

But Banu could see Byron's mouth tightening. Was he was trying to keep himself from laughing, or cursing? Instead, Byron said politely, "'Scuse me fellas, this is a private party." He set the plastic glasses down in front of Marty—Byron's chair—but kept hold of the jug of beer, waiting for Marty to vacate.

Marty began the process, in a languorous fashion, enjoying the way he was commanding the room, or thought he was. That status actually belonged to Dawn and Byron, but it was all the same to Marty. He was in the circle of attention, and that's what mattered. As he stood, his silver neck chains swung, clinking against each other. Marty was a big guy and not a fast mover. He was, thought Banu, like a picture by...they could see the paintings and plucked the name from their memory—Botero. Who painted people's features as if they were upholstered in flesh. Like Marty, with the wads around his middle; legs pressed apart by the girth of his thighs; his triple chin and fleshy neck creating crevasses where his chains were caught, then freed, caught then freed, by his movements. He was open and over-friendly, smiling at Byron. A jolly, everybody's-best-pal kind of guy. He patted Byron on the shoulder, and Banu saw that his wrist chain was the same as the chains around his neck. Sweet, thought Banu. Matchy-matchy.

"No worries," he said. "You're Tammy's lucky fiancé, right? Boyfriend? Party on, buddy boy." Each *boy* with a slight lean in. Huh, thought Banu. Anyone else hear the racist slur? Tammy was going red again, Banu noticed, so *she* had. Byron had frozen, so *he* had. And Dawn had turned towards Byron, so she'd heard it too. But Marty wasn't finished yet.

"Did you know," he said to Byron, "that Donald was our star striker? You don't mind me sharing that, do you Donny? Your amazing past? Donald scored and scored for our high school team. He took every soccer trophy in the case."

"Dawn," said Dawn.

"That's what I said." Marty grinned. "Your hearing gone funny, too?"

Banu stood now. "Too?"

Dawn stood up beside them and said, not so quietly now, "My hearing's great. And it's Dawn, not Donald or Donny, and it's not he, it's she."

The musicians had started to tune up, but now they stopped. Ali moved quickly from around the bar and stood a couple steps behind her brother. "Marty," she hissed, just before he projected, "Woah! She? Whaaaat. Come. On."

Ali pulled at his shirt."Marty! Leave it," louder now, and she turned to Tammy and said, with the least apologetic tone Banu could imagine, "Sorry, Tammy," and Tammy, with the spine of a curled-up piece of kale, replied with the worst words ever.

"It's fine."

Dawn glanced at her sister, a look flecked with disappointment and anger. Betrayal. Byron looked at Dawn's face, then back at Marty, and with an "Oops!" poured the pitcher of beer down the front of Marty's track pants, a long pee stain running into Marty's expensive white leather sneakers, over the chubby ankles spilling out of them.

You could have heard a pin drop, and then after the pin, you'd have heard Byron saying, "Gosh, all gone—so I guess we're done now. Come on, ladies." Byron set the pitcher down firmly and turned to move past Marty, but bumped his shoulder as Marty lunged at him and then slid in the pool of beer, landing hard on his very padded ass. Someone—more than one person—laughed. The freckled, fair-skinned Marty turned scarlet. Bear-like, he lumbered onto his feet, helped by Aisle-Guy. "You fucking cunt," he said. "You on the tranny train too, or have you got a cock?"

Here it comes, thought Banu. Guys just can't resist. And Byron didn't disappoint.

"I've got a cock. That what you like?"

"You calling me a fag?"

They were pathetic, thought Banu. But at least Byron was witty.

"If the wet shoe fits," said Byron, winding up with, "you're the one wearing jewelry."

Nicely done. Banu mentally chocked points up on Byron's side of the board, but as they did, Marty head-butted Byron in the face. Banu thought they heard a crack, but it might just have been that the blood gushing from Byron's nose warranted some sound. Byron backed up, wound up, and landed a smacking punch under Marty's left eye. Another dramatic noise: fist to flesh. Banu had never seen a fight at close quarters like this and wanted out, but—it was weirdly exhilarating.

"Stop it! Get out! Tammy, why'd you let your brother come in here and cause trouble?! Get him out of here!" Ali was pulling Marty away from Byron, her massive belly the referee now, pushing the opponents to their corners.

Tammy had rushed to Byron, but now she turned to Ali and, getting as close as the belly would allow, bawled into her face: "*Her*, it's *her*!" then turned to follow the others out of the pub. Arriving at the door, she opened it, then turned back, the bad fairy delivering her curse: "I hope you have the longest labour ever."

The heavy door banged shut.

Tammy

Tammy joined the others on the street, taking some satisfaction that the final salvo had been hers. But the adrenaline was short-lived. She looked at Byron, blood still spilling down his face.

"Maybe we should go to the hospital," Banu said. "His nose could be broken."

"Don't think so," said Byron. "He got lucky. I always bleed like this. It'll stop. But," he indicated his jacket, "not sure what I'll wear to the funeral."

"You *always* bleed like this? Is this a regular thing?" Banu asked.

"He'll be okay," said Tammy.

"Right," said Dawn. "'Cause it's fine."

"Dawn, I didn't mean—"

"Tammy, just be quiet," Byron interjected.

She whirled to him. "What? Why? What did I do? What could I do? I just—"

"Shut up, Tammy," said Dawn, not facing her sister. "This isn't fine. It wasn't fine. None of this is fucking fine."

"I meant—"

Now Dawn whirled. "I don't care. I don't care what you meant; I care what you did, what you said. Which was exactly nothing except *it's fine—it's fine* for ignorant creeps to abuse people. Because you don't get it. And that is shit. Those people are shit. This town is shit, this," and she bent and picked up a rock, "this bar is shit!" And she let the rock fly at the neon sign.

A crash, a flash, a buzz, and the *Watering* went out, leaving only *The ——— Hole* to light up the night. The crash and flash, the broken glass on the sidewalk, and now the door opening behind them, sent them flying up the street—still a unit, just not united.

They walked in silence, first to the riverside where Banu soaked some tissues from Dawn's purse and Byron mopped at his face.

Tammy didn't even try to help; she knew she'd disgraced herself but didn't know how to fix it. She wanted to cry, and felt absurdly that if they'd only heard her parting shot at Ali, things would be okay. But probably they wouldn't.

Byron did not once complain on the walk back to the car. Tammy, on the silent trudge, fought with herself, swinging between two truths. She hadn't done anything wrong, but why hadn't she done *something*? She felt ashamed. She hadn't reacted with any kind of dignity or—and this was worse—empathy for Dawn. Hearing Dawn say, This town is shit, made her feel sick, because Dawn was actually saying, YOU are shit. To Tammy. In front of Banu. And Byron. And yet, while she was ashamed of herself, she was proud of Byron; of how he was dealing with this foul aftermath, and mostly of how, in that ugly moment, he had defended Dawn, and by extension, their family.

They were back at the car. Byron unlocked, but no one moved to get in. Banu looked at Dawn, Dawn looked at Byron. She could feel the *can you remove my sister* vibe coming off her. Byron felt it too, caught Tammy's eye and nodded towards the car. She came around to the passenger seat and climbed in, and he got in too, closing the door and sitting silent. She had to get things right with him.

"How are you feeling?" she asked, tentative.

"Like some asshole just ruined my suit." End of conversation.

Tammy could not leave it. "Well, the only thing this town has going for it is a really good menswear store, almost as good as home, so tomorrow—"

Now he did turn to her. "Really? The *only* thing? And...is this *not* home for you? Is that the problem?"

Solar plexus punch. What was he asking? What problem? Had it been so awful, so far? On the scale of uncomfortable events following a family death, where did it fall? She felt that Byron was taking sides with Dawn, and it felt shitty.

She weighed her possible responses, then: "Of course it's home. This town, and all its ugly...attitudes—it *is* home, but I meant Toronto. I meant my home with you. Isn't it possible to have two homes? To be split and know that there are different rules in each place?" He was listening, so she carried on, aware that Dawn and Banu were standing close to each other outside, deep in conversation. "I fucked up, Byron. I get it."

The back door opened before he could answer. Tammy turned in her seat to look back at Dawn, and saw Banu walking away. "Banu doesn't want a lift?"

No response.

Another tack. "You...okay?" A plea.

"What do you think?"

"Dawn, of course I didn't mean *it's fine*, I meant—"

"Forget it, Tammy."

"It's just...you're, like, exhaling annoyance." Tammy felt Dawn sit back hard into her seat.

"Sorry. I shouldn't exhale? That would fix it."

"Dawn—"

Quietly, Dawn cut her off: "Tammy. Shut the fuck up. Please."

Byron looked at Tammy as if about to speak, but then dug the keys from his pocket and started the car. Tammy turned to the window and looked into the dark, her eyes filling. She would not cry. She would make this right somehow. This, too, she heard her mom saying, will pass, and this night, this day, would be history.

Miranda & John Andrew

It had turned into what Miranda would call a "naughty night": wind up, rain sideways, trees disco-dancing, limbs akimbo. Only one light shone through the dark: John Andrew was in his office, head bent over his desk. He heard the car door slam and saw Tammy racing for the cover of the porch. She looked back, as if to see whether the others would follow, then slammed the back door too, heading up the stairs without speaking to him when he came out of his office. John Andrew's "Tammy, hang on—" was ignored and he stood at the bottom of the stairs waiting for the slam of her bedroom door. Instead, a careful click. Was someone going to tell him, he said to Miranda, what exactly the hell had happened?

Byron came in next, soaked and covered in blood. "It looks worse than it is," he said, and took the stairs two at a time.

Then Dawn. He wasn't letting her pass. John Andrew took a deep breath and said, "Dawn. Ali called from The Watering Hole." He wasn't going to tell her that Ali had referred to Dawn as *Donald* throughout the conversation. He did have to let her know that Ali had given him a lot of high-pitched grief about the broken sign, and that Dawn would have to sort it out. But he felt sure, if the blood all over Byron hadn't already confirmed it, that Ali had left out a lot of details. That Dawn had been pushed too far, and Byron had gone with her. That was all he needed to know. This wasn't a question of sides; it was a question of expectations. Maybe he had no right to them, but he expected better from Dawn. In his ear Miranda said, Wait, let her go first. But he didn't. As soon as Dawn said, "Dad," he began.

"Make your choices"—no, no, no, sang the rain breeze through window—"live how you want"—wait, wait, stop—"but this is my home"—our home; her home—"here, you have to play the game"—not play, not game, oh—"understand?"

A statue with Dawn's features thawed. Ice to flame. Since she'd been home, he'd not heard her speak with passion or pain. But now—

"No." She didn't shout—she *shot*, and hit him. "I don't. Not when the game is cruel and ignorant." She headed for the stairs but stopped at the bottom. She turned; she'd gathered herself. "And if you think how I live is a lifestyle choice—think again."

Her footsteps receded, up the stairs and into her room. Another door closing with an almost inaudible click. More of a statement than their adolescent slams. John Andrew leaned against the desk and reached for his breath as he listened to the blistering silence upstairs. He pulled his shoulders back, rolled his head trying to loosen his neck and this tight chest that ached for a proper, deep inhalation. Everything was constricted; limited, as though waiting for some kind of signal, resolution.

The singing of the wires outside had stopped; the rain was easing, the wind was dropping. A sudden crash shocked him; the jolt made him gasp and started his breath again. The window he'd opened to enjoy the sweet petrichor of the much-needed rain had slammed and a small bottom pane shattered with the impact. He went to the window and picked shards off the sill and then the floor. As he tipped them into an old envelope, he saw bright red drops on the white flap. Blood from a cut he hadn't felt. Now he picked the splinter—not small—from his hand and examined it. How could he not have seen it? It began to sting. He watched the blood dripping onto the white envelope and wondered if his bleeding would change anything.

Dawn

The thing is, Dawn thought as she pulled her mother's hoodie over her T-shirt against the moist coolness of the morning, the night ends, however shitty or however great, and morning comes. Stuff happens, then it's done, and something else waits just out of sight to ambush you.

She came out of her room as Tammy emerged from the bathroom. Tammy took a breath, about to speak, as Dawn swept past, and that moment was done too. Well, thought Dawn, tough. She wasn't ready to make things okay for Tammy yet.

In the kitchen Byron had filled the French press with coffee and was pressing it down. John Andrew sat tying his boots. He'd never get away with having his boots on in the kitchen if her mother were here, Dawn thought. Her father lifted his head and she saw him having the same thought. Byron poured out three cups, went to the fridge for the milk, added it to her mug and John Andrew's, and offered them in silence. His eye was ugly this morning. Red, plum-purple, navy-blue edges.

"Does it hurt?" Dawn asked as Byron sipped his coffee.

"Not much. Just my vanity," he responded, and John Andrew snorted. When Dawn and Byron turned to him, he carried his mug to door and spoke only to Betsy. "You can stay here this morning." Which was, Dawn thought, what he'd like to be saying to us.

Jerry was already moving the herd in and hooking up the early team. He took a look at Byron and gave a single rueful headshake, then turned back to what he'd been doing. They got busy, working in silence but for the buzz of the fluorescent lights, the chug of the milkers, and the trudge and settle of the cattle. No sliding, no laughter, no cellphone photos. And when the last cow had exited, and the troughs and floor were sluiced, the four of them headed towards the house, still no one talking.

It amazed Dawn how efficient they'd been, how capable Byron was and what a fast learner. He hadn't needed to ask about anything. And now, walking the path back to the house, not a word—until they got to the machine shed, where Dawn peeled off to go to the tractor. Because I am going to fucking fix it. This, I *can* fix, she thought, and he can't stop me. She threw a glance to her dad, who called ahead to Byron.

"Byron! Get Jerry a coffee." And to Jerry, "I'll be right in. We need to do the order list."

Jerry nodded and confirmed. "Yeah. Running short of feed."

Looking at the tractor yesterday, Dawn knew one of the first tasks in getting it going again would be cleaning—or more likely replacing—the spark plugs. She remembered seeing a wire brush on the workbench and went to dig for it. Her dad stood in the doorway. "I'm going into Stewart's after breakfast. I thought you might want to come."

Dawn gave a wry, strangled laugh, and then responded to her dad's puzzled look with, "It was Marty Stewart that butted Byron last night. Happy to give him your money?"

Her dad looked at the tractor, at the window, studied his hand—why did he have that big Band-Aid?—then said, "I've never liked giving the Stewarts my money, but Angus's is the only farm machine shop hereabouts. He has to make a living, just like I do. He gives his asshole son a job because no one else will. Do I punish him because his kids are jerks? Will he punish me because he doesn't like what you are?"

Dawn's hackles went up; her dad adjusted. "Who. *Who* you are. Marty Stewart's been tormentin' you since you were eight. I said then, ya gotta stand up to him. Ya gotta be a—" Dawn watched John Andrew swallow *man* and recalibrate. "Ya can't be a puss—" He stopped again. Dealing with language was torture, Dawn saw, but he was trying. Dawn didn't mind the word *pussy*, but it wasn't one she wanted her dad directing at her. He didn't. He arrived at what he wanted to say and he said it, pulling at the Band-Aid that had come lose.

"He's a coward. You're not. If you wanna start on that tractor, you're gonna need some parts." The bloody Band-Aid came off and John Andrew stuffed it into the pocket of his coveralls as he left Dawn gaping. Stunned, but elated.

John Andrew

You're not going to get everything right, John Andrew thought as he strode towards the house. He knew he was leaving Dawn staring after him. But he had a feeling she'd come along, and that was a triumph. Now though, he needed to deal with the order and the bills and—aw, fuck. All of it. Easier on a full stomach.

He opened the back door and the smell of bacon and...pancakes? He hadn't had pancakes since... His eyes prickled and he swiped at them. Jesus H. Christ. They're just pancakes, he thought, and I'm starving. He went into the kitchen and pulled his oldest daughter to him in a hug.

"Is this a pity hug?" she said into his chest.

"It's a pancake hug. Everyone'll get over—whatever. C'mon. Get Jerry a plate, and let's eat."

Tammy dabbed at her eyes. "They've already started."

"Don't give Byron any more till I've had mine!" and he went into the little cloakroom to wash.

The phone began to ring in his office as John Andrew finished soaking his final bite of pancake in maple syrup. He forked it into his mouth, nodded at Jerry and a disapproving Tammy as he bolted to the office to grab it. He could see it was Nancy from the feed store returning his call. He'd love to let it ring, let her leave a message, carry on a never-ending game of telephone tag, but he knew he'd have to speak to her eventually. Jesus. How many times had they asked this woman for credit. He picked up.

"Nancy. Thanks for getting back to me." And then he listened. To her condolences, her concern, a dash of gossip—was everyone okay after last night? Nancy loved a bit of news of any kind. Great, thought John Andrew, jungle drums already beating it out. But he said, "Yeah, all fine. You know how things go. Time like this, feelings running a bit hot. I guess some steam got blown off. But listen, I've just been looking through the invoices and—"

Nancy interrupted, gently taking the burden from him. Everyone knew, she said, that times like these were *not* times folks needed to be thinking about invoices. And she knew too that Miranda had dealt with the farm accounts, so whatever he needed right now, until things got—he heard her deciding on a word—settled a bit, he could count on their patience.

He was relieved not to have to ask. He felt a bit shaky as he put the receiver down, then picked it up again: this call might be different. He looked up a phone number on the list in Miranda's careful handwriting and pulled the figures from last night's bookkeeping in front of him.

After the third ring he got a recording: Gerrard Thomas, John Andrew's personal banker, was never far from his desk, hated to miss his call, and wanted him to leave a message.

He started talking straight away, was interrupted by a long beep that threw him, and he had to start over again. "Ah...Gerrard, John Andrew here. I, ah...listen, I need to get a sense of where exactly things are... I know you're aware of, well, of course you know that Miranda has, ah..." Gone? Died? He realized he hadn't yet had to say this to anyone. What was correct for your banker, who might seem friendly but who wasn't really, when it came down to it, your friend. And meanwhile, Gerrard Thomas would be listening to a long pause. "Sorry, Gerrard. Just give me a call, please? I need to know if there's any space on the mortgage. Thanks."

John Andrew put the phone down and ran his hand across his forehead. He was drenched. He didn't sweat like that moving the herd around, or lifting bales, or a million other tasks he accomplished every day. Not this cold, unsettling sweat. But contemplating a conversation about money, and confronting his financial failure, soaked him and made his chest ache. He wondered for the hundredth time that week if his heart was failing. Then what? How could he leave this mess to his kids? Jesus. How could Miranda leave this mess to him?

With that thought, he felt ashamed and then angry—at himself and at her father. That ancient fucking history. Victor had told him time and again, leave the business to Miranda: don't interfere; stick to what you *do* know. Emphasis always on the *do*, like he was some kind of halfwit. But especially after the tractor stuff blew up, he *had* left it all to Miranda. Victor mocked and belittled every one of John Andrew's choices, every change he tried to make, and though Miranda ran interference, she'd still deferred to Victor right to the end of his life. But the blessed release when he died: from Victor's anger and sapping scrutiny. Miranda said she'd get John Andrew up to speed, but he'd been—still was—afraid of ruining everything. He'd always found reasons to avoid the paperwork, so that burden stayed with her, even when her illness meant things got left and left and...left. And now, here he was. Afraid again.

"Dad." Dawn was at the door, freshened up after breakfast. "I'm ready if you are."

"Give me five," he said, up and passed her. He had to splash his face and go forward; make what he could, better. Concentrate on this tiny victory.

Dawn

The kitchen still smelled of pancakes and maple syrup. Dawn was hungry; she hadn't eaten much. Feeling the progress with her dad, she was ready to offer an olive branch to her sister, but then breakfast wrong-footed her. Dawn wasn't crazy about pancakes so ate little of what Tammy had clearly taken trouble over. And then someone—Tammy—had helped themselves to Dawn's face cream. Passing on the landing, Dawn had gently let her sister know she'd prefer if Tammy used her own products, and that, combined with Dawn's ingratitude for Tammy's domestic talents, meant things had stayed "right chilly," as her mom would say.

Now Dawn stuck her head in the pantry—a piece of fruit would hold her—but Tammy was putting dishes away. She turned to leave.

"Hey." Dawn turned back to her sister, who seemed to be proffering her own olive branch, tentatively. "You look great." And then, "Pretty fancy for a machine shop." Tammy had a talent for offering compliments wrapped in disparagement.

"Yeah, well, my wardrobe choices are a bit limited here." And she turned to exit again.

"Dawn, listen. Please." Dawn waited. "I'm sorry. Sorry you don't like pancakes. Sorry I used your moisturizer." Dawn shook her head as Tammy defended herself. "I thought it was Mom's! But mostly, I'm sorry I said *fine* last night." She paused, in case Dawn wanted to weigh in. She didn't. Then, "It wasn't fine. It wasn't my fault, but it wasn't fine, and never could be."

She waited again—was Dawn thawing, even a bit? She was. So Tammy went on: "And since I'm going to spend most of my time apologizing while I'm here, I wonder if we can do some kind of credit thing? I'll say sorry a dozen times now, and that'll buy me every fuckup till I go home?"

Now Dawn did respond, smiling a bit. "Only a dozen? How soon you leaving?"

Tammy's over-bright eyes focused on Dawn. "Ha ha," she said, then, "Do you want me to go?"

Dawn stepped back into the pantry, leaned against the counter opposite Tammy. The red *TAMMY* and blue *DONALD* mugs were catching the light through the glass cupboard. "No." Tammy relaxed and Dawn continued, "Let's stay," she said, concentrating on the two mugs, "till Dad says he loves us."

Tammy laughed, stopped, laughed again. Dawn went on. "Till I finish the tractor. Highland Heart Tractor Trials."

"You're going to fix it?!" Tammy was like a dog with two tails, John Andrew would say, both wagging madly now. "That's so great. But isn't that, like—isn't it two weeks from now? I don't know if my work—"

Byron stepped in. "What about work?" He looked from one sister to the other.

"I can't just not go back," Tammy finished.

Byron looked alarmed. "Hang on, what? Not go back to work?" he said as John Andrew entered. Now all four of them were in the tiny pantry space. Cozy, thought Dawn.

"Okay?" John Andrew said to Dawn. She nodded, moved from the counter towards the door, and Tammy lobbed a slow but direct, "Heyy, Dad?" and John Andrew turned back. Pause for effect, then gently, "I love you."

John Andrew studied Tammy, expressionless and still. Then he glanced at Dawn, then back to Tammy. Byron looked from face to face to face, confused.

Finally, John Andrew spoke: "Right. Well. Good." Then, turning to the door, over his shoulder, he threw, "We're off."

Dawn and Tammy grinned at each other. Dawn saw Byron recognizing the truce, but it tickled her that he had no clue as to what had wrought it. The game, she thought, was on.

It was a large morning. Enormous clear sky, warm enough that already the air was pungent with rugosa roses, the end of the lilacs, and linden and fresh manure—Dawn could see someone spreading a load, way in the distance. I've missed these smells so much, she thought, climbing into the cab of the truck.

When she was little, it had been a reward to sit in the front seat of the truck with her dad. So high, such a sense of freedom. They pulled onto the road and Dawn clicked the radio on. A self-satisfied host oozed from the speakers. Dawn and John Andrew reached to turn it off at the same time. He grinned. "She makes me crazy."

"Poor Maria," said Dawn. "She speaks well of you. Music?"

John Andrew nodded, and Dawn dug into the glove compartment. You could tell Miranda had been the disc jockey in this vehicle: Bob Dylan, Brian Ferry Singing Bob Dylan, Bob Dylan and the Traveling Wilburys, Bob and Friends, Bob and the Band, Bob, Bob, Bob.

"How about a little Bob Dylan," she asked as she popped in *Blood on the Tracks*. And then remembered every track and wished she hadn't. Wondered if she should take it out. Thought about how her mother's passion for Dylan's music had made it the soundtrack of their lives. Not in a screaming fan-girl way, but awe and respect for a poet. Curiosity from one artist about another's process. Dawn could see her mother in her workroom, bent over a collage or painting, the music always in the air. She remembered conversations at the kitchen table late into the night: Jenny smoking and drinking red wine, back when Jenny still smoked, the two of them analyzing Dylan's lyrics and joining the dots of Joan Baez's *Diamonds and Rust* to reveal a portrait of Dylan that wasn't, try though they did, flattering. Laying Dylan's life out on the table and examining it: a dissection. Who did what to whom and when and why, exactly. His history tangled inextricably with theirs. His religion and theirs. His politics and, most definitely, theirs.

Now each song spoke to Dawn about this exact moment in their lives. She'd forgotten how every track on this album catalogued loss, tangled moments of blue and wretched pain. She watched her father out of the corner of her eye, wondering if it wasn't all too close to the bone. That as Bob sang about waking in an empty room; about a lover gone but still living in his damaged heart; about confusion and anger because they'd been left behind—if it wasn't all making her father's aching heart ache even more.

She turned it off. John Andrew turned to her and said, "Bit much, eh, old Bob?"

They'd arrived. They turned onto Main Street and pulled up in front of Stewart's Machine Shop. Dawn took a breath, then another. John Andrew looked at her. "He's the jerk."

With those words, suddenly breath was easy again. "Thanks." She flipped down the visor for a mirror and pulled out a lipstick. John Andrew, with only a tiny sniff, got out of the car and waited for her. They crossed the street together and she realized that the coffee shop where Banu worked was only two doors away, and more than anything else in the world right now, she wanted...a coffee.

"Just be a sec, okay?" She turned right, and he turned left.

Dawn opened the door to a space that wouldn't have existed when she was growing up. The whole wall behind the counter was a rainbow, arching over the hatch where the food orders were coming out as the baristas—Banu and a wiry guy with a bright green moustache and goatee—dealt with customers at the counter. It took Dawn a second to realize, watching Banu working and laughing with their mustachioed colleague, that the green streak in Banu's hair matched his green facial hair.

Sweet, thought Dawn. A team. She nodded to Banu, who'd waved and sent her stomach spinning.

"Hey!" said Banu "What'll it be?"

"Just coffee, thanks."

Banu turned to their colleague. "Ethan, pass me that fresh carafe? And hey, this is the Dawn I was telling you about." Banu introduced them as green-face-fur approached.

Ethan was sweet. Spiky and cute. Funny, self-aware, use-it-like-a-weapon *camp*. Unselfconscious and direct. He offered his hand. "Hey, man—"

Banu interjected, “He calls everyone man.”

Dawn took his hand, saying to Banu, “It’s cool,” then, to Ethan, “I know you, don’t I? You were in 4-H? You sing, right?”

“Right. Few years ahead of you. And your sister. Your mom was my—ah shit, man, I’m so sorry about your mom. And—you’ve probably heard it lots—you’re so like her. She led my 4-H group. We all had a crush on her. Anyway. Yeah. I sing to support my café habit.” He smiled, and Dawn dug for money in her pocket and laid it down.

“Uh-uh.” Banu pushed the money back. “First one’s free.” They nodded at Ethan. “Boss says.” And he nodded back, adding, “It’ll get better, man. Town’s not as...”

“Backward?” Banu offered, grinning.

“...queerphobic as it used to be,” said Ethan. “Or at least, they’re better at hiding it these days. Except Marty.”

“As you saw,” Banu said, then dropped their voice. “Whole family’s like that. His dad’s a class-A bully. Apples didn’t fall far from the tree, ya know?”

“Poor bullied Marty,” said Ethan. “Let’s not give him space.”

“Exactly,” said Dawn. “I’m more interested in the matchy-matchy hair?”

“Thereby hangs a tale,” said Ethan, giving Banu’s little green streak a pull. “We’re into dares.”

Dawn picked up her coffee, laughing, wishing she wasn’t going next door to see Marty and his apple-tree dad. Banu held out their hand. “Hey. Phone.”

Dawn felt another little stomach flip as she handed over her phone, smiling, she thought, like an idiot. Banu tapped their number in, gave it back, and said, “We’re connected. Text me and I’ll text back.”

“Just like that?”

“Just like that.”

Marty

As soon as he heard his dad give his big "Well hey, stranger" and "Sorry for your loss," he knew Don MacInnes's dad had come in. And the rest of the day, and however long after that his dad decided, would go sideways and up somebody's—probably his—ass.

He touched his eye carefully, using one of the windows in the back storage room as a mirror. Still colouring up. Still hurt. But a multi-hued face was nothing new to Marty. All through school, if one of his siblings hadn't provided him with bruises on a regular basis, he generally found himself in some kind of bust-up with a teammate or the opposition. Failing those, his dad could be counted on for a good smacking after a few. These days, though, his dad was hitting everyone a lot less. Mellowing. Ha, thought Marty. Just afraid, now that Marty was bigger than him; worried that the worm would turn. Well, maybe.

He eased closer to the door, listening. Parts for—what? Jubilee? What the frig was—

"Marty!" his dad bellowed. Marty went out, squinting in the brighter front shop. There was a cardboard box on the counter and Marty, stopping short of coming through the door, could see a range of stuff going into it: somebody doing a refurb of...something.

"Marty! Go see if you can find a twelve-volt Starter Drive for a Ford Jubilee—8N is fine. Try the back room, left side. Box might say *PARTS WORLD*. Reddish box. Go." His dad never asked for anything; he ordered. Marty went back into the storage room where he'd been, truth be told, dozing for most of the morning. Place wasn't exactly jumpin'. He could hear the door jingling again—wow. Two customers, same hour. A regular fuckin' rush.

He couldn't see anything resembling a starter drive for a tractor. But he couldn't go back out there without it. He climbed the step-ladder, starting in the top corner of the highest shelf: he'd just work his way down. Nope. Nothing. Through to the end of that shelf. Nope. Fuck. He had to find it. Next shelf. Next one. Nothing. Dust. Ancient boxes. Everything but a starter.

He jumped off the steps. God. He wasn't going out without a box in his hand. Not with John Andrew there. His dad would go up one side of him and down the other. He stood back at the doorway: left side, left side. He looked at his hands like he had when he was twelve, when one always had an *L* drawn in marker, and one an *R*. Had he slipped back? Was that left? No. That was the left side and there was nothing that—

"Marty! What are you doing back there?"

Fuck off, old man, Marty thought. You come climb the fucking ladder and move all this ancient shit yourself, you want it so bad. He heard his sister saying, Practically runs the machine shop now, last night. Yeah. Right. King of the shit heap, him. Now he turned to his right. Moved the steps closer to the shelves on the right side of the storeroom. Same thing: started in the back corner—fucking spiders—and nothing. Nothing. Second shelf, noth—

There the fucker was. Middle of the second shelf, easy peasy—ON THE RIGHT. On the right, big man daddio, not the left, that's what I'm doing back here, he was saying to himself as he grabbed the box and scrambled down, brushing the webs from his face, hitting his sore eye, and shouting, "Ow!" then, "Found it."

This time Marty went right into the shop. So, this time, John Andrew MacInnes saw him. And this time, Don MacInnes was there too. Oooh sorry, Dawwwwn.

Fuck. He had cleavage.

What the fuck.

Didn't see the cleavage in the bar last night, but he—she—whatever, was stacked. Were those real tits?

Marty felt weird. Couldn't look; couldn't look away. Stood there holding the box.

His dad came and took it from him. He looked strange, Marty thought. Kind of bowed down or something. Definitely weird. But Angus Stewart covered with, "Jesus. Like pushing string, you. We were gonna send a search party. Take a lunch next time." Angus took the part, added it to the pile of stuff in the larger box, and scribbled it onto the tab. He looked up at John Andrew, waiting.

John Andrew looked at Dawn. "Look okay? Good to get started. All fine for us, I think. We can bring anything back, right?"

Angus nodded. He was trying, Marty realized, not to look at Dawwwwn, too. But Jesus. Disgusting. Scary. Like, can anyone just turn into whatever they friggin want now? There are rules, thought Marty. There are ways of being. And this was—

John Andrew was speaking to him.

"...you didn't mention you all had beer last night?"

Marty looked at him. "Ah, yeah. No."

Now his dad was looking at him. A knowing, hard look around his eyes, his mouth tightening as he bit back words he'd save till they'd gone.

"So, you and Byron hit it off, eh? Great lad. Tammy'll never have to fight her own fights, fella like that around. Bit of a champ, Byron. Light middle-weight. Boxers, eh?"

What the fuck? Boxer? Marty saw Dawwwwn look at his dad with a weird little smile. A joke or something. Angus finished adding up, slipped the chit across to John Andew, then looked again at Dawwwwn—staring openly now. He started to speak, stopped, then tried again. "You're so like—"

"His mother." Then John Andrew turned to Dawwwwn, saying quietly, "Sorry," then back to Angus. "Doesn't she? I know." John Andrew sounded pathetic, Marty thought, sad and pathetic, and that pisssed him right off. Old woman.

"Right," said John Andrew. "We're off. Just add that to my bill, Angus. I'll get you."

"I know where ya live, John Andrew."

Dawwwwn reached for the box, but John Andrew got to it first, picking it up and saying, "Let me get that." Then led the way to the door and held it open. Like he would for a girl.

John Andrew

There was a light tapping on the truck window as Dawn and John Andrew sat at the only traffic light in town.

John Andrew turned and rolled down the window. "Don't be ticketing me for blocking traffic, eh?" he said to the young cop with the buzz cut.

"No worries." The cop leaned in. "So sorry, John Andrew," he said gently. "We're going to miss Miranda at Highland Heart, and... everywhere. I'm just...sorry."

Every time John Andrew felt like he was getting back on track, Miranda's name came out of someone else's mouth and knocked the wind out of him again. Ah well. This lad couldn't know that. Only knew what he was meant to do—and holding up traffic now to do it.

"Thanks, Fuzzy." John Andrew glanced over at Dawn. "Fuzzy, this is Dawn, back home from—"

"Away," said Fuzzy, smiling and reaching in to shake Dawn's hand. The light changed; the cars behind John Andrew waited patiently. "Nice to meet you, Dawn."

"Thanks, and you."

A car behind honked gently, and John Andrew's cellphone started to ring. Fuzzy waved them on, shouting, "Don't answer that!" and John Andrew waved back. Dawn grabbed the phone, and after they'd rounded the corner, handed it to her dad.

"Arthur," he said and listened, his face growing sombre again.

John Andrew slammed the truck door and started up the steps of the funeral home, but stopped when he heard a young voice nearby shout, "Miss? Miss?!" He turned on the top step as Dawn turned towards the voices too.

"Hey, miss. Hi." A pause, some quiet chatter and giggling between them, then: "Is it true you have a dick?"

John Andrew froze, focused now on Dawn. The kids turned tail and ran, probably afraid of being recognized. Dawn sat absolutely still, staring forward.

He'd felt all kinds of things over the last few days. Bereft, confused. Angry, mostly. With Miranda, for withholding and dying; with Tammy, for trying to move him before he was ready; with Byron, for taking everything in his stride; and with Dawn, for not being his son anymore. Even the prodigal would have been better than this... But would it? He stood still on the top step, caught by that thought. So far, this young woman had more dignity than everyone around her. And even as he thought he was coming to grips with who she was, Dawn was still the source of such pain and such—he knew it wasn't fair—betrayal. She was forcing him, he realized now, to come to grips with who *he* was. Shit. Shit. A narrow-minded bigot he was meeting over and over as he struggled to get his head around what had happened to all of them. Every loss, every secret kept because...he wasn't big enough, and Miranda had known it. The wife he'd adored for over thirty years had found him badly wanting. How many other ways, he wondered, had he failed her, and failed his kids.

Fuck.

Now, his child's humiliation and hurt lit a fire in him. Searing anger and clarity, sparked by the young assholes but fuelled by his own regrets.

Miranda. Stop them. They're running away. Let me fucking plough them.

He didn't move. They'd shot off laughing and he'd watched them run, his face flushed, his heart pounding. Now he wished he'd gone after them. They don't know Dawn, he thought. They don't know anything about this person: who she is, what matters to her, what she's lost or found or sacrificed. The ignorant little shits.

He looked at his child, still motionless in the cab of the truck, and wondered if he could ever do anything to make any of this better. Then went inside.

The ride home was silent. A perfectly square cardboard box sat on the armrest between them, the Murray's Funeral Home logo lit by the rays of gold streaming through the truck's tiny sunroof. John Andrew glanced now and again at Dawn, her face slightly streaked. She hadn't cried in front of him, but he'd been inside with Arthur for longer than he'd wanted. She hadn't spoken since the assault by those little shits. He surprised himself with that word. *Assault.* It was, he discovered, an attack. His stomach flipped and landed in a place he recognized as fear. The same lurch he'd felt when Dawn was young, and they'd met a bear when they were tapping maple trees in the woods.

He remembered knowing he had to grow. Raising a thick branch above his head, he imagined himself taller than he was. Stronger and faster and less afraid. He remembered roaring as if his life depended on it—and it had. He wished he'd scared those kids shitless with a roar. He wished he'd been there to roar at Marty, because clearly, what happened last night was also an assault, and these things, he was learning, weren't casual, or flippant, or light, or, worst of all, unusual, for Dawn. And they were hateful. Hate-full. And hate, he knew, was dangerous. He wished he knew if a roar now would make the difference it had made then.

No music on the ride home, so John Andrew's thoughts were free-range, clucking.

If his son had come home from a pub encounter with Marty, he would have said, Stand up, be a man. Don't take that shit from anyone. Hit him back. Hit him back. He'd have settled in the same place that his father, Miranda's father, Marty's father had all been comfortable, watching the world and making it work the way they wanted. Standing up, bumping chests with each other, pissing up the wall to win, and backing down with excuses and anger at losing face: anger directed at the smallest, the youngest, the less-able or less-inclined folks, who couldn't or wouldn't defend themselves.

Miranda knew all this. She'd recognized those tendencies in him, but still loved him and waited for him to...adjust. He wondered if she'd had a plan. He snorted. Of course she did. She had a plan for everything, this woman who paid for her own funeral. Now his anger cooled as his curiosity was growing. He wanted to know Miranda again, more—as badly as he'd wanted to know her the first time he saw her climbing the wooden fence in front of the dairy. And he wanted to know the daughter Miranda had risked so much for.

Byron was in the yard when they pulled in, working at the picnic table by the kitchen garden. He looked up and waved as John Andrew came to a stop. Dawn got out, waited for her dad to collect the box, and passed Byron silently on the way into the house—not responding to his gentle, "What's up?"

In the dining room Tammy was working away on her computer, but looked up when they came in, not clocking, at first, the box in her dad's hands. But then, her "What's that?" was answered only by the tenderness with which John Andrew set the box on the sideboard and looked back at her. Dawn arrived with Betsy padding quietly behind her as her father's eyes spilled over, and Tammy laid her head on the table, sobbing with a force that shook him.

Dawn

Betsy sat on Dawn's feet as she worked in the circle of light in the otherwise dark kitchen, trying not to breathe. Tammy, hands clasped, was perched across the table. She was also focusing on holding and very carefully releasing her breath, so as not to disturb the stream of grey ash Dawn was transferring from the plastic bag in the cardboard box to the childish red clay pinch pot with *Mommy* lettered in a child's painstaking hand. Dawn's artwork from grade two, kept all these years in pride of place on Miranda's dresser, usually held bobby pins and hairclips.

Dawn set down the apple-shaped plastic scoop and considered the pinch pot, now full to the brim. Then she pulled the box closer and studied what remained. She looked up at her sister.

"Won't all fit."

Tammy blew her held breath towards the ceiling then pulled the box towards her. "Oh my god. That's like half of—"

It? The ashes. *Her*? Their mother.

The girls stared at each other, seeking permission to speak and be wrong.

"Should we ask Dad?" Tammy was biting her lip.

Dawn shook her head. "He said he couldn't. For us to go ahead and, you know..."

Tammy nodded. "Right."

Dawn pulled the box back again, tenderly tucked the top in place, set the tiny lid on the pinch pot, and said, "Come on." She picked up the box and headed through the back door into the dark yard.

Tammy reluctantly followed, turning to urge Betsy who was hanging back. "You too," she said, and Betsy got to her feet with a sigh.

The night was clear and warm and bright. The moon was a waxing crescent with a curious and benevolent profile, peeking out from behind the light clouds. Appropriate, Dawn thought: her dad said a waxing crescent was good luck for travellers, and what was Miranda now if not that?

The kitchen garden was neglected, weeds taking over, except for one corner where Miranda's perennial cutting flowers bloomed in profusion. The early flowers were long finished—the tulips and daffs—and now Miranda's peonies in every shade from white to pale pink to deepest burgundy were near the end of their season, filling the air with their delicate, waning scent.

Dawn pulled at the box lid and in the flurry of the untangling, a few ashes dropped onto the petals. Dawn dipped the little green scoop and Tammy reached to still her hand. "Wait. Wait."

Dawn gave Tammy her full attention. "Tam. She'd like this. Her happiest place was digging here—here and the herb garden—imagining what was coming next. Would you rather—"

"I'd rather she was here," Tammy wailed. "I'd rather not be—god."

"Me too." Dawn didn't move. She knew Tammy. She knew it was movement that spooked her. Haste. The little eddy of air was back again, playing at the edges of the plastic bag: pulling it, grabbing a flake or two, spinning and dropping the larger ones, sending the dust off into the night. Dawn watched it. The night settled to stillness again.

Tammy nodded. "Okay."

Now Dawn began to lift the full scoop and lower it close to the ground, once, twice, again, and—

"Stop! Stop! It's in my nose, it's up my nose!" Tammy was flapping and Betsy was pawing her eyes. Dawn looked at the gentlest of movement in the leaves contrasted with the pulling of the plastic—so odd—and knew.

"She's laughing at this—you know that, don't you? She knows us, and she's laughing, and this is...it's good. Good and right."

"I don't want my mother up my nose." Tammy didn't know what to do—rub her eyes, her nose, brush off her sweater? The dust was in the air, as well as on the petals, leaves, and soil around them.

"She'd say nothing changes. She loved to get you going." Dawn tipped the last little puff out and watched as some seemed to take off, blowing gently across the yard to settle in the herb garden. The night exhaled a peony-scented sigh, and the girls felt they'd just finished a long, hard run.

They climbed the stairs—up the wooden hill to Bedfordshire. Their grandfather had said it to their mother, so their mother had said it to them; their father had learned it and he said it, and now Dawn said it to Tammy as they started their climb after their garden adventure. Dawn didn't know where Bedfordshire was, besides upstairs. England somewhere, she knew, but her mom's family was Scottish, so it was nonsense really. But shared, ancient nonsense. She wondered if she'd ever say it to Tammy's child, or—startling thought—her own. Pushing that aside, she committed to going to Bedfordshire someday. I've climbed to it thousands and thousands of times, so I deserve to actually see that hill, she thought.

Tammy had reached the top now. She paused outside Byron's tiny box-room where, through the slightly open door, they could see him on the bed reading. Tammy looked at Dawn and put a hand on the door. Dawn raised her eyebrows. There'd been no sign of any hanky-panky so far.

"What?!" she said to Tammy. "Noooooo touching!"

Tammy responded with a faux glare. It seemed forever ago since Tammy had said that, and her expression as she eased Byron's door open was a testament to the shrinking distance between them. Dawn could hear the pleasure and assurance in Tammy's "Hello" and Byron's "Hello, too." The door closed gently.

Lucky Tammy, Dawn thought. Sex. Touching. Company. She pushed her own door wide to find Squeak on her bed, nudging and arching into her hands for stroking. Ah—touching. Then a conversation, responding to Dawn's replies in between. And...company, thought Dawn. Finally, climbing into bed, the cat settling close with her purr set on high, Dawn thought two out of three wasn't bad.

The morning of the funeral began exactly the way Dawn's first full day home had: with whispering outside her door. This time, Byron and Tammy. And Dawn's cell buzzing.

She reached for her phone to look at the time: nearly ten. What happened? How had everyone slept that long? Who'd done the cows? She started to scroll. Messages from Jill and Tula and her landlord. The landlord was just checking in that she was okay—wow, she'd hardly spoken to the guy—and Tula was telling her Jill was on her way to the funeral, and Jill texted the same. Typical Jill: *Missing you too much and need to say goodbye to your beauty mom. I told her I'm on my way, so don't start without me.*

Dawn put her phone down. She didn't know how she felt about that. Jill was *that* life, not this. Jill was part of the world kept separate from her father, and *this* world, this bubble of family, felt too fragile to expose. What would they think of Jill? Dawn's huge, beautiful, androgynous friend, with her delicate features and massive hands, her smooth, licorice skin and cheekbones like blades? Jill was the most beautiful and smart person Dawn had ever known, but also the most direct, and the possible collision of her two lives was suddenly terrifying. She'd been prepared to be judged by her family, but the idea that they might be confused by, or critical of, the fine gender line her friend trod, and judge Jill—or worse, patronize her—was awful.

Mom, she thought, it was easy for you—can you please make it easy for them?

She realized she'd started to think of her mother as she'd thought of God when she was small: instantly available, constantly making space in a packed schedule to pave Dawn's way with ease or provide what was most desired. God or Santa, she thought. Neither of whom she'd believed in for years. She did believe, though, in the power of her mother. Look what she'd managed so far.

"Dawn?" Tap tap tap. "Can I come in?" Tammy cracked the door.

"Yup." Dawn set down her phone and put aside the conversation with her mother for the moment.

Tammy settled on the end of the bed wearing jeans, ancient ones—where had those come from?—and the old hoodie of Miranda's that Dawn had been wearing in the barn. She looked very pleased with herself.

"You'll never guess what I did." Then, "What's wrong?"

"Nothing. What did you do? Oh my god." Dawn sat up. "You didn't milk?"

"I did. Holy heifers, batman. And Dad says I'm a natural, so."

"So, I've lost my job. Ahh. Too bad. See ya, 5:00 A.M. Fill yer boots." Dawn glanced back at her phone, still thinking of Jill.

"Something's wrong. What?"

"Just...funeral day, I guess. A load more people, like you said the first day, looking at me, not thinking about Mom—"

"I shouldn't have said that."

"We both know you were right. We both hate it. All hate it. Dad is—"

"Dad's okay. He's...more...I don't know. Easy, or something. And we—we had last night with Mom and she's—okay, I think. And everything else, well...we're on this train now, Dawn, we can't stop it, so—"

"You're right." Dawn reached for Tammy and gave her a squeeze. "You're right. I'll shower."

She got out of bed, feeling the lightest she had in...weeks. And Tammy had—oh yeah, thought Dawn. That glow is something altogether different than our re-connecting. She grinned.

"What?" said Tammy "What are you grinning at?"

"I'm thinking about you meeting my other sister today. Jill." Dawn lied, a little. "You're very different and exactly the same. Beautiful, crazy, opinionated, smart—oh, but not tall. She's tall."

"That's so nice. That she'd come up for someone she didn't—"

"—She did. She knew Mom." Oh no. Why did she start this? She took a deep breath. "She was with us, with me and Jenny, when Mom died. Jill sang her off."

Tammy stared at Dawn as though she was something she needed to keep track of. Something that might suddenly change colour or shape and she couldn't miss it. Dawn was waiting for an explosion. Instead, after a long silence, Tammy reached for Dawn's hand.

"Sang her off? That sounds exactly perfect." Beat, in-breath, sigh. "I wish I'd been there. Of course I do. I wish Dad had been, more.

But now we can only do our best, right? And I will love your other sister if she loved Mom. If she loves you."

Where has Tammy gone, Dawn thought, and who's this in her body? If bonking Byron had this impact, well, holy...holy something. All she could be was grateful, and all she could say was, "Thank you."

Byron

"...A loyal friend," Jenny was saying, "...a loving mom—"

Jenny was at the front of the packed church that, when Byron narrowed his eyes, looked like one of those beautiful glass mosaics, multicoloured and luminous. Everyone seemed to have got the memo that "the brighter the better" was requisite for Miranda's send-off. On the table near Jenny was a portrait of Miranda, laughing and pulling at her windblown hair, cut-crystal jars of Miranda's award-winning blueberry jam with their first blue ribbon, a perfect white peony from her garden, and the pinch pot six-year-old Dawn had made for her mom, and filled so carefully the night before.

"She was," Jenny continued, "a keeper of confidences and a giver of confidence. Miranda built people up"—now Jenny was speaking directly to the row of 4-H kids in their green T-shirts—"with her belief in them. She pushed boundaries we didn't know needed pushing until"—now she spoke to John Andrew—"until we did. She kept my secrets, and I kept hers." Finally, Jenny spoke to Dawn and Tammy. "She wanted this to be joyful, she said—no pressure, right?—and she wanted us to close with a couple of her favourite pieces. Tammy?"

Byron looked down the row at his fiancée. She hated public speaking. Amazing, he'd tease her, for someone who loved being the centre of attention. It wasn't the same thing, she said, and from her trembling hands holding the scrap of paper, he saw it wasn't. She stepped up to the podium to join Jenny, who hugged her before leaving. Tammy looked like she wanted to grab her to stay, but instead she leaned into the mic and blasted Jenny with her first words: "My mom"—Jenny jumped, then laughed—and the congregation laughed too when Tammy said, "oops, oops, sorry." Taking a breath, she started again further from the mic.

"My mom was a proud 4-H'er. Growing up, we seemed to schedule our lives around it—around all of you"—she pointed to the row of green T-shirts and smiled—"and that used to really piss me off. Oops." Tammy covered her mouth and got another laugh as she looked to the ceiling to say, "Sorry, God. Sorry, Mom."

The congregation settled as Tammy raised her bit of paper.

"But she loved this, and lived by it." She took a breath and began the 4-H pledge she had heard, and said, so often: "I pledge my head to clearer thinking, my heart to greater loyalty—" And then Tammy stopped. Byron felt her search for him, saw the panic in her eyes, her small shoulders lifting and falling quicker and quicker. He was trapped at the end of their pew, but Dawn was up and out in a heartbeat. Arriving with her sister on the podium, she took both Tammy's hands and held them tight, the two of them face-to-face for a moment. A breath, then Tammy whispered, "Thanks," and Dawn turned to the full church to continue from where Tammy had left off.

This must be the moment, Byron thought, that Dawn had dreaded. On display for all to see. But when she spoke, her voice was clear and strong and confident. She looked at her father.

"My hands to larger service," she spoke from memory, then turned out to the rest of the congregation. "My health to better living, for my club, my community, and my country."

The words landed, like the dust on sunbeams coloured by the stained glass windows, on John Andrew and Byron; on Fuzzy and Jenny and Arthur and Aunt Leny and Ethan and Banu; on Angus Stewart and his tiny wife; on the 4-H children; on Jerry and Sandra and their sons, Andy and Michael, whose focus didn't waver from Miranda's portrait; on the family of Tammy's ex-fiancé; and the community kitchen women that Miranda had cooked with for years; and the teachers who had taught her children; and the doctor who had sent Miranda to the specialist; and the minister of this church; and the women who had done the flowers; and the deacon, who had two children in Miranda's 4-H row of green-shirts; and on Jill, who had known Miranda so briefly but loved her so deeply—the simple words of this simple pledge to live simply and kindly and do your best for others. Everyone heard those words and understood that a life of service had ended.

Byron saw the complexity of this community in the silence that followed, as if a benevolent arachnid had released a silken thread to bind everyone together, reminding them of where they'd all come from and what they all strove for every day. He understood what a gift Dawn had given, on behalf of Miranda, with those words. A reminder of who they were, and who they could be still, because they were alive.

"Thank you for coming to celebrate our mom," Dawn said now, and Byron saw Tammy squeeze Dawn's hand and wipe her eyes while looking at her with such gratitude and warmth that Byron felt proud. He loved Tammy even more, in that moment, for the way she appreciated her sister.

Dawn continued: "Anyone who's ever been in our house, or near our truck when she was in it, will understand that this service wouldn't be complete without something from her constant companion and hero, Bob Dylan." Dawn looked out to the congregation where, on cue, Ethan and Banu stood, and Ethan's full, bright tenor voice began, a cappella.

He asked for blessings always, and for wishes to come true. Banu's rich alto joined, and the wood and stone and sunlight in the church received and returned the effortless power of the two voices in harmony. The profundity of all these connections brought the first tears to Byron's eyes, and he felt John Andrew shaking beside him.

Byron kept his eyes, brimming now, on the picture of the beautiful woman, vibrating with life, smiling at someone she loved, surprised by the wind and death and caught in that frame that would keep her forever young.

Without turning to him, Byron laid his hand on John Andrew's arm.

John Andrew grabbed it and held on, like he was clinging to the edge of a cliff.

John Andrew

Coming out of the church into the sunlight of a perfect summer afternoon, John Andrew felt weak as a foal, not fully trusting his limbs, but held in the benevolence and love of his community. It was, he reflected, the nicest funeral he'd ever been to. He wondered who'd organized the dress code? And who'd asked Fuzzy to deliver the joke-filled piece about the early days of the Highland Society, which, helmed by Miranda, had been fraught with local politicking and organizational inexperience but had also, according to Fuzzy, been full of laughter. Mostly, he said, the result of exhaustion, panic, and hysteria.

John Andrew had expected to confront his pain and loss, but the roller coaster of laughter and joyful recollection had left him totally unprepared for the breaking of a wave of deep blue grief as Miranda's favourite song was sung. Those young people were exactly the right voices to deliver it, and he knew that Banu and Ethan had been chosen by Miranda to send a direct message to him. But as well as the little pinch about inclusion and kindness, Miranda was saying, Keep on, my love, as she always had, and also, Wake up and look around. Things are different now. She might just as well have had someone sing "The Times They Are A-Changin," to put an elbow in his ribs. I get it, he said to her now. Give me some credit, eh?

"Dad?" Dawn was drawing someone towards him. A stunning, tall Black person. John Andrew couldn't confidently determine their gender—and then chastised himself for that thought, that he should need to. Then, look at me, was his next thought. All modernish.

"Dad, this is my friend...my best friend, my other sister, my coach." Dawn looked to the smiling face beside her. "And Mom's third daughter."

That took him aback for a second, and the smiling person saw that, and interjected.

"—Dawn! You'll frighten him. Mr. MacInnes, I'm Jill. Dawn and I worked together and we play on the same soccer team. I'm"—Jill took a deep breath before continuing—"so sorry for your loss. I was fortunate to get to know Miranda through Dawn, when she was in hospital over the last few months, and like every person who knew her, I loved her. I was honoured to"—Jill looked to Dawn who nodded permission—"to be with her as she passed."

Dawn studied her dad before adding, gently, "With Jenny and me, Dad. Jill sang. In Uganda, where Jill's from, her family would sing folks on their way, so—that song"—Dawn waved towards the church—"was the last thing Mom heard."

John Andrew reached for Jill's hand, and, having just managed to regain his self-control, now felt it slipping again, so he said only, "Thank you."

What a massive hand she had, he thought, and how black. He realized in that moment that he had never in his life shaken the hand of a Black person. How could that be?

It wasn't, he thought. Byron was Black: but Byron was...Byron. And this person still holding his hand and looking at him, warm but puzzled, her eyes on exactly the same level as his—was...Jill. He felt overwhelmed with shame and pride in the same moment. He scanned the crowd and didn't see anything unkind or ugly in the faces he knew, so he allowed himself that pride, and gripped Jill's hand tighter.

"I'm so glad you came to be with Dawn. Thank you."

John Andrew could see Dawn relax, and he let go of Jill's hand as Jenny joined their circle, slipping one arm through Dawn's and the other through Jill's. "These two," she said to John Andrew, "you know they're the stars of the finest Halifax women's soccer team, right?" John Andrew raised his eyebrows, and the two young women shrugged modestly.

"Roar's the star." said Jill. "I just assist."

Jenny and John Andrew looked to Jill, puzzled.

"Ah. Roar," said Jill. "Dawn's nickname. When she attacks, kicks for goal, she roars. I called her Aurora—goddess of Dawn, yes?—but the team shortened it to Roar. We're very proud. She's quiet most of the time, but when she roars, it's frightening." Jill looked at Dawn and then continued. "And funny. And now, crucial!"

John Andrew studied Dawn, bright pink and clearly pleased with the praise. But something else. He followed her gaze. Ah.

Across the street, Marty was waiting in his father's ancient, babied Volvo, watching Dawn and Jill with a concentration that was...unsettling. John Andrew heard Jill's "Do you know that yellow-haired person?" and Dawn's "Sadly, yes." He watched the two women: Jill, worried; Dawn, irritated. "Stay away from him," Jill said. "My stomach says bad news."

Dawn turned to John Andrew with a wry smile. "Your stomach's right, Jill. Hey, Dad?" He gave a single nod, looked across to Marty. Angus and his wife—what was her name? John Andrew wasn't sure he'd ever heard Angus call her by name, she was just "the wife"—were crossing the road, and now, climbing into the car. Marty continued to stare at Jill and Dawn and then everyone chatting in front of the church heard Angus bark, "Are you deaf, boy? Drive." Folks turned to watch Marty peel away. Making a show of himself, of them. Angus would have something to say about that at home, John Andrew was sure.

Jill and Dawn had moved away, heads close together. Tall as Dawn was, Jill was bowed down to listen to her. John Andrew wondered if there was more than friendship there and hated that he started to go down the path of how that all worked, what it meant. He stopped as Banu approached them and was introduced to Jill. John Andrew saw Dawn's face light up. Ah. Something more than friendship *there*, maybe.

He watched Jill seeing what he saw, and being glad. How interesting, he thought, observing his children and their peers as...adults. A sense of relief and pride he hadn't expected today. He'd dreaded it all—the wake, the funeral, the focus on him and his children—but everything was out there now, he thought, and people could like it or not. He was taking a page from Dawn's book, and he liked the lightness it was bringing him.

Someone was going from group to group, reminding folks of the gathering to follow—Fuzzy's partner. John Andrew groped for the young woman's name: Sarah. Who'd been at school with Tammy, he realized as he saw them hugging. Goodness. When did these children acquire partners? And start calling them that, instead of boyfriend or girlfriend or wife? When did they start organizing and managing things? He turned to follow Jenny and Jill and Dawn, who were moving on, and overheard Jenny whisper to Dawn as she paused to pull her in for a hug, "Your journey is what kept her going. She wanted to see you through it."

The after-event was a cèilidh. No one had brought instruments, no one said let's sit around a kitchen and sing songs Miranda loved; it just evolved, as these things often did. The gathering was in the home of the woman—Rebecca—who'd taken over from Miranda as chair of the Highland Society's board. Rebecca taught music, and her children—five of them—all played, as did she and her husband, so instruments weren't an issue; the house seemed to be littered with them. Guitars and fiddles and ukuleles, and John Andrew noticed a trombone and discovered that belonged to Rebecca's husband, who also taught music privately. Who was learning the trombone these days? This noisy family home was a whole new world. Interesting for sure, but John Andrew hoped they weren't going to be treated to a trombone concert tonight. Two of the kids, Alistair and Andrea (the others were Adam, Alicia, and baby Anaïs), hoped to make their mark as a musical duo, and though still in high school, were already having some success.

The kitchen was huge and opened onto an even bigger family room with a piano. The music started as the crowd began to thin out, but once it did, everyone stayed, including John Andrew and Dawn and Tammy and Byron and Jill. A sort of competition emerged: who's got a wicked story about Miranda, and a song to accompany it. There seemed to be no shortage of either, but a lull came after about an hour, and John Andrew surprised himself by speaking up.

"I don't sing, and it's a hundred years since I played, but there's a song I would play for Miranda to sing, when we were courting. Stepping out together." There was an oooooh from the crowd, and some laughter. "Yeah, well, I told you it was a hundred years. *Dating*. Anyway, it's this." And to his daughters' amazement, he picked up Alistair's guitar and, hesitantly at first, picked out "The Wild Mountain Thyme." No one singing, everyone just concentrating on listening to his careful picking. The girls recognized it, but they weren't going to sing. John Andrew looked to Ethan and Banu, hoping one of them would. Finally, he came to the last line of the chorus and spoke it, more than sang:

"Will you go, lassie, go?"

John Andrew's voice broke a little. He couldn't speak in the church, but he could play this song that was theirs. He felt the room holding him gently, waiting for what came next as Ethan began to sing:

"And we'll all go together
To pull wild mountain thyme."

Jill watched John Andrew intently, not smiling but sending, sending him warmth. She joined Ethan and sang:

"All around the blooming heather
Will you go, lassie, go?"

Ethan dropped away to let Jill, accompanied by John Andrew, carry on alone with her extraordinary voice:

"I will build my love a bower
By yon clear and crystal fountain
And on it, I will pile
All the flowers of the mountain."

Then Alistair gave the song its bass, and Ethan and Banu and the rest in the circle joined in, harmonizing, finally arriving at the last chorus. John Andrew felt, more than heard, the glorious sound, all these voices singing to his love. The kitchen was full of breath made of music, and it felt like a benediction.

Will you go, lassie, go?

John Andrew held the final note on the guitar, till it disappeared into silence.

There was no applause as there had been for all the other songs. No whoop, or hey remember when, or anything but stillness and sweetness and ease. John Andrew wondered if he had embarrassed his kids with this public display of emotion and lack of talent. He had a quiet conversation in his head with Miranda, to make sure she'd heard the brilliant voices and forgiven the tentative guitar playing, his only public offering to his wife.

He looked at Jill and reached to pat her shoulder. "Your voice is a wonder. Thank you." Jill patted him back.

Tammy took his hand and whispered, "You have to keep playing now you've started again."

The cèilidh broke up. Folks made their way home knowing Miranda had been properly celebrated and sent, wrapped in love, on her travels.

John Andrew and Dawn drove Jill to the station to catch the last bus, and Jill held Dawn for so long that that the driver said, "Hey. Hey. Just take her with you, why don'tcha?"

"Call?" said Dawn to Jill. "When you get home? And thank you. I can't even—"

"I know. I'm so glad I was here. Love you." One last squeeze. "I think you needed a bigger suitcase, yeah?"

"Maybe. Yeah."

Dawn watched her friend climb onto the bus with the same driver who'd brought Dawn home, while John Andrew watched the two women and thought what a wonderful thing a friend was.

Later that night, when everyone's good clothes were in a heap on their beds, the dinner dishes washed and stacked, the animals fed and watered and stroked, John Andrew sat on the ancient sofa in the office with a glass of Scotch in his hand and a pile of sympathy cards at his side. He opened and read, opened and read, then put them aside, wondering what he should do with these, after. Tammy would know, he thought, and there she was, her head appearing around the door. Seeing him sitting in the dim room, she sent Byron on his way and waved Dawn in with her.

There is something so particular about the home of the recently bereaved. A quality of silence that wraps the booming of the future—as it presses and challenges the occupants who remain—in cotton wool, muffling its approach. The girls took their places on either side of their father, Tammy taking his hand and Dawn leaning her head on his shoulder. None of them spoke or cried. All felt the strange relief a funeral brings: the cruel conflicting emptiness that seems more profound in the hours after the celebration of the life that, if not yet fully absent, is vacating.

With every door that creaked closed on its own, every puff that moved a curtain or a tree or swept a curl across a face like a caress, Miranda blew a little farther away from her family. They felt the growing distance and tried to hold her there with the power of their love.

Dawn

Jerry and Andy had declared another day off milking, bringing in the same folks who'd helped the day before, so when Dawn woke early it was like waking on a Saturday. It took her a minute to figure out that it *was* Saturday. A whole day spread in front of her, she thought, as she rolled over in bed. She felt the sun through the window and knew that if she stayed in bed, if she got too much into her head, the lightness she'd begun to find could dissipate quickly. So. She wouldn't.

She inhaled her bowl of cereal. Tammy had bought the cereal they'd always had at Christmas when they were kids: Alpha-Bits—what was that about?—and coffee, then went to the shed. She poked through the box of supplies, planning her next attack on the tractor, starting with the spark plugs, which were rusted in place. So, a good scrubbing with a wire brush. First: find the wire brush.

Methodically Dawn cleared off the bench, organizing bits into "useful," "possible," and "rubbish" piles. The hardware store bag and the brand new bike pump were definitely for the "useful" pile. The peace offering from Tammy replaced the useless ancient pump that Dawn had thrown at the wall. She'd taken the shiny new one out of its packaging and pumped the tires, assuming after all this time they'd be past the point of no return. But she discovered they were good. And going back to check them now, distracted from her tidying, they were still good. Not leaking.

A quick ride, she thought. Flying down a hill's the best way to clear your head.

She aimed the bike down the old railbed that led to the cornfields, knowing eventually she was heading for the hard climb up Paterson's Hill and the long flight down. But first, she zigzagged through row after row of young corn, not too tall yet, but still giving the sense of travelling down narrow enclosed tracks or through a maze, in fields that dropped to the ocean. It felt cozy, somehow, even with the huge sea-edged sky above her and the crops running nearly to the water in places. The relief of a crest and the joy of a drop as she rose and fell with the hilly farmland.

She remembered a day—though nothing about how or why—when she and her mother were out here together. One bike carried them both: Miranda on the seat and Dawn on the handlebars. Miranda was singing at the top of her lungs—which Dylan song, Dawn couldn't remember, but Dawn was laughing. Laughing and hanging on for dear life as they hit bump after bump even going as slowly as they were—so slowly that really it was kind of amazing the bike kept moving at all—and loving having her mother to herself. What age was I? she wondered. Ten? Eleven? Small. They'd ridden up and down the rows of shoulder-high corn and dropped once or twice into the dry, flat irrigation ditches between the fields. Perfectly safe, but it felt daring.

Now Dawn rode and imagined her mother on her handlebars. Imagined how she might have carried Miranda as her mother grew older and smaller, the child to Dawn's adult, still riding these paths, giving her mother an outing, keeping her safe and happy. With that thought, Miranda appeared, and Dawn realized that at least for now, whenever Dawn thought of her, Miranda would be there. In the house, in the shed, on her handlebars, in the wide world.

Dawn struggled up Paterson's Hill, thinking how different cycling was to running around a soccer field for an hour and a half. How it seemed to require more puff. A lot more puff. Wow. She walked the last hundred yards pushing the bike that only had three working gears, none of which seemed to be helping her.

But the prize! She'd forgotten how this spot, so hard-won, provided a view right across their valley, then across the strait, which meant, actually, across the province, because the water separated their arm of land from the distant island of Cape Breton. It seemed impossibly remote, haze clinging to its shores like land rising from the sea in a fairy tale: a land that might just disappear again—like the Scottish village of Brigadoon her mother used to tell her about, visible for only one day every hundred years. Dawn knew, though, that they could drive there in an hour and look back across to *this* shore, equally beautiful and remote.

She gazed down on their farm and the dairy, with Jerry's market garden farm broken into small colourful squares across the old highway from their place; to the cliffs dropping away on the left, growing into the beach to the right. Everything laid out; one physical feature becoming the next, becoming the other. Surprising transitions of colour and texture: the striated ocean of silver and green-blue-taupe; the muddy red edges turning pink then beige then gold; the spring-green where the grass was new and sweet and would be hayed at summers end; the black-green where the pine forest began; and bisecting everything, the river that ran down from these heights then through the valley, sometimes parallel to the ocean, but always glittering silver in the sun.

She looked and looked. Drank it, determined to remember this picture on the darkest, foggiest winter days: the sharp, clear focus on everything, and her family farm at the centre of the silver and gold and red and green. This was her place. How had she forgotten?

She swung her leg over the bar of the bike and started down the hill. The trick, she thought, is fast but not crazy. Not *just* letting go. She tested the hand brakes. Letting go but holding something back. So she kept control. She was halfway down the long hill when she realized she had defined her whole life that way.

Dawn worked on the tractor most of the afternoon, losing track of time. She'd managed to remove all but one of the sparks—scrubbing away the rust with the wire brush, and cleaning underneath every one. Her dad came to the door and stood watching as she worked. She moved on to the final spark—couldn't shift it. She paused and looked up at him. "Whew."

"Yeah. Hot work today," he said. Little pause, then, "Nice to meet Jill. Shame she had to go back."

"Well, she manages the team now and there's a tournament next weekend, so—"

"Manages! Like a real team."

Dawn looked up at her dad and felt her features settle into her *for fuck's sake* face. Yes, a real team. A women's team, but a real team. She picked up a ball-peen and tapped around the spark, trying to ease it, using the taps to work out her irritation. Tap tap tap, and then at it with the pliers again. Nothing. John Andrew watched quietly for a moment and then waved at the tractor.

"Little white vinegar. Dissolves the rust. Steel wool instead of that." He waved at the little ball-peen she was knocking against the spark.

"You don't think brute force'll do it?"

"Ha," he said, "you got any o' that?" Dawn watched him counting up his faux pas from the last few minutes. "Ah, shit. I meant...shit."

Dawn remembered braking on the bike, staying in control, finding such joy in that restraint, and she turned back to him, thinking, he's trying, he's trying, he's here and he's trying. She handed him the ball-peen and pliers and said, "You try brute force and I'll go get the vinegar."

It wasn't perfect. Or anywhere near. But it was better than indifference. Something had happened to her father, and Dawn could see him being other than he was—other than he had been, she corrected herself—and that was enough.

She heard the heat in their voices before she got into the kitchen. Through the pantry door into the dining room, she could see Byron and Tammy facing each other across the dining table. They both had their computers open, tapping and talking, neither of them really looking at each other. Hm, thought Dawn. Maybe I'll just sneak back out...

"Dawn?" from Byron. Too late.

"What's your plan, Dawn?" he called, catching her as she tried to quietly open the cupboard for the white vinegar. No sides, thought Dawn, whatever this is.

"Um...which plan? For...what do you mean?"

"Your plan for—now. What you're planning. When are you...going home?" Dawn read, in his pause, that he was a little confused about where Dawn's home was. Well, so was Dawn.

Byron was watching Tammy, who was still tapping away on her computer, and with everything he asked, she sort of huffed. Like the way her dad sniffed, thought Dawn. Showing her superiority and irritation.

"Um, I haven't got a plan, really. I mean, I'm going to finish this," and she held up the wrench she'd left the shed with and the bottle of vinegar she'd collected. Tammy did look up now. She gave an impression of Betsy, cocking her head to one side.

"What? Tool Salad?" she said.

Dawn smiled. Then straightened her face again: no sides, no sides. "Ha. No, the tractor. I'm gonna get it going and re-painted, and then—well, you know. Highland Heart. The tractor trials."

"What? When? How long?" Byron looked panicky.

"It's about two weeks from now, so—" Dawn's sentence was bitten off by Byron.

"Jesus, Tammy. We can't—"

"You said when we came that we could work remotely, if needed."

"It's not, though, is it? Needed."

"Who decides that?" asked Tammy.

Dawn was trying to sidle back through the door.

"It's not, is it, Dawn?" Byron again, trying to draw Dawn to his side.

"Um. Do we have to figure this out, like, this moment?" What was wrong with Byron? Usually so unflappable.

"What is *with* you?" Tammy was irritated. "Is no one in the office missing you? Is that it? Are you afraid they'll forget how necessary you are?"

"Wow." Byron stood up. "Okay. I'm not sure why it's weird that I want to be able to make a plan and know what's going to happen next, and when I'll get out of the box-room and back into my own space, but it's actually not about me and my fragile male ego, and it's not a reflection on how much I care about...everything here, you know?" He snapped his computer closed. "I'm going to town. If anyone decides anything about...anything, let me know." And he left the sisters staring after him, then at each other.

"What was that?" asked Dawn.

"Not sure." Tammy looked out the window, watching Byron walk towards the car.

"Do you want to go?"

Tammy looked back at her computer screen and shook her head. "I don't know. I want to go back, of course I do, but I can't get my head around leaving Dad yet. It's so short. I feel kind of disconnected or something. Odd." Long pause. "Not odd. It's *not* odd, is it? To feel...odd. Every single thing has changed. I just need a little more time to...process it. Will you go—like, right after the Tractor Trials thing? Or will you—"

"I don't know. Probably go. But—" She was thinking of Banu.

Then Tammy said, "Byron's gone to town to have coffee with Banu." She looked away from her screen and up at Dawn. "Is that weird?"

Was it? wondered Dawn. Maybe a bit. But not in the way Tammy was thinking.

"No," she said. Dawn wasn't going to share her own slight unease with Tammy, but her stomach was suddenly tying itself into knots. She knew that thinking about Banu and Byron would result in useless, spinning, circular speculation unless she diverted herself, and fast, with action of some kind. She needed to get back to work in the shed. "No," she said, definitively, "it's not. He's just had enough family drama and they're great and want a laugh, and who wouldn't?" Wrong answer. Dawn looked at Tammy, still tapping on her keyboard, but with a stealth tear running down one cheek.

"Oh god, Tammy, come on. There is nothing going on with Byron. It's just all too much for him. This week has been intense. For everyone. Look, I can't do this. I'm gonna keep on working, okay? Dad's in the shed. Come out if you want." And she turned, and Tammy returned to tapping.

The next day and the day after moved with a different gait than the days before the funeral. Head up now, eyes forward, shoulders down and relaxed. The days didn't creep or plod like before. And, with the exception of the slight tension between Tammy and Byron, which didn't fully dissipate—but also, Dawn observed, didn't dominate family life the way Tammy's moods used to—things were kind of pleasant, even productive.

John Andrew was in the shed with her a lot. Days were breaking down into a routine now: milking, breakfast, tractor work, lunch, farm office or field, tractor work, milking, maybe a walk or a swim, dinner, *The Google* with her dad, for tractor guidance. Sleep. Rinse, repeat. When he didn't need to be somewhere else—even, according to Jerry, when he *did* need to be somewhere else—John Andrew was with Dawn, working on the tractor or planning on working on the tractor. It was heartening to see how much pleasure her father seemed to be taking in every task, every discovery. His go-to response was still irritation, as if the tractor was a recalcitrant person he didn't much like and was going to put straight. But now, as challenges came—and there were lots—the two of them, and sometimes Tammy, were...cooperating, Dawn thought. Helping each other. Being actively thoughtful. She could see her father biting things back, and she let him.

He never asked her anything really personal. He seemed to have no curiosity about her physical journey, for which she was profoundly grateful. People in general were way too interested in her body. Well, her genitals. It amazed her how almost-strangers felt it was a fair topic when they discovered she was trans: what she wanted, what her process was, what she'd kept or rejected. The gut-punch of a friend's friend saying, within earshot, "What do they want to see when they look in their pants?" Dawn remembered wanting to throw up, hearing that. She understood curiosity but couldn't understand the extraordinary lack of respect that seemed to be meted out to her and her trans friends. Dawn didn't think it was helpful to define that sort of behaviour as transphobic, but in her circles, she was in the minority. It was more basic than that, she thought. It was just rude. Did no one teach these people any manners?

But with all the time they were spending together, her father had never dipped even a pinky toe into those muddy waters. She appreciated that. They went out every day to build something that seemed to matter profoundly to both of them, and that, thought Dawn, was more than she'd ever hoped for.

They were, however, still two people who didn't always know exactly what they were doing, and what they'd found on *The Google*—as John Andrew insisted on calling anything to do with the internet—often just wasn't clear enough. There was a lot of doing things twice, as they discovered and then corrected their errors. Those were moments of tension, and sometimes undignified tantrums, on both their parts. One or the other would stamp out of the shed, then tiptoe back in later. They never addressed what they were *actually* building in the shed.

There were definitely times when they just needed a couple more hands to lift, or turn, or tighten, or adjust the pieces and whatsits and whosits that sat inside, outside, or around each other. And neither of them, they discovered, had small fingers.

One day, trying to squeeze a piece in—John Andrew said it would only slip into position when he and Dawn were both holding their faces right—they'd failed and failed and grown more bad-tempered with each other by the minute. Dawn had tried and lost patience, then lost her temper completely when John Andrew suggested he try.

It wasn't, she exploded, her ability. It was her big hands. Her father replied, "You don't have big hands, not like these meathooks," holding up his own. Dawn took her dad's hand, pressed it against hers, and said, "Oh yeah? Look."

Dawn's hands were smaller than her dad's, but still large and solid, with blunt, chubby fingers. But in this moment what suddenly moved Dawn was discovering that they were, without a doubt, the same hands. The same vein pattern, the same nail shape and both sets bitten nearly to the quick. Dawn looked up, smiling, curious, and realized her dad was seeing the same thing. She wondered about all the things that made him bite his nails, and if she'd ever be able to ask him. She wondered if he saw, like she did, that she was still his. Still made up of everything she'd arrived with as a little preemie, when her whole baby-self could likely have been held in one of his large, capable, and, now she saw, tender hands.

Born a month premature, she'd been a worry then. And a worry now, Dawn thought. But her father smiled down at their hands now, then took his away and put it on the top of her head, as he had when she was small, leaving it there for a moment like a blessing.

She wondered if thoughts could be transmitted by touch; if her father might be reading hers. So she thought as hard as she could, I love you, Dad, feeling a twinge of guilt that Tammy wouldn't be here when Dawn won their challenge, pulling from John Andrew the coveted "I love you too." But what he said now was, "Okay. Tammy has your mum's hands. She wants in on this. Let's get her tiny mitts out here."

Dawn felt only the tiniest disappointment. The rest was a triumph.

They called Tammy out, and Dawn felt these milestones slide behind her, into the distance.

A sense of growing anticipation now.

Instead of dreading a coming event—the wake, the funeral—time was marching forward with its lighter, determined step, taking them all towards the Highland Heart Show and the Tractor Trials with something resembling excitement. The competition was assuming such significance now for Dawn and, she knew, for her dad too. It was their private memorial. The wake had been fine as wakes go; the funeral and reception were, as John Andrew had told himself, the most pleasant he'd been to, but this—this moving, shining (it would be shiny by then!) piece of Miranda's history—was built from their knowledge of her, their planning and effort and what she would have loved most: their connection.

The Highland Heart show had been her mother's brainchild, and as a volunteer on the Highland Society board for so many years, she'd worked with every business and organization in the area to create the Highland Heart Exhibition. While local shows like this were dying out everywhere else, this one was thriving, evolving and growing every year, and, the town realized, driving tourism in the region. There was a newfound interest in the area's Gaelic heritage, so Miranda and her colleagues reached out to communities in Scotland, growing a network of twin and sister towns, devising one program after another.

In the early days, highland dance displays were the focus. Those turned into competitions, and now their little town ran one of the most prestigious events in the country, with local winners heading to Scotland. In the third and fourth years, caber toss and stone put, drum and pipe bands were added to the competition and the parade now put a couple of thousand people on the streets of their little town. Miranda's father had played the pipes in his youth, and there was a time when she had pressed Dawn to learn the instrument. But John Andrew—who declared that his pride in his Scottish heritage was just as strong as Miranda's—wouldn't countenance bagpipes in or near his house. If the sound hurt him, he said, it hurt his herd, and he wasn't having his milk curdled. Dawn remembered "it hurt his herd" with such gratitude. These days, itemizing their similarities instead of their differences, she added their dislike of bagpipes to the list.

Nowadays, the Highland Heart show had less of the Highland, as the competitors had dropped away, and more of the heart. An old-fashioned farming fair with animals, and judging of jams and flowers and crafts and...tractors.

Duncan MacDonald, a schoolmate of Miranda's and fellow society member, was a self-described tractor-fancier. Which meant, basically, that anyone with any issue or question or need for any tractor any time could contact him for an answer. Duncan lobbied for a tractor pull, and the next year, as he was finishing up a tractor restoration and discovering a whole new world of like-minded tractor obsessives, he pitched an event to show off ancient and refurbished tractors. Miranda and her father became Duncan's staunchest allies, and the Tractor Trials were born.

This year, the Tractor Trials fell just two weeks after Miranda's funeral. An incredible, almost impossibly tight timeline to get the old Jubilee that Miranda loved sanded and re-painted, with headlight-eyes that worked, a horn that beeped, and steering so finely tuned it could take the tractor through a series of dressage-like challenges. This was the event that Dawn and John Andrew, and now Tammy, had set their sights on: an event they knew, though never said to each other, that Miranda would attend. Organization was key. So little time, so much to do.

Miranda

They'd moved into a new phase of summer: the heat wasn't threatening now, it was ever present. Work in the shed became sweaty graft, less and less pleasant as they put on respirators and began to sand all the places they had scrubbed rust from, then filled and sanded again. Their grind was underscored by the music of cicadas, and their own jazz-like rub-brush, rub-brush percussion. Tammy came out with drinks, and stayed, perching to finesse little corners, small edges, and clips and rings with her "tiny mitts." More than once she brought their dinner out and sat to make sure they ate it, then left them to continue until it was cool and dark and the jack-o'-lantern shed spilled its warm light through eye windows, the night's stillness broken by frog calls, cows, and conversation: sometimes requests, occasionally demands.

Dawn had chipped away at the jammed windows in the shed, finally managing to lift one on either side, so there was a breeze as they worked. A constant caress that kept them from getting too hot or too cross to continue.

They were close now. So near to settling on exactly the shade of red, the shade of cream. Whether the hubcaps should be cream and red, or black and red. Whether the Jubilee medallion should be the original silver, or painted red with silver and gold like some decals were. Whether the script *Ford* should be left to just show its slightly raised self under the shiny cream paint when that finally went on, or whether they should get an artist to hand-paint it as *The Google* suggested. John Andrew had been amazed when Dawn had shown him all the wonderful sources on the web: treatises like PAINT YOUR TRACTOR (wasn't that a musical, her dad asked?) and YOU CAN REBUILD A TRACTOR!! But none yet, said Tammy, called TRACTOR: A LOVE STORY—that was theirs.

Now they worked later and later, Dawn ending every night with a pat on the tractor's nose.

She'd take off her coveralls, hang them on the hook she liked to use, turn off the spotlights focused on the tractor, and join her dad at the door. Tonight, he leaned by the door waiting to flip the switch, and she paused as she passed, to caress the now smooth snout where the newly painted decal would go.

Goodnight hood, goodnight headlight, goodnight haunch.

John Andrew laughed and said, "You pet that tractor like it's a beast."

Dawn smiled, then suddenly serious, said, "It's our pet. I love it. Her. I'm proud of her." She looked at her dad and considered before she said, "You are too, right? Whatever it was you didn't like, whatever it—she—did...it's fine now, right?" She felt foolish as her voice trailed off. It was a tractor.

John Andrew looked for a moment like he might tell her...something. But then he gave a sniff. Oh, John Andrew. That sniff could break a heart. And he said, "Tomorrow we'll get a new fuel injector. If it goes and keeps going, that might make me really like it. You get the light." And he crossed the yard to the house. Sniff.

Dawn watched him, puzzled. They'd come so far. Still, though, there was some strange threshold left uncrossed. She turned out the light and Betsy waited outside to see her safely across the yard. But the windows of the shed were still open and the breeze, scented now by honeysuckle and rugosa, was drying the decal—*Golden Jubilee Model, 1903–1953*—hand-painted by Tammy earlier that day, and placed so carefully on the work top beside the detailed picture John Andrew had found on *The Google*.

The air moved over the tractor: Goodnight hood, goodnight headlight, goodnight haunch.

Goodnight, Dad.

Goodnight, Miranda.

Ethan

Once things settled after the early morning rush, Ethan had five minutes for his own coffee and muffin. He ground espresso and pressed it into the silver cup: the portafilter, he thought proudly. When he started this whole process, he'd done course after course, making sure he could take the espresso machine apart and put it back together, learning all the names of all the parts. How he loved this, he thought. These moments when there was a lull, when he could inhale the smells of his shop, bask in his achievement, were magic. It was almost unbelievable to him, still. *His* shop; *his* counter; *his* magic coffee machine and *his* portafilter, making, right now, *his* cappuccino. Every day, what he'd managed here, the obstacles he'd circumnavigated to make it all work, energized him anew. The café had grown into a success on so many levels. Good coffee, good food, lovely staff helping him. The first—the only—queer-centric business on the main street of his very Catholic, queer-phobic hometown, was now patronized by...everyone. Everyone including the most homophobic assholes in the community, he thought, glancing to where Marty and his dad sat in the front window, engrossed in their phones. Ethan prided himself on his openness and warmth, but he couldn't manage it for those two. Even Ali, Marty's sister, though she was easier, still carried the family prickle that was part entitlement, part aggression, and part—he didn't know what that other part was, and why the frig should he care. He couldn't tell Banu not to give them any brain space and then let them distract him from a perfect foam.

He was steaming the milk with the wand now—daydreaming, he realized—looking past the big silver Marzocco. He flicked the switch off, wiped the wand automatically, and picked up his cup, starting the delicate transfer of hot milk to espresso. He'd heard—yesterday? Last week? The summer became one long day—a piece on the radio about a barista in Toronto who'd started creating coffee-foam portraits of the stars he had served. Daniel Radcliffe, inspiration to boy wizards everywhere! Tilda Swinton, Ethan's personal gender hero because—what were they? Who knew? Who cared? Meryl Streep, whose accents he hated but whose cheekbones he loved: he was sure he'd love her latte portrait. He wondered if he could— "Ah, shit!" He leapt and waved his hand.

Marty looked up. Angus looked up. "What?"

"Burned myself. Sorry—didn't mean to swear."

Angus shrugged. "Heard it before." And went back to reading his phone. Marty kept studying Ethan. Lizard eyes, Ethan thought—not for the first time. The bells on the door went as it swung open. Turning for his muffin, Ethan smiled to see Dawn coming in. What a beauty, Ethan thought for the umpteenth time. He was aware of Marty being aware.

"Hey!" Ethan said.

"Hey back! Coffee, please? And...those look good—"

"They are good. Just out of the oven. Morning glory." He took out two muffins and held up a plate.

"To go, thanks."

"So...waddup?" Ethan was rooting for a little bag now.

"Same old, same old." Dawn watched him, and then reached for the bagged muffin. "Need a little tiny part. We're so close now. Where's Banu?"

"Getting some groceries. They'll be back in sec, but hey—" Ethan looked towards Marty, lowering his voice, "are you, uh, hanging around?"

"Like, now? Today?" Dawn broke off a tiny bit of muffin. "Mm. Good."

"Like, generally. Inquiring minds want to know."

And at that moment, the doorbells jingled again and Banu came in. Ethan nodded towards them almost imperceptibly. Dawn went a deep pink that would, Ethan thought, give Banu exactly the answer they'd want—if they'd known Ethan had asked the question. But, phew, they didn't know, which was probably a good thing as Ethan wasn't sure Banu would thank him for...inquiring. And Banu, because they didn't know anything was going on, blew in with their trademark ease, and obvious delight at seeing Dawn.

"Hey! I was just gonna call you. We"—she nodded at Ethan—"were thinking a picnic after work—supper on the beach? Wanna join? Maybe ask Tammy and Byron—that's all good now, right?" Banu suddenly looked like they might regret that extended invitation.

"All good," Dawn reassured them. "I think they'd love that. We've all had our heads down so a beachy break would be perfect. What time?"

Ethan noted that Lizard-Eyes was listening hard. Ethan had caught Marty's furtive glance and his equally covert look to his phone as he began texting, feigning indifference. Ethan heard his name and turned back.

"...Ethan specializes in picnics. He's a total foodie—you'll see. Beach Meadows? Bring a suit, towel, and we'll do the rest." Banu grinned.

Dawn grinned back. Beamed, thought Ethan. The two of them were—ah well, he just wished that Marty wasn't seeing their obvious attraction and delight in each other. He would try and fuck it up somehow, because he was a prick. A confused prick, Ethan would bet. No one was that homophobic if they weren't scared of their own curiosity. Frankly.

Ethan slid Dawn's coffee over and she picked it up. "Great. I'll confirm with the others and text, but I'm sure it's fine. We'll meet you guys as soon as you can get away. I'll be in the shed for the afternoon, but I check my phone."

"Yee-haw!" said Banu. Lizard-Eyes looked up, but Banu was looking at Dawn.

"Yee-haw! See you later." Dawn turned to Angus and Marty. "Excuse me. Anyone in the shop?"

Angus didn't look up. Marty narrowed his eyes, looking at his dad before answering "No," like he was speaking to some kind of halfwit who'd asked for something impossible. Angus lifted his head, glared at Marty, pocketed his phone, stood, and said, "Yes." Aiming the word as though his son was the target: an affirmative that was so far from an *affirmation* that in spite of himself, Ethan felt a bit sorry for a young man who got no respect, no interest, nothing that Ethan recognized as love, from his father. Ethan suddenly felt grateful for his own fractious relationship with his parents; however imperfect they were, they saw him. They talked. They revelled in the discursive nature of their relationship, disagreeing about nearly everything, but they listened to him. They liked him, most of the time, but they loved him *all* of the time, and he knew it.

Angus opened the door but didn't hold it for Dawn. She caught it on her hip—coffee in one hand and muffin in the other—with a look back to Ethan. He raised his eyebrows as high as they could go, making her and Banu laugh and Marty look at each of them, pissed for not seeing what the joke was, but knowing it was at his expense.

John Andrew & Dawn

The afternoon was searing: the metal shed turning into a kind of oven, even with the windows open. Today, nothing was stirring and John Andrew and Dawn were soaked. John Andrew knew it was probably time to stop. They were both losing heart, getting further and further into what had become an unproductive cycle of trial-and-error. But, he thought, one more try.

"It must be the wires aren't properly attached," he said. "That was the last thing we did. We'll go back into the points, make sure everything is okay. It should be turning over now...anyways, we'll do it again." John Andrew took a deep breath, trying to stay patient. "Right, take that cap off and let's get the points and the condenser out." He reached for a screwdriver, still glaring at the offending part, and Dawn, like a nurse in surgery, laid a slotted screwdriver in his hand and watched him do what she had just finished doing. He popped off the rotor and clip, then the cover over the points.

"Phillips," said John Andrew, hand out. Dawn was dripping and getting pissed off. She wasn't a fucking nurse. He could say please. She handed him the Phillips, took back the slotted, watched him take out the screws holding the points pad and the condenser and—drop both tiny screws to the dirty, dark floor.

"Shit. Shit shit shit."

"Just don't move." Dawn got down on the floor, trying to see where they'd gone. Under the tractor of course. Head underneath now, she spotted one, then the other, started to ease herself out, whacked her head coming up, and then smashed her hand against—something—reaching to hand her dad the tiny screws from down below.

"Fuuucck. Ow."

"That's not ladylike," said her dad. And as she stuffed a bloody finger into her mouth, he added, "Break a nail?"

She looked at him in disbelief. What the actual fuck. She threw down the screwdriver she still held. “Don’t,” she said. “Don’t do that.”

He straightened up to look at her, sweat running into his eyes. He rubbed it off and, impatient, said, “It was a joke. Hand me—”

“—Well, don’t,” said Dawn. “I am not a joke. Nothing about me is a joke.”

Focused on Dawn, he took his wife’s advice. No sniffing. Just breathing. Then the voices of those asshole kids at the funeral home came shrieking back into his head and all he could think was, How could I? Again? Fuck. Fuck—and instead of a third *fuck*, a kick to the front bumper they’d screwed on right after lunch.

“What are you doing? Dad! Don’t dent her. Shit! All that work straightening—Dad!” as he seemed to be taking aim again. “Stop! What is the matter with you?”

John Andrew turned away from Dawn. He was so angry with himself, so frustrated and fucking hot and all he could think to say was, “Waste of time. It’ll never run.”

“It will,” said Dawn. “You know it will. We’re so close. This stupid points box, these wires, that’s it, then the ignition will work. Honestly. What it is with you and this thing?”

Her dad walked, silent, to the shed door, pulling down the zip on his coveralls. He just needed to catch a bit of breeze, needed to cool down and consider. Could he tell her this without blame, without anger? He glanced across the yard to the house that was his home but that had been owned by his father-in-law, and then his wife, according to the deed, and had, only with Miranda’s death, become his.

And this farm. In the distance he could see Jerry and Andy tossing hay into a feeder: same thing. Victor’s farm, then Miranda’s. Now he could hear Miranda clear as clear: Didn’t you say no one owns land? We caretake it? So why has it mattered so much? It’s time, isn’t it? To let this all go? You two are peas in the same pod. Tell her. Go on.

He took a breath. “I get it, ya know,” he started, his jaw going. He could feel Dawn’s focus on him as she came around the tractor towards him and leaned, he could tell without looking, on the snout she loved so much.

"Get what?"

Jesus. He just didn't know if he had the words to make her understand something he'd only just begun to grasp himself. He threw a glance over his shoulder—yes, leaning on the nose. Arms crossed, head on one side, hair loose and gold—so, so like her mother. He realized it was getting easy to think *her*.

He started, "For years I looked for Victor's approval—"

"—Grandpa Vic? Why?"

John Andrew started a contemptuous sniff, heard Miranda's "John Andrew!" then turned it into a long, slow breath. "I was never good enough for him." Dawn looked shocked, as he'd expected she would. He nodded. "His sights were set a lot higher than a farmhand for his daughter." He wasn't sure if he could keep going. That was a hard, humiliating time he was conjuring up.

"So..." His daughter's voice was gentle. Curious. He owed her. He continued.

"So, he did everything he could to stop it. Stop us. Show me up as an idiot to your mom—he was no fool, he felt her growing towards me—and eventually he fired me. Pretended I'd banjaxed this fucking tractor—I think he loved it more than your grandmother. That dent you kicked out? Yeah, well—"

"Had you?"

Now he did sniff. "Of course not. Everyone drove this thing. But that wasn't the point. It was something to hang on me so he could get rid of me, but—"

Now, Dawn saw something different on his face: pride? Where was Jill and her stomach to interpret when she needed her? "But?" she prompted.

"But your mother packed her bags, said she was leaving too. Seventeen and a firecracker. Your grandmother never said boo to a goose and Miranda didn't seem to have much to say to her, but Victor? Well, Miranda thought the sun shone out his arse, and he thought she was, well, what she was. Amazing. Perfect. And his. But she showed him she *wasn't* his anymore, that she was her own person. When this all blew up, she said to him—well, lots of things, but the part I remember—she said to him, I'm not yours, Dad. Or his. I'm mine. My own self. And my self loves his self, and it doesn't mean I love you less. But I will. If you send us both away—because he won't go without me because I won't let him—I'll never forgive you, she said. I'll never forget that. *He won't go without me*. And I wouldn't've."

"Woah." Dawn grinned. "No kidding, firecracker. Ballsy."

"She was. Can you say that?"

"Firecracker?"

"Ballsy. Isn't that kinda..."

Dawn grinned at her dad. "You learn fast. Mm...probably not great. But—what's said in the shed stays in the shed, right? So? Then what?"

"I stayed." John Andrew turned to look out into the field and beyond. "But he never stopped letting me know I didn't belong."

The cicadas hummed and whizzed and filled the space. Dawn studied her father. She'd never heard such...*soreness* from him. This old anger, she realized, had acted like scar tissue, determined the way he guarded his heart, let people in, or not. Still no answer about the tractor but this conversation felt, she thought, like the work on the tractor: a little nudge here, a tiny push or polish there, moved it forward. She gave a nudge.

"Okay, so it started with the tractor, but you won that battle. Why would you still feel so... What did she do?" She stroked the tractor's nose, a gentle tease.

John Andrew moved back into the shed and sat on a milk crate, facing her. Now a tiny breeze defied the heat, toying with the reddish curls escaping from the edge of his ball cap. She felt him gathering himself.

"Few years after we'd married, I started looking for a tractor. Bigger, newer, that could do more."

"Was that the big John Deere?" Dawn remembered being up in that cab.

John Andrew nodded. "All the bells and whistles. I loved it. Vic hated it. And since he did, your mom took against it. Biggest fight we ever had, the three of us. I was paying for it, but now I think, that was it."

"What? Why? That's nuts."

"It was, but—this stuff isn't logical, Dawn. But it had got so important to me. Too important, I guess. It irritated your mom, made Vic dig his heels in. But it was going to be the one thing on the farm that I chose. That worked for me. Modern, cheaper to run, but mostly, mine. He hated that. Seeing his old tractor shelved—seemed like I was shelving him, I guess. Staking a claim on what had been his. Upstart farmhand, stole his daughter first, then..." He pulled off his hat, rubbed his head.

"Your grandma wasn't long dead then," he continued. "I guess he... he missed her more than I knew. He was kinda...lost." John Andrew paused for an unspoken apology to Victor; to Miranda; to Emily, Miranda's mother, whom he'd really never bothered to get to know. Contributed to her invisibility. Shit. He hoped there was no ledger. No god keeping track of all these—what even were they?—*doings* he regretted. So many in his life.

"Miranda was mad I was upsetting her dad. But you know..." He swallowed and counted, keeping control before he said, "I loved your mother, Dawn, more than anything. But she wasn't perfect and she never really understood how hard her father had made...everything. It...withers ya, livin' on another man's charity. It was his house. His land. She'd say it was mine too, but—it wasn't. I couldn't do anything right. Couldn't turn around without him asking why I didn't turn the other way."

Dawn listened, astonished—to hear her father say so many words. And words about feelings at that. He was delivering this story mostly to his hands, as if the details could be found in the oil on his palms, in the dirt under his bitten fingernails. Finally, he lifted his head and said directly to her, "I know disapproval, day after day, can near 'nuff break someone."

Dawn was still. The cicadas were quiet. The breeze seemed contained in this space; just enough movement, just cool enough now for comfort.

"But I did it to you." He looked at her with such clarity. She felt it all—regret, apology, sadness: so many feelings she never imagined her father could express. When did he learn this? She felt sad for him, for all his losses, but such pride and elation in him too. He hadn't finished.

"The only things your mum and I fought about after Vic was gone was this tractor, and you. She asked, not long after her dad died—you kids knew—if I'd fix it up. And I couldn't. I looked at it and felt small again, always trying to be somebody else. Stupid, eh? That a thing can make you feel like that."

Dawn said, "A person made you feel like that."

He got up, moved around the tractor, his hand running over the work they'd done over the last long days and nights.

"You know," he said, "she never asked for much. She would've liked to travel, but she never asked because I guess she thought I'd feel bad not being able to provide that. But this..." He looked at the tractor as if waiting for it to speak now. "She asked for this. To restore this tractor to its glory days, as a kind of memorial to her dad." Dawn looked at her father, surprised. "Yeah," he said. "And to talk to you. But then you left, and she got sick, and—"

"We were going to tell you, Dad. We'd planned—"

"I know, Jenny said."

Dawn thought of her mother; the times she had sat in her business class chemo chair, imagining all the places in the world she might have gone. If. If. If. She wondered if her mother had been saving her father the hurt of what he hadn't been able to give. Really, Dawn was sure his love had been her mother's whole world. Even with Miranda's illness and Dawn's complicated journey, John Andrew had been to his partner what Dawn hoped she might find someday. Now, John Andrew drew the threads together.

"Five years from when you left, Dawn—might be five hundred. I maybe don't get it," his look now was direct, open, "—but I don't wish anybody ill."

They stood in silence looking at each other. Dawn had nothing to ask, nothing to add, no conclusion she wanted to draw. He took his favourite screwdriver out again, pulled the wires loose from the points, twisted the ends, then waved her over to re-attach them, watching as she secured them.

They worked in silence. The breeze had cooled the shed a little, the points were back in place, the two lost-then-found screws were slotted in, the condenser was secured, the cap on, then the cover. She was a nurse again, but now she didn't mind.

John Andrew put down the screwdriver, took the keys out of the cup, and dangled them. "This time?" he said.

Dawn took the key, got on the tractor, wiggled it into the ignition, turned it, held her breath, and—

Nothing. Not even a cough.

"Fuck!" She wanted to cry. All this knowledge about her dad hadn't fixed the tractor.

"Language! Jump off, I'll do it."

Jesus. He was still annoying. "It's not going for you if it won't go for me!"

He backed away, hands up: don't shoot. "Okay. Okay. Check the key's turned all the way. Put the choke in. Take a breath. Pull the choke out, take another breath. Press the starter and hold it."

She did all that. Every action with a breath. The cicadas stopped as she pressed down on the starter. Everything holding its breath.

The shed door banged.

The tractor started.

Coughed, spluttered, but started. Then ran.

Euphoric, Dawn reached to high-five her father, but John Andrew caught and held his daughter's hand just long enough for her to wonder, committing the moment to memory, if the white tracery on her father's face was sweat, or tears.

Tammy & Byron

"Whistle again," Tammy said to Byron.

"Tammy, I don't think she'll be any too pleased if I'm whistling for her like a pup. Go get her if you're worried. I thought this was so caj, no timeline, nothing to worry about but bathing suits."

Tammy was putting bags into the back seat. For a "beach event" that required them to bring nothing, he thought, they seemed to be taking a lot. Cookies. Drinks. Chips. Towels. An ancient boom box. And so on. Tammy pulled her head out of the car and hollered—she really could make noise when she wanted to, thought Byron.

"Dawn. Dawn! Dawwwwnnnnn! We need to go. It'll be dark." The shed door banged open and Dawn came tearing out. She looked like she was flying a couple feet above the ground. Maybe, thought Byron, levitating with joy, she was smiling so hard. John Andrew was not far behind—not exactly flying, but looking very pleased with himself.

Byron started towards them. "Good news, then?"

Dawn was out of breath, but managed, "She's going!"

John Andrew arrived, cap in hand, rubbing his hand over his head like it was a job, grinning and nodding. Bobbing like a noddy dog, Byron thought. Nod nod nod, grin grin, grin. What was next? World peace?

"Dawn, you're disgusting." Sisterly warmth and support from Tammy. "Your face is covered in, like—I don't even know. Did you rub it all over the shed floor?" Dawn looked at her dad, her grin getting, if possible, even wider. "Just go," urged Tammy. "Get your stuff and at least look in the mirror. Banu's coming, right?"

Dawn ran.

Tammy hadn't been to Beach Meadows for years, so she assumed it was the same for Dawn—at least the five years she'd been gone and probably more. Tammy looked around, delighted that, unlike everything else she'd seen this trip—the town, the countryside, and even the farm—not one thing seemed to have changed. The parking lot might have been pushed a little farther from the beach, but the spot was still an oasis: long, high dunes stippled with feather-like grass and a scattering of lowbush blueberries that Tammy remembered going bright red in the fall. The silver-grey dunes stretched between two high cliffs a long city block apart, and hid the beach and ocean from view. They could hear it, though, as they hauled their beach bags from the car.

Ethan pulled in behind and Banu got out laughing at Tammy, who had a bag in each hand and towels under her arms, and at Byron with the ancient boom box. "You guys came prepared!"

"Ready for fun of any description!" Byron handed the boom box to Dawn and pulled a Boogie Board out of the trunk.

"Oh my god," said Ethan. "I thought we were just eating."

"Nope," said Byron, "surfing first." He held up the Boogie Board, eliciting hoots of derisory laughter. "Then dancing to music about surfing, *then* maybe eating—"

Ethan snorted as he examined the child-sized plastic surfboard. "Did you waylay a toddler on their way to a playdate? And were you by chance a camp counsellor?"

"Camp? Moi?" Byron secured the board under his arm and was off. "Beach this way, yeah?" following the sandy trail through the dunes.

Tammy was trying to keep up with Byron, but did throw over her shoulder, "Counsellor, yes—" and Banu added to Ethan, "But definitely *not* camp." Laughter from Banu and Ethan and Dawn, now a trio behind Tammy. She looked back, stung at feeling left out and her teeth all on edge. Shake it off, shake it off. This *will* be fun, she said to herself. You're allowed to have fun.

Coming to where the narrow trail widened onto the beach, Tammy paused, waiting for the others to catch up. She could see Byron, off to the right and already down the beach. She loved watching him discover something new. His delight never got old for her; it was never forced. Now, he'd run down the empty beach towards the cliffs and the turn that hid a stunning cove—a destination for locals who were prepared to wade around the point if the tide was in, for the seclusion. She wanted to be right there when Byron looked around that corner. But for now, he'd paused, and was standing, feet in the water, looking first one way, then the other, up and down the beach, revelling in the empty strand. Unheard of in the Beaches, their Toronto sand experience. He turned and whooped, seeing her, and threw his arms skyward in his *bless you, bless me* pose. When he was wordless—rarely, but it did happen—this was his stance. Feet apart, arms and head heavenward: a *thank-you, universe* Tammy knew was authentic. Now he headed back towards them, and she could see he'd left his shoes by an improvised firepit flanked by a large V of driftwood logs. She headed there and the others followed.

The wind blowing onshore meant that Tammy struggled to lay out a couple towels and Byron went in search of rocks big enough to hold things down, Banu joining him. Tammy watched them walk, heads down against the wind, laughing, and felt that edge returning. Ethan and Dawn had set up the boom box in a protected spot created by the largest of the drift-logs and were looking through the handful of ancient CDs Tammy had found—her mother's and some of Tammy's boy-band high-school-crush faves. There was a sudden blasting exhortation to rock her body, and Ethan and Dawn began to gyrate to one of Tammy's Backstreet favourites.

Oh. My. God. How many years since she was choreographing duets with Nick Carter in her bedroom? She did a camel one, camel two—what was her jazz dance teacher's name?—then sashaaaay in the sand, camel three, camel four, and as she turned there were Byron and Banu heading back, still laughing, both with rocks in each hand, and why did it matter so much? Their joint effort? And behind them, way down the beach, three tiny figures.

By the time the three tiny figures had turned into three looming ones, Ethan and Dawn had the fire going and Ethan was giving clear instructions about creating a bed of glowing embers for the most efficient roasting. Watching the trio closing in, Tammy felt sure dinner wasn't coming any time soon. Tammy joined Byron and Banu who seemed to be supervising at the fire—encouraging, Byron said—and lightly touched Byron's back with, "Look. Company."

Byron turned. Banu turned. Ethan and Dawn turned. Byron said, under his breath, "Insects at a picnic."

Marty replied as he got close enough to kick sand over their fire, "What's that, douche canoe?"

Byron turned to Banu. "Really? Douche Canoe? What does that even—"

"Byron." Tammy hadn't meant to sound so sharp.

"Want a dog, Marty?" Ethan said, holding up a hot dog, and Tammy remembered *fine* and clamped her lips together. Not doing that again. She went to stand by her sister. She'd offer silent solidarity this time.

Marty had two pals with him. Jimbo, and some other minion whose skin was so pockmarked with past and active acne that Tammy felt sorry for him. Only for a second, though. Because then he said, "We don't eat Fag-Dogs."

Ethan the Unflappable responded, "Oh man, too bad, 'cause they're the only type of dogs we've got. *Sorry*." And he managed to make that sorry the gayest sorry in the history of sorrys. That was a talent, thought Tammy, and an effective tool for winding up rabid homophobic asshats like these three.

Marty grabbed the reins from his pal with the unfortunate face. "Backstreet Boys, huh? Cool," he said. "Historic, right? But this is my cousin's land and he's not a fan, so—you gotta go."

Banu stepped towards him. "Beaches are public access. We came from the parking lot at Cemetery Road."

Edgy as Tammy was about all things Banu, she admired the way they were taking this idiot on.

"Huh. That right? Well, what do you know?" Marty started nice and got nicer. "You can't help it though, you're a lesbian foreigner. You don't know our customs. Our laws. But this happens to be *his* beach, and a fag-free zone, so—"

Byron had started filming with his phone when the trio arrived, and now took a step forward, getting in Marty's face.

Marty's wingmen moved in tight on either side as he swiped a large, loose paw towards Byron, sending his phone flying. Byron lunged at Marty, and Banu pushed between them, shouting and shoving them apart while Tammy was, once again, watching and doing nothing. But then, Dawn wasn't doing anything either, except gripping her sister's hand, painfully.

She could see where this was going. Tammy wrenched her hand away, turned, and switched off the boom box. She strode past Byron and Marty, brushing past Banu, and went to take the rocks off her sandy towel. She shook it hard, turning so the wind would blow it towards Marty. He rubbed his eyes and glared at her, and she stopped shaking the towel and stood in front of him, discovering her power, because she realized he'd do nothing.

He couldn't hit her or make a show of her, like he'd done to Byron in the pub.

Byron was different: he was a come-from-away and Black, and he'd challenged Marty when people were watching, so Byron was fair game. The fact that in her hometown, Byron's hue and Dawn's gender made them targets, while Tammy's gender and colour could keep her safe, pissed her off. Made her gut-wrenchingly sad and disappointed. She looked at Marty with the melancholy that coloured everything lately and thought, this world is actually fucked; I could stand in front of this moron all day and he won't hit me because my dad would kill his dad, and his dad would kill him and his sister would kill him—

And then, joining dots tiny as grains of sand into a constellation of understanding, Tammy got it.

Marty was afraid of his father because his father was cruel. But Marty was afraid of his sister, Tammy was sure, because Ali and he were close—they'd had to be allies—and Ali knew everything about her sibling. She knew things her father would never see, just as Tammy had known *her* sibling's secret before her father had, even before Dawn did. Tammy saw, standing in front of Marty, what a cliché he was. That the years of abuse he'd heaped on Dawn weren't the result of a bullying father and almost invisible mother. Not just.

She started to fold the towel, looking at him with all the compassion she could muster.

She could feel the others behind her, gathering their things in silence. Then over Marty's shoulder she saw Dawn starting towards the parking lot, Ethan on her heels, then Banu. Byron cast a glance at Tammy and Marty before she saw him running to catch up with Banu. Not Dawn. It bit her, seeing him choose Banu.

Now, though, Tammy focused on Marty. She tried to think of something that would let him know that she knew. Who he was. *Why* he was. She wanted to dispense something witty and life-changing. Kind. Big. Bigger than she'd been of late; bigger than she felt in this moment, thinking about Banu and Byron walking together towards the purple-pink horizon; big enough to gently reveal Marty to himself.

But Marty pulled his eyes from hers and turned to join Jimbo and the other guy who were kicking sand over the embers of Ethan's perfect roasting spot. And Tammy turned to head down the beach towards the figures, silhouettes now against the sinking sun, who dropped from sight one by one on the narrow path over the edge of the dunes.

Byron & Tammy

Silence as the car spun along the gravel road away from the beach. The atmosphere like a rubber band slowly stretching to its maximum. Any minute now, Byron thought, it's going to ping in someone's eye.

"Fucking dick." Ethan, to the point.

"That's hard on dicks." Banu, trying to lighten the mood but eliciting only groans and yeah, rights from her companions in the back seat. And then, reliably provocative Tammy, still smarting from—what? Byron wondered. They were all pissed off at Marty, but the target was Dawn, and she was silent. But not Tammy. She turned with her tight, superior smile and launched a little grenade into the back seat, landing in Banu's lap.

"Mother Teresa." She smiled. "I didn't think you were a dick fan?"

For fuck's sake, Tammy. "Hang on, kids." Byron pulled sharply to the side of the road, to the low crash rail, beyond which the edge of the cliff dropped vertiginously to the ocean. Everyone looked at the water and the rocks below and inhaled sharply while Byron got out, went round to open Tammy's door, and nodded down the road behind them. Tammy looked up at him with no intention of getting out. His look gave her only one other option: having this conversation about her shitty behaviour here, in full view, with no danger of anyone missing a single word. So she got out of the car and followed him down the road.

Byron stood near the cliff's edge, looking out, gathering his patience. He knew this woman. He loved her. And these last couple of weeks had been hard—relentless and exhausting. But this flippant cruelty was not—fuck, not what? He wasn't her father—Not nice? Not appropriate? Not...her. It wasn't her. So, he faced her.

"What was that? What is going on?"

Tammy was looking away from him now, chewing her lip. Then,

"I'm losing everything. My mother. My brother..." She turned to him. "You."

"What?"

"You like her. You want to leave. You said—"

"Like who? Oh my god, Banu? Of course I do. And leave? You? You're not making sense. I do want to leave. Here. I don't want to leave you. I want our life back. This weird limbo isn't good. It feels like everything's stopped, but it hasn't. We need a plan. We need...I want you back. I know you've changed, of course you've changed, losing your mum, dealing with, learning about Dawn, but...you'll absorb it. You'll...get it. It'll be—"

"Easy?" Tammy was so ready to fight.

"Not easy, Tam, just fact. Just true. Just—Jesus, Tammy. Banu? You don't know I love you? That I want you? Most of the time?"

"You rushed off to have coffee with her. She's so...she'll step in, she's—"

"*They*, Tammy, not *she*. Yeah, they're ballsy—shit. Spunky. Whatever." He took a breath and continued. "Banu's not interested in men. As you pointed out." Tammy looked away. "I'm not interested in Banu. That way. They wanted to talk about Dawn. Whether she was staying here. And that's good for Dawn. That someone cares like that for her. Now. When she needs it most."

Tammy stared out across the Strait, where Cape Breton was a distant floating log, mist below and dark above. God. She was always letting herself down. Why should Byron love her? How could he? And for how long? Till he knew everything about her, how angry she got, how sad.

"Tam." He reached out a hand. Tammy stared at it. "Please? Please know there is nothing wrong with us, nothing going on. Don't make this into something because you're sad and angry. Neither of us is perfect. I'm not, you're not, but I don't want anyone else. I want you, and I want you to be okay, and yeah, I want to go home. To our home."

Tammy searched his face now, started to speak, but he beat her to it. "After the tractor...thingy. I know. Come on. Let me..."

Now she did take a step towards him, and let him put his arms around her, and stood still. Tammy listened to Byron's heart, still watching the changing shapes across the Strait, and Byron looked over her head into the car. Three heads in row, eyes front, no one looking back, yet Byron felt seen and held in their quiet patience.

When they got back in the car, Tammy didn't say anything. Her embarrassment, Byron knew, had its own circuitous route to travel. He turned on the radio, and The Once was singing "We Are All Running." How did music know? Why did a song come on when you needed it? Because they did: linking moments, choices, people to music forever. His mother appeared in his head sitting in her worn armchair, crocheting herself to the jazz she listened to on Saturday nights, squinting at the wool she hooked under an ancient brass-arm lamp. And now they—all of them—would come back to this road, this moment in this summer, with this song. He looked in the rear-view mirror before pulling out onto the deserted road and caught Banu's glance at Dawn. Dawn was focused on the road ahead, lips only just turned up into what Byron privately called her Mona Lisa *I know, but I'm not sharing* smile. Tipping his mirror down, he saw they were holding hands.

They got stuck behind a combine at Malignant Cove that didn't pull off until Brierly Brook, just before the town limits, so it was dark when they finally got back. They were all hungry, hot, tired, and silent. The car windows were open, the air conditioning having proven itself absolutely *not* up to the task. Ethan was dropped first, and Dawn and Banu didn't shift to relax into the space he'd left but stayed glued together. Now, stopping in front of Banu's tiny house, lights on in every window, cats visible in two, Byron watched covertly as the pair in the back seat untangled their fingers.

Dawn handed Banu a hat as they slid across the car to the opposite door. "Give this to Ethan tomorrow?" she said.

Banu reached for the hat, smiling as their fingers entwined again, then extricated themselves before opening, then slamming the car door and throwing over their shoulder, "Thanks, all. Loads of funnnnnnn!"

Tammy grabbed her door handle and jumped out of the car, running to get to Banu before they climbed the steps to their door.

"Banu?" Tammy touched their shoulder and Banu turned.

Tammy clenched and unclenched her hands before saying, to the ground, "I'm a bitch to everyone." Then, looking up. "Not just you. Ask Dawn. I'm—" But Banu didn't let her finish.

"You're not. It's fine," they said, and Tammy stepped backward, hearing *fine* and wondering if Banu was taking the piss. But they weren't: they too were imperfect, spunky or not, and hadn't thought to find a word that didn't carry the load that *fine* did at the moment. In a breath, Banu realized it. They stepped forward, pulling Tammy into a hug.

Byron and Dawn exchanged looks in the rear-view mirror that, by the time Tammy and Banu separated, had grown to grins. Banu took the stairs two at a time, and with a final look back and "See ya!" was inside. Opening the car door, Byron and Dawn turned to Tammy. She threw her hands up.

"What? Oh my god you two, quit!"

But they didn't. Not until they'd stopped at a fast-food chain then driven to the landing to eat their burgers, sitting on mossy logs on the edge of the silver river, watching loons, and a beaver gnawing on a sapling. The beaver gave them only a cursory glance. Everyone chewing. Tammy's phone rang, and she reached for it. She looked at the name on her screen, and Byron saw the sadness that seemed to have eased in just the last few hours was back, so he looked too.

Mom, the screen said, over a picture of a peony.

"Hi, Dad." She listened, then, "We're nearly home. At the river. Got something to eat and yeah... Miss us?" She listened again, then to Dawn, "Betsy does. Right." And to her father, "Tell Betsy we're nearly home. Okay. See ya. And Dad," to Dawn again, "we love you."

Tammy waited, listening, focused on Dawn, and Dawn waited, watching Tammy. Byron could hear the silence coming through the ether, and then John Andrew's round, brown voice made small and tinny as Tammy held the phone out so they could all hear him say, "Okay then. See ya soon."

JOHN ANDREW

Why was it, John Andrew wondered, that Saturday always carried the whiff of a holiday, even for him? Everyone else might be sleeping in, having coffee in bed and a slow leisurely breakfast—or brunch; brunch was the thing now, wasn't it—but he still rose at five. He made his coffee listening for steps upstairs. Nothing. No assistants this morning, he thought as he pulled on his boots, but no brunch either, as he knew Dawn was joining him at the 4-H meeting. So. He picked up his mug and whistled quietly for Betsy, who padded behind him, and they headed for the dairy through a fine mist. He squinted into the distance. He was fine on his own—well, with Jerry, this morning. The kids were late last night.

They were quiet when they came in. Subdued, he realized, and wondered if he should be asking them more questions. He shook his head at himself. Useless, he thought. They have no idea that I sat wondering, worrying, hoping they'd be home to spend the evening with me. How can they know, he thought, and resolved: I will talk more. I won't burden them with this—he didn't know quite what to call it—this ache, but I will talk about other things. Lighter things. I should make a list of all the good stuff, he thought. The good memories, the joy and laughter their mother, and they, have brought. I will, I'll make a list. That made him smile.

Miranda made lists. Long, detailed lists of needs, jobs—for him mostly. He'd only ever made a Christmas list, and only at her insistence. Always with two things heading it: *Socks*. He never had enough socks without holes. And *books*: because it was important Miranda knew that he wanted to read, like her, though he rarely got through a book. Maybe I'll do that now, he thought. I'll start by reading the books at her bedside. Tonight I'll—

He stopped, his eye caught by a dark pickup parked on the roadside near the path running to the machine shed. A person—he couldn't tell from this distance, through the mist, if he knew them; did he know that truck?—climbed in and closed the door, carefully. Had they seen him, he wondered? He eased himself behind a large stand of pines. Odd. So early. Or late, maybe. Someone pull an all-nighter, need a piss? But here? Nothing out here but their farm, that shed with the tractor.

The truck started, pulled away, as if the driver—was he imagining this now?—was trying to be quiet. An ancient pickup like that could only be so quiet, though; the muffler was only just holding on. The truck passed close to John Andrew and he adjusted position so he wouldn't be seen. What, he wondered, bothered him about this? Then he stepped out and watched the truck accelerate away.

The cows were...cows; Jerry was Jerry; Andy was late, so most of the work was wrapped up by the time Andy arrived only to have a strip torn off him by his dad. Although, having a strip torn off by Jerry was a bit like a kitten pulling a sheet of toilet paper apart—whiskers and fluff, a bit of mess soon swept up. The three men left the dairy together, everything hunky dory again. John Andrew hadn't mentioned his early morning encounter yet, but he did now.

"Hey, anyone you fellas know have an old—I think it was a Dodge—pickup? Dark—blue, coulda been black? Seen one parked out here early."

"Isn't that about every truck in town?" Andy grinned. "Including me. Do I need an alibi for something?"

"Dunno. You tell me, I won't tell your dad." They all laughed. He was making too much of this, he thought, and paused before heading to the house. "Coffee, either of yas?"

"Nope," from Andy. "I'm going to brunch. You coming, Dad? Ma's set it up."

John Andrew was grinning. Brunch. Jerry gettin' fancy?

"Naw," said Jerry. "I'm gonna catch up on paperwork. Keep your mother from buying for the town, will ya?" This called after Andy, now jogging towards home. Jerry turned to John Andrew. "What you up to? Not brunch, I'm guessing."

"4-H. Kids are doing small engines this morning—with Dawn."

"Good for her." Jerry sucked his teeth, shaking his head. "Just as mechanical minded as ever, eh? How's the tractor going? Gonna be ready?"

"If Dawn has anything to do with it. Getting close. It's going. On and off. One coat of undercoat on. She's gonna be a beauty."

They reached their fork: Jerry one way, John Andrew the other.

"She is a beauty." Jerry smiled and *didn't* mean the tactor. Then, "Later. Gonna be hot again, now that mist is liftin'." And off he went.

John Andrew had put this little workshop into the 4-H calendar weeks ago—the spring meeting, when they'd planned a bunch of one-offs, all unrelated to the kids' animal projects—and thought there wouldn't be much take-up with it being the middle of summer vacation. He would have been leading it himself, and usually these mechanical-type demonstrations didn't pull the full group, just a handful of boys. Though that was changing. 4-H was priding itself on moving to more "innovative and inclusive" programming and he was seeing the fruits of that now, as he and Dawn finished placing chairs in rows and a table in front to set the old lawnmower on. The list of names was three times as long as usual.

The church basement had a small stage at one end and a kitchen at the other, and in between was filling and buzzing with young voices, chairs scraped and shifted—with "saved!," "no way, mine!," and "get off!"—re-organizing the work he and Dawn had just finished. He was amazed. There was never this sort of turnout on a summer Saturday morning. Kids from eight to eighteen, nearly equal numbers of boys and girls, and even a bit of diversity (that was right, wasn't it? Diversity?), as he watched one of the Syrian women the church had sponsored ushering three children, two of them girls, into seats. "Be good, be quiet, learn," she admonished, then turned to smile shyly at John Andrew before slipping out.

Well.

He wondered how Dawn felt about drawing this crowd, because of course she had. He'd only asked her to come do this a couple of days ago, but no doubt Ethan and Banu and the network their café provided had something to do with it. Any news travelled like the wind, and John Andrew knew that recent events—the wake, the pub-fight, and the funeral—had given the family a peculiar kind of profile and shot Dawn into the village stratosphere, providing her with an unwanted celebrity status. Those who'd known Dawn before wanted to know her again; those who were just curious wanted their curiosity sated. And—he thought of Marty—those who'd been shitty before...

Ah, Jesus. He didn't want her hurt again. This might have been a bad idea...he didn't know. He was remembering the three young assholes at the funeral home—lodged forever in his memory—and scanned the room. Absent. Right. Good. Better get started. He walked to the front and cleared his throat.

John Andrew wasn't good at getting attention—he was very good. He only needed to place his solid six-foot-two frame in front of any group, lift his hand to run it through his hair, and look ready to speak, and folks went silent, waiting. As they did now.

"Right then. There's a bunch of you. Good. I've brought my—" Shit. Nearly. He thought that was done with. Must be nerves. "—my daughter, Dawn, to—"

"I've heard about Dawn!" piped a little boy in a too-big 4-H shirt. "He's—"

"*She*'s"—John Andrew was a little more forceful than he'd intended, but I'm shutting *that* down, he thought—"going to talk about small-engine maintenance. She's always been great with machines"—he turned to her—"right, Dawn? So sit tight, and I think I heard someone's mom saying, *Be good, be quiet, learn*, and I couldn't have put it better myself. Dawn?" He saw the little Syrian kids poking each other—*our mom, our mom*—before settling into their best, most focused learning postures.

Dawn stepped up to the table and he moved to the back of the room to watch.

She was a natural teacher. Like Miranda, she spoke to the kids like they were people, not stupid and not a chore, asking them questions and making it clear she knew they had the answers. She had that talent for making them feel good about every answer they gave, and created laughter around the more...creative responses. Laughter—not ridicule. He watched and thought about Jerry's comment this morning: her beauty.

His child, who he'd seen operating in public now two or three times, truly was beautiful. John Andrew was surprised again by the delicacy of her. And more, and better: she was kind and quick to laugh. She managed to appear unaffected by the cruelty and judgment that he knew was directed towards her. How? he wondered. How has she stayed, how has she become so...herself, so young. He wasn't sure he'd become himself yet. He leaned against the wall, relaxing. He wondered if and when she was leaving and he wished she would stay, and thought, maybe he should say that.

He saw Dawn talking to a small kid—Kyle Smits. Smallest kid in the group, eight years old, with a single mom who worked on Hans de Koning's farm. Nice woman. Smart. The child looked like a painted cherub, something you'd see on Christmas card. Long-lashed blue eyes, golden curls nearly to the middle of his back. Time someone cut those, he thought. Dawn was speaking directly to Kyle, saying, "Yeah, before you can put things together so they'll work, you have to be able to take them apart. So"—now she raised her voice to include everyone—"I've got a couple of wrenches here." She raised them in the air, one in each hand, like trophies. "Who wants to come start taking bits off?"

Every hand in the room went up. John Andrew watched as the circle around his child grew and the chatter rose. Dawn raised her head to catch her dad's eye, and smiled. He smiled too, then turned his focus back to little Kyle, who was gazing at Dawn with fascination and reverence.

Dawn

That was the nicest thing, Dawn thought as she reached for the reconstructed mower that sat on the edge of the church lawn. Its coughing resurrection had been greeted with a massive cheer from the group of tool-wielding 4-H'ers. One of whom, she realized, was holding a stray out to her now.

"Hey, thanks." She smiled and took the wrench from the serious and helpful Kyle, bending to put it back in her toolkit, and smiling as she registered his bright pink socks. He saw her look.

"My mom says pink is just a colour. I can like it if I want." He had the slightest lisp that he countered with very precise speech.

Dawn straightened up, just to his height, and matched his serious face. "Your mom's smart. She's right."

"She told me you're fixing a tractor for the Highland Heart. And that you used to be a boy."

Dawn felt the cold rush that always came when that truth was so baldly put. She could see her father standing by the truck's driver side. She wondered if he might feel like leaping to protect her—she'd appreciated his corrections inside—but she smiled at the young boy. The chill passed. She was good.

"Both right," she said. "Sort of."

Kyle was fixed on her. She felt so...seen. He was looking, looking, looking. Trying to discover everything about her: her past, her future, and, she knew, himself.

"But now," he said, "you're—" and stopped. He wanted to be clear. "Now you're—"

Dawn said gently, "Now I'm me."

Kyle looked at her with relief and said, "Wow." A long, reflective pause and then he asked, "Was that..."

Dawn waited.

"...weird?"

"Well," she spoke carefully, "it didn't always feel great, figuring out I was really a girl."

Kyle's eyes, thought Dawn, seemed full, but she wasn't sure if it was the bright sunlight making them seem so liquid.

"Yeah?" said Kyle.

"Yeah," said Dawn. "But *my* mom said to *me*, and she was smart too, *There's room around the campfire for everyone. And there's a different view from every spot.* That helped." Dawn could feel her father listening. "I remember that now, all the time."

"Huh," said Kyle, thinking hard. He looked up and squinted at the sun, considering, the light wind moving his yellow curls around his face. He pushed them away from his eyes, and after much deliberation, looked back to Dawn. "I like campfires," he said solemnly, then turned and started towards the other 4-H'ers waiting in the parking lot for their rides.

Dawn looked to John Andrew. He seemed to shake his head—did he, she wondered?—then he shrugged—she *knew* he shrugged—and got in the truck. Dawn lifted the lawnmower into the back, closed the tailgate, and joined him. He started the truck, turned to her as if to say something, and then didn't.

Tammy

Tammy looked out the bathroom window to the patio below and the firepit, only cleared out today. Byron had felt deprived of a beach fire the other evening, so he'd spent today digging the pit clean, collecting kindling, and building a fire that was, he felt, a masterpiece. He was right—it was burning. Tammy grinned to herself. So good. And everyone had relaxed a bit.

Now, Byron was swinging back and forth in the hammock between Dawn, feet pulled up onto an old Adirondack, and their dad in one of those fold-out camp chairs. Tammy remembered them; her mom and dad used to take them to their games, Dawn's soccer and her baseball. God. She hadn't thought about baseball for years. And, she thought, looking in the mirror and studying herself objectively, with good reason: I was awful. She grabbed her sweater before heading back down. It was just starting to cool down a bit and they'd heard some rumbling: heat thunder, her dad said.

Climbing back into the hammock with Byron, Tammy tried to remember whose idea this hammock was. It had to have been her mom's, she thought. Romance over comfort. Her dad was all about comfort and this hammock was a lot of things, but comfort wasn't at the top of the list, not for two people. She shifted again.

"Tam! How many elbows do you have?" Byron adjusted again. "I was so comfy. Ow. Okay. I'm going to take that pillow—wait, just wait. *Now* lean back. Okay?"

"Okay. But honestly, who put this up?"

"Shh," said Dawn. "Quiet time. We're listening for the barred owl."

"You mean barn owl." Byron pulled Tammy in close. Now she was very comfortable.

Dawn shook her head. "Barred, not barn. I don't think we have any barn owls here, do we, Dad?"

"Dunno. I haven't seen one for years. Only just heard a barred owl the other night, so wondering if there's maybe a nest nearby. Won't likely hear him this time of night. Three, four in the morning—that's when he'll call: *Who cooks for youuuuuuu?*"

All three turned to look at John Andrew.

"Do you just *know* that?" Dawn meant the call.

"Nope. Yer mom has"—everyone waited while he nearly adjusted to past tense, then didn't—"an app on her phone. A bird app. I heard him the other night—"

"You get up at five!" said Dawn. "What are you doing up at three or four listening for him?" John Andrew shrugged.

"Or her." Tammy looked at Byron and hooted gently, "*Who cooks for youuuuu?* More likely to be a female, isn't it?" She dug him with one of her elbows.

"Oh my god. Are you still moaning about making dinner tonight? I dug this pit. I made this perfect fire." Byron shifted position.

"Ouch." Tammy pushed him over. "Tonight. Last night. The night before—"

Dawn cut her off. "—Tammy, shush! Honestly, you two. Go inside if you want to debate. We're doing nature."

John Andrew chuckled. "Any self-respecting nature'll keep its distance. I'll warrant that owl's gone out to the back field where the mice are dancing to crickets." He grabbed a log and edged it onto the fire, pushing it in place with a long, charred stick, sending up a shower of sparks.

"I'm amazed there's no fire ban," said Dawn. "I don't remember a summer so hot. Everything's so dry." Her dad lifted the bucket next to his chair and it sploshed gently.

"Ahh," said Dawn. "Right. Be prepared." She lifted her bottle of beer. "I'd pour this on to save us, but"—she put her head back and finished her beer, then tapped the empty on the old Adirondack arm—"it's empty."

"'Nother?" Byron was beer monitor.

"Nope. I'm going up soon. Big day tomorrow. Undercoat must be dry now, then the main event! Right?"

John Andrew was nodding. He looked, Tammy thought, as close as she'd seen him recently to relaxed. Happy. "Think so," he said, raising his beer in a sort of toast.

"I can't believe it's done, or nearly," Tammy said. "Mom would be so..."

No one rushed to finish that sentence. Eventually John Andrew said, "Yup," and drained his bottle. He looked at Dawn. "You were great with those kids today."

Dawn lifted her chin in thanks.

"So sweet the 4-H kids wanna help with it at the trials," said Tammy.

Byron was scrolling, but asked, "Trials?"

"Byron." Tammy took the phone from his hands and looked in his eyes: "Tractor. Trials. We've been talking about nothing else for, like, ages. Part of the Highland Heart county show. The figure-skating beauty-pageant for tractors." John Andrew barked a laugh at that. "What?" said Tammy. "That's right, isn't it?" She looked at her sister, who nodded, smiling.

"It actually is," Dawn said.

"Thank you. Mom drove that tractor in, like, prehistoric times. Right, Dad? Before you? Can I drive it?" Tammy asked her dad, shooting a look to Dawn. She knew the answer.

"Nope." John Andrew just dipped his head towards Dawn.

Tammy pretend pouted and Byron pulled her closer, tucking her head under his chin as he scanned the sky. "So clear," he said.

"Callin' for rain tomorrow." John Andrew looked up.

"No way. Look at all those stars." Byron adjusted again as Tammy sat up.

"That's nothing. Wait," and she took off around the side of the house.

In a moment the outdoor light went off, and the fire was the only source throwing shadows around the yard. Strange how turning that light out created a sense of hush, thought Tammy, reorganizing herself in the hammock. Even the cicadas seemed to have dialled down the volume. Somewhere towards the dairy a dog was baying. Such a lonely sound, thought Tammy, reaching to stroke Betsy, quiet beside them. A vehicle with a muffler that needed work was approaching the farm and slowing. Not someone coming? She lifted her head. People didn't just turn up around here, not this late. Past eleven now.

John Andrew heard it too, he was sitting up a bit, listening, and Betsy, watching him, sat up too. The car—truck, more likely, Tammy felt sure—accelerated just when she thought it might have turned into their drive, and now, beyond the edge of the back porch past the corner of the house, she could see the tail lights in the distance, heading for the bend. They all watched it go, but no one commented.

Tammy looked back at the sky. "Shooting star!"

All eyes looked where she pointed. The delicate end of a lace tail, just a strand, was fading now—gone. "Mom looked for those."

"Your mom *made* them fall." John Andrew was still looking up, then glanced from one daughter's face to the other's before saying, "Well...*she* said. We'd come out, she'd say, I need a star to wish on, and bam—"

"*Bam?*" Dawn doubted *Bam*.

Byron offered, gently, "Probably *whooshhhh*."

John Andrew studied the sky again. "There'd be one, then two... if she got three, there'd be a prize."

Tammy looked at her dad. Why had she never heard this? "Oh yeah?"

"What?" asked Dawn glancing at her dad, then Tammy, knowing.

John Andrew didn't look at either of them, now. The red-gold fire had changed their father; something played in his eyes that wasn't the light thrown by the flames. Memory. Intimacy. The girls looked away from him and at each other. They understood; were amused; embarrassed; sad.

A piece of wood popped, sending another shower of sparks outside the circle of the fire into the dried grass. John Andrew took a few handfuls of water from the bucket and threw it down, and they heard thunder again, far off. From the direction the tail lights had disappeared.

Dawn

It got late, and later; cool, and cooler. The logs were coals, then embers, and the four of them stopped talking. The barred owl called and four heads went up together to listen, then turned to each other to confirm. The nod of John Andrew's head signalled a complete and kind of perfect night; the hiss and sputter of the dying fire the punctuation as they headed inside. John Andrew locked the back door. Tammy looked back—he never locked the door—then followed Dawn and Byron upstairs.

On the top step, she headed to Byron's room instead of hers, pausing at the doorway when she realized her sister and her dad were watching.

"Getting my, uh, book," she said to her dad.

Dawn grinned. "Bam," she batted to Tammy, and Tammy looked daggers at her. Then, from Byron in his room came, "Woooooosh," as he reached a hand to pull her in and close the door.

Dawn couldn't look at John Andrew then; she turned and went to her room, gently closing her door, too.

Something woke her.

Betsy, she thought. Odd. She never cries to be let out at night. Dawn rolled over, expecting it was a dream: hers, or Betsy dreaming outside on the landing. Dawn closed her eyes again, then—

She felt, rather than saw, the curtains move with a waft of—

She sat up. Betsy was barking now, not dreaming, and not outside her door. Downstairs. And the breeze was—

Smoke.

She was at the window, pulling at the curtains, revealing gold and orange and red light.

She was screaming for her father, for Tammy, for Byron.

She was grabbing a sweater and running, her father on her heels, Tammy and Byron close behind.

"Dad! The shed! The shed! Dad—"

"Dawn, wait! Wait! Tammy, call 911."

Now they were in the kitchen, John Andrew at the back door pulling on the first thing he could grab—his rubber boots—Dawn had already opened the door, struggling to unlock it. "And Jerry. Call Jerry. Keep Betsy inside. Dawn. Stop. Dawn!"

But she was gone, racing across the backyard, past the firepit, past her mother's kitchen garden, towards the burning machine shed, crackling and fizzing and popping and brighter with every second. Dawn couldn't run fast enough.

The tractor. The tractor. The tractor.

She reached for the shed door—the side door, the *man-door* they called it—the tractor the tractor the tractor—and pulled her hand back. Hot, and her father right behind her, pulling her by the waist and Byron behind him, pulling off his—what? Sweater? Why? She reached for the knob again.

"No. No, Dawn. Stop." John Andrew had grabbed Byron's—whatever—and used it to pull open the door. Ugly, dark-grey smoke poured through the man-door, stinking tendrils wrapping around them. The paint, the oil, so much *stuff* in the shed. The tractor. John Andrew held the sweater up to his face, turned, and pushed the others back. Dawn strained against—who? Who, now?—Tammy, holding her tight saying, crying—

"No, no, no you can't, Dawn, let Dad, let Dad." And Dawn watched John Andrew vanish.

How can you see someone vanish? That's nonsense—but he was gone, disappeared into the smoke; heading, she knew, she knew he was, towards the far corner, near the bench, near the window sill where the cup with the key was, where the tractor sat, nearly finished, with its dry nearly dry undercoat nearly nearly dry nearly done nearly ready nearly finished for her father and her mother and her grandfather and all the stories and the words and all the truths and where *where* was her father now? Where was he now when she could hear—starting so so so so so quietly and so far away—a siren? Come fast come fast come fast. Dad! *Dad!*

Jerry ran up behind them and Sandra. Dawn heard Sandra saying Oh my god, Jerry, Oh my god, and Jerry yelling, Tammy, where's the hose? And Tammy handing her, handing Dawn to Byron, like she was, like—then Jerry and Tammy running—Dawn turned to watch them run: two three four five, she was counting now. How far would she count before her father came back came out.

Dad. Dad. Dad. Dad. Dad. Dad. Dad.

Eight. Nine. There was a breath a tiny little pull on her hair, Dawn felt it, thought, maybe it will rain now. Thirteen. Maybe. Dad.

The sirens were louder. Closer. They were coming from two directions. Further away and closer—the closer ones from town, the further from the firehouse in the village down the—how far? How far. Dad. Dad. Dad.

Dad.

Tammy

Tammy ran as fast as she could in the boots she had grabbed—hers, but ancient and too small. Jerry was three times her age and twice as fast. She headed for the outside tap and hose, and he passed her and went straight to it, turning it on, pulling it past their firepit, soaking the ground as he went, getting as close as he could to the shed, but not close. Not close enough. Tammy was running back to where Dawn and Byron stood; she paused by the firepit. It wasn't even steaming. There wasn't a coal remaining from earlier—John Andrew had created a thick black soup before they'd gone in.

The fire truck—the first one, from town—was pulling in. Men jumped out and Jerry ran to help as they pulled the hoses, started connecting and setting themselves. In seconds, it seemed, they were aiming water at the building.

Dad. Dad. Dad. Where are you. Come out. My Dad. My Dad.

She ran to tell them her father was inside.

John Andrew

He couldn't keep holding the sweater to his face, he knew, and he was afraid to put it down, but he had to. God. If there is a God, show me. Show me where the fucking key is.

He'd gone straight into the wall of smoke—thinking, did we do this, did our fire light this fire? So dry so dry did we do this?—feeling his way to the sill, found and picked up the cup. The key that was always, always there, was not. Not there. Now. Where then? Where, God? Where is it, God?

He held his breath, tried to hold his breath. Tried to tuck his head in so his face was against his own body, making a little cavity, a little cave of air that felt less dense, he thought. Less foul. Less hot. Jesus, it was hot. He kept his head down in that cave and ran his hands over the bench. Hot metal but no key. No key. He felt his way to the ground, chin on chest. The little cave of fresh air went with him, a strange little breeze blew around him, keeping the smoke away as he felt the ground, the edge of concrete, the dirt, felt the stones under his knees, the side of the tractor, put his hand in some oil they'd spilt, found a rag he'd left. But no key, no key. Fuck. God, just this, only this. Everything else has been shit can't you leave this thing that has done us—wait. Waitwaitwait.

The light of the fire above and in the corner was shooting from something directly above him, but not fire, just light. Just light thrown by—

The key.

That hung in the ignition of the tractor, dangling, a delicate piece of silver fruit.

Tiny. Perfect. There. He climbed into the seat, breathed in—shit—and coughed and dropped his head back to the cave, called the breeze and it came. It came while he turned the key and the tractor hacked but didn't start. God Jesus fuck! He put his head almost into his lap. He felt like a child; he wanted to stamp and cry and yell. He took a breath and coughed—the cave was getting smaller and tighter and the breeze could no longer fill and refill it. He pulled the choke out, again—count three four five and turn the key. The sound of fire whoosh-roar-whoosh behind him rose; it was a creature waiting to consume him. It won't, he thought. He stood on the tractor, still counting—five six seven—it won't, you won't, he yelled, he roared back into its face, then bent down again to turn the key, sat to push the starter, and—

The window behind him exploded. The glass flew outward, into the night: a screen stopped it from showering him. He'd put that window in backward. In and finished. Who does that? Idiot, Victor said twenty-eight years ago. Screen out, not in. Useless. Hopeless. Stupid. True. True. Now he knew which way a window went. But then? That window only ever opened from outside—big joke—and John Andrew wouldn't change it and give Vic the satisfaction, but now his useless hopeless stupid saved him maybe, but also fed the creature, because the window shattered, bits falling on the other side of the screen into the night whose breath rushed in. But the tractor started and he urged it forward: a charger pawing the earth, testing the air, then racing for freedom.

John Andrew aimed where he thought the doors met, behind the thick drape of smoke, where the board set in its two brackets was its most vulnerable, fragile, and he was right; it splintered, the doors flew open, and John Andrew and the tractor exploded into the night, shot to safety.

Go. Go. Dad. Dad.

Dad, he heard, as if he was under water. He put his head up. He had to have air. Taste it. Sweet. The breeze brought him breath as he drove. Into water. Into air. Into men yelling stop stop stop turn the hoses.

Into Dad. Dad. Dad.

Now with his head down, face dripping, the man-machine centaur convulsed and shuddered. He was panting and, he discovered, weeping, stopped midway between the shed and the house. An ocean of space around him and now a sea of faces lit and unlit by the revolving lights of the emergency vehicles and the flickering fire.

Sounds in strata: topmost, the roar-hiss as water from the huge hoses, held by three men who used each other's backs for purchase, began again and met the fire, and repeated, over and over and over; a babble-chirp-mumble of voices questioning replying consoling explaining; the rustle and thud of heavy fire suits and equipment being moved and the start-stop of pressurized water as it hit the building—wood, glass, and something metal. Different metals, different materials: musical almost. Deep in the mix and far in the distance, an occasional low rumble, the thunder they'd heard earlier that teased, but didn't deliver, rain.

John Andrew felt rather than focused on Tammy and Dawn in the distance—everything was a blur—but he raised a hand to where they were being held behind some tape by a firefighter. He squinted. Couldn't tell who was who, though he knew them all. Now he looked around the yard, his vision clearing, recognizing a face here, a vehicle over there. Jenny had arrived and was with the girls now. Sandra was putting blankets around them. Ethan. Banu had just pulled up. The town was awake and present. His gaze continued its sweep—then bumped to a halt.

Oh no.

Between the kitchen garden and the shed, in a sweet south-facing spot, was the peach tree Miranda had planted years before, when her dad died, sprinkling his ashes round the base. It'd had a full blossom this spring, promising a big yield, but now...the tree was a slender torch. Glowing debris had floated from the shed and dropped into the tinder-dry foliage setting the top alight. Amazing the whole yard wasn't ablaze, he thought calmly. How was he calm? The peach was protected from north winds by a stand of pine; the pines were next to an ancient maple; and the maple dropped its limbs over the house. Jesus, the peach.

Oh.

Under the peach tree stood Miranda.

Her pale hair was loose, glinting with dancing red and gold. She wore the dress he'd chosen for her weeks ago and lifted a hand towards him. Not a wave, just the barest acknowledgement, and she looked upward to the flames. As she did, a stream of water arced over John Andrew's head and he turned towards its source: another set of firefighters, another pumping vehicle, with their attention focused away from the shed, which was, he saw, under control now. Nearly. One side of the building was gone. The side he'd been on, struggling with the tractor. The side with the window.

He turned back, wondering if Miranda was seeing all this—the window finally resolved—but she was gone.

The stream of water had shaken the peach branches where the flames—exotic birds—had settled, evicting them. The peach, the pines, the maple, the house, the yard stood soaked, immunized against the diminishing threat. Hands helped him off the tractor, someone handed him a bottle of water. His legs shook then gave way, and he slid down the hot tractor to the ground, head down again, people kneeling beside him—*John Andrew, John Andrew, drink this, here; this is cool, wipe your face; here, John Andrew*. He sat still—head back now, eyes to the sky, clouded now, no shooting stars but no rain either—hoping for the return of that breeze that had brought him calm and breath.

Byron

There was a gash of light at the world's edge, like lifting an upside-down cup. But it was a half-hearted sunrise, Byron thought. Desultory.

The four of them plus Jerry and Sandra and Jenny remained, the last of a sombre crowd. Wrapped in blankets, everyone clutched the latest mug; he'd lost count of the number of cups of cocoa, tea, and now coffee, they'd consumed in the last four hours. Both fire trucks had just rounded the corner of the house, driving into mist that seemed to have dropped over the fields and roads in the last hour, appearing just before first light.

The mist and smoke, thought Byron, would've been beautiful and mysterious if it hadn't all been so frightening. The steam rising from the heap of black rubble that had been the shed was mixing with mist that Byron had seen on other early mornings: it had always been a new-day, new-world reassurance of morning. Not the filmy toxic fingers of an amorphous monster released when the man-door to the shed had been pulled open. Imagining John Andrew grappling with it alone in the shed made him feel sick.

The time John Andrew was inside had been dreadful—like nothing Byron had ever experienced. They'd been powerless: no options, no agency. They couldn't follow him inside, there was nothing they could provide except...hopes and prayers. He hated that phrase, co-opted now by ineffectual politicians. His mother believed in the power of prayer, though. She had long chats with her creator, believing the conversations made a difference. Her son had long since stopped trying to explain his understanding of the urgency of need or want, how change—success or failure—was due to the strength of manifestation. Maybe what he'd been doing last night was praying, but he thought it was manifesting. Saying it to make it so.

He'd held Tammy's hand and Dawn's, saying over and over about John Andrew, he's okay, he's okay, he'll come out, he'll come out soon. And he talked to Miranda. Byron suspected they'd all talked to Miranda last night, called her to be with them and with John Andrew. The night had been full of chaos and then other-worldly calm. The peculiar quiet that fell over that big group of people when John Andrew burst out of the building on the tractor, then sat there as if the fire had welded him to it. When he finally did get off and collapse, it felt as though the yard, the shed, the whole property was a boiling pot, pushing a lid up and off. Now the lid was gone and the boil subsiding. The fire had crescendoed to its climax, then finally begun to diminish, the crowd calming too. Everything became practical, careful, rational.

Now, hours later, John Andrew seemed okay. Subdued. He'd apologized to Byron about losing his sweater. Byron watched him—standing with an arm around each girl, Dawn and Tammy almost asleep against him—talking to Jenny. Byron heard her say she was leaving now, and they should all go to bed; she'd be back later to take stock, to call her if they needed anything. Sandra and Jerry nodded. Jerry. What a champ.

Byron had never seen someone Jerry's age run the way Jerry had run last night: to get the hose, to meet the trucks, to John Andrew on the ground. Then dragging a bucket wherever he thought a hose might not reach, foot by foot, scouring for sparks, eyes to the sky for fliers. He was everywhere, doing everything. Byron saw how he watched John Andrew now, with love and sympathy and concern and respect, and Byron thought, give me one friend, one neighbour like Jerry and I'll be satisfied with my life.

Tammy came and took his hand. "Jenny's going. We should go in. This has been—" She was too tired to finish.

He nodded, then shook his head. He didn't know which was what now. "Yeah. What people, though."

She nodded, said, "I have to go to bed," and turned to the house. The door slammed behind her. Byron waited for Dawn to follow, but she and John Andrew were dark statues draped in blankets, focused on the tractor that stood where it had landed. The new undercoat had blistered and was mottled, but as the sun rose, everything in the yard—the steaming remains of the shed, the relics saved, variously leaning or sprawling—was touched with pink.

Byron swung a last look over the remnants of the night's havoc, and the tractor, a silhouette against the rosy-tinged sky, looked unblemished.

Dawn & John Andrew

The old clock was chiming ten as Dawn came down the stairs and into the empty kitchen. No one else seemed to be up, though the back door was open. Had they left it open last night? She remembered how when they'd been rushing to get out to the shed, the back door had been locked. They never locked the door, and yet... Those thoughts were curtailed by the still steaming French press. They were up.

Through the kitchen window, just on the edge of the frame, she saw Tammy and Byron standing, mugs in hand, looking to where the shed had been, and to where Dawn knew the tractor stood. Betsy was with them. Poor Bets. The hero of the hour, kept inside all night, going crazy probably. All those people, though. Dawn poured herself a coffee, added milk. What is this? she thought as she stirred, what do I feel?

More loss. Their goal, and everything it had come to represent, impossible now. What do I feel? Too much and nothing, both. She went to look for the others.

The pink promise of early morning had disappeared. The day was heavy, the air still thick with the scent of fire. It wasn't raining, but it wanted to: a sneeze that wouldn't come, a tickle in the throat. The tension was an ache.

Her dad was up too. Four hours of sleep, maybe. But here he was, moving around the tractor—itemizing the damage, Dawn knew. *Injuries,* she had thought first, not damage: the tractor as a living being. And that made her think about the cattle. At one point last night, she'd heard cows crying and she didn't know who'd gone to check on them, or to milk them this morning. Someone must have. Someone from that huge crowd—how had they all known to come? Why were they all awake to hear the sirens?—must have asked Jerry or Sandra and they'd organized it, because she knew her father hadn't.

He'd gone so slowly up the stairs ahead of her last night Dawn had been afraid he wouldn't get to the top. Everyone was exhausted, but John Andrew spun through so many emotions, or rather, states, last night. He'd been fearless. Efficient. Worried. Intent. Distraught. Angry. She'd seen all that *before* he went into the shed. How had he stayed in there so long? And when he blew out—flew out, exploded out—in the minutes after that, and even after the shed collapsed, he wasn't adrenalized or wired or triumphant or whatever, she thought. He was...it was like he was trying to hide on the tractor, in full view. Head tucked down.

Now he stood on the opposite side of the tractor, lifted his head, and gave her a little nod. Byron was beside him and across the yard, Tammy was poking at the edges of the still steaming black mess with a stick.

Dawn came around to look at what her dad and Byron were focused on: a long, straight scrape down the side of the tractor, like a blade had been dragged along it. As Byron pulled his cell to take pictures of the metallic scar, Tammy started yelling, running towards them.

"Hey! Hey, look, look!" She was holding something on the end of her stick as she ran, dropping it then picking it up again just before she reached them. "Look."

They all focused on what was glinting in her hand.

"Jesus," breathed Dawn.

"What?" asked John Andrew

"Dick," Byron spat.

"What is it?!" John Andrew looked from one to the other, frustrated.

Tammy lifted a swinging silver chain to eye level: it scattered droplets of water as it spun and shone in the sunlight.

"It's Marty's." She wasn't even accusing him; she knew.

John Andrew stared at the dangling chain, feeling himself once again under the tractor, unable to breathe, looking up at the dangling key, knowing he hadn't left it in the ignition. Dawn hadn't. He called up the moment—they all did—of the truck near their driveway so late last night. He took the chain from Tammy, pulled his keys from his pocket, and walked towards his truck.

"Byron, go with him," Tammy called, taking Dawn's hand and pulling her towards the house. "Have you got your phone?" Byron waved his cell in the air at her. "I'll get my keys," she told Dawn, who shook her sister off to turn and watch the truck tear down the drive, before asking, "Where is he going, Tammy?"

Tammy squinted after her dad and Byron. "We'll find out."

Dawn

Tammy was hard on their dad's bumper as he turned the last corner, pulling up opposite the machine shop, near the café. They watched him and Byron get out of the truck and have a conversation across the hood.

Tammy opened the car door and turned to Dawn. "Come on."

Dawn sat, unmoving. She felt sick, watching her father and imagining the confrontation between him and Marty, him and Angus. But John Andrew didn't go towards the shop. Instead, he strode past the post office and up the steps to the police station. Now Dawn did get out of the car.

"Dad. Wait." She ran after him. "What are you doing?"

He slowed only slightly. "Talking to Fuzzy."

Dawn's heart was thumping like she'd run a mile. She couldn't catch her breath. "You can't. Please. Don't. It'll make it worse." Tammy arrived beside her dad, and Byron too. She felt the three of them—a wall of solidarity and righteous anger—ranged against her.

"Dawn, it's a hate crime." Tammy spoke quietly, as if trying to contain not her own anger but Dawn's fear.

"It won't matter what we call it if we can't prove it." They didn't know, they didn't understand at all. There wasn't a chance in hell that anyone would call what had happened last night by any name that faulted Marty and favoured Dawn. Even a friend like Fuzzy; he hadn't been there. He hadn't found that chain. They couldn't even prove that the chain had been where they'd found it. There were a dozen reasons why Marty wouldn't be blamed for this.

"Dawn, we can't *not* say what we found. We can't *not* report the damage, the mess. We didn't pluck this out of the air." John Andrew was speaking slowly, carefully. "Our suspicions aren't from nowhere. They have to be heard. Even if...maybe even a suspicion can change how folks see things. And it's time, isn't it? Time Marty stopped getting a free pass? We heard that truck, Dawn." John Andrew pointed at the navy blue pickup he'd seen days before on his way to the dairy. The truck they'd all heard last night. Even from here they could see the muffler, low slung, in need of repair.

"Dawn," said Byron. "He's not just an asshole now. He's a dangerous asshole."

Dawn didn't move as her dad turned to pull open the door to the police station.

Tammy stood beside her, torn.

Fuzzy appeared at the door. "John Andrew, heard about last night. So sorry. Everyone okay?" John Andrew shot a look back to Dawn, paused, then took a step inside, saying, "Not exactly. Got a minute?"

Byron followed him. Dawn turned to Tammy. "Let's just go. Please?"

Thunder cracked and Dawn ran for the car. Finally, the rain they'd wanted arrived, with the sound of a colossal, cosmic tree splitting in two. Something that had promised shelter, breaking up around her.

Tammy

Tammy didn't know what to do now, with her sister sobbing in the seat beside her. Had she seen Dawn cry? Recently? Ever? There was so much crying lately she wasn't completely sure who'd been doing it all. She couldn't stay there in front of the police station near the machine shop—someone would see. Marty would look out the window or go for a coffee and glance across the street and clock them in front of the cop shop and...anyway. Something bad would happen if they stayed here, so they were going. She put the car in gear.

Dawn looked up. "Where are we going?"

"Where do you want to go?" Tammy was aiming down the main street, away from home, towards the river and the landing, and then onto the Cape Road.

"I don't care. Not home."

"Okay." Tammy just kept driving. The rain was heavy now. "Raining stair rods," she remembered from somewhere. Mom, probably. It sounded like something Grandad Vic would have said. What a weird expression. She shook her head, watched the water hurtling down as they passed the old convent. Oh. She got it. Long, straight rods of water, creating a wall, like banisters. She didn't relish heading towards Cape George in this. She crept along—past the old chocolate shop, past the landing, past Cemetery Road, but after the turn to MacDonald Beach, a tap above them was turned full-on and she had to stop because now she couldn't see much at all. She pulled over, easing towards a gravel road she knew was just ahead.

This road: she used to come here in high school for the—what were they called?—oh god, the submarine races. Every guy she'd ever dated had said let's go to the beach and watch the submarine races. Yeah, right. In the strait. Or maybe just park and neck.

She sat forward in the driver's seat, squinting through the downpour, and crept to the top, stopping near a large stand of sheltering fir trees. Any other day they'd see the harbour laid out in front of them, dotted with tiny islands. She turned the car off, relieved. Not a cliffside, thank heavens, thinking of her conversation with Byron earlier this week. It seemed like months ago. A lifetime. She looked at her sister, who'd stopped ugly-crying.

They sat in silence, staring straight ahead into the monsoon-like deluge, with no hint of the landscape around them. They were in a box in water. Loud water, as if the clouds above were intent on producing every drop they'd withheld for weeks.

Minutes passed. Minutes are months in rain like that.

Tammy wondered what had happened at the police station. She wished she'd been there; was glad she wasn't. She knew Byron and John Andrew were absolutely the right people to start this—whatever *this* would be. Not because they were men, but because neither of them ever reached for a fight—despite Byron's uncharacteristic response to Marty in the pub. Tammy remembered her mom saying her dad liked the quiet life. She'd thought it a criticism at the time, though she couldn't remember the context. But there was nothing wrong with wanting the quiet life, she thought, because if you valued it, you understood when it was threatened, or your people were threatened. You knew what was at stake and you would fight for it. She hoped her dad was fighting for the right thing. Because they all knew it wasn't the shed. Or even the tractor.

She studied her sister. "Are you okay?"

"I wish it had rained last night." Dawn rubbed her face hard, pushing the heels of her hands into her eyes like she had when she was tiny.

Tammy gently pulled the closest hand from Dawn's eye. "He'd have done something else." She held Dawn's hand with both of hers and thought about Marty, what she knew about him, what she'd discovered on the beach, and she wondered if Dawn knew, if she should tell her. No, Tammy decided. She didn't know why she thought it would make it worse for Dawn to hear out loud what she suspected Dawn already knew, but the idea of someone who might really have the same—

Tammy couldn't connect her thoughts. She was struggling towards understanding recent events as some kind of betrayal by Marty, but couldn't put the pieces together because, after all, Marty didn't owe them anything. You just expected that at a basic level, people were human, that they understood they were surrounded by other humans. But some—too many—seemed not to understand their own humanity and the connections it should create. Every day's news proved that.

Should.

Should create, should feel, should understand.

Should behave...the way I want you to.

Byron was right. It was a dangerous word, loaded with unreasonable expectations. She felt exhausted. She wished that everything could be the way it once was.

That her mother was fine and waiting at home.

That her younger sister was her little brother getting ready to finish high school and launch himself on a fine, gay life. A gay life would be great, she thought. Not so hard as this. Then yelled at herself: what the fuck do you know?

She wished that Betsy was still a puppy. God, if only time could go backwards.

She said, "Dawn, do you ever wish—don't get mad—that things—"

Dawn cut in calmly, firmly: "I can't go back to something I wasn't."

The rain continued.

"Sometimes there's shit," said Dawn. "Mostly there isn't. I try to focus on the mostly."

They looked out, wondering if the music of the rain was changing.

"Tam, do you know what's going on with Dad?"

Tammy turned. "What are you talking about? Like, everything. Come on. *Everything's* going on with Dad. Mom. The fire. You." She hadn't meant that all to come out so hot. Bad choice, saying *you* like that. Adding Dawn to death and destruction. She started again. "Not *you*, not like that, but, you know, it's been...a journey. And Mom: it's hard because it *is* everything. Mom did everything. She managed everything, organized everything. Dad got up and did what Mom expected...every day."

"That makes him sound pathetic," Dawn said. "He's not pathetic."

"Isn't he? He's not in this world. He can't use the internet. Sorry, *The Google*. He's never done the bills, he left Mom to figure them out, and now there's a fucking mess. You can see it, can't you? The piles of bills on his desk. Who's gonna fix that, Dawn? Are you? I can't. He can't. What if he loses the farm? What's that if it's not pathetic?" and Tammy started to bawl.

"You don't mean that. He won't lose the farm, Tammy. He's not an idiot, he can learn stuff. He just hasn't had to yet. It's not like he sat around being...fed grapes or something. Come on. He didn't force Mom to manage things, the money stuff, they agreed on how it would work, right at the beginning, way before us. Grandpa Vic insisted she look after that stuff early on and she was good at it—she told us that enough times when she was trying to get us to do our math. It must have been true. And Dad was great at other stuff. Managing the dairy. Dealing with animals. All the people he's helped. Delivering calves all over the county. He could have been a vet probably. People call him for any kind of help and he always goes. He's kept the farm going. He'll keep it going. He'll figure it out. Why are you suddenly all mad at him?"

All this truth, this knowledge, this defense of the father she loved so much, made Tammy put her head back against the seat, tears streaming. "I'm just...I'm so tired. Tired of being sad. Of crying. I've never cried so much in my life. I'm tired of being mad. At her. At you. At him." She hiccupped. "And scared. I'm tired of being scared."

Now Dawn turned fully towards Tammy, intent. "What are you scared of?"

Tammy drew a long breath, let it go in a shuddering exhale. She was ashamed of this. "Of getting it. I check myself every day. It feels so shitty to miss her so much, and still just be thinking of myself. It just proves...what an asshole I am."

"Tam—"

"You said it. I am."

"You're not, Tammy. It makes sense you're scared. It would be weird if you weren't."

"Are you?" Long pause. "Can you get it?"

Dawn considered, then, "I guess."

Tammy knew this was dangerous territory but still stepped in. "Are yours...real?"

"Tammy! Jesus!" Dawn exploded, stared into the rain, and Tammy felt her counting, the way their mother had, to contain her anger. She answered, calmer, "Yes."

Tammy should have left it. But she didn't. "So then you *could,* I guess. Because...it's genetic, right? And hormonal, so now for you, with hormones—"

"Wow." Dawn was mouth-breathing. Never a good sign. And flushed with—what exactly, Tammy couldn't tell, but it wasn't a happy, rosy glow.

"You are..." Dawn turned back. "You're glad. That's so...wow. You're glad that we could *both* get it."

Tammy realized how absolutely correct her sister was. Dawn had always had the ability to read Tammy's finest print, her tiniest footnotes, and she'd done it now. She'd hated it when they were young, but she loved it, loved Dawn for it, now.

"I am." She realized she could see the field around them now, the edge of the harbour: the rain was beginning to abate. She smiled. "I'm fucking warped."

John Andrew

The girls pulled up in front of the café where John Andrew and Byron sat in the front window. They watched the two of them get out: Tammy coming around the car to Dawn and hugging her until Dawn looked like a too-loved puppy in the arms of a toddler. Released at last, she pulled the café door open, Tammy on her heels.

"Did ya go to Cape Breton and back? We've been here ages." John Andrew was only half kidding. The girls had been gone nearly two hours. He and Byron had had coffee, then lunch, and were just embarking on more coffee and a second dessert—cookies just out of the oven, delivered by Ethan. On the house. John Andrew wondered how Ethan made any money—he was always giving stuff away.

"Got stuck in the rain, and then actually stuck. Drove the car up to that spot above MacDonald Beach and it was sticky getting out. Sorry. Doesn't look like it's been a massive hardship though?" She prodded Byron in the side. "Tell."

Byron looked across to John Andrew. "Your dad'll say. Oh. Look."

Dawn and Tammy turned to John Andrew, who'd suddenly focused outside. They all went silent watching Fuzzy cross towards them and disappear into the machine shop.

"He wasn't sure they could do much." John Andrew turned from the window to all of them around the table, which included Ethan now, "but he said he'd feel Marty out. See if he was wearing or had anything like what you found, Tam. I didn't know he meant *now.* And where he was last night, with who—anyway, I don't know what the cops really do. What they chose to follow up on is a mystery to me."

Banu had been listening from behind the counter, watching Dawn, their gaze both helpless and vibrating with connection. Now they brought coffee and cookies for Tammy and Dawn. Setting them down, they cocked their head towards the street and said, "Must be something they can do."

Fuzzy was back outside with Angus and Marty. Marty was remonstrating with his dad, his voice raised, Fuzzy speaking quietly. Then Angus's voice above the other two.

"Off you go," Angus Stewart said to his son, turning back into his shop. Marty looked after him, open-mouthed. A sad little scene, John Andrew thought: Marty watching his father leaving him to deal with whatever happened next, on his own. John Andrew couldn't stand Marty, but still felt a tug of something like sympathy for the young person whose father didn't for a moment consider protesting his son's innocence. Fuzzy put his hand on Marty's shoulder and propelled him across the road and into the station as the door to the shop swung shut, and John Andrew didn't feel satisfaction or triumph.

Ethan broke into his musing with, "We'll see if that sticks."

John Andrew shook his head. "I reckon he's just taking him over to scare him. Then he'll leave his dad to deal with him. Poor bastard."

"Poor bastard Angus?" Tammy was indignant. "Or poor bastard Marty? Either way—"

"Either way," said John Andrew, "big family"—he sipped his coffee, still looking to the station door that had just closed, and shook his head—"small town."

He thought he knew what he felt now, and it wasn't relief.

When they got back to the house, the rain had truly stopped. Tammy bolted upstairs, claiming the bathroom for a hot bath. John Andrew went inside, leaving Dawn and Byron in the yard surveying the shed, the mess of tire tracks in the yard, the trampled garden, and the tractor.

He sat at the desk, hung his hat on the back of his chair, and considered: the desk was in order now, the pile of invoices on one side, the condolence cards on the other. He shoved the first aside with contempt, then carefully took the second pile and placed them—just for now—in a drawer. He put a sticky note on the drawer: *RESPOND*.

There. Clean desk. He picked up the phone and dialled.

"James! John Andrew here—oh yeah? Yeah—I'm not surprised, there was a crowd here last night, helping, so I was pretty sure the word would—yeah. Thanks. So, I know you'll have to come out—or, right. Someone. Adjuster. That's not you, then? Anyway, just to get the ball rolling...couple questions? Great. I, uh, haven't got the policy in front of me... Do you have quick access? Great. 'Course I'll wait."

John Andrew picked up a photograph that had been in the same place for probably twenty years without being moved. He studied it now: Miranda with Dawn in her arms. John Andrew beside her, Tammy on his knee, and behind, Victor, one hand on Miranda's shoulder and the other on John Andrew's. He thought he remembered that day. Dawn couldn't have been more than two or three weeks old and Jerry's brother and his wife had come to wet the baby's head, celebrate the birth of John Andrew's son and heir. Confirmation for Vic that the farm would go on, handed to another generation. Sandra brought a casserole, Jerry's brother took pictures, and Jerry's gift for Dawn was this photo that Vic had presided over, thrilled with the baby boy. Time's a shit-stirrer, thought John Andrew, then heard James's return.

"John Andrew? Couple things. So, all the outbuildings are listed separately."

John Andrew felt his shoulders relax as James talked through, building by building, finally landing at the machine shed.

"So," James was at the end now, "contents there? Significant losses?"

John Andrew paused. The shed's contents and their value hadn't occurred to him. Insurance barely had. He looked Vic in the eye. He felt the old man nudging him.

"Yeah. Well, the shed of course. And one thing of value—yeah. Badly damaged, but"—he stared back at Vic and Miranda, both smiling now, Miranda ruffling his hair with her sweet hand—"repairable."

He put the phone down, went to the window, and pulled it up. What was that word? One of Miranda's favourites: she loved the word because she loved the smell, the world after rain. *Petrichor*, he remembered. Petrichor flooding into his office now, the smell of relief—the long summer drought broken—but tinged with smoke.

Present joy, mortality riding its back.

Thank you, James, he thought. And also, as he picked up his hat from the back of his chair, present joy, riding the back of...malice. Thank you, Marty.

John Andrew opened the back door to voices that were raised. Well, Dawn's voice was raised and Byron was trying to contain whatever was going on. They were sitting on the old picnic table, facing the tractor. He paused and heard:

"Dawn. We're so close. You can't just—"

"There's no *just* here, Byron. I *can* choose to stop now. We've *been* stopped. I mean, I don't even know how we'd go on from here—and knowing when to stop is just as—"

"Aha," Byron shouted. "*Just!* You see? He's *just* one person, Dawn. We have to—"

"Oh my god, Byron. You don't get it. And you know what? You're not equipped to comment on this tractor. You don't know anything about... Fuck it. I'm not going to talk about it. Anything I do will be fucked by that jerk and his pals."

John Andrew stepped outside. Dawn flew from the picnic table, past her dad and into the house, slamming the door behind her. He watched her go, then turned back when Byron sighed, "That's me told."

John Andrew walked slowly round the tractor. Water dripped from the telephone line, to land inside his collar and run down the back of his neck. He looked up to see the grey slate of the sky had splintered, slivers of blue now, with shafts of sunlight slicing through here and there. The long, malign scrape on the tractor's haunch caught and bounced a slim beam of light; the tires were a sticky melted mess; the grey undercoat was a bubbled black sheath. But.

"Take no notice," said John Andrew. "She needs a plan. I think I've got one."

Tammy

After a bath to get the chill of the summer storm off her, Tammy thought that relative peace was, at least for now, restored. It lasted long enough for her to get dressed, dry her hair, and go into her mom's closet and start the awful process of deciding what to put in bags for the charity shop and what to keep.

It wasn't so much the *what* that was painful, but the *why*. Everything she touched was attached to a memory, and she wanted each one—but in this profusion? After the events of the last twenty-four hours, inflicting this task on herself seemed perverse: a heaping on heaps. But she needed to distract herself from an even worse thought (though a day ago she wouldn't have thought there was one): the idea that someone who'd known her sister for Dawn's whole life not only wished her harm but would act on it.

She wondered if Marty was chastened now. He'd looked younger, frightened, when he stood on the sidewalk with his dad. But when he'd glanced back to their window as he and Fuzzy crossed the street, he'd still looked like Marty. Lizard-Eyes, Ethan called him. Marty in the pub. Marty on the beach. She realized, with a sudden, sickening clarity, that her sister's life might always be like this. Someone somewhere would want to hurt her, or hate her, or determine where she could live, what job she could have, who she could love, because she was herself.

Tammy dropped her head. She felt her heart beating. It grew louder and louder. She stood up and—it had to be all right—sat down again.

She'd steeled herself to do this and she'd chosen to start with what felt the easiest to discard, a pile of Miranda's scarves, in the quiet of the afternoon. Her racing heart, the slam of the back door, and the rush of feet up the stairs, confirmed that the nanosecond of tranquility she'd had in the bath was just that, and it was over.

Dawn's bedroom door slammed. With scarves draped over her arm, Tammy went onto the landing, listened for a moment, then went down the hall.

"Dawn?" Tammy knocked, then carefully opened the door to her sister's room.

Dawn had pulled her little suitcase out: it sat with its mouth wide open, waiting to be filled. And now Dawn was grabbing and throwing small piles of clothing—she hadn't brought much—from the drawers onto the bed.

"What are you doing?" Tammy watched in dismay. "You can't leave, Dawn. Not now."

Dawn didn't answer, just kept taking things from the dresser and bedside table. Now her T-shirts were going in; now the skirt and top she'd worn to the funeral. Her sneakers. Socks.

"Dawn. Dawn. Stop. Please."

Dawn turned to Tammy about to say—what, Tammy had no idea, because instead of speaking, Dawn reached for a silky, multicoloured scarf on Tammy's arm. She took it with such care, opening the rainbow to its full length, then crumpling it with both hands against her face like she was trying to inhale it. She sank to her bed in the midst of all her things.

"Dawn?" Tammy was being so careful, so tender.

"I gave her this."

Tammy nodded. Of course. "Everything smells of her. That peony soap."

Dawn nodded; otherwise, she was still.

"Please don't go." Tammy didn't reach for her, didn't cry. "He hasn't said it yet."

Her sister looked at her, looked down at the scarf in her hands. From downstairs they heard Byron laugh, and then John Andrew. Such a strange sound after this peculiar, sad, angry day.

"Okay," said Dawn.

Dawn & Tammy

When Dawn and Tammy went downstairs a bit later, they found an atmosphere transformed. Both John Andrew and Byron were on their phones in John Andrew's office—John Andrew at his desk, Byron pacing with his cell. The sisters looked at each other and waited. There seemed to be a lot of listening by each of the men, and questions that couldn't be tied to the cloud of *bleak* that lay over the house earlier in the day.

Byron finished his call with, "Great! Eight A.M. is perfect! Thanks—bye!" He did a little happy dance, slipping his cell into his back pocket. "Soooo hungry. Anyone else?"

Now John Andrew was hanging up, a more protracted goodbye. "Anything else I should— Great. Thanks, Jock. See ya then." And he put the receiver down. "I'm starving."

"I don't get it," said Tammy. "You guys had lunch, dessert, dessert after dessert, and then more dessert, less than two hours ago. How can you possibly be starving?"

"Burning calories with this." Byron tapped his head before hugging Tammy. "What do we want?"

"Not a casserole," said John Andrew.

"Pizza? Night out?" Byron was reaching for his coat and John Andrew nodded, picking up his hat. "Perfect." John Andrew was on Byron's heels, following him out the door.

Tammy looked at Dawn, shrugged, and followed Byron.

Dawn stood. What the hell was going on? Where was all this... *delight* coming from? She didn't feel delighted. What the actual fuck had happened over the last couple of hours to—

"What are you doing?" Byron had come back in.

"What are *you* doing?" Dawn countered.

"Going for pizza. With Team MacInnes. Come on." He grabbed her hand. She felt like she was being pulled onto a speeding train, destination unknown, but she let herself be dragged through the door and into the slightly frenetic, definitely weird energy coming off Byron and her dad.

The pizza place was always packed. It didn't matter which night, or what time. It was the after-school haunt, then the young-family-early-evening destination, the middle-aged not-making-dinner-tonight eatery, the late-night-snack-after-a-beer-or-six haunt. Tonight, they were smack in between young families and middle-aged, and the place was teeming: a veritable orchestra of kids crying, fighting, and laughing, and adults remonstrating or coaxing, all conducted by Sandra, who seemed in her element managing the other two run-off-their-feet servers.

"Exactly what you need! A quiet, relaxing break." Delivered with her lopsided smile, Sandra set down menus and four beers. "Beer's on for half," said with such warmth that Dawn finally forgave Sandra fully—she'd been well on her way and half-priced beer cemented it—for their very first interaction. John Andrew gave Sandra a large, wide smile. He was, Dawn thought, positively beaming. How could this day, on so little sleep, produce this genial, easy man who said things like—

"Fire sale on beer?" John Andrew quipped. Dawn had never heard her father quip. Tammy was examining her dad like he was a specimen, but Sandra patted Dawn on the shoulder, as if her father had lost his mind and she should be gentle with him—which, Dawn thought, might be the case—then left with their order.

"Okay," said Dawn, "are either of you two going to spill?"

Byron and John Andrew simply raised eyebrows at each other.

Tammy poked Byron, looking at Dawn. "He can't keep a secret. He'll tell eventually. I'll pinch him."

Dawn got up. "I can't stand seeing cis guys cry. I'm going to the bathroom." They laughed; she dodged a server, heard her dad say, "What's cis?" and smiled, heading to the back of the restaurant. On her way she passed a booth, and the occupants made her stomach plummet.

Marty, his sister, and her husband sat, heads close together, until Dawn passed. Then Marty and Ali turned—Dawn felt it—to watch her.

She passed a serving station before the hallway leading to the washrooms: an ancient blue fella with a top hat for *GENTS*, and farther down the hall an hourglass-shaped pink silhouette for *LADIES*. Traffic was sparse here, the din of the main room muffled. The back of Dawn's neck prickled: footsteps—heavy and fast—advanced behind her. As she reached for the door to the Ladies', the footsteps dodged in front of her, as fast as Marty's bulk would allow.

"Hey," the oily, amiable voice. Unctuous and polite. "Sorry, but you can't go in there." Marty managed to get an arm each side of Dawn, trapping her against the wall opposite the door, speaking quietly, sweetly. Dawn knew this moment, the split second when she could still scream or kick or fight, and she ought, she knew she ought, to be able to do any of those. One of those. But she couldn't. She couldn't before, other times when shit happened, and she couldn't now.

Her breath didn't stop but she was afraid it would: the distant noise of the restaurant was an underwater roar and she was swimming up now swimming rising rising up to the top, watching from above the water now, listening to a scratchy ancient recording submerged and playing on the wrong speed saying what she thought the voice was saying but she wasn't sure she could tell because now a hand pink hand strong fat pink hand like the one next to her face pink with nails like hers bit to the quick, bit to bleeding, the other pink hand was under her skirt—

"You can't go in there you don't have"—grabbing

squeeze squeeeeeeeeeze squeeze, shitogodogodshit and in her face

"the right junk"

holding her crotch squeezing the oily voice said

"You can't go in there you don't have—"

god it hurt it hurt she turned her face up towards herself floating, bumping on the ceiling where she didn't feel pain she just watched how her face her eyes were nearly closed her mouth was pinched she couldn't speak she couldn't he said in her ear— "you can't go in there you don't have the right JUNK"

squeeze squeeeeeeeeze squeeze then closer in her ear:

"Or. Do. You?" he whispered, treacle.

Mom. Mom. MommyMomMom was she yelling jesus JESUS was she making any sound from her pinched mouth? Can you hear me, Mommmommy—

"HEY! STOP! Stop that! Leave her." Tammy arriving. Ali behind her. No one else. The restaurant still so noisy, so crowded, safe.

Marty let go. But in her ear, "sexysexysexy," he said. "Next time it'll be the house."

He swung around, his sister hissing as she passed Tammy, grabbing Marty and pulling him away. "You asshole"—to Marty? To Tammy? To Dawn?—"Why the fuck couldn't you just stay in your own fucking weirdo...fucking gay world. Fuck off back."

To Dawn.

Then they were gone and only Tammy was there. Tammy led Dawn into the bathroom. Dawn slid down the wall, in a corner, making herself smallsmallsmall. Jesusmothermummymummy.

"Shh, Dawn. Oh Dawn, did he hurt you? Oh Dawn...oh Dawn." Tammy held her sister—rocking, rocking. They stayed there and stayed there. Women came in and out of the bathroom, looked, looked away. Drama in the bathroom. Small-town life.

"Don't tell Dad."

"Dawn, we can't—are you okay? Are you hurt? Did he hurt you?"

"Don't tell Dad."

"Dawn, how can we not? What are we doing? You can't go back out and—eat a pizza. What do we...how do we get through tonight? Dawn, we have to go to the police. Please."

"No."

"Dawn."

Silence now. Ragged breathing.

"Call Jill." Dawn handed her phone to Tammy.

Tammy stared at her. "What can Jill do?"

"Come get me. Take me home."

“Dawn.” Tammy wanted to cry. “I’ll take you home. Let me take you. I’m your sister. We’re home—this is home.”

Outside the bathroom Tammy heard, softly: “Tam? Tammy? Y’okay?” Byron.

She got up and went to the door. “Hey. Dawn’s”—she looked to her sister, hidden from view—“feeling shitty. It’s been a day. I think it’s just all been...” She paused again. Everything in her screamed for her to run to Byron, to her dad, they’d sort it, they’d—but this wasn’t The Watering Hole. It wasn’t the beach. It wasn’t even the blackened heap of cruel mess that had once been the shed. This time he’d touched *her*. His filthy hands—the thought made Tammy sick. “It’s been too much.”

Byron watched her, deciphering as she continued. “She needs to go home. If you grab my keys, I’ll take her—we’ll go out the back—you guys finish and I’ll just get her home, to bed. She doesn’t need to, you know, come through there—okay? Okay?” She looked from Dawn to Byron to Dawn. A long pause. Laughter in the restaurant, a hoot, a cheer from some group. Dawn gave the barest drop of her head. Down. Up. Tammy looked to Byron. He nodded. This wouldn’t be understood now. It couldn’t. Though, she thought, maybe he did understand, so Tammy just kept moving her head up and down, thinking as loud as she could, so he could hear her: Just the keys, the keys, not Dad. He can’t see her.

Byron nodded, one hand on the wall, the other clenching, unclenching—then he turned towards the restaurant. Don’t say anything, don’t do anything, Tammy sent to his back receding now. Byron, she thought, just the keys.

Tammy

Tammy got up off the bed. If she stayed any longer she'd be asleep, and she couldn't leave the next conversation till morning. It was after one-thirty now, about the time they'd discovered the fire the night before. How could so many things happen in one day? The fire. Marty's chain. The police station. The crazy rain. Marty's—what was it? Arrest? Apparently not. What the fuck *was* it? And then the restaurant. Too much.

Dawn was asleep. They'd talked, eventually. But first they'd silently moved Dawn's suitcase from where they'd left it earlier. Today. Tammy shook her head again. It had still been perched on the edge of the bed with all the stuff transferred from dresser to bed and now to floor. Dawn had crawled, still dressed, under the covers and called Jill—who was out. Tammy loved Jill after one meeting, but she was beyond glad that Jill hadn't answered her phone. She knew how important her sustaining friendship was to Dawn, but Tammy needed this: to be here for Dawn now, to make up for all the times she hadn't been.

Communication was monosyllabic. Starts and stops. The conversation from the car—*sometimes there's shit*—rang in Tammy's mind. Eventually, Dawn started to talk: she'd expected stuff here, at home, but not like this. These attacks weren't generalized transphobia, they were personal. These were focused, planned, dripping with vitriol and hate. What had she done to him? She talked about the way the rest of the town had reached out: from Aunt Leny and other family at the ultimately triumphant wake to Ethan and Banu; the 4-H'ers and that little person, Kyle; Jerry and Andy and even, finally, Sandra. Dawn said she'd sort of stopped imagining this stuff happening, even after the pub, because things seemed to get easier and kinder, and she'd felt safer and...

She stopped, was silent, then started again. She felt that sometimes people take—what she was going to say would sound strange, Dawn said, though Tammy got it when she said it—a kind of *ownership* over her. *Our* trans person. *We* get her. *We* welcome her. Look at us, *getting it*. So maybe, Dawn said, she'd let her guard down when her biggest fear began to abate.

"Which fear?" Tammy asked.

"You," said Dawn. "Dad. Losing you, leaving you, forever."

After that, Dawn got tired beyond sense—maybe a good time, Tammy thought, to broach this. With a lot of pausing. Space for Dawn to interrupt.

"If you feel that...that relief in...me, then we need, you and me, to tell Dad, Dawn. Not to—no police, but—"

Dawn had been adamant, almost hysterical, when Tammy tried again to get her to involve the police. Dawn knew from every story she wouldn't tell—her own and others'—that what Marty represented was a tiny frozen tip of a massive global iceberg. Death sentences in Arab states and African countries. Murders in Uganda. In Kenya. Jill had wept. In the US. Sports team and bathroom bullshit from the States—ironic and awful. Hundreds of new anti-trans bills there in one year—and looking worse every day. Shootings in a queer bar in Colorado. A trans woman left for dead in a Toronto ravine. So close to Tammy's home. Too close, she thought. *Toronto the Good*, dear, gentle Canadian friends, she thought.

The iceberg's bulky body of shame with its cruel pink snout—so similar to Marty's—above the waterline in this small town, almost unknown, almost invisible on the map. But how many invisible towns, Dawn asked, had people like her—visible and invisible—just trying to BE.

That, said Tammy, was why they had to tell their dad. He might not be able to say he loved them, but he did, fiercely. He wouldn't go to the police if they told him not to, but he had to know what had happened, Tammy repeated. He might want to chuck Marty off a bridge, but he wouldn't. Their father was a master of holding himself tight, she thought. But he would do something, said Tammy, something that would matter and be the right thing. If they told him, she said. If they trusted him.

"He's earned it, Dawn. He saved what matters to you—to you both—because he loves you and because you matter, and now," said Tammy, exhausted, "please. Let me tell him. So we can figure out what to do."

They'd heard the back door open very quietly, hours ago now. They'd gone silent for a time to listen to their family moving about downstairs. Dawn's window was open, and the sound drifted up on the breeze that stirred the curtain and stroked the girls' heads. A tap was turned on. The kettle boiled. The small metal sound of a cupboard latch, then the clink of glass against glass. Tammy knew her father was pouring a Scotch into his crystal whiskey glass, a birthday gift from their mom years ago. Byron coming quietly up the stairs in his sock feet to his little room, carefully turning the noisy handle, giving the sticky door a push.

Everyone being, Tammy thought, who they are, quietly. She stroked her sister's hand.

"You said you brought sleeping pills?"

Tammy nodded. "I don't use them much, but I always bring a few."

"They work?"

"You never take them?" Dawn shook her head. "They're magic." And Tammy went to get her one.

Fifteen minutes later, Dawn was asleep. Tammy slowly withdrew her arm from under Dawn's, eased herself off the bed, switched off the tiny dresser light, and stepped onto the landing, listening for the sounds of her dad.

Dawn & John Andrew

There was a theme to mornings at home, Dawn thought, groggy, but coming to. Let. Dawn. Sleep. She rolled towards the door, awake now. The whispering in the hall outside her bedroom today was so different from her first day, and the funeral day, but why did the family conferences happen on the landing right outside her door, contravening the Let Dawn Sleep rule? And why, this morning, was there was a large rock in the pit of her stomach?

Oh, she remembered. A decision sitting there. Except it wasn't really a decision.

She had to go, now—how could she stay?

The whispering descended. She lay in bed watching the sunlight create leafscapes on the wall as coffee and maple bacon wafted up the stairs. She felt so desperately sad. They'd gotten so close: so much made good here. Her home, her safety, her sense of place had been restored as she'd rediscovered everything she'd loved—everything she'd had to push away while she'd been gone. It was, she realized now as she imagined leaving it all again, a kind of affliction. Home*sickness*: longing for, imagining, hoping for, dreaming of. But when that crack of thunder had come yesterday, she hadn't been afraid, she'd been bereft. The loss of shelter, just when she'd begun to trust and believe in it: that was the boulder in her gut now. She rolled to face the wall and thought, I have to go, but I can't get out of bed.

Oh, dear girl, she heard.

And rolled over again. Her mother's voice. Peonies. Was it a breeze blowing up from the garden? Dawn knew the peonies were long gone. The curtains billowed, settled.

"Mom?" she whispered.

The curtain moved.

"Mom, I don't know what to do. I'm exhausted from the work of being me. I'm sick of the work it is for other people."

She listened to a tap, tap of the lightest branch of the maple against the sill and heard her mother say, "I know. I know."

"I can't stay, Mom."

"You can't go. Not yet, not yet." Tap tap.

And the lightest tap on her door.

"Dawn?" John Andrew was using a voice she hadn't heard since she was little. The voice her dad used when they were ill and he was worried, or tending to a new calf, or— "Dawn. Are you awake?"

She got out of bed and was surprised to realize she was still in her clothes from the day before. She didn't remember getting in bed—oh yes. The sleeping pill. She looked at the clock: just before eight.

"I'm up."

She opened the door. Her dad looked awful. "Want a coffee?" he said. "Will you come down?"

Tammy's told him, she thought.

"Dad—"

"Dawn," he interrupted gently, "come down. We'll see what's what, okay?"

She nodded and closed her door. With her mother's visit, and now his gentle bedside demeanor, she couldn't cope. Their love so tangible. Visible, almost. How could she leave this?

Dawn thought Tammy would be in the kitchen when she came down, that she'd have to cope with two sympathetic faces. She couldn't bear it.

But the kitchen was empty, except for her dad—even Betsy was gone.

"Where is everyone?" she asked, taking the coffee her dad offered her.

"Out. They'll be back. Ya hungry? Bacon?"

"No, I'm..." But he was holding a plate out in front of her and she discovered she was hungry. She'd not had dinner last night, she remembered, and thought of why, and how, and what it had felt like, and thought too that the heaviness in her stomach might also be emptiness, and she might as well put some of the sweet-smelling bacon into that pit that felt like a rock. So she took a couple pieces, and then a slice of bread and loaded it with jam, and sat in the still kitchen.

The clock ticked her father's patience. The birds sang her mother's refrain, not yet, not yet. Finally, John Andrew said, "Would ya come for a walk?"

It was chilly this morning. The heavy rain of yesterday had brought down some leaves. There was something autumnal in the cool damp, though it was only the start of August. But sometimes, Dawn remembered, the autumn did start now, creeping in on the heels of the heat and taking the legs out from under you. You were running in summer, then autumn laid a tripwire of mist and rain, and dahlias instead of peonies stood heavy-headed and bent. Melancholy and apologetic.

They pulled on sweaters and gumboots and set out across the field towards the dairy. Dawn could hear voices at the front of the house but her dad didn't stop, just strode that half-step ahead that he always had. Then slowed to make sure he was walking beside her.

She studied him. She'd been right when she first saw him.

"You look awful, Dad."

He gave what would have passed for a weak grin yesterday, but today was a grimace. "I didn't sleep much."

"Tammy gave me a sleeping pill."

"Ah. Those things work?" He slowed his stride again.

"They do. Well, this one did. You never take them either?"

"Nope. Truth be told..." He paused. "I'm a little scared of all that."

"What. Like, pills?

He nodded. "Hard to explain when I know lots of things do so much good, but..." He paused again. "I've just always been scared of...losing control, I guess."

Dawn realized that she had never in all her life seen her father even a bit tipsy. He'd have a beer, a glass of whiskey, but he was always solidly sober.

He looked at her. "My dad was a drinker. Never knew where we were with him. I guess that's it."

"I didn't know that."

"Ya wouldn't. I didn't talk to you. Should've, but—" He turned to her. "I am now."

They'd reached the circular path that would lead back towards the house and the machine shed, near the road crossing the dairy lane. John Andrew stopped. "The morning before the fire, day before yesterday—Jesus, yesterday—morning. Feels like a month. When I got here on my way to milking, there was a truck parked here. Marty's truck, I know now. Low-slung muffler. Its own sound. I didn't know, though. Didn't know what anyone was doing out here at five in the morning, but I thought just night owl or early shift or...something. But it niggled me. All day. I kept coming back to it. And I should've thought to do something because I heard the car in the morning and I heard it that night and I knew it was the same one—didn't have to be Marty's, I guess, but—you know how ya just...know? He's been poison as long as we've known him. And you've been—you've amazed me. Made me..."

Dawn watched him. Her father continued as though he was navigating stones in a stream, checking his balance with every step.

"You've made me proud. Curious—like, in a good way. I've wanted to know you: know *you*, who you are now. You're not the kid that ran off. You're not my son, I know, but you're all I ever wanted in my son—I just couldn't see it, didn't know it was there till we worked on that fucking—sorry, French—tractor. But what I've loved? Seeing you turn a blind eye to that prick. Seeing your mother and you with the same stubborn...just-get-on-ness. Must be a word for that. I'll bet your mum would have a word. But I watched you and thought, she's something else. And I thought, thank God you came home, because God knows, I can't have made it something you would've looked forward to. And I'm sorry for that but, ya know, I think two things."

He stopped, took off his hat, and rubbed his head hard, like he was trying to press the thoughts out of it. And he started walking again, up the hill away from the fields towards the woods. "I think we...neither of us, were ready till we were ready, you know? I think you had to grow into yourself and I had to—your mom would say get over myself, but it wasn't that. I had to let go of that fear, ya know?

It's the same fear, the pills thing, the same thing, I think. Control, I guess. Or loss. Anger maybe. I felt it when your mum got sick and I couldn't...I could do nothing." John Andrew was finding it a bit hard to see; he was blinking a lot.

This was only the second time in her life Dawn had heard her father say so much, reach for feelings and examine them in front of her. It was disorienting. He saw that.

"Y'okay? It's a lot, I'm sorry, but I have to say it all now." He stopped and took a breath. "Tammy told me what happened. I don't blame you for wanting to leave."

She waited for him to say something about the police, but he said nothing. He turned and kept climbing, in silence now. She saw they'd climbed up towards the grove of wild sugar maples. Dawn couldn't remember the last time she'd been up here. Probably the *only* time she remembered being up here—the time with her dad, tapping the trees for her school project. That day. With the bear. He spoke her thoughts.

"This place. I haven't been up here much. It spooked me, that day."

Dawn nodded. "Yeah." A moment passed. The wind blew her hair, and her dad held his hat for a moment as a zephyr pulled at it. "You said *two* things. What's the other?"

John Andrew looked around the glade. So beautiful. Tall grass he could tell had been flattened by deer bedding down there, and the heavy rain maybe. He looked to the corner where he'd seen the bear that day, then to the other corner where his younger self had stood, taller than himself now, stronger, holding up the tree limb, ferocious with fear for his child.

"Five years I wasted," he said, turning away from the memory. "Worse than wasted, because your mother was angry, every day. Every day. Things got so hard. Why'd she stay? She made herself sick, I think, because of me. Because I was scared. Of what?" He picked up a stick, measured it against his side, imagined a walking stick. "Of having to put everything I'd ever imagined for my son aside. That loss. I didn't hear her losses. You and..." He squinted at the sky. "Me. I was scared to silence—afraid of having to justify my child's existence to people like Marty. There's lots of them, I guess. But Marty's been a gift to me, Dawn. Marty's the lesson: what your everyday must be like, what you deal with. Your losses. But you walked into the shop the day after he beat on Byron and shat all over you, and you were quiet and clear and..." He searched for the right word and could only come up with: "dignified. Ya know? You have, you've always had, something he never will. You know who you are, what you want, and what you need, and he only has some need he can't name, can't understand; and can't... direct, so he—he just *does* shit. And you confuse him. You're quiet. You don't swan or flash around like he does, but you're..." He looked back to the other corner of the glade. "Remember when that bear came? Remember I stood up and...."

"Yes," said Dawn.

"I think about that a lot now. Of how your life is one long...roar. One long...standing up, looking taller, looking stronger, looking more—I don't know—who you are, so you can just hold your place. I think of that, and I think that Marty has given us the gift of you knowing you can do it, and he's given me the gift of seeing you do it and knowing what it is. I never would have known what a roar should be but that I've watched you do it. And do it. So..." He reached and took one of her hands. "Don't give him the satisfaction of seeing you go. Don't give him the power. And"—he dropped her hand, pushed his hat back, and pressed the heels of his hands into his eyes like she did, Dawn realized, when she needed to stop herself from crying— "you don't have to stay long, or forever or...whatever, but please, stay and finish what we've started? For your mum, and for me—'cause I can't bear for you to go now we're both grown-ups. Ya know?"

They came back down the hill in silence. Companionable. Easy. A silence Dawn had longed for, though she'd never defined it or known what it might signify. She still didn't have an answer for what to do, wasn't sure how to decide. But...whatever, she thought. Breathe. Then breathe again. And wait, rustled the leaves. Listen and watch, flapped the clothes Dawn saw Tammy hanging out in the distance. Tammy lifted a hand to them, waving excitedly. The breeze drying the clothes was carrying voices too, from the other side of the house.

Many voices, any single one indistinguishable. By the time they got to the yard, though, she could hear Jerry and Byron and—Andy and Ethan? Banu? She started to jog from the edge of the blackened heap of shed, to Tammy who ran to meet Dawn and grab her hand, saying, "Wait'll you see. C'mon."

Together they rounded the corner, John Andrew close behind, to see—

A kind of circus.

A strange blue-and-white tent with a zippered opening through which the tractor, though protesting, was being eased by Jerry. He waved to them as he disappeared inside.

A large group of people, known and unknown: Fuzzy, Ethan, Banu; the town mayor and her secretary; Arthur and his wife, Joy; Duncan, Miranda's old tractor-fancier friend, and Jenny, of course, with Karen from the Highland Heart board; Owen, an old pal of her dad's from the county council; parents of 4-H'ers; some of the youngsters, including young Kyle who raced to Dawn, pulling her into the centre of the crowd and pointing people out, explaining "The Plan."

Jock over there—see that big truck?—he brought everything they needed to fix the tractor: Kyle had named it—her!—Mucky Mackie. A fully appropriate moniker, Dawn said. Kyle whooped, delighted. John Andrew stood grinning and silent except for nodded, monosyllabic acknowledgements and clear delight in Kyle's explanations, given as though Kyle was fully responsible for the events underway.

John Andrew took a cup of coffee and a muffin from what was a groaning table—the 4-H parents had outdone themselves: everyone had coffee and seemed to be eating. But this was a work party, Jock MacIntosh informed Dawn, so the socializing would have to wind up and folks get down to it; there was a lot to be done and not much time. Jock was the owner of a local auto-body shop; Dawn recognized him now as the dad of one of her former soccer teammates and remembered the big, soft-spoken man with his shiny bald head, massive, tattooed arms, and—now greying—beard as ever-present on the sidelines. He told Dawn he was managing what would be Mucky's transformation. Kyle was grinning like their little face would split, seeing the name was already sticking.

Byron came up, followed by two men close to his age that Dawn had never seen, but who were now, apparently, Byron's new best friends. They listened attentively to the list of chores that Jock began to lay out. Byron put his arm around her shoulder and whispered, "Hey."

She looked at him, shiny-eyed. "Hey. This was it. All this."

He nodded. "Glad Tammy didn't pinch me?"

"You need to pinch *me*. I'm dreaming. All these—who are these people? Where did they come from?"

"You're asking me? Well these two"—he nodded to his new pals—"are Allan and James. I think they have last names, but we haven't got that far. One is dad to your bestie," nodding at Kyle, "and one is," he looked at James for confirmation, "Kyle's teacher? You get your coffee at Ethan's?"

"Exactly," said James, a serious guy with an—Irish?—accent. A come-from-away, thought Dawn. "Ethan and Banu rounded up some folks: mind you, that tent's only so big, but we're here for the duration to do whatever. Jock says it'll be a couple—three?"—Jock nodded—"days getting Mucky ready for the trials on Saturday. We're waiting for our work assignments, and the timetable, including helping Fuzz with overnights the next few days. He might not be able to do a lot to keep, um, trouble *contained*, but we figured it shouldn't be too hard to have a little sleepover, to keep Mucky company. You know?"

Dawn turned to her dad. "You knew all of this?"

"Not *all* of this. Didn't know this many would turn up. Byron and me only made a couple calls each."

Byron nodded. "But oh, the quality of those calls!"

Now Banu joined, and slipping a hand into Dawn's said quietly, "Takes a village, eh?" Dawn squeezed their hand, not trusting herself to speak.

And work began. The crowd thinned out. Jock pulled out masks, heavy-duty respirators, sanders. Banu followed Byron and Jock into the tent, grabbing a mask.

John Andrew stayed back with Dawn. "You comin'?"

"I don't know," said Dawn. "I kind of can't believe we can do this, but I know, I really do know, we have to try. But I can't bear..." She didn't want to be negative—they'd come so far in so many ways—but she couldn't help feeling that anything they did would only encourage Marty. She heard him close in her ear saying, *next time it'll be the house*, and felt sick again. Her dad watched her.

"What?" he said.

She told him. He nodded, and nodded, and looked away and thought before saying, "Here's the thing. Maybe I should be worried about more shit from him, but I'm not. Because I think he's done his worst now. He's a coward. He knows we know, now—that all these folks know. Good thing about small towns. He'll be terrified of word getting back to his dad. Whatever swagger he had on, his dad's the boss of him and Marty's afraid of him. Angus is the gravy train; Marty can't fall off it. So, I think he's gone about as far as he dares. He'll keep being an asshole, but..." He shrugged and reached for a mask, handing one to Dawn and taking one for himself. "I think we should be in there, yeah?"

Dawn heard laughter coming from the tent. Her dad studied her, waiting. Would she get anywhere imagining further disaster scenarios? And someone inside was making folks laugh; Byron probably. I could use a laugh, she thought, so she took the mask from her dad and went into the tent.

The day was water on a hot griddle: it landed and disappeared. The gods of summer rethought what August should be, and the cool morning became a hot afternoon. Food appeared and disappeared; work began again, one group handing over tools to another. A circle of cooperation. It was, Dawn thought, what a barn raising must have been like a century ago.

She'd been energized by peoples' skill and generosity. The group kept morphing as the day went on. Folks, including Dawn, came and went—on errands to collect material, tools, or other experts. At six, Dawn had gone to get groceries while Byron and James picked up

Jock's co-owner at the body shop after he'd closed. Harley—as in Davidson—was bringing more tins of primer. After a rigorous group sanding, they'd washed, dried, and primed—first coat on—and set up huge fans. It was so hot; everything was bone dry and ready to start again in a couple hours. Sand, blow it off this time, prime again, with this coat putting Mucky to bed.

Tomorrow, the main event: top colour in the morning, *fans on full blast (fofb)*, light sand blown off; then second coat soon as possible in the afternoon, *fofb*, then see how it all looked—maybe-a-bedtime-coat? *fofb*. A long day. The next day for the accents, both coats *fofb x 2*. Another very long day.

This whole week though, thought Dawn, had been about time expanding. Or maybe collapsing. Elastic. Something. Because somehow there was so much more *content* crowding the length of a day than Dawn had ever experienced. So when Jock went through the timeline, punctuating everything with "all being well," everyone knew that meant as long as no one fucks this up intentionally (Marty) or otherwise (rain, disasters, World War III), they would squeak into the Tractor Trials on Saturday morning. With the freshest paint job in the competition. No prize for that, Jock said. Shame.

By nine o'clock, daylight was nearly gone and Jock and John Andrew had been leading the changing team in the tent all day. They were tired, dirty, thirsty, but exhilarated. What they'd done in a day. They came out of the tent, following Byron, clapping each other on the back, heading to the circle of seats around the firepit where Dawn and Byron and Tammy and John Andrew had sat the night of the fire. So long ago now.

Tammy had filled a cooler with ice and beer and pop, and she and Jenny and Sandra had food—more food!—standing by. James and Allan were back, without Kyle, and had set sleeping bags near the tent. Ah, thought Dawn, that's the "all being well" guard.

At ten-thirty Fuzzy pulled up. He stood by the fire a few minutes, saying nothing; listening, laughing occasionally, until just before he left, when he knelt beside Dawn who was sitting close to Banu. He looked at the ground, speaking so quietly that Dawn knew no one else could hear over all the chat and laughter. "I'm not allowed to say anything, you know? So here's me saying nothing."

Now he did look at Dawn, and Banu focused on something in the far distance. "I didn't join the force to let assholes be assholes, but sometimes there's nothing I can do—officially—to stop them. But I see you, Dawn. I do. And I see him. His dad sees him now—finally, really sees him. His sister. They have to live here, work here. The town'll make the difference, like now." He waved to the circle. "There'll be other jerks. There are, for sure. But..." He stood up. "Folks are figuring it out." He huffed a little, the way her dad would sniff when he was annoyed with himself. He shook his head as if he was puzzled. "I wish I'd done better for you."

He turned away, heading to his car, saying over his shoulder, "Y'all got your designated drivers? Night!" A chorus of "night, Fuzzy" followed him. He gave a siren-blast salute, a flash of the cherry-light, then disappeared down the drive.

That was day one, night one, in what would eventually be referred to as "The Tale of Mucky Mackie: A Race to the Trials." But the whole story had yet to solidify its place in MacInnes family history. The Tractor Trials were still to come, and they would likely be their own story. Before that, there were two more days and nights, very like the first, with more people arriving—many more. Folks who'd heard a little or a lot about what had happened, heard about Dawn and about Marty (Fuzzy was right) and came bringing food, drink, laughter, skill, stories to pass the time, and pairs of hands. Hands that released John Andrew and Dawn and let them step back to watch something they'd known about their community, but had never seen before so tangibly. These people brought with them an energy of cooperation so sweet, it felt as though nothing—no injustice, no cruelty, no hardship—couldn't be righted by them.

On day two, just before noon, John Andrew said to Dawn, "Gotta run into town. Want to come?" Puzzled—they had everything and everyone they could possibly need—she nodded and followed him to the truck. She knew the tractor was running "like a top," because Jock had said it was tuned to within an inch of its long tractor life. So. Now what?

A beautiful day, like the first time they'd driven together into town. No music this time. Dawn didn't ask where they were going. He would tell her, or she would see. When they pulled up in front of the machine shop, her dad turned to her before he got out, a silent question. She answered with a small shake of her head: she'd come this far with him, but no further. A little nod, and he went in.

Dawn watched Angus straighten from reading something on the counter to upright and—even through the window, she could tell—hostile. Marty came out from the back room.

Her dad spoke to Angus; Angus barked at Marty; Marty disappeared.

Then Angus stood silent, facing John Andrew. John Andrew stood silent, facing the window and Dawn. Dawn was sure the haze she was registering was a smog of tension filling the shop. Time—in its new-and-improved, elastic form—stretched a few minutes to feel like a week of wet weather, and then Marty returned with a small box in his hand. John Andrew reached into his pocket, pulled out his wallet, and Angus waved it away. Marty disappeared. John Andrew picked up the small box, nodded to Angus, and came back out to the truck. Dawn looked into the shop where Angus sat, unmoving, staring at them through the window.

John Andrew settled in, slammed the door, put the key into the ignition, then held up the box: spark plugs.

"Let them know we're not done yet. You know?"

Dawn nodded. Opened the glove compartment. "Music?"

"Got any Queen in there?" John Andrew swung the truck into traffic and Dawn turned the volume to max, so that "We Are the Champions" could be heard all the way down the road and probably, inside the machine shop.

Night two, Dawn went over to Banu's for a sleepover.

Byron and his new best friend James camped outside the tractor tent.

John Andrew might have gotten, for the first time that anyone could remember, a bit tipsy, and promised Fuzzy he wasn't driving anywhere because he was going to sleep by the fire.

Night three, Dawn told Banu she had to sleep at home: she wanted to wake up with her dad and sister on the morning of the trials. "Cool," said Banu. And Tammy said, "But you can join—hey, Dawn?" And before Dawn could respond, Tammy said, "Great, I'll make up the guestroom."

Banu and Dawn looked at each other and Banu said, "How about I bring an air mattress and we do the 'all-being-well' tonight?" Tammy looked from one to the other not knowing what the hell they were talking about, but Dawn said yes and beamed at John Andrew who'd joined them, thinking that Dawn looked happier than he'd ever seen her.

Night three slipped past. Dawn and Banu laughed a lot during their watch—so much and so loudly that Tammy came out at three-thirty and said, "Shut the fuck up. I love you both, but no one in the house can sleep." And went back in.

Dawn and Banu kept counting shooting stars, quietly now, and eventually, after their rewards, Banu fell asleep, and finally, Dawn.

Dawn

There's no Nova Scotia morning more glorious than a morning when summer has chased autumn away and reasserted her ascendancy. No sky a richer blue, no sun more lucent or gold, the green of the fields and trees restored each to their own particular shades, plumped and vivid again, enriched by the day of heavy rain and the lingering mists.

This was what Dawn woke to. Light and colours so bright they stung her eyes. So she did what she'd done as a child: hands over her eyes, fingers slightly spread so she could view the world in slivers. The beauty was too much all at once. She turned her face and hands slowly like a camera, panning across the house, the garden, the yard, the field with the black-and-white cows—and that sweet Jersey, Martine—in the haze at the base of distant hills. Then, the roof of the far dairy and beyond that, the steeper hills, all carpeted in a diaphanous mist, drifting slowly upwards as she watched. Taking her hands from her eyes, she studied the sleeping form beside her. Spikes of black and a delicate green braid escaping from the top of the sleeping bag. She felt "all fulled up" as she used to say to her mother when something was too big to explain or contain. Good or bad. The moment was enveloping, complex. It was a multitude of *fullnesses* and it made her euphoric and afraid. As Dawn watched Banu, still sleeping in their cocoon, her stomach jumped and spun like a fairground ride.

She'd never been kissed like Banu had kissed her. She'd never felt she wanted anyone close enough, until now. But it wasn't just Banu. It was everything this homecoming had delivered: things still undiscovered, or registered but not yet emotionally catalogued. That was her joy, and fear—to have discovered so much, and to wonder if it could possibly remain intact. She shook the thought away, looking around her.

Stop it. Be here. Sit in now, not tomorrow. The breeze bent the treetops, nodding. Here, now.

Tammy came out of the house, saw Dawn sitting up, waved, and called: “Coffee! Want some?”

Dawn waved and nodded, started to climb out of the two bags zipped together, and was...encouraged back down inside with a tug, a caress.

Coffee would wait.

But it wouldn’t wait long. The activity in the house ramped up, and Dawn and Banu joined the others for the breakfast Byron had taken responsibility for. He had Tammy working as sous-chef as he created his *everything* omelette, using, he informed them, “every-sing I find in ze freege”—his terrible French accent sending everyone over the edge. Except John Andrew and Jerry, who were already at the table eating and planning the transfer of the tractor to the fairgrounds.

Jock would be bringing his tow truck any time now, John Andrew threw over his shoulder to Dawn as he glanced at his watch—cuing the sound of something enormous rolling up the drive. This day, a large day already, was about to become huge.

Jock arrived; so did Andy to help his dad, Harley to help Jock, and Allan and James to help Byron. Dawn and Banu watched Jock and Harley get the tow truck backed right up to the tent, and John Andrew handed Dawn the key.

“Here ya go.”

“What? Me?” Dawn eyed the narrow ramp onto the truck.

“You’ve had her through her paces.”

Dawn took the keys and went into the tent as Banu and Tammy rolled and tied the sides tightly back. She stood alone in the tent with Mucky Mackie—now a long way from mucky. The ugly duckling transformed, Dawn thought. The tractor was gleaming red and white, the chrome polished, the tires so new and clean they were blacker than fresh licorice twists. Mucky was a magical confection, a candy tractor sweet enough to eat, with the Jubilee medallion, scraped and blackened by the fire, now scrubbed and shining diamond bright. The medallion flashed a tiny light around the inside of the tent, catching sunlight from—where? The opening was shaded. Dawn looked around, not finding the source. She knew it, though, and she watched the flashes dance inside the tent—first here, then there—as though a spark was being blown to and fro.

She climbed onto the tractor and started it—not with a fart or a splutter or a cough but, as Jock had promised, a rolling purr: only a hint of the roar Dawn knew Mucky was capable of. Dawn eased her—like butter, another Jock promise—through the swags on either side of the tent, onto the ramp, and into position. The straps went on, around, and under, Jock and Harley taking no chances, strapping under front, middle, and back, then front to back as well. That's it.

"Belt and braces," said Jerry. Blank faces turned to him—what?

"Better safe than sorry. Measure twice, cut once. Belt and braces."

Blank faces turned to each other.

Jerry shook his head: did no one speak his language anymore? "Belt"—lifting his shirt—"and braces!"—he twanged the red suspenders across his chest.

A collective "Ohhhhhhhh."

Jock laughed, started the truck, and, grinning at Dawn, patted the seat beside him.

Epilogue

That day was a success. Mucky behaved well and was recognized and rewarded. The MacInnes family was surrounded—mostly—by excited well-wishers, but also gossipmongers keen to dissect and pronounce on the last few days.

Marty was there. He stood on the fringes of the event, lizard eyes focused on Dawn until a pal of Fuzzy's moved him along. Heads turned to watch, and saw Angus follow his son and deliver a series of smacks across his head. Then Marty raised a hand to his dad and Fuzzy's pal intervened again, turning Marty and escorting him away. Angus went back into the arena, white-faced, and watched expressionless as Dawn put Mucky through her paces: figure-eight and stop on a dime—they actually put a dime on the ground. The figure-skating beauty pageant for tractors was judged by the mayor. The warden of the county. The fire chief. The town was out in force to watch and was visibly divided: those who watched Dawn and cheered, and those who stood silent in judgment.

And then?

Mucky took the blue rosette, of course. From Duncan MacDonald the tractor-fancier, who delivered the rosette with first one pronoun, then another, followed by a waterfall of sorrys, but shining eyes and a vigorous handshake. Mucky and Dawn were cheered and beribboned, patted and hugged. Then, while Tammy and Dawn stood arm in arm talking to Jenny, John Andrew turned from the judges' table to put his arms around them both, looking from Dawn to Tammy and back to Dawn, and saying so softly what they'd been teasing from him for weeks. So simple.

"I love you two." Pulling them in tight.

The family went home. John Andrew and Byron had a glass of whiskey; Dawn parked Mucky in her temporary blue-and-white shelter and opened the tiny bottle of Henkell her sister had produced from her purse when Mucky won, took a long drink herself, then poured almost all the rest over Mucky's nose.

Tammy had walked into the field between the house and the dairy to stare at the sky and look back at the house. Now that she knew she'd be leaving soon, she needed to catalogue everything. She had to cement all this, forever, because every time she came back from now on, things would be different. Not so complicated, perhaps, but changed. Her grief would ease, she knew, with the remove that time would bring. This snapshot of her family and their home was captured at a complicated junction: joy colliding with grief; pride and accomplishment with anger and fear. Tammy studied to memorize the picture, attaching, to everything she saw, its singularity. She must not forget.

The kitchen garden that her mother always started planning in February, drawing a new design every spring, harvesting with delight throughout the season and then mourning its end every autumn—even while planting garlic for the spring.

The flowers that had survived their trampling the night of the fire. Dahlias: one given every Mother's Day that Tammy could remember. And peonies, though not flowering now, that would bring Miranda to Tammy forever.

The laundry line: Tammy realized she'd hung this morning's load—she seemed to have done more laundry in these last few weeks than in her whole life—exactly as her mother had. Small whites, growing to large colours. Prayer flags, Tammy thought, calling for a sweet and gentle domestic order. This brought tears: thinking of the lack of sweet domesticity in her mother's last years. But Tammy focused on her task: collect the joy, she heard her mother remind her. She continued.

Byron and John Andrew settled with their drinks on the back porch, laughing—she smiled to herself: Byron was almost always laughing, or on the edge of laughing.

And then her sister, coming around the corner of the house, holding something out to her. The tiny bottle of sparkling Henkell Tammy had bought, just in case.

"Here!" said Dawn, "I poured most of it over Mucky, but then—"

"—thought you'd pour the rest over me?" said Tammy.

"Nope. Slug each."

Tammy reached for the bottle, then, about to drink, turned to collect her final fragment of joy. She watched her father, who was laughing and shading his eyes, and she raised the last draught of sparkling wine to him. "He said it!"

Dawn took the bottle back. Glittering gem drops were gathered on the green-glass edge but Dawn scattered them, tipping the bottle up and draining it, the sweet breeze pulling her hair around her face,

And roared.

Acknowledgements

ROAR could not have been imagined or written, without:

My son, **T. Thomason**, for the trust and confidence he had in his father and me: taking us on his journey and sharing his insights and community. T. you are my North Star.

My lovely, patient husband and first reader, **Ed Thomason**.

My fantastic editor, **Whitney Moran**, from whom I've learned so much about my own writing, giving me clarity and honesty and confidence. I'm so grateful, and so fortunate, to have had your expertise. Thank you, **Nancy Regan**, for the intro!

Members of the trans community who've responded to or advised on this story, in either of its forms: **Savannah Burton, Maya Henry, Sydney Sarayeva, Dana Levinson, Jack Jackson, T. Thomason**.

My mother, **Alice Williams** (1926–1999), who grew up on a farm in Northern Alberta, was a maker of things, learned to drive on a much-loved tractor, ran away from home to become herself, and taught me the importance of stories.

My father, **Albert Thompson** (1917–2004), who always believed I was a writer. This book would have thrilled him.

My beautiful stepmom, **Willy Thompson**, who's taken such pleasure in the evolution of this project and pride in our family's journey.

My dear pal **Maggie Huculak**, whose journey in "business class" inspired so many of her friends.

My lovely friend from Antigonish where *ROAR* is imagined: **Karen Fish** gifted me the kernel of *ROAR*. Her friend **Sandy Forbes** and his particular tractor relationship also impacted this story.

The kind folks at **Grande Pre Service Station**. They introduced me to **Chris Pinch** of TRACTORS PLUS who advised on all repair segments. **Barron and Deborah Blois** (Gore, NS) for early and detailed information on dairy farming. **Paul Taylor** (Windsor Forks, NS) for his excellent milking tutorials. **Dr. Michael Cussen** (Wolfville, NS) for medical information.

My friends who offered patience, curiosity, and support through the creation of this book, especially **Paula Rockwell, Molly DeShong,** and **Pam Cooley.** Your love and belief is sustaining.

For support of the early stage screenplay that inspired this book, thanks to:

Egale Canada—**Helen Kennedy**, Canada Council for the Arts, **Savannah Burton, Noel Baker, Lynn Matheson**, The WIDC (Women in the Director's Chair): **Carol Whiteman and Linda Coffey, Terry Greenlaw** (Producer, *Dawn, Her Dad & the Tractor*), New York Writer's Lab: **Nitza Wilon, Elizabeth Kaiden** and **Pamela Gray**, Nova Scotia Department of Communities, Culture & Heritage, Harold Greenberg Fund, Telefilm Canada.

A feature film is unlike any other project: the cast and crew all brought something that's been absorbed into the bedrock of the MacInnes family's journey. I heard your voices as I wrote and thank you all for your impact.

Sensitivity readers—thank you so much for taking the time to consider and respond. **Ronnie Ali, Veronica Merryfield,** and **Matty Grace**. Your thoughts and generosity have helped so much.

The responsive, positive, and creative team at Nimbus/Vagrant. What a pleasure it's been!